I0824550

SISTERS *of a* HALVED HEART

ALSO BY NAYANTARA ROY

The Magnificent Ruins

SISTERS
of a
HALVED HEART

---

a novel by

NAYANTARA ROY

ALGONQUIN BOOKS OF CHAPEL HILL
LITTLE, BROWN AND COMPANY

The characters and events in this book are fictitious. Any similarity to real persons, living or dead, is coincidental and not intended by the author.

Algonquin Books of Chapel Hill / Little, Brown and Company
Hachette Book Group
1290 Avenue of the Americas, New York, NY 10104
algonquinbooks.com

First Edition: June 2026

Algonquin Books of Chapel Hill is an imprint of Little, Brown and Company, a division of Hachette Book Group, Inc. The Algonquin Books name and logo are trademarks of Hachette Book Group, Inc.

ISBN 9781643757698

LCCN 2026935534

Printing 1, 2026

LSC-C

Printed in the United States of America

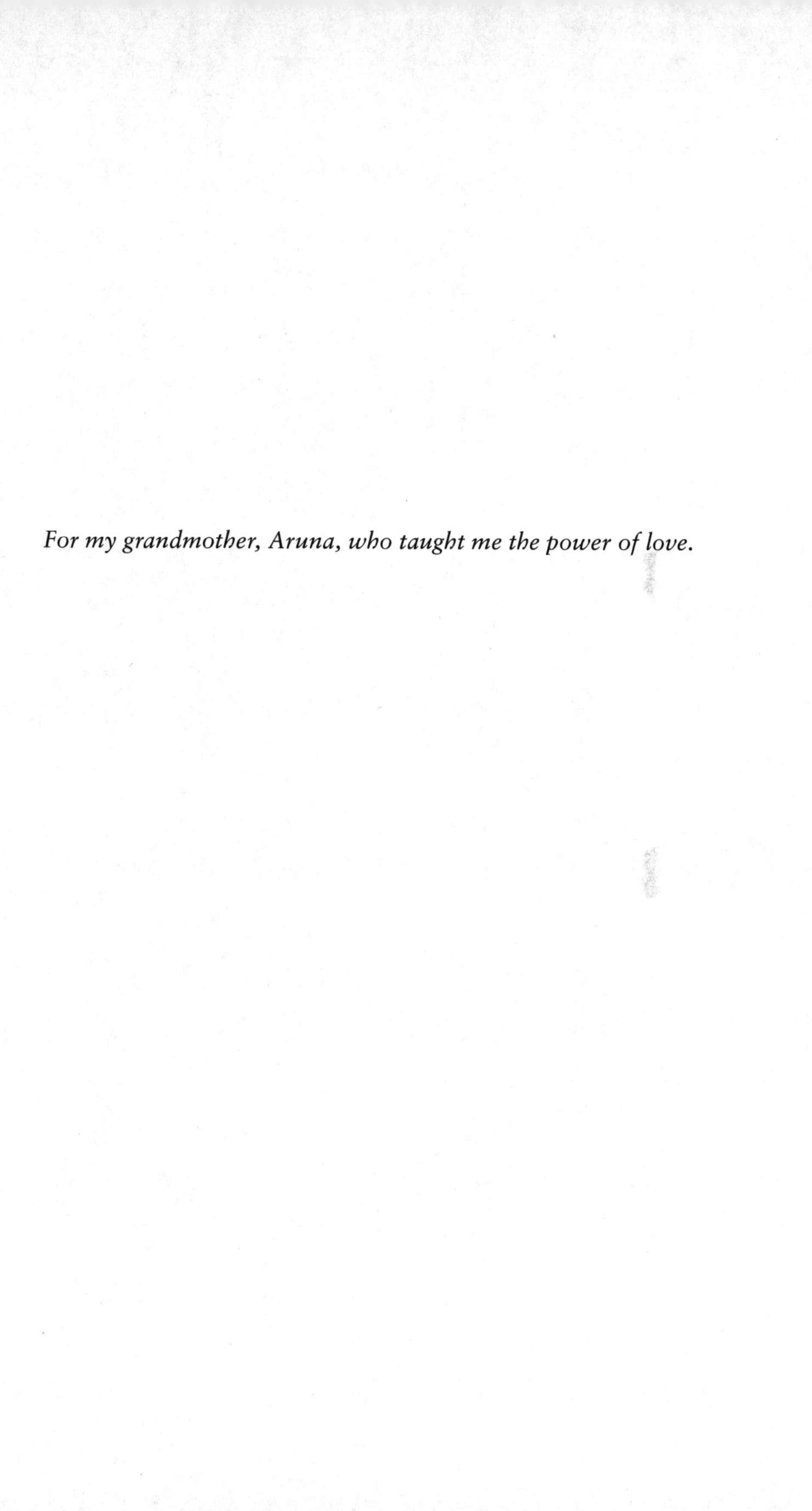

For my grandmother, Aruna, who taught me the power of love.

Of two sisters
one is always the watcher,
one the dancer.

—LOUISE GLÜCK, *Descending Figure*

A story has no beginning or end: arbitrarily one chooses that moment of experience from which to look back or from which to look ahead.

—GRAHAM GREENE, *The End of the Affair*

SISTERS *of a* HALVED HEART

PART ONE

CHAPTER ONE

SHE WAS MY half sister and through our lives, we bore this label. Half of our father. Halved by race—her blood half mine, her skin lighter (whiter, brighter?). We were confidants, bound by the secrets only we could know, and enemies, divided by the cracks and fissures in our father's attentions. We were reluctant to share (sweets, a bedroom, life itself), and so close to the bones of our father's face that you might do a double take at a photograph despite the eight years by which I was older. But Joy and I were in search of something that might turn us whole in each other's presence, grateful to have been gifted even a portion of sisterhood. And so we strove to turn it into the real thing with an uneasy combination of best behavior and secret jealousies, devoid of the open chafing of other siblings. We were the chipped pieces of our family's urn, bound by common traumas and absent mothers; you could tell where the fractures had been. In this manner, we were inseparable and learned to swim the same strokes, taste the same pleasures, our bodies and fashions a trick mirror of each other. It was natural therefore that the two of us learned to seek the same things, and what came to pass should have surprised no one, except that it nearly destroyed me.

IT WAS RAINING, the morning I returned to New York, the early light piercing through a pale gray cloud cover, a soft blinding in my eyes despite the drizzle dotting the aircraft's window, spotted snow and skyscraper blanketing the city below—an aerial homecoming. Somewhere in the city, Jack was waking up, his alarm bursting into Bach (*Sonata in E Minor*), his arms reaching for the covers, pulling them over his head. Soon he would swing his feet to the floor, willing himself to be awake and walk to the kitchen (*yellow kettle, steel toaster, lactose-free milk, his ugly globe bar cart from the flea market on Broadway*) as he started his day (*chemex, steam, his breath on mine*), inhabiting a life that held only my ghost.

FROM THE AIRPORT I took a taxi to Lena's house, chilled by the icy, wet weather, the cab driver in a temper because someone had broken his taillight an hour ago. Lena and Sebastian lived in a brownstone they had bought next to Prospect Park, a few blocks from the botanical garden. I would have liked to live as near them as possible, but nothing in their neighborhood, or for miles around, was affordable. Instead, I was forty minutes away, in the heart of Bushwick, above an Ecuadorian restaurant and a jazz club called Birdlore. In the photos, my apartment had looked charming, with wooden floors, a tiny second bedroom I could turn into an office, and a French window that got sun in the late mornings. It was not far from Bed-Stuy, where Lena and I had lived after college, not knowing how we might divide up the furniture and winter jackets we had shared for three years in student housing. We had met at Brown in a class on avian poetry taught by a professor we both hated for his small meannesses, Lena's popularity creating bridges to social events that my shyness and lack of glamour might have prohibited otherwise. Like me, she had not known Jack well, but he had occasionally appeared on the periphery of her large social orbit. Lena had always been a precipitous force in my life. At her insistence, in my senior year, I finished a poem I had worked on all year. It was called "Evening Skin," and the first draft had been written quickly, after a night that I had found difficult to forget. In revision, I had liked the simplicity of the poem's structure, and Lena had convinced me it held more depth than I thought. Despite my reservations, giving in to her urging, I had submitted it to Brown's college magazine.

By morning I mourn you,
Our shedding long past
In fickle light. Your senses come to
Word, breath, limb. I unpeel, last.
We nod, cool
As ice. You ask if I want to play pool
Tonight, as a thousand times before.
I eschew rapture and riptide for yore
Erasing all trace of liquid body. Drinking
Inhaling. Sweat and saliva surrogates for thinking.
Our acquaintance of sturdy years of leisure
Dissolved by a single call to pleasure.
A harsh noon. Clothed
Our colors no longer stark against the other.
To university and community and bro
Once more betrothed.

FIVE WEEKS LATER, it was published and received a maelstrom of praise; and then a year later, "Evening Skin" won me a prestigious award. For reasons I attributed to luck, timing, and the student body's emotional state, the poem had touched a nerve on campus, after which word of mouth had carried it wider. The shock of my sudden (fleeting) fame was diluted by the confusion of being seen as a Promising Young Poet overnight. I put it down to fortune and spent the prize money on a writing desk and records and tried writing more poetry, but it was as if an artery had clogged. Soon after, I was commissioned to write a poem for an anthology. When I sent my verses in, I could almost taste the editor's disappointment. Perhaps I could write something more like "Evening Skin"? He had made the inquiry, tapping his earlobe, as if in search of a missing beat.

After graduation, we went separate ways—Lena into publishing, while I tried to assess what I might be good at. We talked daily about our dreams and our friends, the state of the world and the state of our hearts, the movies and music we both loved and the frugal recipes we could afford to make. She had gone to work for one independent publisher after another, working her way up to editor. I landed first at a rare bookstore, shelving books and running the register and later, evaluating worn hardcovers, looking for flaws and markups. Then, I was an assistant editor at a tabloid, where I edited the scorching Letters to the Editor section and summarized the scoops and speculation published by other outlets each week. Eventually, and with relief, I applied for and got a position as a poetry editor at a small but beloved literary magazine called *The Janus Review.* Once a week, I taught a foundation class in poetry at the New School. That year, one afternoon, Lena went on a blind date and returned at one in the morning with Sebastian, a Mexican-American pediatrician with green eyes and the hint of a beer belly, who saw through her armor and had the ability to make us both laugh. I knew then that I would have to make sure Lena stayed in my life even if she gave herself up to a man.

As the cab pulled up, Lena opened the front door and came running down the stoop stairs through the gate, Gino hanging off one hip.

"Be careful, it's slippery," I said as the cab driver pulled out my suitcase.

I got out and threw open my arms, my purse sliding off my shoulder to my elbow. Gino smelled of sour milk and candy, his toddler arms pulling on my hair as I took him from Lena, enveloping them both.

"Good god, he's a grown man," I said into his fine, dark hair.

Lena's face was wet with a mix of tears and rain as she pressed her cheek to mine, Gino fidgeting between us.

"Goddamn you, Mira," she said.

"Stand," said Gino, emphatic, pointing at the sidewalk with a tiny finger, but I held on to him, taking in his tan, flushed face, the many folds in his little arms and legs, their color that of a milky latte.

"This is Mira mashi, darling," said Lena, stroking his head. "Mama loves her so much."

I set Gino down and immediately, he ran back into the house.

"Be careful," called Lena after him. "Sebbie, Gino's run inside."

She turned back to me.

"I'm glad you're back. If you ever leave like that again, I'll kill you."

INSIDE, THE HOUSE smelled of children and crayons and Bolognese, cushions everywhere, a large cat asleep by the radiator, height marks on the kitchen wall, the stamp of a family in every cranny. Seven years ago, Lena and Sebastian had had their twins, Mirabel and Alice. Four years later, Gino was in their lives. I was godmother to all three. I watched them throw peas at each other—Gino caught in the fray between his havoc-causing sisters as Lena tried to referee—and thought of the empty apartment that I hadn't seen in person yet, a mere forty minutes away. I would be in the same city as them, this family I loved, and it sent a brief ripple of happiness through me.

"You look athletic, Mira," said Sebastian.

"I can literally see a bicep," said Lena, wiping red sauce off her neck.

Self-conscious, I shrugged. "I went running a lot in London. The office was in Canary Wharf so it was nice to run along the river. Got myself some dumbbells, too. Exercise was the only thing I didn't want to do in a mask."

"All that rain," said Lena. "Runners get mowed down by traffic in London all the time."

"Okay, mom," I said. "I'll wear all neon when I run in the rain here. Maybe you'll come with me."

"I have three children, Mira. You stop by here when you want some real exercise."

Sebastian yawned, stretching his arms over his head. "Will you miss London? What made you want to leave? You'll miss the pubs at least?" Sebastian grunted with longing.

"You're such an anglophile, Seb," said Lena, looking at her rumpled husband with affection. "He'd do so well living a quiet life in the English countryside." Lena turned to me, her flaxen curls catching the light. She could go from harried, sweatpants-clad editor and mother to extraordinary in seconds. She was pretty to look at but there was something startling about her sweetness and the devotion with which she focused on people.

"I'd be the village doctor," said Sebastian, pleased. "If I were you, Mira, I wouldn't have left. England feels so much more... real than America." He rubbed the tips of his fingers together, as if feeling for texture.

I felt something constrict in my chest and make its way into the base of my throat. "It was time to come home," I said after a pause.

Lena and Sebastian's eyes softened together, interconnecting emotion and memory in the way that long-term couples did.

"How do you feel, M?" asked Lena, gentle above Gino's clamor for more peas.

"About being back," said Sebastian, his voice dropping as if we were talking about things that children should not be privy to.

I lifted a shoulder, trying to locate the answer in my knotted limbs. "I wasn't going to disappear forever."

AFTER LUNCH, THEY let me fall asleep on the couch. I woke up with a start to an empty house and a note on the table.

Taking the twins to their recital—come by for dinner if you're hungry after movers xx

The cat blinked at me as I pulled on my jacket, as if making note of an intruder in the spectacle of domestic happiness.

"I'm leaving," I said to her.

Suitcase in hand, I took an umbrella from a stand by the door and pulled it shut behind me. But outside, it had stopped raining and Brooklyn was alight with a burst of afternoon sun, the snow melting into rivulets, bits of it still clean, sparkling in the light. I lifted my face to the sun, letting the warmth seep into me. It was a trick that I had learned in therapy, which might make one feel better if only for a moment. I had been lifting my face to the sun for almost five years. The walk from Lena's house to the train station was only two minutes, made pleasant by the calm of the park's green. From there, it was seven stops to City Hall, where I changed from the 5 to the J. Ten more stops to Jamaica Center, and finally, a fifteen minute walk to my new address on Palmetto. Even with my heavy suitcase and the subway stairs, it would not have occurred to me to take a taxi—every dollar in my life was accounted for. The apartment was too far from the increasingly white bar scene around Maria Hernandez Park to be trendy, and the friend who was leasing it to me had confessed that, despite the lack of street lighting and the three junkies who lived below the building, it was a mostly residential, dead area. As I turned the corner, I saw the mover's truck outside a three-story building that looked like a house, just as it had in the photographs, a brief happiness coursing through my veins at the sight. At the van's open back, two young men were lifting my small piano. I quickened my pace, suitcase trundling over the pavement.

"Be careful," I said, out of breath as I stopped in front of the men.

Inches away from setting the instrument down in the slush, they stopped to stare at me.

"It's maple. You can't get it wet," I said, a pinching in my ribs from the sudden rush of air.

Their eyes widened at my panic. I tried to smile.

"I'm Mira Guhathakurta," I said. "Apartment Four. It's got an elevator."

IN UNDER THREE hours, Mitch and Ramin of the MakeAMove company assembled the parts of my renewed life. Shelves and books, my beloved ancient coffee maker with its miraculously unbroken glass carafe, the piano, a record player with an oak turntable I had found thrifting with Lena, and my father's frayed Victorian velvet armchair. The objects of another life, now spread across bedroom and living room, as if I had lived in these rooms all along.

"No couch or kitchen stuff?" asked Ramin, stretching out a muscular, veined calf on the floor. I handed him one of the three coffees I had bought from the bodega around the corner.

"I got rid of almost everything when I moved to London a few years ago," I said. "This"—I looked around—"was the stuff I kept in storage. The chair and piano were gifts. I didn't want to sell them."

"Good little neighborhood," said Mitch, the taller of the two, bending to avoid the doorframe as the men readied to leave. "Not glamorous but it has character." He made an emphatic fist in the air, intended to reassure me. "And you found yourself a solid spot."

"There's a great empanada stand around the corner," said Ramin. "My girlfriend's aunt lives across from it."

"You're going to like it here," said Mitch. "But if you do move again, remember MakeAMove."

For the first time, I realized they were brothers, an unmistakable resemblance in the way they grinned at me. I watched them drive off in the slush of the street, their easy banter having lifted me out of my own head for a few hours. I was home, that much I knew, but the loneliness felt as if it might never leave my bones. Would I ever take a breath and not feel hollowed out, the life scraped out of me? It felt like a crime that three thousand miles between us had abated nothing. That I could not breathe knowing Jack was now near—I did not know if I would survive it.

CHAPTER TWO

BEING ALONE IN the apartment felt unbearable. I pulled my warmest coat on, retrieving it from the depths of my suitcase, and left quickly. Outside, the evening sky was violet, the cold air a relief. I circled the neighborhood a few times and looked through glass windows at the faces of shoppers and lovers and patrons of a bar who leaned in toward each other. I was dazed by their cheer, ashamed of my own bitterness. Somewhere on a park bench, I remembered that I could go to Lee's. After Lena had moved in with Sebastian, I started taking the train up after work to her office on Wyckoff Avenue. We would walk to Lee's Heights, a neighborhood bar we loved for its simplicity and cooking. Lee, an unflappable bear of a man with joy in his eyes, had moved from Canberra to Brooklyn to be with his American girlfriend and had opened a bar that served strong cocktails and had a grill in the back. Lena, Sebastian, and I became regulars. Over the years, I would sit at the bar with Lena or my laptop or, later, with Jack, our elbows touching, and Lee would want to know how we really were.

EVEN OVER THE course of just a few blocks, Bushwick felt changed. The plant store was now a kombucha bar, the pottery workshop shuttered, small businesses with graffitied windows ravaged by the pandemic, only the behemoth pharmacy still standing. But the Bolivian grocer was still behind the counter at his store, and the magazine stand and café had survived. It felt good to see any semblance of familiarity, any consolation that the past had not disintegrated entirely. The lights inside Lee's looked warm. I hurried in, the tips of my ears so cold that they hurt. It was not full and I made my way to the bar, but it was a stranger and not Lee behind the counter. The bartender nodded at me as I clambered onto the seat, shrugging off my parka.

"Be right with you," he said.

A woman, sprite-like with tortoiseshell glasses, leaned over the bar, her elbows resting on its surface as she cupped her delicate face in one palm and smiled at him. The bartender smiled back at the woman as he mixed her drink. I hung my coat on a hook below the counter, imagining their lives. It was another trick learned in therapy, to focus on the possible existences of others when one might drown in one's own. There was a lithe quality to the bartender's body, the shape of lean muscle under his shirt as if he might be athletic, his wiry curls a soft halo around his face in the dim light. I felt the same hard indifference I had felt toward men in London and looked away, longing for Lee's easy warmth. When I looked up again, the bartender was in front of me, one hip leaning against the counter.

"What are you thinking about?"

I raised my eyebrows. "Is that your usual question for a customer?"

He smiled. "Well, I like to think of them as humans first. It's a good question for one human to ask another, don't you think?"

He was older than I had realized—late thirties, early forties?—his forehead lined with faint ridges, his glasses prescription. I was thirty-five with one suitcase to show for it. I shrugged.

"What if you gave me three guesses?" he asked. "About what you were thinking about."

"Would one include the cocktail I want to drink?"

There was something about the man that felt surprising enough to not be invasive, a softness to his intense interest, but I wanted Lee back.

"Why do I feel like I'm being questioned by a con artist psychic?" I heard the hardness in my voice and felt a quick regret.

It was his turn to look surprised.

I paused. "Could I please get a menu?"

The bartender paused for a moment, his head at an angle, as if he were listening to music. Then he nodded, his face polite as he placed a menu in front of me. "I'll be back," he said.

I felt a sharp stab of anger at the bartender, for asking too much of me. I read the menu twice, waiting for the stinging behind my eyes to subside. Once, I had been capable of ordinary conversation with overly genial strangers. I watched him exchange pleasantries with his other customers, all of whom seemed to want to shake a hand or touch his forearm or shoulder. When he returned, there was a wariness in his eyes.

"You ready?" he asked.

I exhaled. "I'm sorry. That was rude—earlier."

He did not agree or disagree, but his slight smile was gentle. "What can I get you?"

"I haven't decided yet. I'm sorry. What were your guesses?"

The bartender took off his glasses. For a moment, he looked tired. "You're good at apologies. Not too little, not too much."

"I've had some practice."

"Oh yeah?"

There it was, his curiosity that felt almost alive. I tried to be carefree with my words. "My boss thinks I apologize too much. It's nice to hear that I've gotten better."

He looked amused. "My three guesses," he said, placing a palm on the counter in front of me, "would be that you were thinking about your life, liberty, and/or your pursuit of happiness."

"How very American of you," I said, disappointed. He had a British accent that slid off his breath, leaving an echo in the air. I realized that I wanted him to be interesting.

"I'm not wrong, am I?"

"Only because our generation thinks of nothing else," I conceded.

The bartender looked at me, searching. His hand on the counter felt intimate.

"I feel like I could guess a few things about you," he said.

I shook my head at him. "A psychic after all."

But this time I could hear the softness in my voice. The overhead lighting moved his shadow over my limbs as he cracked his knuckles.

"You've traveled to four continents, you have no trouble eating dinner alone in a restaurant, and you're secretly a romantic," he said.

"All this because I sat at the bar and was rude to you?"

"You wouldn't be the first," he said, easily.

I felt the banter die in my throat. He touched my wrist on the counter for just a moment, the sensation lingering on my skin.

"All this because you walked in and I wanted to know more," he said.

Something about the bartender made my body warmer. I had been cold for so long that the feeling was surprising.

"Five continents," I said, after a pause. "My dad took us to Antarctica to look at fjords. I was sixteen and complained about the cold and not having cell service the whole time. Then we got to the coast and it was the most beautiful, wild thing I had ever seen."

He nodded.

"Nature like that, the untouched, jagged kind, makes me feel alive, too. In a way I can't reach in the city," he said.

It felt like we were alone in the bar.

"Look, you're smiling," he said, a mild cockiness in his voice. "You looked sad when you walked in here and now you're happier. Being curious about people is underrated." He plucked the menu from between my elbows and held it to his chest. "Now, what can I get you?"

"You like to know about the private thoughts of strangers."

"Yes, but if you put it that way I sound like a creep." He leaned by the bar again, a man unrushed by a burgeoning crowd. "I'm not a creep," he said.

"I'd like a martini. Gin, olives, very cold."

He reached for a bottle of gin on the rack behind him, the cluster of expectant customers expanding even further around the bar's island.

"This one's new," he said, cradling a pale blue glass bottle between his palms. "If you want to be my taster, it's on the house. I'm told it's botanical and very good."

"You want a guinea pig," I said, an unexpected lightness to my being.

He laughed and waved behind me. "Hi, be with you shortly."

"Hello Marlon," said an elderly man, with affection.

Marlon set the bottle down and leaned toward me, his eyes serious, both palms on the bar this time. "Listen. Don't go anywhere," he said. "I'll come back with the greatest drink you've ever had."

I watched as he made my drink and listened to people with attention, pouring draft beer and water into glasses, his energy a clean, easy line behind the chaos of the counter. I pulled out the copy of *Silent Spring* I had been carrying around in my purse and tried to focus. The bartender had been flirting and something inside me had responded, the slightest tremor in a hard knot that had stayed in place for so long that it might have fused into my organs. I felt a surge of hope at the flicker—maybe there was life in me yet.

"Rachel Carson said, 'in nature, nothing exists alone,'" I heard Marlon say.

I looked up, startled by his nearness. I had disappeared into the book, forgetting the swirl of the bar for a few minutes.

"Just a little light reading?" he asked as he shook my drink.

There was a grace to the way he moved, as if he might be a good dancer. I waited until he was done with the shaker.

"Yes, my idea of a comedy," I said.

"She certainly thinks humans are a joke."

He smelled of beer and a citrus I couldn't place, his teeth imperfect and disarming, a dent of missing skin in the thickness of his left eyebrow. I wondered what his injuries were.

"You've read it," I said, stupid to my own ears.

He smiled at me, as he scooped olives from a jar.

"Yes," he said.

"What's your idea of a light read?" I asked, suddenly striving to make casual conversation.

"Jane Austen, actually. Or the Brontës." He tasted my drink with a teaspoon and, satisfied, poured it into a coupe.

I laughed. "Really?"

"What's not to love about a love story?" He put the glass down in front of me. "Here, try that," he said. "And then tell me what you were sad about."

I laughed. "Do you always ask your customers very personal questions?"

Marlon shook his head. "No," he said simply.

His warmth felt infectious, making its way into my cheeks. "Where is Lee anyway?"

He looked surprised. "You know my brother."

"You're Lee's brother?" The sentence slipped out of me involuntarily.

"Half brother," said Marlon. "My mom's Black."

He radiated a kind of happiness that felt foreign to me. What might life be like, if one lived it as this man?

"Lee let me take over the bar while he decided to go on his long honeymoon. His first vacation in a decade. I'm thinking of renaming the place while he's gone. The Poppyseed or something lovely like that, that he'd kill me for. Big signage outside."

"Classic little brother. You sound more British than Australian," I said.

"Did you know, you'd make a great cop? All you do is return a question for a question. I am British. I was raised by my mum near

Cornwall. After she died, I was in a bad way. Lee and our dad took me in. I was sixteen."

For a minute we stayed in place, taking in each other. "I'm sorry about your mother," I said.

"These things happen," he said, softly. "I thought it might kill me, being alone like that." He shrugged, a flicker of memory in his eyes. "But I'm here now. The heart learns to love again." His grief returned to lightness. "Here I am, telling you sad stories instead of making sure you have a good time."

"It's unfair, the amount of loss life expects of us," I said.

"What do you think of your drink?" he asked, holding my gaze.

"It's almost as good as Lee's," I said, the teasing in my voice taking me by surprise again, my neck tilting, my body suddenly liquid.

I had been a husk only an hour ago and yet now an unfamiliar electricity washed over me, my skin tingling at the idea of the man in front of me.

"I've just moved back from London," I said. "I used to be a regular here."

"Listen, your next drink is on the house if it'll help you become a regular again," he said.

Regulah.

I swallowed. "Look at you, running Lee's business into the ground. Don't you have to get back to the rest of the bar?"

He smiled. "Deedee just started her shift. Let me make you another one."

As he reached for the bottle of gin again, the opening bars of a familiar melody ascended over the murmur of the crowd. I would have known it anywhere but my body stilled to let it be a mistake, to not let life be so cruel as to snatch tiny happinesses from me—the respite of a sexual encounter that might, for a moment, ease the body I inhabited daily.

"Do you want the same gin, I forgot to ask?" said Marlon.

He stopped to look at me.

"What's the matter?" he asked.

"I . . . the music . . . is there a way to turn it off?" I asked, as the song exploded into its full magnitude.

Confused, he looked up at the speaker.

"Oh—I mean, they pipe it through a laptop, up in the office. I don't know that we could turn it off entirely. Is it too loud?"

"It's fine," I said.

I shook my head, as if to shake water from my ears, the song insidious, in my bloodstream. Marlon made my drink, then looked up at me, cautious.

"That song, 'Lived in Bars,' used to be one of my mother's favorites. She played that record a lot."

I nodded, taking a sip of my drink.

"You don't like Cat Power?" asked Marlon, after a pause.

"I do. What made you move here?" I asked, desperate to recapture the first feeling of life that I had had in years.

He waited for a beat, scrutinizing me as the wretched, joyful melody finally faded away.

"It felt like I needed to take a leap of faith," he said, finally. "I had a job that didn't seem to be going anywhere. And it began to get to me. I took the world too personally, started fights with my customers. Lee thought I'd have better luck here. He needed help and he enjoys bossing me around."

"And now you're going to rename it The Poppyseed in return," I said.

Marlon laughed. "Okay fine, maybe not The Poppyseed then. I'll call it something more manly. The Last Drink in Brooklyn. One Hundred Years of Temptation. Lee's Drunken Way. Fries and Prejudice."

"You're a poet," I said, giddy at the darkness having passed. *Maybe I could do this.*

"Thank you. If you're back tomorrow night, I could write you a few bad poems."

"I'm actually a poetry editor," I said, flirtatious. "I can't take unsolicited submissions."

"Oh come on, you can't make up stuff like that. It's unfair to the spirit of ban-*ter*," he said, breathing out the final consonant.

"It's true, I am. I promise. At *Janus Review*. For nine years now, actually."

Marlon looked taken aback.

"Well, Lee was right when he said you could get all sorts of jobs in New York."

He wiped his hands on the towel on his shoulder, set it down, and came around the counter. He was taller than I had expected, as he swung his frame onto the barstool next to me, our knees inches from each other, looking at me in a way that reminded me of the way Jack had once looked at me.

"What were you doing in London anyway?" he asked. "Tell me everything."

A familiar heaviness began to descend into my brain, its fingers of memory cold as the reality of who I was. My breath caught in my ribs. I felt myself shrivel. I wondered if the weather had given me a chill or if the drink had gone to my head.

"I have to go," I said, fumbling for my keys in my purse. "Early morning tomorrow."

I heard him begin to say something, but everything felt at a distance as I stumbled from the barstool, the couple on my left averting their eyes at what must have looked like sudden madness. I inhaled as I stepped outside. It had started snowing again, the flakes pooling on my face. Allowing myself to breathe again, I began to walk.

"Hey. Hey."

I shook my head.

"I have to go," I repeated, as he caught up with me. Reluctant, I turned around.

Marlon lifted up his palms, as if to reassure me that he was no threat.

"Hey," he said again, gentle as he touched my shoulder.

I flinched and took a step back. For a moment he looked at me. As if coming to a decision, he nodded.

"Okay," he said.

I looked away. The snow had begun to come down heavier, the branches bare.

"I realized I don't know your name," he said, slowly. "And you don't know mine. I just wanted to say that I'm Marlon. That's all."

"I'm Mira," I said as I began to walk away. "Thank you for the drink."

Soon it would be above my ankles, the steady swirl of a thick, unanticipated storm I had been warned about, but paid no heed to, when returning to Brooklyn. I felt the ice seep into my boots, my footprints leaving a trail that the falling flakes erased in seconds, as if I had never walked there at all.

CHAPTER THREE

I HAD TAKEN to running in London. In New York, everyone ran, but there was something about it that had felt foreign, one more thing that seemed to come effortlessly to white people in particular. When she was in high school, Joy had begun to run, in an effort to lose a few pounds before prom. Red in the face and breathless, she had looked pained, hunched over, sweat dripping off her even after she returned home. In the end, she had worn her usual size eight, in a silver jumpsuit that gleamed against her skin. After being crowned prom queen, Joy had sworn off cardiovascular exercise for good, relaxing into exultant curves. Joy was eight years younger than me but had three extra inches of height and an extra two sizes on her body, inherited from her Caucasian mother, who had once been on a national rowing team. Joy's feet and skin were several shades lighter than my dark brown. Yet we both looked like our father, and in photographs, unless you paid attention, we looked alike, pronounced by our sharing what clothes we could, she stealing oversize jackets and sweaters and scarves from my closet in later years as if they were her own, an abundance to her at all times.

Joy's renunciation had erased any interest I might have had in running. But one morning in London, awake before dawn and desperate to ease the grief that shook me awake as a migraine might, I pulled on sneakers and headphones and began to run. I ran without purpose, but as the morning light broke, and the chill of the Thames mixed with my breath and sweat, I felt a dizzying release. The incessant noise of my mind emptied into a silence. Even if temporary, there was a blessed escape in the way physical exertion forced my body to return to the ground. For a few minutes, it had felt as if I might even be capable of euphoria. Since it was my only refuge, I returned to it time and again.

THE DAY AFTER I had unraveled at Lee's, on an unusually warm morning for February in Brooklyn, the snow a distant memory as New Yorkers took to the streets in T-shirts and sunglasses, I had gone running past the promenade, following the Hudson all the way up to Vinegar Hill, trying to reclaim a sense of refuge before I had to get ready for work. It was a Monday, my first day due back in the New York office of *Janus*. On my way, I walked past all the old friendly sights: fire escapes, garbage bags bursting at the seams, bodegas and cafés. Sweating through the English sweater I had chosen in a hurry, I entered the brick building that stood next to five other buildings exactly like it. It felt like the years had slipped away, liquid through the hourglass of a pandemic.

Janus was on the third floor, and when you entered, it felt more like an author's apartment than an office. Turkish carpets and bookshelves lined the floors and walls, and people worked on mismatched couches and desks. There were piles of books everywhere, including the floor, because we published essays, poems, short stories, and excerpts of novels, plus art and photography depending on the issue. We were funded by patrons who believed in the cause of literature, but every now and then, we had to cut back on the number of interns and editors that we could hire per year. My work involved reviewing submissions, selecting poems, and editing the poetry section, and it made me happy on most days. My father liked to say that Joy, ever practical, laser sharp, with a penchant for argument since childhood, had turned into the fearsome attorney that she was always meant to be; whereas I was his emotional, absent-minded child, perpetually late, with a fondness for the abstract. He was grateful that I had found a calling that suited me even if he would have preferred that I, too, had chosen more sensible terrain. Desperate to leave the tabloid I had worked at in my early twenties, I had applied for the job of a poetry associate editor at *Janus*, with no real relevant experience. But Lena, who was already being taken seriously by her peers, had sent "Evening Sun" to the poetry editor. Soon after, *Janus* requested an interview and sent me a packet of poems to critique. My phone had died in the night and so I had slept through my silenced alarm and rushed to the meeting in wrinkled slacks. But I had done well on the critique, and I got the job. I had been at the magazine since, for almost a decade. *Janus* prided itself on being fearless, and as a result received the most arresting submissions in contemporary culture—debutantes and stalwarts alike. If ever the doubt assailed me that poetry might someday become irrelevant or be replaced by an artificial intelligence, all I had to do was return to that which I had read since I was a teenager, poets and musicians having offered me life through every storm.

THE MAGAZINE, EAGER to stay lean while still publishing monthly print issues, had hired only two new editors to replace former staffers who had moved away from New York for good during the pandemic. *Janus* did not offer remote work, and Ulrike, the editor-in-chief, had been relieved five years ago when I had asked to be relocated to the London office, instead of expressing the desire to move permanently to the Catskills or Woodstock. In London, I had submerged myself in submissions, discovering a few voices that had haunted and delighted our readers. I had worked obsessively and stayed up late for countless time-zone unfriendly meetings, and eventually, Ulrike had promoted me to senior—and sole—poetry editor. When I had wanted to return to the New York office, she had agreed immediately.

"I'm so glad you're back, Mira. We've missed you," she said now, hugging me, a bright yellow scarf wrapped around her long, pale neck, jewelry hanging off her ears and arms and fingers, a vivid bird of the literary world.

"I've missed this, too. London was lonely. People didn't come into the office much."

Ulrike nodded, sunshine illuminating the silver-gray strands in her dark hair as she pushed her glasses up on her head, rubbing the bridge of her nose. There was a new exhaustion to her that I had never seen before, despite the fact that she was almost sixty.

"It's been a nightmare, these last few years. It felt for a minute like the city might not recover"—Ulrike smiled tiredly—"but here we are. But you don't have to worry; the poets have been on overdrive given all the desperation in the air."

I loved Ulrike and the room she made for my often esoteric taste. I felt a quiet happiness to be back in the office, with its stacks of papers and books, the smell of coffee in the air, the soft chatter of editors emanating from the kitchen as they ate breakfast pastries. I could see my office through Ulrike's glass wall, my desk framed in the door, the striped fabric of the chair I had had reupholstered light-years ago. A square of sun fell over the handful of wildflowers wrapped in brown paper that Binyamin and Gigi, the senior fiction editors, had brought to me that morning.

"What's being a grandparent like?" I asked Ulrike, turning back to her. I realized that she had been watching me.

"We love it. Greg and I are devastated that Isiah and Jill took the baby back, so now we drink martinis every night." Ulrike's face softened with compassion. "How are you, Mira?"

I felt my cheeks warm as a familiar sinking spread through my chest. I had integrated Jack so deeply into every facet of my life that any person who had knowledge of me had seen us as a whole. Jack and

Mira. Mira and Jack. Without him, I was fractured. In that moment, I felt something close to hatred for him. Even as I tried to rebuild, everyone knew the secret of my cracked-open heart.

"I'm here," I said, bitter, shame rising like bile inside me. "Like New York. Still standing."

THE PEACE THAT I had felt in Ulrike's office returned in fits and starts. My work felt vital in a world that was in pain. Writers were making sense of mountainous grief, reminding us that we were not alone, that there was meaning left in the world. Even the clichéd felt better than ever before. The March issue was themed around weather, and to embrace it fully, I had been reading the Carson. The thought of Marlon passed through me—thrill followed by a fleeting embarrassment. By five in the evening, piles of submissions lay around me, and I could no longer tell the rejects pile from the accepted or edited. My strength lay in my ability to see what a poet meant and help them sharpen that instinct; organization was my fatal flaw. Even as a girl, Joy would shake me awake to make an early morning flight or organize our family vacations—in return, I had held her through the loss of boyfriends, the absence of a mother, the endless meannesses of a mostly white private school. I pushed my chair away from my desk, standing distractedly, extricating myself from the day's work—it was always better to make sense of things in the morning, preferably with the help of one of the assistants. Binyamin, a worn laptop bag slung over one arm, his hairline having receded further since the last time we had worked in the same office, stopped in front of my desk.

"We're going to Franny's. Everyone wants to know if Pam in the London office is really a monster."

IN MY GRIEF-STRICKEN haze, I had forgotten that I enjoyed my colleagues. To return into the fold of fellow editors who seemed genuinely happy to have me back in New York felt blissful.

"Maybe the weather theme was a bad idea," said Gigi, glum, her forehead wrinkled in concern as she chewed on her index finger's lime green nail, her long legs squeezed under the tiny table. "People are on edge and every writer feels like they're writing themselves out of a hole. It's going to be such a depressing issue," she said.

Ana, the junior fiction editor, nodded, rueful. "I thought it was going to be all, Spring is upon us! Here, come cavort with us in the changing of seasons, gambol a little in the sun of our lives, forget the news, leave that frightful virus behind. But no, it's all beautiful rumination on like, mortality and morgues as a metaphor for the climate crisis."

"At least Ulrike agreed to run a few more cartoons," said Binyamin as we laughed.

Jansson, the art editor, shook his head. "It's all very black humor, funny-while-in-a-freewheel kind of stuff. We're making great art born of great pain now. You're not reading *Janus* for the fun of it this time, I'm afraid, not even the cartoons."

"I don't know, guys," I said, finishing my glass of wine. "I've got some really lovely stuff. Poems focused on the beauty of time slowing to a standstill, the seasons entering different corners of your one-bedroom apartment as a reminder of their passage, the anonymous joys of locking eyes with a stranger on the street behind a mask in the depths of an extra-cold winter on a first date, the opera of protest—that sort of thing. There's a lot around bodies and minds crumbling, of course, a lot of darkness, but there's also a noticing of what came of the great slowing down, too. We got one from a writer in Northern California about the plethora of wild birds that flocked around her father's grave after traffic came to a stop. He used to be a birdwatcher and it was the first time she was able to mourn."

Ana and Binyamin rolled their eyes.

"Well of course the poets are thrilled," said Gigi, grumpy. "They're always searching for eternal joy in dumpster fires. I'm going to get another drink. Anyone else want a second?"

Ana and I nodded. Binyamin stood up.

"I'll come with you. My turn to get this round," he said.

"A beer for me this time, Bin," said Ana. "Can't do another cocktail on a school night."

He nodded and joined Gigi at the crowded bar. We were at our usual cramped window table at the diner around the corner from *Janus* that served pancakes and breakfast burritos in the morning and transformed into a dive bar after six except that you could still order the burrito.

"Mira, do you think Ulrike will let me relocate to London?" asked Jansson, reflective as he reached for a packet of cigarettes. "I hear British men are the salt of the earth. Funny in their brutish ways and those accents. Mmm."

"Jansson wants a husband to cook him bangers and mash," said Ana.

"Jansson just wants a husband to bang," said Jansson.

"I don't know why I bother looking through the slush for gems when the two of you are such poets," I said, as Binyamin set a second glass of the house red in front of me.

IN LESS THAN an hour, I felt myself fading, jet lag still in my veins. I hugged them each in turn, holding on for the few extra seconds it took to communicate my gladness to be back in their fold. The streets had emptied out on a Monday night. As I began to walk toward the subway, the night air cool on my face, my heart felt lighter than it had been in five years. I was home again, emerging from a long and bitter frost. The fading sunset had turned into whirlpools of pink and gold, rapidly darkening into slashes of purple against the piers. New York was putting on a show for me. But when I reached the station, limp yellow tape crisscrossed the entrance. The only other train that could take me home was a two-mile walk away and the next bus would not come for an hour. I felt light-headed with fatigue, the city blurring around me. A lone rat scurried in the direction of a half-eaten sandwich on the sidewalk. I turned around, stepping onto the curb to hail a taxi, the breeze flipping my hair around my face. The split-second whim gave me a jolt of adrenaline, and I smiled at a stranger, a woman in an expensive suit, eating potato chips from a bag. She cautiously nodded back as a cab stopped inches from my loafers.

"Hi," I said to the elderly driver. "Palmetto. Between Wilson and Central Avenue."

"Brooklyn," said the man as he turned around to look at me, his shaggy blond eyebrows raised in surprise, his accent thick in the way of Eastern Europe.

I nodded.

"Didn't feel like the subway," I said.

He must have been pleased at the amount he was going to make, triple that of a Manhattan stop, but he had not been able to hide his feelings at the extravagance. A cannonball of dread lodged itself in my stomach. What had possessed me to take a taxi? I calculated—it would come to sixty or so dollars if I was lucky, likely more. It felt like an insane act of hedonism. I thought of my father, who would have worn the same disapproval as the cab driver, except that he would have reminded me how hard he had worked as an immigrant to enter the country and build a life so that Joy and I might have privilege that he had never experienced. It was a speech we had heard often through our childhoods, whether over purchases of sequined jeans and romance paperbacks or uneaten portions of shaak paneer ("Blended spinach, yuck. It's like a green smoothie with curry in it, Baba," Joy had said, aghast, making him laugh despite himself, as was her way). Now I longed for my father's shaak. We sped past Brooklyn Bridge, the water calm below us, the odd planet and stars in the now dark, clear sky overhead. I willed my shoulders to relax, dispelling thoughts of bills and overdraft fees. The indulgence had been worth it for the beauty of the moment, I reasoned with myself. A Harry Styles song was stuck in my head from the bar, and I hummed the chorus softly to myself.

"You are having a good day," the cabbie said, startling me.

He must have heard me hum, but something in the flat statement in his voice made me smile.

"Yes," I agreed. "Something about the season changing."

"It will be the spring before we know it," he said, stoic.

I thought of the green of Prospect Park, the tulips I might buy from the bodega for my little apartment, as we rolled off the bridge, entering Dumbo. I could take Lena's children to the botanical garden and teach them the names of flowers.

"I can't wait," I said. "Feels like we're all coming back to life."

"Where are you from?" he asked, in his staccato, abrupt way, but it was a question I was used to, and there was a softness in his voice now.

"Well, Manhattan, but both my parents are Indian."

"India. Very nice country," said my cabbie, a new warmth to him. "In Prague, where I am from, in springtime we have the Prague Spring Festival. A lot of operas and music and flowers."

"Sounds beautiful," I said. "Do you ever go back for it?"

"A plane ticket is too much in the spring. So I go in the dead of winter. When the Americans go to the Caribbean." He guffawed.

"There is a spring festival in India, too," I said. "Holi. The Indian students in college would celebrate it."

"That's right. You have Holi," he said, rolling the word off his tongue. "India is an interesting country. You throw the colors of spring at each other. I used to be a history student a long time ago. Have you ever been to Prague?"

"No, but I'd love to go. I've read Czech writers though, Karel Hynek Mácha, Václav Havel of course."

My cabbie turned around to look at me for a second, his thick eyebrows quivering in pleasure, as we swerved through the streets of Brooklyn. He had gray eyes, the color of an overcast sky.

"Really? My sisters and I studied them both in school," he said.

"Really," I said back, delighted.

I thought for a minute.

"'A haze of stars in heaven hovers— / That church of endless love's communion— / Each jewel blanches and recovers / As blanch and burn long-parted lovers / In the high rapture of reunion.'"

My cabbie shook his head, his voice thick with emotion.

"It's not the same in English but I'd recognize Mácha's 'Maj' in any language. Hearing you say these words, it reminds me of the school I went to as a boy."

He was silent for a few moments.

"I miss Prague," he said.

The cabbie did not know it, but we were both adrift from the lives we had left behind, from bodies that we no longer held close. I felt a kinship with him that I could not have spoken of, but just as I started to ask him about his boyhood, about the life he had made anew (*how did one make a life anew?*), we were confronted with a violent, reverberating explosion of sounds as a truck hit a large tree at the curb of the street corner a few feet in front of us. I heard screaming as a heavy thud threw me forward, as I descended into a darkness, my last thought that it had at least been a memorable conversation.

WHEN I CAME to, it felt as if my shoulders might be broken, so blinding was the pain in my torso, but hunched over between the seat and floor, I realized that I was alive. I opened my eyes, dazed immediately by red and blue LED light, the blare of sirens pouring into my senses. I heard voices nearby. It felt like a monumental effort to lift my head. When I did, I realized that the rear of our taxi had pressed up toward the front, sandwiching my body, the leather seat's faint scent of tobacco in my nostrils. I felt the first stirrings of a headache as I craned my neck in the direction of the driver's seat. It was empty. Wincing, I lifted my body upward. A rush of relief swept over me as my knees performed their required action, my limbs in pain but unhurt. I fumbled with the handle of the door and it gave way immediately, detaching abruptly from the vehicle and hanging by its hinge. As I climbed out of the taxi, I heard an urgent voice.

"Hey. Hey, hey. Miss. Take it easy."

It was a firefighter, his hand extended toward me, the moonlight mixed in with the streetlamps and police car lights shining off his helmet.

"My driver," I tried to say, as he took me by my elbow, his grip and motion speedy yet gentle.

"You can't just come barreling out of a crash like that," he said. "You could have a concussion. Here, let's go over here and sit back down. Easy now."

Very slowly, the firefighter walked me a few feet away from the taxi and lowered me onto a curb as I registered the chaos around me.

"Where's the taxi driver?" I asked again, fear making its way through my stomach.

The firefighter stretched out my arms and legs at an excruciatingly slow pace. "The driver's okay," he said. "He broke his arm, but he's over there, getting it looked at. He told us you were in here."

I looked in the direction that the firefighter tilted his head toward. My cabbie was sitting on the opposite curb a few feet away, a paramedic leaning over him. An open ambulance with its headlights on bathed them both in a floodlight. The cabbie had been watching us and raised one hand in my direction as the paramedic examined the other one.

"What happened?" I asked the firefighter, but he was walking back toward my taxi. He leaned into it, looking for something. After a few moments, he returned to me.

"Here, miss," he said, handing me my phone and purse. "There was a crash—a Sprinter van rammed into a fallen tree, skidded, hit another tree and overturned on the curb. Major pileup because of it. Seven cars and they think two people died inside the van. They're still pulling folks out of there. You got lucky—a pretty bad rear-end, but you seem okay. You need to get your leg cleaned up—it's bleeding. The window shattered so it's probably a piece of glass. Do you want some water?"

I nodded, a wave of nausea coursing through me. The front of the taxi was crumpled into the back of the vehicle in front of it. My father's face floated into my brain. I closed my eyes. When I opened them again, a man with a microphone stood in front of me, backlit by a halo of blue light.

"Are you okay, miss?" asked the man, his eyes worried and alert.

He was younger than me, about Joy's age I thought, earnest in the same way.

"Yes," I said. "I'm just waiting for the medic. My leg."

I felt a tiredness taking hold of me.

"Can you tell us what happened?" he asked, pointing his microphone at me.

Joy, bossy and determined, said into my brain, *Tell me what happened.*

"I...they said it was a crash—a van fell over or something."

I couldn't focus, the lights getting brighter in my eyes, the headache beginning to throb in the back of my head.

"Did they say who was to blame? Was the Uber driver driving recklessly?" At my bemusement, he explained, worriedly, "It was a private van. I'm with ABC7. We're just trying to get to the bottom of what happened."

I realized that, as he spoke, a second man was behind him with a hefty camera pointed at me. The reporter turned around to face the camera.

"We are live at the site of the crash near Barclays Center," he said. "We're told there are multiple fatalities—three dead so far. We've got a survivor here."

An image of Jack making breakfast, buttering toast, the television on in the background as he listened to the news absent-mindedly and without fail in the mornings, his blue eyes widening, took amorphous shape inside my mind.

Tell me what happened, MG.

I felt myself physically shrink from the reporter, raising both arms to cover my face with my palms.

"I...I can't," I said as I raised myself to my shaky feet, clutching my purse. "Please, I have to go."

Pushing past the reporter and his cameraman, I walked as steadily as I could until my faculties began to trust my body again. I walked quicker before breaking into a slow, painful run through the night streets. I had made a promise to myself a long time ago and I would not be found by those who had left me.

CHAPTER FOUR

I RAN OUT of breath in two blocks, my purse leaden on my arm, my coat too heavy for my body. I had not broken anything, of this I was certain, but somewhere on my leg there was an open wound on fire, and shards of pain shot through my shoulders and ribs. I needed to sit down. I leaned against a brownstone gate, trying to get a sense of my bearings. Prospect Park was to my left, so I could not be too far from home or Lena. I reached for my phone in my purse with an intense gratitude for the firefighter who had remembered to collect my belongings. The map glowed up at me, reassuring, as tiny black Ubers raced across my screen. I stared at them, trying to make a decision, the throbbing in my right leg taking on a life of its own. For the second time in two days, I was only a few feet away from Lee's Heights.

INSIDE, MARLON WAS alone behind the counter, a CLOSED sign in curved gold font hanging on the door. The lights inside were dimmer than usual, his body behind the empty counter against the streetlamp's light reminiscent of a Hopper painting. I stood outside for a few minutes, undecided, until he looked up. Seeing my shape in the dark through the open window, he frowned, his muscles tensing immediately. As his eyes adjusted to the darkness, widening in recognition, I raised a hesitant palm in a wave. In seconds, he had unlocked the front doors of the bar.

"Mira?" he asked into the darkness, as he stepped outside. It was the first time he had said my name, the syllables rounded in his specific, tender manner.

"You must think I'm insane," I said.

He smiled, cautious.

"We are all a little—" he began to say and then abruptly stopped. "Good god, what happened to you?"

I did not know what I looked like, but I felt my chest tighten as something snapped inside of it. In dismay, I realized I was crying, taking in mouthfuls of air, my body shaking in release. I tried to get a few words out to explain myself, but nothing emerged, and instead, Marlon gently took me in his arms, my face wet, pressed into his collarbone, cotton and sweat, the concentrated smell of alcohol, and a long-ago aftershave engulfing me. I felt his palm and fingers on the back of my neck as he let me cry.

"I have a sister," I said into his shoulder, the shoulder of a stranger, yet it felt natural. "I haven't seen her in three years. The last time I saw her I told her that I hated her. She could see I meant it. I could have died tonight and that would have been the last thing I ever said to her."

I felt him pull me a fraction closer, his heartbeat quickening.

"I could have died"—I felt myself gasp, through my tears, on the words—"I could have died, and no one would have known for days."

Marlon said nothing as my weeping escalated, then subsided.

"I'm sorry," I said. "You don't even know me."

I took in a breath, as his arms released around me.

"Sometimes people can see each other," said Marlon, his face a mix of confusion and compassion.

I swallowed, uncertain, the lack of judgment in his eyes unraveling me further.

"Maybe you just thought you could trust Lee's brother?" Marlon shrugged very slightly.

"I should go. I just needed to sit down for a moment."

"And you came to my bar to sit down, Mira?" he asked, so softly that I had to strain to hear him.

I looked away. It did not feel as if I could lie to him.

"Look, your leg, it's bleeding. Just come in for a moment and I'll wrap it up. I've got a kit behind the bar." He looked at the wound, concerned. "Although maybe it needs stitches," he said. "Maybe we should go to the ER. How did you get that gash?"

"A car... van... crashed into a tree and fell on its side. People were hurt—some of them dead." I felt delirious, my eyes beginning to burn again. "My taxi crashed into the car in front of it, the car behind us rear-ended us. I—I got lucky."

"Jesus," said Marlon, soberly. "Fucking life."

"My leg and ribs hurt, but it isn't too bad." I paused. "What if you just came home with me?" I heard myself ask. "I live right around the corner."

Marlon looked taken aback; quickly, his face dissolved into a grin.

"Not like that," I said, smiling back at him.

"You are a bit mental, you know that," he said, as he touched my elbow, a now-familiar charge passing between us.

I looked at a passing taxi. I wondered if my cabbie had made it home yet but then again, home was Prague.

"I don't want to go to the ER and I've got Band-Aids at home and I don't want to walk home alone and even though you have no reason to want to, I could use the help," I said.

For a long moment, Marlon and I looked at each other. I watched as he made up his mind, nodding in the direction of the bar.

"Deedee and Carlos are back there—they'll close up," he said. "I'll walk you home."

I felt an irrational relief. "Thanks."

"Hold on one moment," said Marlon.

He disappeared into the bar as I stood on the street, my leg throbbing. Lamplight spilled over rust-brown exteriors and stone stoops.

Dance music emanated from an open window nearby. Two men, absorbed in each other, held hands as they passed me by. A child was asleep on his father's shoulder across the street as they left the chop-house around the corner. The bookstore, co-op, and café had shuttered for the night. Marlon reappeared, wielding a plastic red box.

"A Band-Aid isn't going to cut it on that gash, I'm afraid. I'm going to fix you properly."

I OPENED THE door to my apartment, self-conscious about the dishes I had not done, the half-eaten bowl of cereal still on the table, magazines and books everywhere, the sofa covered in loose-leaf poems. I had bought packages of toilet paper and Kleenex and left them on the kitchen counter. Even if I had not lived in it long, the evidence of my teeming, messy life had inhabited the apartment. Marlon and I had not talked much on the ten-minute walk. When my leg had given me enough trouble to make me wince, he had extended his arm for support. In this manner, I had taken a stranger home.

"You better not be an ax murderer," I said airily, slowly taking off my coat, my limbs still congealed from the crash.

"You don't think that I'm the one who should wonder if you're the murderer?"

I worried that my joke had offended him, but Marlon stood in the center of my apartment, taking it in, his sinewy frame occupying a large portion of the suddenly cramped living room. He seemed to be a taker of mental notes, the most vulnerable parts of me exposed by his observation.

"I did lurk outside your bar tonight," I said, rueful, gritting my teeth as a flash of pain seared its way through my calf.

"Sit down, Mira, please," said Marlon, pushing back the cushions on my father's armchair.

I dropped into it as he moved aside issues of *Janus* from my ottoman and pulled it closer, propping my foot on top of it. He opened up his first-aid kit, and began to cut a piece of gauze into squares.

"What does a poetry editor do, anyway?" he asked. "Outside of any murderous skill, you seem like you might be good at it."

I laughed. "What makes you say that?"

"You're unpredictable and feel a lot of things and seem like you want to know more about the world."

I shook my head at him. "Anyone ever call you presumptuous?"

"Yes." He smiled up at me as he applied three lines of ointment on a precise square of gauze. "But you didn't answer the question."

I stretched out my uninjured leg. Marlon bent over the first-aid box—I saw him make note of the brief flash of my upper thigh as my skirt moved slightly. I felt powerful, and it was inexplicable, unfamiliar.

"I read poems and spend a lot of the day thinking about them, about the ways in which language has the ability to rearrange itself to mean new things. Once in a while I'll think about a word for hours. Mostly I just choose the poems that move me most. Sometimes I have to pick a big name whose work I don't necessarily love but it'll bring new readers to the magazine."

Marlon looked up at me again, a flash of something in his eyes.

"What poems move you?"

I took in an involuntary breath between my teeth, his nearness as acute as the flashes of pain I felt.

"Langston Hughes. Gwendolyn Brooks. Danez Smith. Oliver. Linda Gregg, Jack Gilbert, Vikram Seth. Ada Limón. Tagore."

I quelled the urge to chatter.

"Pushkin," I said, feeling the pain that Pushkin now brought with him.

"'Everyone forgets that Icarus also flew / It's the same when love comes to an end.'" Marlon placed the gauze, now with tape attached to its underside, on the table and pulled out an antiseptic wipe from its wrapper. "I always loved that one," he said.

I paused as I looked at him. "How do you know it?"

He shrugged. "My mother liked Gilbert and Gregg and their love story. She must have introduced him to me."

"I fell in love with Gilbert in college," I said. "'I believe Icarus was not failing as he fell / but just coming to the end of his triumph.'" I shook my head. "Can you believe that line is about divorce?"

The words soothed me as I watched him work, but the spaces between our bodies felt finite and dangerous, and my mind felt fragile. Marlon looked at the magazines on the table next to him as he came closer to my skin.

"So do you have a kid in the back somewhere?" he asked. "Fine if you do. I like them," he added quickly.

"I'm hiding him in my closet," I said.

"I won't call the cops on you. I like you too much."

There it was again, the feeling I had forgotten, the one that emboldened me.

"No kids on the premises, I'm afraid," I said.

Marlon tilted his head as he examined my wound. "Do you want any?"

Something sudden, its kernel hard and bitter, caught in my sternum as I shook my head. "The kids' magazines are for my closest friend's youngest—her son," I said.

In the next instant Marlon had the wipe on my raw flesh. I screamed in agony.

"There," he said with a grin, wiping it down, his fingers light and quick as he wrapped up the center of my calf. "All done."

"Jerk," I whispered, breathless. "You didn't warn me."

"You gotta get through the nightmare in one go." He leaned back, satisfied. "You got any water nearby?" he asked. "I could use a drink."

"There's a Brita in the fridge. There's also a bottle of white wine in there, if you're into that."

"I'm into it," he said, rising from the floor in one motion, his linen slacks deeply wrinkled.

"You don't feel like a bartender," I said, leaning back into my chair, as the stinging subsided into cold relief. "And you read poetry. What are you hiding, sir?"

I heard the pop of the wine stopper leaving the bottle.

"Ah, the sound of sweet, sweet discrimination," said Marlon from the kitchen. "Are you saying I'm too well read to be a mere bartender?"

I felt my ears warm.

"I'm sorry. I only meant that Lee, and...and every other bartender I know in Brooklyn, feels—dresses a certain way. More...practical. T-shirts or shirts over jeans, dishcloths on shoulders, you know. They look more...at home in a bar."

"Ah, impractical discrimination. What about Jules over at Pete's Candy, who dresses like he lives in the 1920s and performs jazz standards by night?"

Marlon emerged from my kitchen, a glass of water in his left hand, a bottle of wine under an arm, and two flutes, expertly held by their stems in his right hand.

"I'm sorry I forgot my dishcloth," he said, with mischief.

"I'm sorry," I said, shame bubbling up in my stomach. "I was just trying to be funny. But it wasn't. I've berated my dad so much for preconceived assumptions about people, and here I am, doing it myself. Something in my blood."

"What's wrong with being a bartender?" asked Marlon, amused, as he filled my flute.

"Nothing. God. Nothing. My dad will slip into this headspace every once in a while, of what a career means, and it's just silly prejudice born of a culture that values success in a certain way."

"That's a lot of cultures," said Marlon, handing me the glass. "Being Black comes with its own baggage."

"Yeah."

He laughed. "You're sweet when you're miserable, Mira."

"Oh good," I said, rolling the flute's stem between my palms, my hands seeking anything that gave them purpose. "Then you'll find me sweet all the time."

Marlon looked at me even as I regretted what had slipped out of me. I shook my head.

"I'm really making an impression here. Girl who almost died alone and found a stranger to bring home and cry about it. And offended him for good measure."

As I lifted my glass, Marlon leaned over and caught my wrist between his fingers, stopping me from drinking. He raised himself nearer to my face and kissed me. I closed my eyes, his tongue luxuriating into my mouth, his fingers pressing into the interior of my wrist, a long-forgotten lightning rod of desire making its way through me. When he drew back, there was hesitance in his eyes.

"I thought...that might be okay," he said.

"Yes," I said, disoriented.

He looked as surprised as I felt.

"Good," he said, as he rose to sit on the edge of the ottoman, my bandaged leg propped next to him.

Marlon took a long drink from his glass of wine.

"You have a really beautiful job, the poetry thing," he said, as he set his flute down.

"Yes. It's the best thing that's ever happened to me. I feel like it was an accident, falling into something I love that much. Some days I have too many meetings and I whine about it and then I have to catch myself, because the truth is, I lucked out."

"That's a big deal. What a stellar lot in life. More than what a lot of us can claim to have."

"You win some in this life, you lose some," I said.

Marlon, even in the few hours he had spent in my presence, seemed to catch trace remains of my hardness when it floated to the surface.

"Do you have a good lot in life?" I asked.

He smiled. "I'm working on it," he said.

I held out my flute. Marlon refilled it and then his own. I examined my leg, perfectly bound. "Where'd you learn how to do that?" I asked.

"There's a lot you don't know about me," he said as he stretched his legs out in front of him, an ease to his body amongst my belongings. "I contain all sorts of multitudes I'm eager to impress you with."

He reached for my left ankle and cradled it, his touch thrilling.

"This is nice," he said.

I was aware that my palms were beginning to sweat. The lamp I had turned on was flickering, a bulb left in storage too long, but it cast a dreamlike haze around us.

"What's the most important thing in this life for you, Mira?"

"Is this a bit you do with women? You ask these questions, and make them feel special?"

"Do you feel special?"

I paused. "In this moment, yes."

He smiled at me.

"Good. I'm always interested in people, yes."

He paused.

"Rarely this much," he said.

"You have to say that."

"No, I don't. I'm so good that I don't have to say it. Ladies still want to come home with me."

I laughed, charmed by his audacity. "It's my home you're in, mister." I took a deep breath. "Love. I think love is the most important thing for me." I closed my eyes and my father's face floated up at me again. I opened my eyes, embarrassed at the intensity of the admission to a stranger.

"Your turn," I said.

Marlon blinked, both of us made a little heavier by desire.

"Truth, I think. To the point where I can be too difficult about settling for less. Art, people, feelings, sport—I like it all to feel true. And that's no easy ask of life."

"That's the only rule I have for a poem," I said. "It has to feel true."

He nodded. I felt my breath rise into my throat.

"Can I say one thing to you, even though I'm a stranger?"

"You're not a stranger," I said.

We looked at each other. Marlon set his glass down, his irises serious and larger in the light.

"Before my mother got sick, I told her I was leaving for Australia," he said. "I wanted to get to know my dad and Lee. She didn't like it. It made her feel like she hadn't been enough for me. She was diagnosed a few weeks later—and her body went quick, almost overnight. There was no time to say anything but goodbye. She was gone so quickly."

I reached for his hand, the grief in his voice extending its reach into the grief in my chest.

"What you said earlier, about not having seen your sister in years"—he shook his head—"regret is a knife in your heart and it can stick in there for good sometimes." Marlon looked at me. "Although I'm pretty sure it's not my place to say anything."

I waited for the stiffening in my body at any mention of Joy, the hot trickle that made its way from the back of my head into my spine and veins, so much so that Lena and my father had all but ceased to say her name to me. Instead, I pulled him toward me, temporarily blinded by what I wanted most, my knee immobile but the rest of me pliant as this time I took the collar of his shirt in my damp fist, meeting no resistance as my body lowered over his, my bruises forgotten, as his breath of tart wine closed over mine. As we lay back on the floor and I took off his glasses and his shirt, after all of the dance, we were able to move quickly, urgently with each other, furious longing that had come alive in me after five desolate years, buckling under heat and skin and teeth and sweat, in the relief of knowing each other's bodies. Afterward, as we drifted into sleep, our arms around each other, I thought of Jack, and if he might feel any pain at my finally having experienced real pleasure for the first time since he had left me.

IN THE MORNING, I woke up in a sweat, Marlon's body next to mine. It was too hot under the covers, the sun streaming in on our faces and bodies. His face was in my neck, my leg intertwined with his, the smell of his naked body unfamiliar. Gingerly, I stretched out my bandaged right leg, while trying to extract the one under him. Marlon's arm slid around my waist, its weight heavy on my stomach. I winced—even though I was certain I had not broken anything, I was in pain.

"Are you getting up?" he murmured against my skin.

I turned my neck toward the alarm clock on my nightstand, my great grandfather's, from Bengal.

"In about twenty minutes, at seven, that thing is going to jangle you awake. The trick is to be up before it can get you."

I slid out from under him. In seconds, I was pulling a T-shirt from my closet over my head. Marlon propped himself up on one hand, blurry from sleep as he put on his glasses. He looked at me, quizzical.

"Regrets?"

I paused for a moment. I shook my head, unable to fathom how someone could live life with his easy transparency, my own guard lowering because of it.

"None," I said. "That was pretty great."

"Come here," he said, sitting up.

As we kissed, I felt desire seize me again, followed by relief—it had not been a fluke. The life in me could rear its head as it once used to, as it had last night, and come roaring back. Grateful, I lingered in the kiss, my body pressing against him. Marlon groaned. "You said it was almost seven," he said. "I open Lee's at seven for breakfast."

I slipped a hand inside the sheet, suddenly fearless. *Nothing had been lost to me.*

"What if you came back later? After I'm back from work?"

"Ah, an invitation," he said, pulling me closer. "Yes. Maybe dinner at the bar before? I make a mean steak and fries. Well, Carlos makes the fries because I'm afraid of that much hot oil."

My desire felt heady. Even so, I knew I owed him the truth. I placed a palm on his chest, the soft hair beneath springing under my touch.

"Marlon," I whispered into the space between us. "I like this. I like you. But I'm not looking for anything."

Marlon drew back to look at me. What was I thinking, sending away the first man in years who had stirred something in me? I felt his hand stroke the top of my head. "You're not looking for anything," he repeated, quietly. "I assume you mean love, a relationship, going steady, that kinda thing?"

"Are you trying to be funny?"

He shrugged.

"Yeah. But Mira, we've just met. What do you know about what you want or what I want from anything? I'm just saying yes to your invitation and I'm suggesting you eat the damned good steak I make at the bar. You don't want to, you want to just bring me up around the block and upstairs and have your way with me, that's fine"—he shrugged again. "I'm in."

I rolled over on my back. "You're crazy."

"Look at us, two peas in a pod," he said as he slid his hand under my shirt.

I caught it and held it above my breastbone.

"I have no idea right now how to be anything else but hurt. Someone... my ex. He really broke my heart."

He nodded, compassionate again.

"Ah, that's a tough one. How long ago?"

"It's been years," I said, looking away.

We lay on our backs, looking at my cream ceiling. I wished the landlord had put in a fan. After a few moments, Marlon sighed and reached for my hand.

"What you are is here and so am I. And that could be fun, you never know. One day at a time."

He kissed my fingers and swung himself off the mattress in one motion. "You're going to want to keep that leg out of the shower today—I'll change it when I see you later."

Marlon walked out of the bedroom. A few moments later, I heard the tap run in the kitchen. I followed him in.

"My neighbors are ordering telescopes off the internet right this minute," I said, as I watched him drink water, naked.

He laughed. "I'll be out of your hair in a second."

I leaned against the entrance of the kitchen. "You just move through life, easy like Sunday morning huh?" I asked.

From the bedroom, my alarm let out a long, ringing screech, followed by another. I ran into the bedroom and banged a palm down on the bulbous top, the sudden silence afterward, deafening.

"Not anymore," he said, from behind me. "I'll be shaking in my shoes from that sound all day."

"I haven't set up my coffee maker yet," I said. "Maybe I'll come drink a cup of coffee at the bar before work."

He turned around to look at me. For a moment neither of us said anything.

"You're in luck. I also make a damn fine cup of coffee."

THERE WAS A chill in the air, but it was sunny and I had decided on a floral summer dress that I felt taller in. The skies outside were blue, yellow-rumped warblers arguing outside my open windows, the promise of a warm afternoon burgeoning, despite the season. As I neared the corner of Lee's Heights, I wondered if Marlon had had a few minutes to himself for a coffee before the bar's breakfast rush. I would ask him something flirtatious about where he had been last night, I thought to myself, reaching to pat a collared terrier drinking from the dog bowl outside. I had left my hair loose and smoothed it into place. As I pushed open the doors of the bar, my body was half inside Lee's but it felt departed, as I looked at Joy—older Joy, more rounded, more beautiful, softer, more fragile Joy, her dark curls falling to her collarbones as they always had, her pants tucked into the boots we had bought together at a sale in Saks, as she leaned over the counter, her familiar, brilliant smile focused on Marlon.

PART TWO

CHAPTER FIVE

JOY AND I had fought over our father our entire life, but it was always a language of small barbs. Once she had borrowed my favorite coat—a silk floral Jacquard that my mother had sourced from an auction in London—and proceeded to lose it at the afterparty of a party where she had had too much wine. It was the only time in our lives that we had screamed at each other, shedding our usual chilliness for an inferno—me, incandescent with rage over her careless disregard of what I loved and her, furious with disbelief at my refusal to accept an apology. But we both knew the argument was the capsizing of a cauldron we had inhabited for too long. I was my father's favorite, the first time he had experienced the rush of fatherhood; I had inherited my whimsy from him, our humor identical in wordplay that incited both scorn and jealousy from Joy. We loved music and nature equally, both easily distracted and wounded, neither able to forgive quickly even as we loved without boundary. My mother, unmaternal and gifted, had left my ordinary, comfortable father for the pleasures of academic stardom in the classics department at Oxford when I was three. At Christmases, I received first editions, rare records, and the galleys of newly minted poet laureates in lieu of mothering, but we were both certain that this was for the best. Joy had lost her mother at birth to sepsis, yet Joy was her mother's daughter, more glamorous than my father and me in persona and vocabulary, with the quicker wit and tongue, her nails and lips a habitual deep crimson or pink, an expert at mastering the details of family life. Even as a teen, she was the glue that organized our vacations and haircuts, mailed in our votes, returned books to the library, called cousins and aunts on birthdays, and ensured that groceries appeared at our doorstep on Sundays. If my father and I argued (politics or the choice of a motorcycle-riding boyfriend or a late curfew), Joy would play referee, reminding us that we were a unit, which was more important than the emotion and egos that rose so easily to the surface for both of us. The fierce love between Joy and I was rivaled only by the unspoken competition over the only parent we had ownership of, the only constant we had ever known. In Joy's diaries, she mourned that my father denied her his innermost musings, his acute honesty and the gift of his friendship, choosing instead the safety of his older daughter's opinions, which might have been mirrors of his own. In my opinion (I refused to keep diaries, certain that Joy would read mine), my father felt constant guilt over his own favoritism and overcompensated, paying for Joy's student loans in full (not mine), allowing her to stay out later (until college, I had had a strict curfew), allowing her the material pleasures she craved—expensive coats and high-end salons, gadgets and trinkets—while I had been raised to be frugal and second-generation, the recipient of harder, higher standards, while she occasionally failed French, a subject I assumed she had chosen for its sexiness. At eighteen, Joy applied to law school at King's College in London to win over my father, her acumen devoted to proving that she was his perfect child. I had floated in the other direction—rebelling with directionless jobs until I found *Janus*, a disappointment until I wasn't. Neither of us felt wholly seen by him, and we compensated by loving each other with an absorption yet letting our resentments rankle politely below our skins, never fully certain in our belonging to each other but this unease overridden by the feeling that we needed each other, as might surviving passengers on a single raft.

IN THE SPRING of 2017, Joy had left for London and I had been at *Janus* for three years. Ulrike had been there for nineteen years, since the sixth year of the magazine's life, and had made me deputy editor of the poetry section despite my inability to remain interested at long administrative meetings. She had recently left her husband of twenty-four years, proclaiming herself "over the ways of the American man."

"What I really need, Mira, is a man to fuck," said Ulrike to me over a second vesper at Franny's one Sunday afternoon, her German accent shooting out syllables in emphasis. "A hot-blooded, hilarious man who will show my poor, old, neglected clitoris that I am in my *prime*."

"You are in your prime," I said.

It was true—Ulrike at fifty-three was undisputedly an icon. At publishing events, photographers would follow her around, to capture the drama of her gray bob, angular against her sharp nose, her forehead high and smooth, an imperial quality to her, whether in sweatpants or couture, in the way she would clap her hands often in delight, her amber eyes slits of mischief.

"I would like to be a cougar, Mira," she said, unhappily.

"I imagine that would make a lot of men in Manhattan very happy."

She frowned. "You are single, yes? No one on the radar yet?"

"Well, there's Leon. Remember? He picked me up from the office last week." I had been on four dates with a well-mannered, entirely capable man from New England who, on paper, was perfect even if he had yet to inspire any strong feelings from me.

Ulrike narrowed her eyes in investigation. "The man you met on the internet? But it is not...a real thing?"

"It's new. I'm giving it a chance."

"Is he rich? Why are you going out with him?"

I shook my head in protest as my caftan billowed around me in the warm breeze. There were spring blossoms everywhere, falling into

Ulrike's hair, their tickle readying for an allergic reaction in my nostrils, the leaves of the city young and green.

"Stop it," I said. "I like him. He's a little on the serious side, that's all."

Ulrike leaned forward. "My dear, one likes"—she flung a palm around—"a park. Or a summer day. A doughnut perhaps. One must be *stirred* by a man."

"I've been stirred by some summer days. Some doughnuts, too."

"Ha ha ha," she said, grim. "Unless a man makes you feel the way your poems do, it is a waste of your time. Just ask me, a few decades later."

I softened. "Oh Ulrike. It'll get better. I promise."

"You don't know that," she said, suddenly miserable. "Anyway, what does Leon do, remind me?"

I leaned back, sipping my vivid orange cocktail, a regrettable combination of salt-sweet mysterious ingredients the bartender had talked me into trying, the alcohol lightening the innards of my mind. I tried to conjure up Leon in my mind and, for a moment, drew a blank.

"He's a professor. An anthropologist. Very smart." I hesitated. "He's from Boston and wants to take me to a great little museum there, the Isabella Stewart Gardner Museum, when we visit. He's great at unearthing little gems everywhere. We have a good time."

Ulrike nodded with satisfaction. "Academic, like Greg. They will turn you into a thesis paper that even you will find boring. Mira, you can't date some *regular* guy from a university."

"It's regular pickings for us ordinary people, I'm afraid," I said. "And that sounds pretty great to me, actually. You, on the other hand..." I waved a tipsy hand in her direction. "Who doesn't want to fall in love with you?"

"I've had enough love to last me a lifetime." She took a drink from her coupe in disgust. "It's an excuse for neglect," she said.

"If that isn't the beginning of a poem, I don't know what is," I said. "Have you tried the apps?"

"No," she said. "Can you imagine—'Ulrike Bernard, editor in chief, ender of marriages, seeks a stallion...to get laid.'"

We collapsed in hysterics. She leaned forward again, this time conspiratorial.

"But there is someone I have my eye on." She had the same look in her eye as when she discovered a new talent.

"A young writer," she said.

"Oh no. You can't. What will people say?"

"Oh be quiet," she said irritably. "He's a novelist and has exhibited no signs of wanting an excerpt published in goddamn *Janus*. He's just besotted with me and quite bright and devastatingly handsome."

"How old is he?" I asked, worriedly.

"Mmm." Ulrike smacked her lips, as if tasting a particularly delicious ingredient, her mouth puckered over her olive, her gray bangs stirring in the breeze. "I want to say he's in his forties, but it could be a late-thirties situation."

"I thought you were going to say, nineteen."

"'Oh oh oh oh, Mrs. Robinson,'" sang Ulrike.

"'Jesus loves you more than you will know,'" I said.

She suddenly turned businesslike. "You work too much, Mira," she said, with an unexpected air of largesse.

I looked at her, suspicious. Ulrike had many qualities but admitting to overworking her staff was not one of them.

"Oh yeah?"

"Yes. And I am here to make it right. I propose we go to a party." At this, Ulrike clapped her hands, as if confronted with a miracle, her many rings glittering in the sun.

"Really? And will there be writers at this party?"

"There are writers at all our parties. This one is no exception," she said, dismissive.

"I'm not going to be your wingman and follow you into a publishing scandal," I said, amused.

"Oh please, darling Mira." Ulrike's shoulders slumped a little, a genuine trace of sadness in her eyes. "I feel old and silly. Starting over—it feels alien, like I've had all my powers taken away. I don't know how to be just a woman, a person anymore. I can't bear the idea of someone laughing at me." She looked away. "I met him months ago. I haven't been able to bring myself to go to the things he's invited me to, or see him. I'm afraid I'll never be ready."

I felt my heart constrict. "Of course I'll come with you." I placed my hand over hers.

"Excellent," said Ulrike, clapping her hands again, instantly revived. "It's on eighty-seventh and Columbus, tomorrow at eight. I'll pick you up in a car."

"I've been had," I said, resigned.

"It's going to be such fun," she said, furiously texting.

I drained my cocktail, my social anxiety rearing at the thought of a party where Ulrike went off into some sort of dim corner with a man and I did not know anyone.

"What's the name of this writer who's turned you into a madwoman?" I asked.

"Sam," said Ulrike, prolonging the syllable. "Samuel. Samuel Smith."

"A novelist I've never heard of. Great."

AS IT TURNED out, Samuel Smith was a red-faced, very tall man of Irish descent from North Carolina with a hearty laugh that filled the room and the beginnings of a paunch. It also turned out that his debut novel was poised to be the talk of the London Book Festival. Incredulous, I watched as glamorous, powerful Ulrike unraveled at his jokes, once even snorting mid-laugh. Ulrike's ex-husband, Greg, was a reed of a man, handsome in a pale, classical manner, a professor of literature who liked to pair wine that he had brought back from corners of France with rich lamb stews that he slow-cooked in their mid-century kitchen. I had never seen her laugh with such abandon, long and hard, standing in that living room. Sam turned from Ulrike, frowning at the bookshelf next to them, as he ran a chubby finger along the spines of hardcovers. I watched as he extricated a book and opened it and read something to Ulrike, who looked at the page, rapt, tracing her finger over the lines, their mouths too close. Ulrike must have felt my stare because she looked up and met my eyes with an embarrassed recognition of my shock. She half smiled, and lifted a shoulder in a slight shrug, and I understood then that Ulrike was in love.

I WANDERED AWAY, in an effort to stop staring at Ulrike and Samuel Smith. Love seemed mysterious and filled with new minefields just as you detonated the last of them. Ulrike had loved Greg deeply, of this I was certain, their marriage a formidable oak with roots spread thick into family and community. Once, he had accompanied Ulrike to a conference in Geneva and I had been envious of the way in which he unpacked for both of them, the snacks they bought for each other, her gentle surrender as she laid her head on his shoulder at a dinner table. Even their squabbling seemed born of known rhythms—an assurance that this, too, would pass. Just after I joined *Janus*, Ulrike had taken me to an awards party where she was being honored. Greg had turned to me, his cheeks bright with pleasure and said, “It’s insanity that I get to have this woman as my wife.”

And so it could be true then, that a person might wind up married for decades to a version of a soulmate and life might yet have the latter falling in love with a ginger Irishman at a book party. The party was for Samuel Smith’s birthday and I looked around his Upper West Side apartment with judgment. A basketball lay in a corner, behind an extra-large flatscreen television and a framed poster of the film *Chinatown* hung over a leather La-Z-Boy. I caught a glimpse of an unmade bed, as I passed by the second bedroom. A single sock, unpeeled from a foot, lay in the crevice of the door. Samuel Smith was a manchild. In the kitchen, the remnants of a chocolate cake from Citarella sat on the counter, nestled between an empty wine bottle and a withering trail of ivy that emerged from a gilded planter. I sliced off a wedge of the chocolate cake with the plastic knife that was still in the box and held it between my fingers as I took a large bite. With my other hand, I filled a glass of water under the tap. The frosting was dense and rich, unexpectedly wonderful, and I closed my eyes in pleasure as I poured the water into the plant.

"It's really saying something when your guests are forced to keep your plants alive," I heard a voice say, behind me.

Chocolate on my teeth and fingers and the edges of my mouth, something in the recesses of my memory clicked softly into place, a feeling of the inevitable.

"Hi there," Jack said, his fine dark-blond hair tousled, his ears sticking out (*Obama ears, we had called them*), his face flushed from the party, a boyish delight on his face as if he had planned to sneak up on me. He was dressed in corporate clothes—a formal shirt rolled up to his elbows as if he had recently shrugged off a blazer, his gray slacks pleated over leather dress shoes.

I laughed and apologized for the overstep.

"You're a friend of Sam's then?" he asked, his eyes alight with the kind of infectious enthusiasm I would come to know was his way of life—a desire to experience fully all that life had to offer him.

"Ulrike Bernard's," I said. "She's—Sam's friend."

Jack nodded, knowing. "Sam's talked about her for a while now," he said. "He's my older brother. But I'm the fun one. Can I get you a drink?"

He reached into the fridge. Cans of craft beer and seltzer stood next to a cluster of Chinese takeout boxes, the shelves empty otherwise.

"A soda would be great. Do you always let your brother have his parties in your apartment?"

I tore off a section of paper towel and rubbed at the chocolate on my hands, the underside of my fingernails stained brown. Jack opened a can and handed it to me.

"It can get lonely, rattling around here by myself after work. Feels like I just sit around sometimes waiting for football season to start. Sam lives upstate."

He leaned against the refrigerator, inches from where I stood by the sink and plant, and brushed a thumb against my cheek, as natural as if he might be touching his unwatered plant.

"Do you always water dying plants?" he asked.

As his fingers left my skin, I said, "Not always."

"Chocolate," he said, looking at his thumb.

He exhaled, as if exhausted. "Thanks for watering her. Her name is Mom's-Birthday-Gift-from-Last-Year-in-an-Attempt-to-Get-Me-to-Have-Some-Children. One living thing leading to another, y'know?"

"Well, the plant is pretty much dead," I said. "So it's bad news for the kids."

He laughed.

"Mom's an optimist. Sam and I get that from her. And I'll have you know I'm great with kids."

"Something tells me that's true," I said.

"The plant has lovely strangers rescuing it. So I guess I'll have to find myself someone who'll help water the kids, too."

He grinned at me, a sweetness exuding from him, and held out his hand.

"Did I mention, I'm Jack?"

"I know," I said, slipping my palm into his. "We went to Brown together. I'm Mira Guhathakurta."

CHAPTER SIX

JACK HAD NOT recognized me at first, but back then I had been shy, with glasses and untamed hair and a persistent glaze of uncertainty.

"I'm Lena Reed's friend," I said. "I used to come with her to watch you and your friends skateboard up and down downtown Providence."

He looked at me with astonishment, frowning as if I might be joking. Slowly, his eyes had changed, recognition and memory entering them. I wondered what he remembered and if it included the night I had never forgotten. And then he had pulled me into his arms and hugged me as if we might have been long lost to each other. It was the first, most specific thing that I would always remember about him—the way he had hugged me in that moment in his kitchen, his thin, long arms encircling my body as he savored his own astonishment, the surprise of his quickened heart under his shirt as I placed my palms on his shoulder's blades. *How is Lena? How long has she been in New York? And you? Did you know Gemma?—she married Rudra. You used to take such great photographs for the magazine. Do you still write? "Evening Sun," no, "Skin," that's what it was called! You were always floating around in those floral dresses, reading something. Of course, I remember. How could I forget?*

And so it was, a thousand questions, a thousand delights.

"I was a deer-in-headlights, through most of college," I said, recovering quickly from how natural his embrace felt, as if we reached for each other often.

Jack had been a mixture of earnestness and youthful abandon in those years, exhilarated by skateboards and the spoken word jams on Friday nights, where I had first spotted him. I remembered him arguing against structural racism at parties, a young anarchist ready to topple presidencies, entirely unaware of me at nineteen. When I had told Lena that he was cute, she had said that he was Jack Smith, history major, and despite his resemblance to a friendly meerkat—Lena, acerbic and puzzled, had shaken her head—girls were always trying to date him, which meant he was always taken. I had never had the chance to find out if that was true; Jack had been a senior when I was a sophomore and we had had no classes together, so he existed purely on the periphery of Lena's social circle, of which I was a sporadic member. But we were not teenagers anymore, and Jack sat next to me on his fire escape that night, as we drank beers in the silent, fragrant spring moonlight. The party had slowed and most people had left; only Ulrike, Sam, and a few others remained, listening to music inside. It had felt right to follow him outside, to squeeze into the tiny space on the metal step below him, my elbow touching his knee. I was a girl again, fizzy with anticipation, a lightheadedness to my speech, but I had had only half a beer. I told myself that the reaction I was having was born of my teenage self, that he was a long-forgotten crush; a mix of thrill and fear rose from my center into my throat. He was from Wilmington, North Carolina, where he described long afternoons skateboarding with his Walkman in his ears, looking out at Cape Fear, wondering how he could escape.

"I loved my folks. But I wanted to get out, get to know the world a little. Then I got to New York and felt like a hick." Jack laughed, the sound of it pure, without cynicism.

"You used to write those beautiful think pieces about

skateboarding," I said. "What was that one called, the one about sport being as subjective as art? You compared skateboarding to dance forms."

"I haven't skateboarded in a while. I should." Jack paused. "How Do You Judge Je Ne Sais Quoi," he said, with a touch of self consciousness.

"When I read it, I thought you were the best writer the magazine had. I took the photo they used for your piece, the one of the dance team emerging in a ring formation with the skateboard in the center— "

"You took that photo?" Jack interrupted, turning to look at me.

"Yes."

Jack looked back to the sky. "I still think about that photo."

It felt like he was going to say something, but a siren barreled through the streets below us and he let the car finish its scream.

"Weren't you going to become a poet?" he asked. "Didn't 'Evening Skin' get you into the big league or something?"

Over the years, too many people had asked me that and something inside me inevitably clenched at the question. Next to Jack, I felt only relief as I said the words. "It was just that one poem. I needed to write it. It didn't mean I was going to write others."

He nodded. "And not a photographer either."

I shrugged. "I didn't become a pianist or a painter either, you know, even though I did a bit of both. The magazine found me. I let it."

Jack nodded, melancholic. "I thought I'd become a writer, but here I am. Jack Willem Smith, Esq. Your friendly local entertainment attorney. Not even the district attorney I planned on. Sometimes you wonder about the life that finds you."

"You like it, though. I can see it in your eyes."

Jack raised his slightly unkempt eyebrows, making himself comical. "What do you see in my eyes, MG?"

He had used the name I had gone by in our college magazine's photos.

"Fulfillment," I said. "Some pride. The je ne sais quoi you've evidently been able to extract from the drudgery of amoral dealmaking and I assume, plenty of money."

Without thinking I reached out to push his hair out of his eyes. He blinked, both of us taken by surprise, his face breaking into a grin.

"Sometimes I fantasize about all the half-written stories at the bottom of my closet seeing the light of day but you're right, I do like it," he said. "I like the wins. Maybe it's my male hunger for power."

"What makes you think I don't hunger for power? Who told you I'm not incredibly powerful?"

He laughed again, but more softly this time.

"I think you are. Tell me about your life."

He knocked his beer bottle softly against my knee, the condensation cool against my skin, the night growing muggier, our sweat beading on our foreheads and necks, our shoulders pressed against each other.

"I love the magazine I work at. I love our poets. Most of them are gentle and sweet and sharp." I shrugged, feeling my shoulder blades loosen. "I was an English major. It's the degree you get when you don't know what you want to do. Ulrike hired me because they had an opening in the poetry department and she thought I would be good at it. She was right."

"I remember now, that night at the spring fling," said Jack. "You were the DJ." He nodded slowly, as if piecing together a math problem. "You played the piano, too."

I felt a soar of happiness. "You remember."

"I remember because they were songs that made me stop and listen. I remember turning around to look at you and thinking, I should make friends with that girl, get her playlists."

"Here I am," I said.

The sounds of the party inside wafted toward us. I felt the silence between us fill and expand with my own awkward desire for a connection with him. Ulrike's laughter was faint but sharp in the distance. Someone was running the kitchen tap, or maybe the bathroom, and over it, music rose.

"This is a great song," I said, desperate to fill the pause.

Jack cocked his head to listen, his body stilling beside me. He looked at me, pleased.

"Cat Power," he said.

"'Lived in Bars.'"

Something inside me calmed as the song began to swell, my right forearm resting against Jack's thigh, his hamstring taut, his palm cupping my left shoulder as he turned his torso toward the living room.

"Sam, turn up the music," he yelled.

The song washed over us, louder now, reverberating in my veins.

"'Out of here,'" said Jack, repeating the lyric softly, looking out at the glimmering skyline.

THREE DAYS LATER, Jack texted me to see if I wanted to have coffee and maybe walk through Riverside Park.

Or if u want to stay in Brooklyn, I could swing by Prospect. But the Riverside leaves are special—just beginning to go green. Later in the fall, they get golden.

I grew up in Manhattan, skater boi. A few blocks from where you live.

I'm a dingus. Prospect, then? U can show me around.

I'm seeing a concert at Lincoln Center with some friends in the evening. Was going to be up there anyway. How about early, around 4?

Sounds grt. What concrt?

Kamasi Washington. At the Jazz festival. Have you heard him?
No but thank goodness we found each other, MG. Now I can get all those playlists.

AT FOUR, IN the third outfit I had changed into, my silk dress already a mistake on a warm day, my armpits damp beneath my jacket, I met Jack at what it turned out had long been a favorite coffee shop for both of us on the Upper West Side—a Dutch arthouse café that had stroopwafels and strong coffee that one could consume while stretched out in wide wooden armchairs, looking out at the expanse of Riverside.

"I used to listen to music in there, with giant headphones on, and read or study," I said, as we carried out our paper cups and crossed over to the park.

Jack shook his head. "Me too. All those years. I can't believe we never ran into each other."

"I ran into you. You just didn't notice too often."

We descended the steps of the park, the green immediately engulfing us. I breathed in the dewy air, filling my lungs.

"This was my favorite park as a teenager," I said. "I'd come here, alone or with my sister, and we'd lie on blankets and picnic and read or she would paint my nails."

"You sound close."

I nodded as we walked, sipping our coffees, the warm liquid spreading like happiness in my chest. "We are. She's at law school, studying to become you. I miss her."

Jack lifted his eyebrows. "A lawyer in the family. Comes in handy. Does she like it?"

I laughed. "I hope it won't come in handy too often. I think she likes the feeling that comes with having a classic career, you know. Feels more reassuring to her, I think. And my dad."

Jack looked at me, his eyes bluer, clearer with curiosity.

"Well, she'd better like it for itself. Law school ain't for the faint of heart."

"She likes security. And power."

Jack raised an eyebrow. "It sounds like you disapprove. I like those things too, and now I'm worried."

I felt a flicker of something that was a betrayal to Joy.

"I didn't mean it like that. My dad and I freewheel too much. We needed Joy's desire for a real home to have stability. She gave us structure. Made sense of our lives, even when she was just a kid, about when we ate and what movie we watched. Without her, we would have had no rules. She's wonderful."

Jack looked at me with shrewdness but he did not say anything.

"You're an entertainment lawyer. That's got to be fun," I said, quickly.

"Sometimes. And sometimes you're just a cog in the wheel of the record label, trying to charge a student filmmaker five thousand dollars to play music in their short film which is on a budget of ten dollars. I like the pro bono stuff. Working with young or indie musicians." Jack shrugged, embarrassed.

I nodded. "A lot of laws feel arbitrary. Like they were made by certain people in a certain mood at some point and should be revised every decade. I can't imagine the music industry's protocols are any different."

Jack bit into his pastry, amused. "You'd make a good criminal. You'd float into a bank, distract them with your ways"—Jack waved his hands around—"and before they knew it, you'd have them handing over the crown jewels."

I laughed and looked at the swell of the park, children playing on the green mounds. "I'm more of a long-con girl. That's how I'd get my sister to agree to anything. I'd figure out a way to bribe her. She kept all my secrets—didn't rat me out for sneaking off to raves, did all the dishes, made the case for separate rooms to our dad, you name it."

"It's nice to hear you talk about her," said Jack. "You light up a little. Sam and I, we just went to war over bikes and baseball cards our whole childhood."

"Are you close now?" I asked, unwrapping my pastry with one hand and my teeth. Jack took the coffee cup from my other hand.

"Yeah. By the time we grew up, it felt like we were all each other had. Our parents divorced when I was ten. Remarried and had second families. They're still friendly though. Wilmington is too small not to get along with your ex."

I laughed. "My mother lives in England, probably so that she could put as much distance between my dad and her as possible after their divorce."

Jack nodded. "I always think it's a waste, to not stay friendly after a breakup. All those years together and people who once loved each other—I don't really get it. Enmity, I mean."

Stricken, he looked up at me.

"Oh god, Mira, I'm sorry, I didn't mean that—about your folks. It's just something I believe in. I'm an idiot; that was rude."

I smiled, touching his arm. "It wasn't rude. I happen to agree, if the circumstances allow for a friendship."

He shook his head. "I'm always saying things like that. Gets me into trouble. Lawyers aren't supposed to have big mouths."

He handed my coffee back to me, remorseful.

"You seem pretty great to me," I said, meaning it. "And my parents are actually good friends now."

I uncapped the lid from the coffee cup, letting the liquid cool. I met his eyes. The late afternoon light glinted through the trees as the sun began its descent.

"Do you want to maybe sit for a minute?" he asked.

I nodded, wondering if I had sounded earnest in the way Joy sometimes made fun of me for. "Here, let's sit on that one opposite the water fountain," I said, pointing a few feet from us. "The Silver Jews took a group photograph on that bench."

He laughed. "I once sent David Berman an email about 'Random

Rules' and asked if he had written that song about someone real, in his life. If he had had those feelings for someone."

Jack took my coffee cup again, as I wriggled out of my coat, self-conscious about sweat stains, but he had a way of looking only at my eyes, focused on what I said.

"Aren't you going to ask if he replied?" asked Jack, with mischief that felt like it belonged somewhere with fields and open, blue skies instead of Manhattan.

I laughed. "I assumed he didn't."

"One-line reply, within the hour. 'Jack, *everything* is personal. Love, David.'"

The sun began to dip low, streaks of fuchsia across the purple sky, mothers beginning to lift babies into their strollers, people beginning to fold up blankets from the grass.

"What did you mean earlier, when you said I didn't notice you in college?"

"Not in a 'I'm too cool for you' way, though you probably were. I just meant that I had a giant crush on you and was always hanging onto Lena's coattails in hope that you *would* notice me, when you said hi to her. Toward the end of college, I think you did." My face felt warm with the memory.

He nodded. "You were shy. I remember thinking you were very pretty, that night you were DJing."

"You had a girlfriend," I said. "Clarisse James. *She* was pretty."

He laughed, the sound traveling through the emptying park. "We broke up that night. Clarisse is very happy in Quebec with a very Canadian husband, as I understand it."

My breath caught in my throat. "Do you remember dancing with me, after Clarisse left? You were so sad."

Jack looked at me, gentle. "I do."

I looked away, unable to allow what I was feeling to rise to the surface. Jack and I had danced till the early hours that night. I was no more than an acquaintance to him, but to me, he was the boy I had pined after for too long. Afterward, intoxicated, we had snuck into his dorm room, giggling like children. We had kissed, and I had taken his shirt and my dress off, but in the end, he had been too upset over Clarisse. Jack had fallen asleep, his arms around my waist, his head against my chest. I had stayed awake, breathing him in, until six a.m., when Lena had texted to ask where I was. Soon after, Jack had graduated, but I had never wanted to let go of the memory.

Now, he shifted, uncomfortable. "I'm sorry I didn't say anything after that night. I didn't know . . . "

I touched his wrist. "There was nothing to say. You were pretty gallant."

He took a breath. "I wanted to. It just wasn't the right time."

I leaned against Jack's shoulder, the action entirely unfamiliar yet natural. He relaxed against me as we watched the final dazzle of the sunset. When Jack had hugged me in his kitchen, I had felt at home in the same precious and dangerous way I had felt in his dorm room.

"Mira, I'm with someone." I heard regret and principle in his voice, a softening and hardening at once, even as his palm folded over my wrist.

For a few moments we stayed that way, my head on his shoulder, his fingers on the underside of my wrist. I raised myself up and turned to him, hiding nothing because that would have been difficult. I nodded, bewildered by the crushing of my breath in my chest. "Lena said you were always taken."

"Did she?" He looked away.

"Yes. I understand why. You're a nice guy. What's her name?"

"Frances. Frankie."

I nodded. "One of those names where you know the person is pretty great, without having met them. Frances McDormand."

"Frances Bean Cobain."

"Frankie Valli," I said.

"Francis Bacon," he said.

"Frank Capra."

Jack laughed. "I'm so glad we've run into each other. Can we be friends? You're such a great person."

"Sure," I said, looking at the clouds in the darkening sky. "Friends it is. So much better than enemies."

AND SO BEGAN our friendship as we folded each other into our lives, despite my recognition of its perils. Jack met my friends from work, attending, often with Sam, the *Janus* monthly salons where new writers showcased their work. Our Venn diagram of mutual friends from college began to swell. Meanwhile, Ulrike and Sam circled each other like shy ballerinas for weeks, after which she threw fear to the winds and gave in as only hot-blooded Ulrike could. As they began to date in earnest, I was invited to Jack's Friendsgivings and holiday parties, he to my birthdays and trivia nights at Lee's. We became regulars at the movies and at dinners at Lena's house and the four of us—Frankie and Jack and Leon and I—would double-date every few weeks. But music became a specific, private language between Jack and I; we went to shows frequently, and when Frankie was busy, it would just be the two of us. Jack was cooler than I was, with more knowledge of indie bands and lyrics and obscure facts about Thom Yorke's solo albums. He could disarm my visiting father with his analysis of a Knicks game while cradling both of Lena's daughters, whispering a nursery rhyme into their newborn faces as Lena and Sebastian took an overdue nap. Jack was self-conscious about his pale, skinny legs and his relationship with his stoic, alcoholic father, but his wounds were open surfaces, offering vulnerability. Frankie looked at him in the way I imagined the girls at Brown had, a glint of ownership in the way she slung a devoted arm over his shoulder. They teased each other with real affection, an easy chemistry in their sips of each other's cocktails, in the way his arm went around her waist, their bodies and personalities undeniably a match. Frankie was half Chinese, half American, a publicist for musicians and an extroverted baseball fan who favored jewel tones and helped me paint my apartment wall the exact shade of pale rose I had imagined. The first time we met her, Leon and I were charmed by her big laugh and the way she told stories about her father's Chinese-fusion restaurant's menu and customers in Orange County, where she was from. Sometimes, Frankie's voice would rise above the chatter of a bar or restaurant, and people would turn, surprised to see a petite woman with delicate features emanate a larger-than-life confidence. Once I had come back from the bathroom and found them arguing at the bar at Lee's.

"For fuck's sake, you could have just been a little more interested, that's all I'm saying," said Frankie, her dark eyes flashing as she and Jack huddled over a plate of fries, their body language like every other couple who did not want the world to know that they were fighting.

I fiddled with the jukebox, unwilling to go back and sit next to them, trying to find the right song that might restore peace. Instead, I heard a low, strained whisper from Jack: "Please, Frankie. Not here."

"Where then? When? You're never going to want to talk about it. Everything to do with us disappears inside you like a black hole."

I heard the tremor in her voice and chose a song by the Cure, exchanging a look with Lee, who had parked himself on the other end of the bar from them.

"I'm sorry I wasn't more attentive to a group of publicists talking about the marketing campaigns of bands I don't know very well," said Jack. "And I was interested. I just needed to get some air for a second. That's all."

"You don't like my friends, my world," said Frankie.

"Can we talk about this at my apartment?" said Jack, his voice taut and low, the bass string of a musical instrument.

"Would you even consider living with me? Having an apartment together?"

I heard the wine in her anger, in the uneven dips of her speech, but there was a raw plea to her words. I wanted to tell Frankie of the spaces Jack occupied that I had discovered in the last seven months, of his intense need to be alone—unexpected and swift—and it was not personal to her that Jack would always return to the loneliness that he carried because of his father. It was none of my business and yet I could not move.

I heard Frankie whisper, her breath catching. "You went home. You told me to come over after I was done. It made me feel like—a booty call."

When I next turned around, they had their arms around each other, unpeeling from a kiss, his hand stroking her thick, straight hair that fell in a single, shiny curtain, almost a wall shielding their privacy from me, their onlooker.

A FEW DAYS before Thanksgiving, I broke up with Leon, who had finally admitted to me his suspicion that all contemporary poetry was navel-gazing. Joy had decided to remain in London to finish an internship at Kirkland & Ellis, a plum job that she was miserable doing but determined to complete. It felt like a minor betrayal. Thanksgiving was my favorite holiday—being grateful for our tiny family was an American idea that I had easily adopted, and it reassured my unmothered anxieties. Joy liked the holiday but did not see sense in making a trip home when she was returning for good in a few months.

—Don't you want Baba's turkey?

I tried and failed to keep the note of blackmail out of my text.

—U just don't want 2 have 2 house 15 lbs of leftovers in ur dinky little freezer all year.

—Fine. But you're going to miss it. Plus mango pie.

—Send photos. Don't forget to call when u guys sit down 2 eat. I

been sleeping on a couch in this office. No time 2 shower. These British blokes r mad. They work all day and go 2 the pub hard at night. Rinse and repeat.

—We say blokes now, huh?

—Lol. 4 years in London will end in a few blokes.

—If you get lonely, Margot in the UK Janus office said you could go over to hers for Thanksgiving dinner. She's nice.

—K. Got2go. Love u. No fights with pops at the table please.

—Stop lecturing me. Try to get some sleep xx

AN ANIMATED IMAGE of a puppy with an icepack on its head, reclining on a couch while typing furiously on a laptop, appeared on my screen as Joy disappeared into the abyss. My phone lit back up almost immediately.

"Hey," I said on the first ring.

"Hey to you, too," said Jack. "What's so funny?"

"Oh, I was laughing at a dumb GIF my sister sent me."

"What was it?"

"Doesn't matter. She's just a goofball. Bossy goofball."

"I can't wait to meet her. What are you guys doing for Thanksgiving?"

"My dad and I are having his annual twenty-five-pound turkey with all the fixings by ourselves because Joy can't come home. Why, do you and Frankie want to join us?" I felt a zip of happiness at the idea of a large table. All of my childhood had been spent wishing for a big family, and when Joy had come along, it had felt like a gift.

"Frankie's going home to California. Sam and Ulrike are going to Barbados and my parents are each having their own family thing, which I'm invited to but don't want to go. Can I come solo to yours?"

"My dad will be overjoyed to overfeed someone else. You're really doing me a favor."

Jack laughed. "Leon coming too?"

"We broke up. Sorry, I meant to tell you. In person." I felt an odd embarrassment, as if I had flunked a class I wasn't any good at.

"What? When? He came to game night last week. You're so secretive."

"We want different things. I want to community garden and he likes electronic Swedish music. We're staying friends. You can stay friends with him, too."

Jack let out an exhale. "Poor guy. He never stood a chance."

"What? Whose side are you on?"

"I'm on your side, MG." Jack chuckled, deep and warm into my ear. I felt a bristling in my ribs, my ears suddenly hot.

"We were together for almost a year. I gave it a shot."

"Come on. You were killing time. Leon probably figured it out. He has to be heartbroken somewhere in a bar right now."

"Fuck you, Jack. I don't know who you think you are, but you can't just say the first thing that comes into your head. I wasn't using him to kill time."

"Hey. Sorry." Jack, chastened, grew quieter, "I didn't mean to make you mad. With you, I do always say exactly what I think."

For a few seconds we were both silent.

"I didn't see it that way," I said, finally.

"I know you didn't."

"Well you should have told me. That's what friends are supposed to do. Call out their friends for being jerks." I felt a burn of shame and resentment, upset at my own reaction.

"Okay." I heard the easy decision in Jack's voice. "We haven't been friends that long, so I didn't mean to overstep. And you're not a jerk. You believe in love like nobody's business. Leon wasn't your soulmate."

"Since when do you wax eloquent about soulmates?" I asked lightly, sitting down on my bed.

"You're making fun of me," said Jack. "The idea of someone who you're meant to be with because they make you feel a way no one else can, what's wrong with that?"

I lay down among my pillows, closing my eyes. "Isn't it kind of silly, to attach that kind of sweeping lock and key on monogamy?"

"You're going to ruin all your poets with all that cynicism, MG." Jack laughed. "I'm a romantic, I suppose. Sure, there might be lots of right people out there for each of us, but I like the idea of someone existing who gets me in a way that no one else can. Whose personality and temperament and joie de vivre fits like a missing piece, as mine does for them. Someone who changes the whole thing and upsets the rational applecart I've lived in my whole life and will make us both want to keep reaching for whatever the fuck it is that makes us happy and alive, together. Someone who is worth the inevitable uphill. I think when that happens, the sky explodes and there's a ringing in your ears and a thousand sirens go trumpeting from one nerve ending to the other. Happy?"

When I did not reply, Jack laughed again. "Fine. Laugh at me. I can imagine your face now."

"Well, as long as you're convinced about the matching joie de vivres and sirens, I suppose there's some sort of science in there."

"That's enough from you. I'll at least have you in my potato cult, if not my theories about love. I can make my grandma's scalloped potatoes for your holiday spread? I make 'em better than a Victorian chef."

"Yes. Hey Jack?"

"Yeah?"

I swallowed. "It feels like we've been friends forever."

"You're the best. Go cool off and I'll see you Thursday."

"Okay," I said, joy bubbling up inside of me. "You can stay the weekend—Baba's got plenty of room."

CHAPTER SEVEN

AS A TWENTY-ONE-YEAR-OLD immigrant with a law school loan and only a small allowance that my strict grandfather had meted out to him in tiny amounts, my father had felt most at home when cooking, in the beginning only for himself, out of a tiny kitchenette in his room at Stanford, self-conscious about the smell of fish fried in mustard oil and Indian spices. Later, he had begun cooking for my mother, his high school sweetheart who had moved from Kolkata to New York to be with her aspiring lawyer husband and go to graduate school herself. Together, they had created a new kind of Bengali-American cuisine for their home—whole spices meeting whole chickens, potatoes and spring onions roasted in butter and nigella seeds, salmon marinades fused with garlic and ginger, cinnamon, yogurt, and green chilies that they sourced from Berkeley. My parents had given themselves a thorough kind of permission to be both American and Indian and, before divorcing on account of wanting different things out of life (the truth in their cases), had made Thanksgiving their personal ode to a culinary repertoire that made them legendary dinner party hosts, first in Stanford and later on the predominantly white Upper West Side of Manhattan, their four-course meals feeding both my mother's literary and academic circles and my father's legal friends. At forty-one, after having found who he considered a soulmate, my father had found himself alone again, suddenly a devastated widower, his beloved second wife gone just a few hours after she gave birth to Joy. Joy's mother had filled a void in my life too, making school lunches, driving me to swimming lessons and soothing my adolescent worries with an instinctive ability to parent. After her death, I was adrift, too. But my father rose to the task of single parenthood with grace, reading textbooks, making mistakes, and taking advice from every parent he knew. During the stretch of years that he raised us alone and without complaint, he also threw himself into the act of creating a legacy of food for his children and the community that had helped him nurture his children. He cooked often and for anyone who stopped by, dispensing with tradition and criticism and, instead, fusing all of his beloved terrains together in the kitchen. At Christmas we ate Berkshire ham smothered in Kasundi and for both western and Bengali new year, we ate lamb shanks slow-roasted in the oven in the same spices that my great grandmother had made her famous dry mutton curry, kosha mangsho, with. On Thanksgiving, my father blended green chilies, mustard, and poppy seeds with ginger, sugar, and parmesan cheese, and slathered it on the turkey.

Jack looked up from his second plate of food, incredulous. "I've never eaten turkey as good as that."

My father's eyes softened with pleasure, his glasses smudged, as he licked his fork clean.

"These potatoes are excellent," he said.

This was generous, I knew, because the cream and parsley potatoes that Jack had made with giddy enthusiasm that afternoon, standing in my father's prewar apartment that he had bought with an immigrant's acute pride in the eighties, was too one-note for my father's taste buds. But Jack had already won his affections, with an exuberance for my father's vegetable garden and handwritten recipes and their common love of sports and legalese. My mother had once carelessly mentioned that my father had always wanted a son to play the sports my sister and I detested. As I watched him and Jack exclaim at replays of American football, I could not help wondering if Jack was the missing piece of my father's heart, so naturally were they on the same team.

Jack looked crestfallen. "You don't have to say that. Everything on this table outshines those potatoes by miles. And they're the best thing I can make."

"Nonsense," said my father, leaning forward, the cuff of his sweater dipping into the gravy on his plate. "I can appreciate a classic. These are better than the potatoes at Keens."

"That's high praise," I said to Jack, rising with my plate. "Keens is his gold star steakhouse, crime scene of Baba's birthday martini and mignon nights."

"Mr. G, you are my hero for making this meal," said Jack.

My father, a Brown, bearded man whose youth on foreign soil had taught him a private, inherent suspicion of white people, a flicker that only Joy or I might catch in his eyes since he moved so predominantly in their circles, regarded Jack with genuine fondness. "You know, Jack, you remind me of myself in my twenties."

"Ma says you were an armchair revolutionary and a prude in your youth," I called from the kitchen, extracting the pie I had made from the fridge.

"Your Ma was and remains a hedon so naturally she considers everyone else a dampener," said my father.

"Don't worry, they're quite fond of each other," I said to Jack, setting the pie down on the table. "They just also excel at taking potshots at each other."

"Secret to a rollicking friendship, but not so much a marriage," said my father, winking at Jack. "Are you married? Or perhaps a girlfriend?"

"My father, the nosy Bengali auntie," I said.

"He doesn't mind," said my father, to Jack.

"It's true, I don't. Yes, I have someone I've been seeing. She's very nice. Look at this pie, MG." Jack inhaled as he gazed at the confection.

"I like this moniker, 'MG,'" said my father.

"MG is an improvement on Sweety, which is what my entire extended family and all of their friends call me. It's bananas," I said, slicing into the pie and serving Jack a piece.

"MG makes the best mango lassi pie you've ever had," said my father.

"I've never had one before but I believe it," said Jack, at the precipice of gluttony as he ate.

"Everyone has a nickname in Bengal," said my father, a sigh escaping him at the memory. "Mine is Khoka, meaning 'boy.' Joy, my younger daughter, is called Muniya, meaning a kind of bird. In India, your nickname is what your loved ones are allowed to call you, a special seal of their insider status in your life. The name itself could be anything from a favorite dessert to an animal to a color, adjective, even a city."

"Sometimes it's just a noise," I said. "My cousin's nickname is Boomba."

"Well, I think Sweety Guhathakurta is a great name," said Jack, straightfaced as my father laughed.

"Eat your pie." I threw a napkin at Jack, my happiness catching in my throat, suffusing me.

"MG, it's so good," said Jack, looking at his plate in astonishment. "It's light as air and so complex at the same time."

"And you haven't even tried my other daughter's garam masala gingerbread yet," said my father, pleased, opening a bottle of wine. "We should start a restaurant. Mihir and Daughters. I can see it now."

I stood up in a panic. "Joy. I said I would call her when we sat down to eat."

I DIALED JOY thrice, with no answer, fretful at having forgotten her.

"She's the one who didn't come this year and isn't answering the phone," said my father. "You're behaving as if you forgot to invite her." He turned to Jack. "These two behave like Siamese twins who share bloodstreams. And then when they fight, you should see the Cold War. I have to put on two sweaters and turn up the radiator."

"She's calling, she's calling," I said as my phone began to vibrate.

"Look who remembered they have a third family member," said Joy, clearly a little drunk, Shoreditch alive behind her.

"Hi," I said. "I'm sorry we didn't call earlier. We wanted to show you dessert."

"Happy Thanksgiving Joybird," said my father, trying to get into the frame from where he sat.

Joy frowned, swaying a little as she leaned against a telephone pole. "Happy Thanksgiving," she said grudgingly.

"Don't lean against the pole," said my father. "I once read about a man who died from touching an electric pole."

"Are you with friends?" I asked. "Who's driving you home?"

"Man, are you guys just going to be giant buzzkills after you forgot to call me on my favorite holiday?" Joy sounded more petulant than angry as a siren blared behind her.

"But it's not your favorite holiday, it's MG's," said my father. "Your favorite holiday is your birthday."

Behind Joy, a group of revelers fell out of Nikki's. She looked at them distractedly, pointing the phone to the sky, then the gutter.

"Who the hell is MG?" we heard Joy say.

"That's my new name for your sister," said my father. "Put yourself back on the screen."

As Joy meandered back on the screen, her eyes upset and unfocused, I saw Jack looking at her image, his eyes crinkled in curiosity. We exchanged a half-smile, mine born of embarrassment.

"Show me the turkey," demanded Joy.

"Here, look, here's the pie." I turned the phone to Jack, who held up the half-eaten pie.

"It's fantastic," said Jack, beaming.

"Who the hell are you?" asked Joy, as I held the phone upright, toward Jack.

"Joy, he's my friend from Brown," I said, a little desperate now. "Lena's friend. I told you about him."

"Hi, I'm Jack."

Jack's sunny friendliness had a way of disarming even the most irate of our friends, but I heard a shard of meanness in Joy's voice as she said, "Oh, right. The one that got away."

I turned the phone around immediately, as Joy's eyes flashed in victory.

"That's for not calling me when the turkey was whole. You wanted to get me back for not coming this year." Joy's voice hardened even as her speech slurred. "Even the damn pie was just leftovers. You and Baba just having your Thanksgiving with your new boyfriend and leaving me out of it. Hi, hi, taxi, *taxi*."

Joy flailed her other arm, presumably at a cab.

"He's not my boyfriend," I said, my voice tight with anger.

"Joy, we will talk tomorrow. Please go home and go to sleep," said my father, wiping his glasses as he turned away, his voice distant even though he sat right next to me, a tone my sister and I knew by heart.

"You can't make me go to bed, Baba. I'm a grownup and three thousand miles away," said Joy. But this time I heard the trace of familiar fear, the unmistakable lilt of worry that Joy, no matter how tired and irritable, always had in her voice, if she was uncertain if she had crossed a line with someone she loved. Joy pushed our buttons and boundaries until we snapped and, immediately afterward, turned into a frightened little girl, one whose hand I had to hold until she safely crossed the street. I watched her as she got into the cab and gave the driver instructions to her address, all the while keeping one eye on me watching her, her phone angled on her face, because she wanted me to make sure she was safe, wanted me to reassure her that I still loved her, as I had done a thousand times before. Joy needed to be sure that she was integral to us, the missing piece to our family's collective heart. My father rose, taking off his glasses, and went in the direction of his bedroom.

"I went to Margot's for dinner. She made everything, even pie, but it was pumpkin," said Joy, her voice frail and defiant at once, a whisper such that I had to bring the phone closer to hear it, even though it was one in the morning in London. The early light caught the loveliness of her face, her long eyelashes swept upward, her eyes wide in apprehension, her jaw set even as her cheeks gave her a baby-faced sweetness.

"You're such an idiot," I said softly. After a moment, I sighed. "I should have told Margot you hate pumpkin."

She looked out of the window, the sound of a rush of wind making its way through the phone. "You should have called me. Even if Baba forgot, you should have."

"I'm so sorry," I said. I felt Jack stir and leave us alone in the living room. "We missed you. Baba was talking about your gingerbread."

Joy looked mollified. "I'll call tomorrow," she said as she yawned. "I can't wait to come home. I hate London."

"Don't fall asleep in the cab," I said. "Let's keep talking until you're home."

"Okay," said Joy, settling back into the seat of the London black cab, her features softened by sleepiness, leaning her head on the dark leather of the headrest, the same way she had fallen asleep on my shoulder so many times in the past.

IN THE MORNING, I woke up to snow. A thick blanket had spread itself over the street and the tops of cars below. My father was in the kitchen, making French toast the Indian way, the spicy, savory kind I loved and Joy hated. Combined with the smell of coffee, the morning roused a fierce hunger in me. I kissed my father's cheek. "Mmm, I'm hungry."

"Good. Did your sister get home safe?"

"Yes. You know she's sorry."

"She's always sorry," said my father, turning back to the stove. "How many for you?"

"Two, maybe three. Where's Jack?"

"He's outside, on the verandah, wearing my coat. It's two sizes too small for him." My father lowered the egg-and-onion-coated slices of bread into the bubbling oil. "Stanley, the new doorman, got a flat tire this morning. The snow was too deep to drop off his daughter at his sister's place in Harlem, before his shift started, so Jack took my car and dropped her off. Quite a hero, Jack. Stanley was very grateful."

I looked outside, at Jack, for a long moment. "We have a new doorman?"

"Yes, Eddie is taking a well-deserved vacation in Puerto Rico."

I looked at the time. "All this before nine a.m.?"

"Stanley's wife is a nurse, my dear. They rely on his sister to watch the toddler when they go to work. You and your sister led lives of wanton luxury at your overpriced daycares. Anyway, I went to the bodega for eggs around seven and Jack needed a razor blade so he came with me. I would have taken Bea myself, but the dear boy saw how upset father and daughter were and swung into action. A very good boy, I have to say."

Jack turned to wave to me from behind the glass sliding door of the small balcony. He was almost comical in sweatpants, rain boots and my father's too-small overcoat, as he held a cup of coffee, a childlike wonder on his face.

"He really likes the snow," remarked my father.

"Yes," I said, laughing as Jack mimicked an upright snow angel to me. "He's from North Carolina, and growing up, they spent Thanksgivings and Christmas with relatives in the Blue Ridge mountains. Reminds him of home. I'll take him a piece of toast and ask him how many more he wants."

When I turned back to him, my father was watching me. "I've never seen you this way, Mira," he said, gently.

I looked at my father, and in that moment we both knew, like every instance when he'd asked me a question for which he already knew the answer, that there would be no obfuscation because he had already discovered the truth. I placed my feet into slippers, carefully. "He's my friend."

"Sometimes in life you have to go after what you want," said my father. "For us, in this lifetime in America, nothing is on a platter. We must look deeper into matters and work hard to earn what might belong to us. To take what's ours."

My father paused and patted my elbow, a kindness, one that I recognized from whenever I had been in pain as a child. He turned back around to the flame of the gas range. "Now please let me know quickly how many slices the two of you want. I can't be standing over a hot stove all morning—I have to finish the crossword before the game starts."

OUTSIDE, JACK STOOD, his teeth chattering in the cold, delight on his face, his cheeks bright pink from the cold, snowflakes melting on his freckles. "Can you believe it? November snow."

"I was going to make a joke about climate change but you look too happy." I held out the plate. "My father wants to know how many of his famous French toasts you want."

"About ten more," said Jack, ripping into the toast with his teeth, his fingers glistening with butter from the slice he held.

He took in a long breath as I felt snow descend on my face.

"I feel happy, Mira. Work, life, everything can get so empty. Endless, like some sort of repeating loop in my head. Being here, with you and your dad, feeling like a part of something"—Jack turned to look at me—"it feels like a different kind of life." He exhaled. "Sorry. Maybe it's just having been alone for the holidays so often. It feels really good to be with you guys, even if it's for a weekend."

As I looked at Jack, at his clear eyes and his focused absorption of the world, of my father and myself and the toast he was eating with his fingers, something inside of me began to give way. I looked away, toward the thick cover of snow that draped across the streets.

"Do you remember that night we first met, when we were sitting on the fire escape, listening to music and talking?" I asked.

"Yeah, of course. I can't believe that was only eight months ago. Thanks, Ulrike and Sam."

I could feel Jack's eyes on me, the frank happiness with which he regarded me.

"Remember that song that was playing? You asked Sam to turn it up."

"Cat Power," he said. "I went home and listened to that album for a few weeks on repeat."

Something in my voice must have changed because I heard a whisper of concern in Jack's voice.

"It's a beautiful song," I said. A calm filled me even as my heart beat faster, the color of the snow deepening in its brightness, a silvery quality to the city in front of us. "When I heard it that night next to you on that staircase, I thought, if this could be the day we met, and this moment became the moment we realized that we were going to be lovers, then this would be our song." I turned to him, meeting his unwavering gaze, the house and city a blur around me. "I love you, Jack. I know you have someone and I know how wonderful she is, but you and I—I think we belong together. Things like this—the way I feel when I look at you, when we laugh together and no one else knows what it's about, the way we know each other as if we've known how to do that forever—that doesn't come along too often in a lifetime. When it does, you have to reach out and take what's yours, take it in both your hands or it could be lost to us. You feel like my family, like a missing piece of myself."

I looked back at the snow as I ran out of breath. I filled my lungs again and turned to him.

He blinked as he stood still, as if listening for some sign of life in the snow. He shook his head almost imperceptibly, as if to shake loose a thought that might have remained a fragment otherwise, a trace of something he couldn't quite get a grasp on. We stood there, the snow falling around us, examining each other with careful precision, waiting for sudden movement or a flicker of what might mean an irreversible departure. After what felt like an eternity, Jack took a slow step toward me.

"Mira, I have to call Frankie," he said.

CHAPTER EIGHT

JACK BROKE UP with Frankie four times in the next month. Once in person, once over email, once during a long phone call, and a fourth time in person again. She was my friend, too, and in her incessant grief and bewilderment (*How long had we been doing this? Was it ever real between us? She could never have believed that we would do this. Were we mad without fear of God or Karma?*), she needed every last detail before she was done with the both of us. Insidious guilt seeped into our pores, filling our individual existences. We missed her easy laughter and big opinions, which suddenly seemed a void, erased from my life—I would never hear from Frankie again. For Jack, it was a piercing loss, the sudden absence of someone he had held in affection and regard, who wanted nothing more to do with him, her radio silence in the end more painful than her desire to dissect events and memory. When it was over, we approached each other, ragged and with caution, my desire immediate at the sight of him standing at my door. But Jack was raw from his wounds and it frightened me.

"I'm sorry this has been so hard," I said, my platitude inane to my own ears.

He shook his head, disbelieving. "You never know how much pain you can cause someone."

I nodded, saying nothing. We stood at a distance from each other, my wants beating through my ribcage, even as I tried to reason with myself.

"Do you want something to drink?" I asked.

He nodded, unmoving as he stood at my door, between existences. I wondered if leaving Frankie had erased his desire to be loved by me, the nature of loss and grief all-powerful—that much I knew from my father. I pulled out a can of sparkling water, the kind he liked, from my fridge, and handed it to him.

"You miss her," I said.

"Yes."

Jack's sadness filled my living room, vaporizing in my imagination, between the stacks of books and records, into the crack on the windowpane, filling the crevices of my apartment.

"I should have seen how little I was giving her, a long time ago," he said. "I thought that we were happy—that she was happy, with our—lack of definition. She said she didn't believe in marriage." He shook his head, defeat in his shoulders, in the way the tendons on his neck strained. "We would have eventually become friends, I guess, maybe had a natural separation because we were who we were."

Jack stopped, leaning his head on the door behind him.

"But now she's lost all respect for me," he said, his voice breaking. "She hates me."

I felt my eyes fill with tears. I could not imagine then what losing him might be like, but I did not know if it was Frankie's loss or the threat of my own that sent sharp sorrow through my body.

"If you've changed your mind, if you need to rethink things," I said carefully, "it's okay. I just need to know." I heard the rush of desperation in my voice and willed myself to sound more even and compassionate, but I was incapable.

"I don't think I could bear it if we lost our friendship," I said. "So if you're in a different place, if things have changed, I get it. But you have to be honest with me."

Jack frowned, the cleft between his eyebrows deepening as he let out a short exhale. He paused, as if undecided on what to do next. Shaking his head, he reached into his pocket, and pulled out his phone.

"Mira, you're always running," he said, quietly. "Sometimes, you have to stop."

He frowned again at his phone as his thumbs worked over the screen. He had said my name instead of the nickname, I thought, my emotions rogue and unmoored, clutching at any formed thought that might present itself to me. Jack looked up at me, placing the phone on the side table that held my keys.

"This is so we remember," he said.

As the first chords of the song filled my living room, emerging out of the tiny phone speaker, the luxurious lyrics ballooning around us, Jack took me in his arms, one hand slipping into the curve of my waist, the other on my left cheek and ear, his breath cool against my skin, as we kissed for the first time, the beginning of consuming each other in a way that would change me forever. We were soft and heated and urgent all at once, that first time. When I opened my eyes, there was a look in his eyes, the kind that I had been waiting for.

"Out of here," I whispered into his ear, the lyric fading as I rested my head on his collarbone, exhaling as if I had held my breath for a year.

I HAD BEEN in love before, unwound by men before. But every relationship that had eventually felt too complex or demanding, more trouble than it was worth for someone who had enough already with sisterhood and a father, had been relatively painless to unpeel from. I had remained amicable with most prior lovers. With Jack, all of my ease and guardrails faded. I had always been a romantic, in tears over music or descriptions of heartbreak or the possibility of divinity in people or nature, but this was my very first rodeo at a love that held me in an exhilaration that I was perpetually afraid of losing. In Jack, I saw the person I wanted to be. He was a skillful lawyer, precise and as fluent in parsing clauses as their loopholes but with a core of empathy that made him beloved to his musician clients. He built shelves in my apartment, where he saw emptiness or need—for my cookbooks and my hair-dryer, spice bottles, and the plant that I had absentmindedly set down in a dark corner. He built a chicken coop for the eighty-six-year-old woman who lived on my street and, while I was at a conference, drove my father to the emergency room for a broken ankle. At his worst, he was fidgety, his mind changing constantly, unable to finish the book or half-built side table that he had started, video games and sports channels his only refuge. Even in those instances where my need for stillness would chafe against his restless energy, Jack found grace. He was gentle with himself and me, when our anxieties about work, love, perfection, the climate, or the devastations of a foreign war took hold. I worried constantly that I would lose myself in love's riptide, but instead of dissolving into him, it taught me greater kindness, with a renewed appreciation for all that the world had to offer us. It felt as if my motherlessness, my clinging to my father, my jealousies with Joy, were resolved by the sense that perhaps life had been waiting to show me that I could have what I needed after all.

OVER THE NEXT year, Jack and I moved slowly but surely, allowing the bedrock of our friendship to bear new romantic fruit, one at a time—a trip to the seaside or my father's house; a week at his mother's cabin in the mountains, where I fell in love with her; a milestone birthday, six, then twelve, then eighteen heady months together; our playlists for each other; and the piano he bought me on my thirtieth birthday. His mother saw something in me that was motherless and she extended me an affection that included reminders to eat lunch and not work through the hour, presents from a candle shop I liked, and the assurance that I was beloved to their family. We filled our lives with shared people and objects and memory, such that when we found an apartment together in Brooklyn—Jack giving up Manhattan with happiness—our home seemed to emerge fully formed. That I would wake up and find him in our yard reading the paper, or back from a bicycle ride and drinking coffee, gave me a peace that I had never experienced before. We found Millie together, an injured pit bull the color of flax who rested her head in our palms and looked at me with large, trusting eyes. Jack and I rarely fought, a calm to our existence, the occasional squabble over what to watch or order easily forgiven by the other, so eager did we seem to preserve the prize that we had stumbled on, that night on his fire escape. I had never been religious, but I felt grateful to the universe, the idol of Ganesh on my father's writing desk, and the church I passed on my way to work, leaving our home a few minutes before nine so that I might experience its bells fully each morning.

The only missing piece was Joy. She had not yet met Jack or come home for Christmas as promised. Instead she had plunged into the first year of the job that Kirkland & Ellis had offered her a month before the internship ended. In being a lawyer, Joy had suddenly found an excellence within that she had never been sure she was capable of, and as my father exhibited visible pride on our phone screens, we all knew that this was the happiest Joy had ever been. In many ways, that year felt like Joy and I had each found a purpose that bound us closer together, able to love the other more gently and fully for it. On my way back from work each evening, before Jack would get home and after I would pick up an ever-buoyant Millie from the dog daycare across Prospect Park, I usually called Joy, because, even at midnight, I knew she would still be in the office.

"Hi Didi," said Joy, her voice exuberant despite the hour. "Do you have Millie yet?"

"She's yanking on her leash. We're walking up Park Slope to meet Lena for a quick drink at Lee's before I head home. Why do you sound so perky? It's"—I looked at my phone—"ten thirty-six p.m."

"I feel perky. We won a pretty big case. Against a gas company. Well, they settled. But it's still a big win for my team. My first."

"Joybird, that's incredible. Congratulations. I'm so proud of you." I stopped by a park bench, restraining a reluctant Millie as I sat down, sweaty in the summer humidity. "Did you tell Baba yet?"

"He's perky, too."

I felt a familiar twinge of jealousy at the unmistakable satisfaction in Joy's voice.

"Said I was his retirement plan now," said Joy.

"That's great," I said.

The sky was still bright in the early evening. Jack would be home around eight. I could stop at the local butcher for a couple of steaks before I saw Lena. The quiet pleasures of domesticity with Jack sent a ripple of pleasure through my stomach. Joy was talking about her inevitable promotion, and with relief, I felt genuine happiness for her begin to permeate me.

"I'm so happy for you, Joybird," I said.

"What? Thanks. Are you trying to avoid the subject?"

Joy sounded suspicious and I realized she had asked me a question I hadn't heard.

"I'm sorry, it's a little noisy in the park. Can you say that again?"

Millie growled at a passing toddler and I put a hand on her head, offering up an apologetic smile at the child's horrified mother, the latter clad in patterned overalls I recognized from the vintage shop in Park Slope that I sometimes went into. I leaned back on the bench. Millie was immediately reticent at my feet, both of us happy in the fading light.

"Your birthday," said Joy, frustration in her tone.

"Oh, sorry. Yeah. My birthday." I realized that I would turn thirty-one in less than a week. "On Saturday," I said, with mild surprise.

"Are you saying you only just remembered that?"

Joy sounded outraged. She loved any occasion to celebrate, and without her, we often forgot how.

"Well, it's been a big year. The magazine has been keeping me busy plus Millie and Jack—"

"I know all about your perfect life," said Joy.

"Without you, it isn't perfect," I said, pleased at the jealousy in her voice.

Joy was happy for me, but that I would love a man as I did Jack was a reality she had been unprepared for.

"With a man I haven't even met," she said. "It's weird that you're obsessed with some stranger."

I laughed. "It's your fault. You haven't been home for two years. You see him on FaceTime all the time. He loves saying hi."

"It's not the same."

I heard a genuine sadness in Joy's voice.

"Joy, this promotion"—I felt a stab of fear—"it doesn't mean you'll permanently live in England, does it?"

"Not a chance," said Joy, decisive. "I'm coming home the first chance something great turns up in New York."

"Good," I said, with sharp relief.

"Do you promise you'll do something nice for your birthday? I can't seem to get you and Baba to understand that life is supposed to be celebrated. Make Mr. Perfect plan a party. If he was all that perfect, he wouldn't need reminding."

"I promise," I said.

"Fine. I gotta go. The fish and chips place near me closes at two. After the drunks trickle out."

"Mushy peas. Mmm."

"Call me tomorrow," said Joy.

Once she had decided on a course of action, Joy needed to execute it immediately and I could hear her impatience to get off the phone.

"I love you, Joybird."

ON FRIDAY MORNING, Jack had woken up early and brought home a cluster of white ranunculus from the farmer's market a block from Lee's Heights. I opened my eyes to the smell of coffee and found Jack toasting bread in the kitchen, the flowers in a large mason jar on our breakfast table, sunlight filtering through translucent layers of petals. I stood at the kitchen entrance, taking the whole thing in. Jack turned from the toaster and slid a piece onto a plate.

"I thought I heard you get up," he said. "I got some of your sourdough from the market."

"How'd you know about the ranunculus?" I asked. "Have we ever talked about flowers?"

"Why wouldn't I know?" Jack kissed me as he handed me the plate of toast. "Happy birthday, MG."

"My mother used to put ranunculus out on my birthday. When Joy grew older, she found out and started doing it." I wondered now if it was Joy who had told Jack that the flowers gave me peculiar comfort on my birthday, as if some part of my mother was at the table. I took a bite, the tang of the fresh bread punctuating its sweetness. "This is amazing, baby. Where's Millie?"

"Out in the backyard. Sunbathing. Want another slice?"

I shook my head and sat down at the table, looking at Millie through the window as she swiped at a butterfly and scratched the back of her ear. Jack sat on the chair next to me, a piece of toast between his teeth, the sports section of the paper in his hand.

"Want to go to the aquarium in a bit?" he asked.

I laughed. "Just a lineup of greatest hits, huh?"

He shrugged. "You should feel like it's a special day."

I narrowed my eyes. "That's a Joy line. Have you been talking to Joy?"

"You think I can't come up with the idea that your birthday is a special day on my own?" Jack tilted his head in disbelief. "You give me no credit."

I leaned close to Jack, inhaling the lingering smell of soap and coffee, and kissed his cheek.

"I give you too much credit," I said.

"That's true." Jack grinned at me. "Say around nine, the aquarium? I hear they've got new clownfish and stingrays."

"I have to go to work," I said, regretful. "We've got the twenty-fifth anniversary double-size issue coming out and I don't want to risk Ulrike's wrath with any delays."

Jack shook his head. "Incredible. That a few poems will cause you as much stress as a class action suit."

I swatted him playfully with the Arts section. "Careful there, skater boi. You couldn't possibly be trivializing my job, could you?"

My leg was stretched out on his lap. Jack grabbed the sole of my foot and squeezed it, sending a thrill through me.

"I'm *Janus*'s most devoted subscriber. You do know we have doubles of every issue since we met?"

"Yes, but do you *read* them?" I said the words with mock belligerence, shaking a playful fist at him.

"I will someday, I promise."

Jack raised his palms in mock surrender as I got up and went over to him, straddling him over the wicker chair we had picked out together. He slid his arms around my waist as I kissed him. "Someday, when we are both retired and sitting on a porch somewhere and Millie's too old to play, I'll read all the back issues of *Janus*," he said.

"A porch, huh?" I reached under his shirt, my palms sliding over his back. Pulling him closer, I wrapped my legs around him.

"Two chairs on it. The kind with arms and you can read in, like my pop has. A couple kids, long gone to their own lives, good riddance to them. Some chickens in the backyard. Our own vegetable patch. A shed, where I can build stuff like pop does."

Jack, despite his desire, rattled off the words as if he'd thought them a hundred times before. As he stood up, my legs still wrapped around him, and walked us back to the bed I had left unmade, it struck me that Joy was right. Life, and its unbidden miracles, was meant to be celebrated.

CHAPTER NINE

I WAS LATE to work. On a normal day, I could come in as I pleased—Ulrike knew that I had my own methods, scattered as they might seem to the outside eye. She had never managed my time before, leaving my department to our odd yet dependable ways as we emerged from a mountain of disorganized sheaves, with a handful of poems each quarter. Lately however, Ulrike had been irritable, sending several emails and texts to me before I had even begun the day. Jack and I had invited her and Sam to a barbecue a week ago, but they had both declined. I assumed she was at the receiving end of our biannual pressure from the owner of the magazine, and therefore I had taken to coming in at nine, a little before she did. But it was ten-thirty that Friday morning. Ulrike opened the door of her office and looked at me with a reprimand in her eyes.

"Mira, would you come in here for a moment, please."

As I shut Ulrike's door behind me, I began to speak quickly, my nervousness betraying me.

"Sorry I was late this morning. I had a—a personal thing come up. But everything's on track. Jenna's working on the final placements of the second Akbar piece and then we'll be all set for you to take a look. The Kenyon estate signed off on 'Blue Bowl' and— "

"Mira, stop babbling," said Ulrike tiredly as she sat down at her desk.

She swept her glasses onto her head and rubbed her eyes.

"Happy birthday," she said, sinking her face into her palms.

I stood in silence for a moment. "I—thank you. Ulrike, what's wrong?"

Ulrike took her hands away from her face and opened a drawer beneath the wooden writing desk her novelist grandfather had left her.

"I got you something," she said, pushing a small package wrapped in white tissue and green silk ribbon toward me.

She was crying.

"What's wrong?" I asked again, going around her desk and crouching beside her chair.

"The blinds," she said, her whisper cracking on the words.

I looked up at where the glass of Ulrike's office wall looked out at the sprawl of tables and couches around which editors and assistants clustered. As I drew the fabric blind, patterned in Ulrike's taste for the baroque, the ornate swirls swam in front of my eyes.

"The magazine, it isn't shutting down, is it?"

I loved the job I had and often worried how I would never have the same autonomy at a bigger magazine. I had never seen Ulrike shed tears, not even when she had left Greg in despair.

She shook her head. "Everything's fine," she said, leaden. "The board is excited about the anniversary issue."

"What on earth is the matter then? You're scaring me. It isn't—a health issue, is it?"

Ulrike looked at me. "Sam," she said, pronouncing his name with soft pain. "He left. Last night."

I held her in my arms as she cried. We both knew she did not want anything else from me and certainly not the verbal reassurances and soothing that Joy would have needed in her place.

Eventually, Ulrike reached for a Kleenex, exhausted as I let her go. "I wanted to tell you before you heard," she said. "He is Jack's brother," she added pointlessly.

"Did you have an argument?" I asked. "Don't tell me if it's too much," I added quickly, wondering if I would have to choose between Ulrike and Sam.

She shook her head. "In the beginning it didn't matter, his age, being so much younger than me. But it mattered. I was always trying to be someone else around his friends, always trying to catch on, catch up in a way I don't around other younger people. Around my friends, he was always bored, or only interested in them in the way young writers find older people interesting."

"Ulrike, age has never mattered a shred in our friendship. Sam should be so lucky to have had you in his life." I felt a spark of fury at Sam, who had succeeded in making beautiful, fascinating Ulrike feel aged and worn.

"Don't, Mira. Don't say 'had.' Even if it's true, it's too painful. Don't say anything at all."

I nodded. Not knowing what to do, I sat down on Ulrike's couch. "You don't have to worry about me—or Jack. We love you. There's no way anything changes that."

"I wonder if I deserve it," said Ulrike with sadness. "I left Greg, you know, when I knew it couldn't work. And even though Greg knew it too, he wanted to keep trying. I wonder if that's what real love is, trying, no matter what. Because it all goes to rot in the end anyway, those early feelings. It all gets hard and uphill anyway and you never have sex anymore and you're rude and you take each other for granted and maybe that's just what love is and maybe I'm getting my just deserts for not trying to save what I had for all those years with Greg. Sam doesn't want to try anymore—'it's too hard,' he says. Oh Mira," she said, beginning to cry again. "I lost my temper so often with Sam. I wish I had tried to be nicer. Less vicious and controlling."

Ulrike said each word with an escalating misery.

"But I felt like he was slipping away already." She shook her head, strands of her perfectly cut hair catching on her wet cheek. "Nothing is worse than the fear of being left. It made me the worst version of myself."

I rose and tucked a strand of Ulrike's hair behind her ear. She stiffened, unused to the gesture, and I had to remind myself that Ulrike was not Joy. I stepped back and sat on the edge of her desk, placing my hand on her shoulder as she composed herself into the person who would have to run our staff meeting in fifteen minutes.

"If you need a place to stay, while you're figuring out things, Jack and I have room. You're always welcome in our house."

Even as I said the words, I could not imagine her in our tiny spare room, the bed a pullout from a couch I settled into when I worked from home. I wondered if Jack would be unhappy at the position that I would inevitably have put him in.

"Where on earth would I sleep?" snapped Ulrike. "On your couch?"

Despite myself, I smiled.

She shook her head. "I went back," she said. "Home. To the house."

"The house? You mean to Greg?" I tried to contain the incredulity in my voice.

Ulrike bristled. "It's my house, too. We bought it together and I lived in it for over two decades."

I nodded, repentant. "Of course it is. I'm sorry. I was just surprised."

She looked away. "It's an . . . adjustment."

"When did Greg move out?"

"He hasn't. He's there. He's glad to have me back," she said, with a trace of defiance. "As a . . . friend."

For a few moments neither of us said anything.

I squeezed her shoulder again. "I'm here, for anything you need," I said. "I love you, Ulrike."

She sighed, bowing her head. "At least it's home and comfortable and what I know to be safe. Maybe at the end of the day, that is all we need."

"SHE WANTS TO settle for a life she was lonely and unfulfilled in. That's not what she needs," I said, my disapproval ringing out over the chatter and Chinese pop music of the tiny Szechuan restaurant in the East Village. "Their son is grown," I said, my outrage rising in my chest. "Ulrike deserves to live for herself."

The waitress, a redhead in a crop top and silky palazzo pants, her arms covered in intricate, tattooed vines, brought over a plate of boiled peanuts and an ice bucket with the bottle of wine that Jack had produced from his computer bag, as we had sat down.

"Twenty-dollar corkage for the pét-nat. That okay with you guys?" she asked, apologetic.

"Totally," said Jack, smiling at her.

"I love your brooch," she said to me.

"Thanks. It was a birthday gift from my boss this morning." I touched the gold sparrow that added a Ulrike-esque glamor to my plain shift.

"Nice boss. Lucky you. Happy birthday." The waitress popped the bottle open expertly and poured us a glass each. "Enjoy. The food will be out in a bit."

"Thanks," I said, my cheeks warm with pleasure. I reached for Jack's fingers. "Thanks for making the reservation. I couldn't believe you picked it."

Jack looked embarrassed. "Well, I knew you liked it. But I thought you might want something else, something fancier for tonight."

I laughed. "Was it Joy?"

Jack shrugged, resigned. "She just knows you like a book. She insisted. And she was right. I could tell the minute we walked in."

"Birthdays are for favorite things. This is my favorite restaurant. I'm easy."

"You might have told me at Per Se last year that you wanted a plate of six-dollar noodles served cold instead."

"I had the greatest time last year, too. You could take me anywhere and I'd be happy as a clam."

"Really? A Yankees game it is next year then."

I kicked him playfully under the table. The candle the waitress had placed between us flickered in the dim lighting. "That's called taking me hostage, skater boi."

Jack caught my knee in his hand, his palm warm beneath my dress. "Maybe basketball then."

I leaned closer to him as I popped a peanut covered in chili crisp into his mouth.

"Tell me that isn't the finest taste in the world?" I asked.

Closing his eyes, Jack nodded. "Affirmative," he said. He opened his eyes. "Listen, I'm sorry I didn't tell you about the breakup. Sam asked me not to and I didn't like it, but he's my little brother."

I stopped, mid-chew.

"I didn't realize you knew before I told you," I said, after a pause.

Jack looked uncomfortable. "I'm sorry. I told Sam it was the last time I would ever keep a secret from you."

"How long have you known?" I realized I had pulled my knee away from Jack and tried to relax my shoulders and the flare of anger I felt.

"A few weeks."

"A few weeks?"

Incredulous, I placed both my palms on the pink Formica of the table.

"Jack, I work with her. She's one of my dearest friends. She said he was cagey and made her miserable for weeks. I would have told you if it was the other way round."

"I know. I'm sorry. I feel really bad. Sam—he's my little brother. I've always kept his secrets."

"Clearly," I said, furious. "But if she'd known sooner, she might not be as heartbroken. Or make a knee-jerk decision to go right back to her ex. Sam should have just been honest with her, if he was going around telling people."

"I'm his brother," said Jack, his voice tight. "And Ulrike is a grown woman. She knows what she's doing."

"Chicken with taro root and dan dan noodles," said the waitress brightly as she set the dishes down between us. Her eyes widened as she registered the atmosphere. "I'll be right back with chopsticks and plates and the cucumbers," she said, exiting with efficiency.

Jack sighed, the few moments of respite having softened him.

"I really am sorry." He slid his chair closer to mine. "I know she's your friend. I promise I won't take sides—I said as much to Sam already."

I tried to dislodge the knot of betrayal in my throat and instead let the damp sweetness of his touch unravel my resentment.

"I'm sorry, too. It's just that she's so hurt. And she's really a force, you know. And kind and generous. She deserves to be happy."

Relieved, Jack kissed my cheek. He picked up his glass and raised it. "Let's not talk about Ulrike or Sam. Let's toast to you tonight. We're going to have an amazing year, MG. Lots of greatest hits in it."

I nodded as I sipped my drink. For a few moments we were both silent, the food untouched in front of us. I set down the glass, unable to let it go.

"Do you disagree that Ulrike is making a mistake by going back to Greg?"

Jack sighed again. He studied the paper lantern above us.

"Well, people need different things, you know," he said, carefully. "Ulrike and Greg share a lot of history, a lot of memories, Isiah, their families. You never know if that's the real thing or not. They may have just let it wither on the vine, as marriages do. And Sam—he's still a little bit of a boy in some ways. He doesn't know what to do with someone like Ulrike."

"What's wrong with Ulrike?"

"Jesus, MG, don't bite my head off," said Jack, gentle as he touched my wrist.

I felt quick shame creep into my cheeks.

"I'm sorry. I know what love can feel like, and Ulrike deserves that.

And maybe I'm also frightened by what love can turn into, if you're right. I—I don't want you to be right."

Jack stroked the knuckles of my right hand, tracing the veins on it. "Real love doesn't always go bad," he said. "I didn't mean to imply that it did. I just meant that the decades-long love affair is also interesting. Maybe this was Greg's wake-up call—I imagine it was the only way Ulrike would have returned to him. Maybe they'll find a way to renew love, assuming they had it in the first place."

Jack paused, reflective.

"You never know, Greg and Ulrike might be the great loves of each other's lives. This might be the swift kick they needed in order to find their way back. Big love is worth the long fight." He sighed, as if burdened. "I'm a romantic, can you tell?"

I let my shoulders drop away from me. "Where does all this wisdom come from?" I asked, softly.

"I read a lot. *A Dummy's Guide to Girlfriends*, for starters."

I smiled, willing away the low hum of anxiety that lingered. "You're sure it's not that you just don't want Sam to date Ulrike?"

"Soon, Ulrike will understand that she was too good for Sam." Jack began to fill my plate with chicken. "We better eat before they kick us out."

"I love you," I said to Jack, quietly.

"Good. If you ever leave me, I'll hang around just waiting for you to take me back. Like poor Greg. Maybe this was his master plan all along."

I laughed, slicing into the meat in its glistening pool of gravy.

"I'll just stand outside our window reciting poetry all day long," said Jack as he drank from his glass of wine. "What languor would his silence show / How full of fire his speech would glow! / How artless was the note which spoke / Of love again, and yet again." As Jack said the words, theatrical over the dancing shadows of the candlelight, I felt a shiver over my skin.

"Joy really set you up to sweep me off my feet," I said.

"What if I knew that whole poem by heart and it was my favorite piece of verse from high school or something?"

"You took carpentry and government in high school. Name one other Pushkin poem that you loved."

"That Eugene one is so long. It would have taken me all of high school to finish." Jack laughed, raising his palms as I raised an eyebrow at him. "Listen," he said, suddenly serious. "I wanted to make sure you had all of your greatest hits today. Everything that makes you happy. So I did the research, you know? I don't want you thinking this is all her."

I looked into Jack's eyes, dizzy with love. "I know."

His eyes crinkled as they did when he was pleased, each freckle on his nose and cheeks a beloved map that I knew by heart, his forehead slightly sweaty from the hot food and summer night.

"I'm a lucky guy, MG," he said.

AS WE GOT off the subway at Park Place, Jack turned to me. "I have one more surprise," he said.

"Almond Joy," I said, in anticipation. "Or the mint chocolate ice cream cake from Carvel's."

"Close but not quite," he said, scooping me up from the last step of the subway stairs, as we ascended into the coolness of the night, my dress fluttering in the summer breeze.

"Where are we going?" I demanded happily as he set me down.

"Back to the apartment. That's where the surprise is."

"Sticky rice with mango," I yelled to the stars above.

Jack laughed, holding me by the waist. "Careful, MG, or you'll float away."

I grabbed his buttock and kissed his mouth. Surprised, Jack responded immediately. As we came up for air, he raised an eyebrow. "That was a good bottle of wine."

"This is a wonderful birthday," I said.

He could see I meant it. We walked the rest of the way, two and a half blocks back to our apartment, hand in hand. I yawned despite my excitement as Jack used his key to let us into the brownstone.

"Whatever it is, can I change into pajamas and enjoy it on the couch?"

"You sure can," said Jack, ahead of me on the stairs as he took them two at a time, his legs bounding over the ancient stairwell with the same loping, graceful quality that Millie had.

"Did you put Millie in the bedroom?" I asked. "She's usually barking at the window."

Jack smiled down at me from the stairwell above as I stopped on the third floor, out of breath. "You ask so many questions."

I trudged up the final flight to where Jack stood outside our door.

"Okay, I guess this is how thirty-one feels," I said. "Cardio starts tomorrow." I paused for a moment. "What is that? What's that music?"

I felt my heartbeat quicken as I listened—the familiar strains of the song, but quicker, more lightness and air and then, a little exaggerated flicker of the wrist on the final few bars, more than an ordinary rendering of *Happy Birthday* might deserve, a flourish I would have recognized anywhere. In disbelief, I pushed past Jack and there, bent over the little Donner wooden piano Jack had found for me the year before, playing the birthday song with her usual intense focus, was Joy, unchanged by the two years we had spent apart. As she finished, she looked up at me, her eyes gleaming with pleasure at having executed the moment exactly as she had wanted it.

"Happy birthday, Didi. Told you I'd be back."

Jack looked resigned and Joy, triumphant. "I told you she would love it," she said.

They hugged awkwardly, part strangers, part family already.

"Did you take her to the aquarium?" Joy asked.

Jack looked at me, embarrassed at having been found out, but I was only delighted.

"She had to work," he said with sadness.

Joy snorted, the sound emerging as a single note of contempt. Before I could look apologetic, Jack opened the freezer door and pulled out a bright green dome covered in hard plastic.

"I still get points for the mint chocolate ice cream cake that was sold out in seven different Carvel locations until a nice old man in Queens let me come and pick it up at lunchtime."

Joy grinned, brazen and happy as she took the cake from him and slid it, sans dome, onto my wooden countertop. "Clap clap," she said to Jack. "Come on, Didi. Let's blow some candles, make some wishes."

JOY HAD FOUND a job at a firm in Connecticut that had gone the distance to woo her into a well-paid position that worked remotely three times a week. As a response to this, Kirkland & Ellis had upped the Connecticut firm's offer by 30 percent and agreed to let her work out of their Manhattan offices starting in the fall. Satisfied that her plan had worked, Joy packed her bags and came home to us.

That summer, Joy and Jack got to know each other. The three of us swam in watering holes in the Hudson Valley and went to music festivals in Asheville and Pioneertown. It was my habit to take Joy where I went and I had forgotten what pleasure it gave me. We spent a week in Jack's family's cabin in the Blue Ridge Mountains and, in the heat of August, drove up to Maine and barbecued by the water with my college friends. Jack and Joy were like match and tinder, arguing incessantly about the law and ethics, about politics and healthcare, bandying theories and countering each other's defenses—everything from whether or not the water was warm enough to swim in, to the measures taken by the Supreme Court in a class action suit on opioids. I watched Joy laugh at Jack's acerbic yet goofy wit, as they discovered a common love of basketball and animal memes, Italian red sauce joints, and my family's peanut phyllo samosas. We began to form an identity as a trio at our friends' backyard gatherings, the three of us going to dinner or meeting our father in Manhattan.

There was a softness to Joy when she made fun of Jack, as if his inherent goodness was able to dissolve the brittle edge that my father and I had been afraid of since Joy was a girl. With Jack, her meannesses turned into good-natured digs. It filled my heart to see it, and all summer long I marveled at the luck that had brought my little family together in this way.

ONE NIGHT, WHILE Jack was away on a business trip, meeting a band in New Orleans, Joy and I curled up on my childhood bed in my father's house, as if we were girls again, midway through a rewatch of *The Apartment*. Joy was asleep, having pronounced that Baxter was a fool for not telling Fran the truth sooner, as she had the dozens of times we had watched the movie together since she was a child.

I turned my body to face hers and whispered—"Joy?"

She opened her eyes, drowsy, her body warm as she tugged on the comforter we shared.

I pulled it back irritably. "Stop taking the whole thing."

She closed her eyes again, scooting into the tiny space between us. "It's cold, Didi."

Remorseful, I covered her in half the blanket. "Go to sleep," I said.

She forced her eyes open, a frown of interest lining her forehead. "What were you going to ask me?"

"It can wait," I said.

"I'm awake now." Annoyed, she raised the edge of the blanket. "Here, you have to come closer if you want to stay warm under Baba's extra small leps."

"Imported all the way from Shantiniketan, West Bengal," I whispered, mimicking my father as we giggled under the cover.

"Well, what is it?" Joy sounded impatient.

"Do you like him?"

Immediately, she knew what I meant—I could see it on her face as she frowned, and tried to focus on the blanket stretched tight over our bodies, like a ridiculous tent.

"I do like him," she said, reflecting on the words. "It's funny, I thought I wouldn't. I found it suspicious you were so head over heels in love with this random white boy who likes sports and can't cook. But—I see why. He's—funny. And sweet."

"You don't seem happy though, about it?" I offered up the words tentatively, voicing what worried me. "You know that I love you more than anyone, right?"

"I know," she said. "I think I feel like he could be my best friend, you know? We just have this instant friendship I've never had before. Like, he's my buddy. And he's also going to probably be my brother-in-law or something. It's weird. I can't seem to label him as one thing or the other. But I like him."

"That makes me really happy, Joybird," I said, feeling my love for her swell in my body.

"Goodnight, Didi," said Joy, sleep muffling her words under the lep. "I love you more than anyone, too."

PART THREE

CHAPTER TEN

STANDING IN THE doorway at Lee's, looking at Joy, my instinct was to turn and run.

I wanted distance between Joy and myself, irreversible distance, the kind she would not be able to close, despite her relentless pursuit. But as I stood there, Joy looked up at Marlon, nodding and laughing with the confidence that she had with strangers, even the white-collar criminals she prosecuted. Joy could make you feel like you belonged to her, but she had always been ruthless about it. I took a step backward and stumbled into the person entering Lee's behind me—a woman, likely my own age, with a cascade of dark ringlets, who was now regarding me with a bemused expression as I stood mute and frozen, my back to Joy, who must have turned around. In the collision, the woman's book had fallen to the floor. I picked it up—a worn copy of *Frankenstein.*

"Great book," I said, handing the paperback to the woman. "About a lovely guy."

She smiled. "You okay?"

I saw concern in the woman's eyes. Maybe her name was Alex. Or Faith. She looked like a Faith. Or a May. No one would ever think I looked like a Mira, I thought as I tried to focus on the way the book's paper surface had felt, glossy, the pulp of the cover cracked open with age against my fingers; the woman's faint trace of lavender oil in my sinuses; my feet warm against the grainy leather of my sandals, my toes curled; the steamer of the coffee machine whistling explosively behind me. Anything but my sister at the bar.

"Sorry," I said again.

I pushed past the woman toward the light outside. In the sun, I wondered if I might pass out from the sharp pain in my side—a stitch, my father called it, the kind you get when you're out of shape and try to run too hard. I was out of shape. I had let my guard down. Yet my legs were rooted to the ground, unable to move or run from her, my heart feeling as if it might shatter in the confines of my chest, shards in every direction, here my esophagus, lung, small intestine, the parts of me that were broken already, needing only a splinter to crumble.

"Didi," she said, and I turned around, my scalp burning.

"Get away from me." I spat out the words but I knew they had formed only in my brain, the sight of an afraid, exhilarated Joy too much to allow me speech.

"That woman probably thought you were drunk at nine a.m.," Joy said, a terror in her eyes that felt unfamiliar.

I focused on the dim outlines of her body to make sure that it was in fact Joy in front of me, and not the image I had conjured so many times before, when I had rehearsed the things that I might say to her. When my body had not betrayed me by turning to stone.

Joy's face dissolved, eyes and nose and ears merging together, her tears blurring my own vision as her arms closed around me, an imprisonment against her taller, tanner, wider, more vital body.

"I can't believe it's you, Didi," she whispered, against my heartbeat, or maybe it was hers, hammering into my consciousness.

She looked up at me, overcome with something—grief or fear or a dawning horror that I had changed into the gaunt, shriveled monster that I felt like in front of her, capable of tearing a body to shreds.

"Why didn't you call?" she asked.

She asked it again, weeping, as if posing a query to the past five years or the last hour. We stood there in the sharp daylight, passersby blinking, curious, but New Yorkers would allow us our ugliness out in the open.

"How did you find me?" I heard myself say, hard and yet not as hard as I felt.

Joy gasped, as if remembering something, classic Joy, all breath and breathlessness.

"The accident," she said, releasing me. "You called Baba. I heard him talking to you."

At this Joy flashed an accusation into her eyes, as if I had betrayed her.

"I made him tell me," she said.

We stood on the street, looking at each other. Joy's eyes filled with tears again.

"Were you in pain? Are you okay? There was no information anywhere, not even at the hospital, and neither Lena nor Ulrike would call me back."

I felt a rush of gratitude for Ulrike, who had known what I would have wanted without my ever having told her.

"Baba didn't know anything else. I was going crazy trying to find out, so I figured that I'd come and ask Lee if he'd seen you." Joy ran out of breath. "But Lee's gone," she said, inhaling. "And his brother"—she turned around, where Marlon, behind the bar, was talking to a customer as he wiped a glass—"his brother knew you immediately."

I felt my spine curl and stiffen. "What did you tell him?"

Joy turned back to look at me. "What? Nothing," she said, fear and a defense in her voice. "I said you were my sister and that I was looking for you."

When I met her eyes, Joy looked away.

"I didn't say anything," she said, suddenly belligerent. "I can't believe you didn't tell me about the accident. Did I have to pump Baba for information to know if my sister might have died?"

I willed my limbs to turn around and walk away from her.

"Are you okay?" she asked, looking at me again, the flip of a switch, her anxious examination returned.

"I'm fine."

Joy's mood shifted again, lightning quick in the face of my contempt.

"Didi, you can't know how it's felt," she said, in a half-whisper. "This whole time." She reached out, both of her hands clasping my shoulders. "Will you ever forgive me?"

I felt an odd certainty slide into my bones, the intensity of my emotion rolling away from my shoulders, the tingling on my neck and the back of my head abating slowly. The street came into sharp focus. A yellow school bus slid past a taxi, their colors merging, a woman in a black coat despite the sunshine, pushed an infant too quickly in a stroller, the green of the tiny dog park bloomed across the street. Through the bar window, Marlon, wearing his glasses that had been on my nightstand light-years ago, tried not to look at us as he leaned against the counter reading, the rush of the morning hour at an end.

"I hate you, Joy," I said softly.

She leaned forward, as if trying to hear the words better, decipher them, even as her eyes filled again, betraying her. I knew her by heart and what lay behind the ebb and flow of her reactions. Joy wanted fury to come to her rescue, but we both knew I had won the battle of rights to anger.

"And what about Baba?" she asked, in an oddly restrained hiss, her torso moving with her breath.

"What about him?"

"Do you even care? He's been sick," said Joy, raising her voice, the temper-tantrum trick that had served her so well in childhood and her legal career. "He is destroyed by everything. Everything that's happened."

"I've talked to Baba every week since I've left," I said into her face, looking straight at her. Cruelty felt good. Cruelty felt natural. In leaving, I had never abandoned my father. Only Joy.

Joy, struck, bolted back, like a feral puppy.

"Well he's lying to you," she said, eyes flashing, this time with real fury. "He's sick. The doctor put him on a truckload of medications after he passed out in the kitchen last month and hit his head on the floor. He's had to cut out red meat completely. He gets pitter-patters here"— she clapped her long fingers over her sternum—"and has to sit down even on short walks. He's out of breath all the time. Even when he's"—Joy threw up her hands—"baking or whatever. You've been living your cute little life in London and Baba's been lying to you. I'm the one who's been taking care of him."

This was us at our truest—sisters grappling with the fear of losing our father, locked in bitter competition over who was best equipped to earn the title of Best Offspring.

"Oh yes, my cute little life," I said to her, and Joy had the grace to look ashamed. But even so, I felt a surge of real fear. "He wouldn't lie to me," I said, but Joy had caught the whiff of uncertainty and lunged toward it, a fearsome vision in a white pantsuit—but she did not scare me.

"Yes, he would. He wanted to protect you. That's all he knows how to do. I told him you would want to know the truth." The fight went out of Joy. "He's on your side," she said, as if coming to the idea for the first time, a slack grief in her words.

We were still for what felt like an eon but it must have been less than a minute, both of us deflated, my mind heavy with guilt and worry. I had been back for three days but had not seen my father in person yet, despite our phone calls. I had put it off, not wanting to be anywhere near Joy. To think of my father debilitated by illness or injury felt like whatever remaining bedrock I had left was slipping away.

"Come to Sunday lunch," said Joy, a plea in her eyes. "For his sake. You can see for yourself. If you don't believe me," she added, her jaw set.

I shook my head in disbelief, unwilling to entertain a long-lost ritual that had been sacred to us for so long. The idea of spending hours discussing recipes and world events and our lives over plates of food with Joy felt absurd. A small, hysterical laugh escaped me. Joy's wrath returned immediately.

"We still keep your place at the table," she said, with muted fury. "He'll cook if he knows you're coming. He hasn't cooked in so long."

At my silence, Joy shook her head in desperation.

"It'll only be the three of us," she said. "You don't have to talk to me. But it would make a huge difference to him to have you there, I know it would. He would feel like there was hope. We might—we might be running out of time."

It's you that wants to feel hope, I thought. Begging was not in Joy's nature.

"Joy, get away from me," I said aloud, suddenly exhausted.

For a few moments, incredulous, she said nothing. Then, she turned on her heel, enraged and defiant, storming out, away from her difficult juror.

But Joy was always readying to prepare a defense, this I knew. Cunning Joy, canny Joy, Joy of a thousand subclauses and loopholes and reframed analogies, but she could not hide the grief in chin and eyes, in which I took such monstrous satisfaction.

THAT NIGHT I dreamt of our childhood. Joy was five or six, her hair slick with coconut oil and combed into the two braids that I would plait for her before we went to bed. She was too big for us both to sleep comfortably in a single twin bed, but in the dream night, like so many nights before, she had left hers and crawled into mine. In the dream, I felt the warmth of her body, the soft cotton of her pajamas, little spoon arms and legs, pale skin lighter than mine, uneven blotches of dark rose on her overheated cheeks, a dairy smell to her sweetness. Outside, war raged, bombs rained from the skies, my father dead as I held down Joy in our bunker. We muffled our grief under the duvet that had the Spice Girls printed into every square, the objects of our infancy floating around us—a suspended fugue. When the horror subsided and we were no longer ready to die, I uncurled from Joy in the dream. *We're safe*, I whispered. *Joybird, get up*, I said. But it was not my sister who looked up at me, only a stranger with her eyes, mocking the magnitude of the joke that had been orchestrated. *Baba is dead*, the demon whispered, gravel in her throat. *You killed him*, she said, with a delicate laugh. When I woke, the sheets were damp with my fear. There was no room in that bed, alone in my home, to pretend that I was not terrified of what Joy was capable of doing to me.

CHAPTER ELEVEN

WHEN I WAS emotional in any way, even if I hid it from the world, Joy would not rest until she had excavated it out of me, not until she found a solution. This was the glue that bound our family together—Joy's relentless ability and need to preserve us as a tightly bound unit. When Lena and I were in our third year of college, we had kept a secret, one that made me desperately unhappy, but Lena had sworn me to secrecy. Joy, twelve at the time, turned into a bloodhound. She could smell sorrow on my limbs and pursued the truth with a tenacity that shocked me, interrogating me constantly and commanding my reluctant father to do the same. I claimed that nothing was wrong, that Joy was the bane of my existence, and she became silent and mutinous, her jaw set in the knowledge that I was lying. Weeks later, Lena came to our house over spring break. One night, finally giving in to my entreaties and collapsing in exhausted suffering, she told my father that her then-boyfriend had assaulted her and that she needed legal help. I could see the shadow of Joy behind the urn in our hallway, aglow in fury that she had been right the whole time, and lied to. In later years, Lena, too, had seen through my shields and the motions I made in order to function in the world. Whenever I had been desolate, Lena had sought to make me happier. But hers was a gentler love, an unconditional one that did not include the fear that Joy's did—that I might someday abandon our relationship, given that our ancestries were not perfectly matched.

TWO WEEKS AFTER Joy had come to Lee's in search of me, I met Lena and Sebastian in the morning at the greenmarket between Prospect Park and Fifteenth Street. It was very cold, but a sunny morning, and our breath formed white curls against the cloudless blue sky. Produce was freshly heaped on tables, colors deepened by the sun. The market lifted my spirits a little, as Lena had known it might. She picked a strawberry off a mound, the fruit made jewellike by weeks of unseasonal weather, and put it in my mouth. I closed my eyes in pleasure, the juices mingling with the aftertaste of my toothpaste.

"Tastes like life, doesn't it?" Lena lifted her eyebrows in knowing satisfaction.

"Maybe your life," I said. "God, that's the sweetest fruit in New York."

"Sorry to burst your bubble, but in March, they are flown in from Florida," said Lena. "Still, perfect fruit." She laughed at the dejected look on my face. "God, your naivete, M."

Sebastian lifted his arms in the air, stretching. "Ah, to be child-free and outside."

Lena picked another strawberry off the mound and, plucking the leaves around its stem, placed the berry in her husband's mouth.

"Screaming to go in a tart," said Sebastian.

"I'll look forward to it. Knock yourself out," said Lena, fondly, as Sebastian ate another berry.

I raised an eyebrow.

"What?" said Lena. We're regulars. We buy mountains of berries from them. The kids are eating us out of home and hearth."

"It's true," said Sebastian, filling a brown paper bag with large quantities. "Each one consumes about fifty berries a day in the summer, and would eat more if unsupervised. Our retirement blowup party fund, wrecked by ripe fruit."

"Tell me more about this fund," I said to Lena, as Sebastian paid a pigtailed teenager who called him Seb.

"You'll find out," said Lena meaningfully.

"The fund is toward the no-holds-barred rager existence that we imagined we'd have together before we had kids," said Sebastian as he waited for his change. "Sky's the limit. Concerts, trips, every restaurant we want to go to. Maybe we learn how to fly planes."

"We'll be seventy," said Lena. "It'll be a great time."

"I'm going to be your third wheel, obviously," I said.

"Obviously," said Lena, linking her arm through mine as we made our way out of the stall, into the sunshine.

"I wish you'd brought the kids though," I said. "Now that Gino's in daycare, I barely see them."

Sebastian stopped in his tracks. "You be quiet," he said to me. He lifted a finger to his lips. "If you talk about them, they *appear*," he said, in an exaggerated whisper. "They have ways."

He shook his head as Lena and I laughed.

"I haven't worked out in five years," he said.

"You look perfect," said loyal Lena.

"Wrangling babies," said Sebastian, flexing a bicep. "Great strength training."

Lena held my arm a little closer. "They're at a playdate sleepover. At my sister's. Gino wanted to join the big kid club and spend the night with his sisters and cousins."

"Len brought all their pillows into our bed last night so that she could smell them," said Sebastian, rolling his eyes.

"You woke up clutching Gino's this morning," said Lena.

Sebastian sighed. "Can't live without the rascals. Should we buy some sausages from Allen's stand?"

Lena nodded. "Maybe a couple of whole birds too, for the week. I'll get some greens and lemons."

Their gentle rhythms usually soothed me, but I felt on edge. The crisp air, initially charming, had turned. The unseasonal sun was scorching against my skin, my T-shirt damp under my sweater.

"You know, guys, I think I'll just go home," I said. "I might have a headache coming on."

"Are you sure?" A maternal worry laced Lena's tone.

"Yeah, I just feel like I need a weekend of catching up on sleep and watching episodes of something good. Maybe I'll get a drink with Ulrike or Gigi later."

Sebastian nodded, approving. "Sounds like a childless dream."

He stopped in front of a cooler-laden table, the last stall in the market's long line, and asked for sausages. I hugged Lena.

"Call me later?" she asked, concern in her eyes. "And maybe come over for dinner this week."

I nodded. "I'll get some sleep and be good as new."

"What's the commotion over?" asked Sebastian, turning. A large group of protesters with signs were gathered at the front of the park's entrance.

"It's a protest against whaling, looks like." Lena squinted at the chanting crowd, a few feet from us.

"We'll walk you out, Mira," said Sebastian. "Anti-whalers seem like a peaceful lot but you never know."

"We're done shopping anyway," Lena said, hoisting a shopping bag onto her shoulder. "I think I've got some lemons left from last week."

We walked toward the entrance of the park and pushed into the throng. I jostled past the bodies of protesters, caught in their limbs and chants. Finally emerging from the sweating crowd, I took in a long breath of air. When I looked up, a familiar face was watching me, a few feet away.

"Hi, Marlon," said Lena in delight, from behind me.

"Good to see you, man," said Sebastian, giving Marlon a hug as he reached us.

I stood on the edge of the clamor, as Marlon met my eyes. It felt as if the two of us acknowledged silently that I had not been at Lee's Bar since we had slept together and Joy had visited.

Marlon smiled. "Mira."

"You two know each other?" asked Sebastian, raising his voice to be heard above the protesters.

Marlon looked at me as Lena and Sebastian turned to me expectantly. I felt my mind go blank even though the answer should have been the simple fact that yes, I had run into Lee's brother at the bar that he ran, that I frequented. And even if I were to tell them that I had unabashedly taken him home after, Lena and Sebastian would likely celebrate my rise from the living dead with gusto. Yet I remained at a loss.

I heard Lena say, quickly, "You guys must have met at the bar, right?"

Marlon nodded. "Mira's come in a bunch of times."

"Without us?" Sebastian sounded annoyed.

I felt jolted out of whatever had taken hold of me. "By the time Lena gets home from work, it's bathtime, storytime, and bed," I said.

The protesters, milling about us, began to disperse.

"I work from home sometimes," said Sebastian, peevish.

Lena took Sebastian's arm. "Mira has a life without us. You just have to accept it, Sebbie."

"It's a sliver," I said, holding my fingers up in a pinch, to Sebastian.

"How do you guys know each other?" asked Marlon.

"Lena and Mira went to Brown," said Sebastian. "They're like sisters. I came into the mix and they allowed it. Had to work for it."

I thought of Joy, her face flushing in displeasure at the idea of anyone sharing in our sisterhood.

"It's true," said Lena. "Mira's the love of my life."

Sebastian put an arm around Lena. "I'm a close second unless my socks are on the dining table."

"Should we ask you about the elephant in the park?" I asked Marlon, pointing at his tote. The bag was bursting with leeks, the stalks rearing out of the top. "Are you decorating the bar with those tonight?"

Marlon grinned. "They had a sale. And I really like leeks. It's actually my day off. Deedee's got the fort. I thought I'd make my chicken leek stew."

"Ah stew, that sexy one-pot dinner," I said.

"Wait till you taste mine, you'll never mock again," said Marlon, leaning a fraction closer to me.

I felt Lena and Sebastian's curiosity, knowing that they had made note of whatever it was that I could not contain in Marlon's presence.

"Should we pick our offspring up then?" asked Sebastian.

Lena looked at her phone. "It isn't even noon yet. This is the third time he's wanted to go pick up the kids. He can't wing even a whole twenty-four hours. Marlon, do you want to come over next weekend? We're going to barbecue in the backyard. Fire up our new grill."

"Yes," said Sebastian, clapping a palm on Marlon's shoulder. "Also, you can help me with the grill. I'm going to prove to Lena that Beer Can Chicken is really a thing."

Marlon laughed. "That sounds great. Let me know if I can bring anything."

"He's got plenty of extra leeks to spare," I said.

Marlon looked at his tote. "I'm going to use every single one of these, I'm afraid."

I could feel Lena watching me.

"Just bring yourself," she said, after a pause.

"It'll be us, Mira and the many children we have," said Sebastian.

"I happen to enjoy children," said Marlon.

"What were you doing at the anti-whaling protest?" I asked.

Marlon shrugged. "Listening, mostly. I love whales, these massive mystical creatures of song, moving through the depths of the oceans. I remember the first time I read *Moby Dick* and thinking, there's a little whale in each of us. It can get buried as we grow older, but it's in there."

"That's beautiful," I said.

"Who was organizing the protest? Greenpeace?" asked Lena.

I turned, surprised. Lena had a fragment of wariness in her voice that only I might have recognized.

"Yeah. I get their newsletter." Marlon shook his head. "It's crazy how colonialism is at the root of almost everything that's wrong with the world. The Inuits started whaling in the most sustainable, respectful way to feed themselves and in five minutes, the English and the Dutch had launched a mafia stronghold all over it. It's like white people can't help themselves." Marlon looked up from his speech at Lena. "I didn't mean— "

She shrugged. "Most of us are in agreement with that sweeping generalization."

Sebastian looked at me, a current of knowledge passing between us that Lena had gone from her usual sweet self to something a little different with Marlon.

"I'm a good dinner guest, I promise," said Marlon.

His regret made me want to take his hand.

"That, I can testify, is true," I said, without thinking.

For a beat, no one said anything. Lena turned to me, authority in her voice. "I forgot lemons. Mira, come with me. We'll be just a minute, guys."

"I thought you had lemons at home," I said pointlessly, as we neared the produce stall.

"Are you flirting with Lee's brother?" asked Lena, her voice lowered, as she pretended to examine a grapefruit.

I looked in Marlon's direction, where Sebastian was deep in conversation with him. "We slept together. The night of the accident."

Lena raised her eyebrows in disbelief.

I nodded. "There's something about him. It's easy. I feel like he's someone I've known for years. It just... happened." I paused. "I'm glad it did. It felt like I came alive for a few hours." I looked at Lena. "I thought you'd be thrilled."

She nodded slowly. "I guess I am." Lena frowned at the grapefruit in her hands. "He's Lee's brother. We see Lee so often. It could be complicated."

"Maybe it was a mistake." I exhaled.

Lena set down the grapefruit and squeezed my hand. "It doesn't matter. I'm glad it made you feel better." She looked in his direction. "I just can't let anyone hurt you again."

I laughed. "You sound like Joy."

Lena looked grim, having blacklisted Joy in her heart. I touched her shoulder.

"What is it, Len? I promise you, I'm okay."

Lena shook her head. "I guess I just don't know Marlon." She smiled at me. "Maybe it's having kids. You tend to become this weird, suspicious gatekeeper. Seeing shadows where there aren't any. I'm sure he's fine."

Lena had reason to mistrust men, but something made me want to defend Marlon.

"I feel good around him. Something in my gut trusts him."

"And you're sure it's casual?" she asked, examining my face in the way Joy might, searching for clues.

I nodded, suddenly tired. "What more could I be capable of?"

For a moment, we were both silent. Lena exhaled.

"Goddamn life," she said.

I kissed her cheek. "Buy your grapefruit. You've squeezed it a dozen times."

"WE BETTER GET going Sebbie, if we want to catch a movie before the kids descend," said Lena as we walked up to Marlon and Sebastian. "Trish said she'd drop them off at two. She also asked if we could watch Beatrice so she and Robin can go to dinner."

Sebastian groaned. "Fine," he said. "Bring your bike to dinner next week? I want to see what you've done with it. Maybe even go on a ride."

"Try to keep the longing out of your voice, Sebbie." Lena hugged me, tighter than usual. "Call me," she said.

Sebastian kissed my cheek. "Love you," he said distractedly, yet with an assurance as was his way, a source of solidity in my life that I had been lucky enough to inherit by way of Lena.

After they left, Marlon and I were left standing on the curb, outside the gates of the park. A fresh crop of recently awakened Brooklynites trickled into the market.

"Hi," said Marlon, his grin cheekier this time.

I felt a warmth creep into my ears. "I'm sorry I haven't called. Or been to the bar. Things have been— "

Marlon shook his head, with ease. "You never said you would. I'm happy to see you."

"It's nice to see you, too," I said.

The sun had cooled again. White clouds bobbed overhead. We stood, smiling at each other, the morning bustling around us.

"Do you live in the neighborhood?" I asked. "I'll walk with you."

AS WE WALKED, I thought of the time we had walked to my apartment together in near yet comfortable silence, inexplicable since we were little more than strangers.

"Do you want me to carry some of those leeks?" I asked. "I feel like I should help."

"You think you're so funny," said Marlon. "But in that stew, you'd eat your words."

"Maybe you'll save me some for when I'm next at the bar," I said, without thinking.

Marlon did not miss a beat. "Gets even better with time," he said.

"Did your mom cook? Is that how you got good at it?"

We stood at the light, waiting to cross the street, a cyclist with headphones and long hair streaming past us, swerving dangerously between bus and taxi.

"Stay safe, brother," said Marlon, softly under his breath, in the cyclist's direction.

The light turned green and we stepped into the street.

"No, the opposite," said Marlon. "She was a nurse. Constantly working multiple shifts. When she'd get home, Mum'd kick off her shoes and pour a glass of wine and read a paperback in the tub or we'd watch a movie. She knew how to defrost things or the best places to get a still-warm rotisserie chicken and a side of greens. Sometimes it was just Tesco." Marlon smiled at the memory. "We ate well though. A roast chicken is still one of my favorite things to eat. I've put one on the menu at the bar. Sells out every time. Lee's going to throw it out probably 'cause it takes so much oven time, but I love it."

"Sounds like your mom loved the heck out of you," I said.

"Yeah, she knew how to love."

"My dad, too," I said, softly.

Marlon looked at me and nodded. For a few minutes we walked in silence again.

"Some afternoons if she got off a shift early, Ma would pick me up," said Marlon. "My high school was a couple blocks away, and we'd go to Ritzy's and watch a movie or pop into Book Mongers by the Brixton Street subway. Once I was filling out a form in school and ticked a box marked for race as 'white.' When Ma heard about it, she got so mad she pulled me out of class and took me right in the middle of the day to the Black Cultural archives next to Ritzy."

I laughed. "She sounds like a force."

It was late morning and a peculiar happiness took hold of me.

"Ma was that and then some," said Marlon. "I was thirteen and so bored at the museum, my face nearly fell off. Afterward, to make up for it, she took me to see *The Sound of Music* at the Ritzy. In her words, the 'greatest white-ass movie I'd ever see.'"

"Why did you say you were white?" I asked.

Marlon shrugged. "I mean, it was ridiculous. Look at me."

He was wearing a lavender wool scarf, the color a contrast with his dark hair, skin, cream sweater, and jeans, the leeks vivid in his tote. I remembered what it had felt like to place my arms on his bare shoulders.

"I'm looking," I said. Marlon laughed at the appreciation in my voice.

"I think I just wasn't sure about the right box I could fit in, for a big part of my childhood," he said. "My dad was so white, you know. And the Black kids were always making fun of me for it. The white kids definitely didn't think I was one of them. I figured I'd just say it and see what happened." A corner of his mouth lifted in mirth. "Caused a stir, is what it did. Black kid tryin' to rebrand."

Marlon came to a stop, outside a stoop, so suddenly that I looked up in surprise.

"Do you always make men talk this much, Mira?" he asked, with something in his eyes that sent a thrill through me.

I thought about it, the quiet street sleepy and sun-warmed around us, the still-bare branches beginning to show the first signs of new life.

"No," I said. "But I like hearing you talk."

He looked at me, a long moment. "This is me, up here. 2B."

I looked up at the brownstone's second-floor window. A thriving houseplant stood behind its glass pane. I thought of the night I had met Jack on Sam's birthday.

"What if I invite you up, for a bowl of stew?" He held up a palm, before I could respond. "Just stew. I know we're in this weird place where it feels a little loaded but what if we forgot about that, and kept it to, I don't know, stew and talk and maybe a little friendship? What if you just made a new friend? I can see you have enough of your own people and they love you, but an extra one can't hurt?"

His face relaxed into a simplicity.

"It really does feel like we should at least be friends," he said.

I paused, shifting my weight from one foot to the other, in search of balance.

"You can say no." He smiled. "It's Saturday. You probably have grand plans that don't involve stew."

"Stew sounds like a pretty good Saturday," I said, at last. "Although, those leeks have a lot of hype to live up to."

"They will," he said, bounding up the stoop.

"MAKE YOURSELF AT home," said Marlon, tossing his keys into a carved wooden bowl.

The apartment was surprising, simultaneously orderly and lush. A vivid portrait of James Baldwin, an oil painting in reds and yellows, hung on the central wall of the living room, surrounded by plants. Cushions sat in an organized lineup on the couch, their bright fabrics unique to each pillow. A metal sculpture of a crane, wings spread, stood on a massive bookshelf. A fiddlehead fern's leaves fanned over a motorcycle helmet cupped on the corner of a wooden accent chair. A notebook with a pencil wedged in the pages, as if abandoned mid-thought, sat on the windowsill next to the chair. There was a dizzying effect to the multitude of his objects, and the pencil felt like the only thing that had not been placed in a beautiful, strategic manner in the apartment.

"Is it always this clean in here or were you conspiring to bring someone back from the market?"

Marlon laughed. "I have been told that I've got a bit of a perfectionist streak. It's a desirable trait, right? I could have had laundry on the floor and pizza under the couch."

I patted the cushions as I sat down. "Over half of all psychopaths tend to be very organized."

Marlon blinked.

"I'm sorry. It was meant to be a joke. A bad one." I felt embarrassed. It was Lena's fault that I was wary.

He smiled, his face relaxing from its surprise. "I get it. It's hard to tell who a person is, under all that folded laundry and stacks of paid bills? When I walked into your place, I knew exactly who you were."

"A mess."

"Real. A kind of warm chaos."

I could see that he was telling the truth. Something pleasant made its way up the base of my neck.

"Maybe you're just perfect?" I leaned back into the pillows.

"Nobody's perfect, Mira."

Marlon flipped open a laptop on the kitchen counter and clicked a few keys. A British pop song I did not recognize floated into the room from an invisible speaker somewhere on the many bookshelves. He had over a thousand books, it felt like. The kitchen was an open layout, with an island that separated it from the living room. Marlon emptied his cloth bag of the leeks and watched me as he rinsed the vegetables under his tap.

"Order comes from the desire to take control," he said. "My life felt—feels pretty up in the air sometimes. The apartment helps me think."

I nodded.

"Do you want something to drink?" he asked.

"Coffee. But I could make it myself. Do you need help?"

"There's some in the pot. I made it an hour or so ago. Are you any good at peeling potatoes?"

I went around the island, into the kitchen, the Britpop sending a sense of fizzy well-being through the apartment. Reluctant, I shrugged. "I could peel a potato."

Marlon laughed. "Don't look so eager."

I poured the coffee and took a sip. I looked up at him. "This is really good coffee."

Marlon soaked the leeks and then sliced into them as if he had been doing it his entire life. "I told you, I make a good cup of coffee. You almost drank one, the morning your sister visited the bar."

I felt dread as I sat on a barstool, facing him.

"Where do you buy your beans from?" I asked.

Marlon looked at me, puzzled. "A place upstate called Overlook."

If Marlon detected my reluctance to talk further about Joy, he did not say anything and instead moved from the leeks to garlic, slicing so thin that he might have been using a mandoline. He paused briefly to wipe his forehead with the edge of his sweater.

"Did you ever think about being a chef?" I asked, as I peeled the potatoes. "I once considered it when I was a kid but decided I didn't want to cook for people I didn't love."

Marlon sizzled butter in a pan, dropping chicken thighs into it.

"I think I might have thought about becoming everything under the sun. When I was a kid, I'd tell Mum I wanted to be a rock star, or a sculptor like my friend Alfie's mum. But she would shake her head and say that Black people needed to have a few practical skills before they went out looking for pie in the sky." He laughed. "My mother was not one for much romance. When I went to uni in Leeds for an arts education, I thought about what she would have said if she were alive. 'Marlon, you dumdum—are you goin' around thinking you're white again?'"

Marlon turned away from me, the sound of leeks sliding into a hot iron pan enveloping him. Even though there was a genuine lightness to him, I heard the unmistakable note of isolation in his voice and felt a sharp kinship to it.

"Don't worry, I'm not aimless," he said over his shoulder. "I had a good little store that made money up in Perth and I like running Lee's place now. Maybe I'll be someone who runs things, y'know?"

"Sounds like you're a good guy to have around. Do you have a picture of her—your mother?"

Marlon nodded. "Over by my writing desk. She's the one with the big brown eyes."

I finished the last potato and wandered over to the corner of the apartment he had pointed at. A large, open window looked out at a furniture store across the street.

"This is a great table," I said, running my hands over the old-fashioned wooden desk. "Look at these drawers."

"Flea market," called Marlon. "I'll take you to my favorite one in Queens sometime, if you like."

I looked at the framed photos that hung with precise spacing on the ten-inch wall between the desk and the windowsill. In the first one, Lee, a burly teenager, had an arm around a young Marlon.

"You look mad at Lee in this photo," I said to him, across the room.

I heard Marlon laugh. "I was mad at everything at that age," he said. "Lee got the brunt of it but I loved him from the start. Have you met his wife, by the way?"

I paused, for a fraction of a second. "No, he met her while I was in London."

Next to Lee and Marlon, there was a photograph of a young Black woman, graduating from something. She had Marlon's lean grace and she looked intensely at the camera, with a little defiance.

"That's Mum," said Marlon from behind me.

Startled, I turned around.

"Sorry." He grinned, holding up a cup of coffee. "Stew's a stewin'. Thought I'd give you some company."

I felt a familiar current at his nearness. "She's so fierce," I said, looking at the picture.

Marlon said nothing for a moment, nodding slowly. "I think you'd have liked her. And she, you. You've both got that inner life going on."

"What do you know about my inner life, exactly?" I heard the flirtation in my voice and regretted it immediately. Marlon leaned against the window and looked reflective.

"I couldn't say," he said. "But I can feel it. There's the sense of an odyssey in you. I thought that later, about my mum, too. A lot of lives wrapped in one. A few secrets." Marlon straightened. "Sorry, did I make you uncomfortable? I can say things sometimes that are too much."

I shook my head and pointed to the fourth photo in the series. In it, Marlon, likely in his twenties, had an arm around a woman, close to his age. She was smooth-skinned, with high cheekbones. At a glance, they seemed like affectionate young lovers and I felt an inexplicable bloom of envy.

"Ming," said Marlon with affection. "She's my best friend. Mum and I lived next door to their family. We were inseparable, two little rug rats terrorizing the other kids in daycare while our mothers went to work. Her parents owned a dumpling spot and would feed me on the regular. Their house is still my first stop in London."

"It's a nice picture. Did you guys date?" I said. "She's so pretty."

Marlon smiled. "No. We saw each other naked in the kiddie pool and left it at that. She's more of a little sister. She's a vet in the posh side of ye olde London now with a couple boys of her own. They're the greatest."

"Lena's kids are the greatest, too. I'd do anything for them."

Marlon and I looked at each other as the album came to an end. He regarded me with interest.

"I really did mean it, you know. I invited you up here just for a bowl of my famous stew."

"I know."

"And yet it feels like there's this unavoidable thing between us. Even when I'm trying to not make it the only thing between us."

"Yes," I said. I felt his arms go around me, our bodies suddenly familiar and urgent to each other.

AFTERWARD, WE LAY naked in his bed, the early afternoon sun warm on our skin, despite the growing chill outside. I felt a lightening of my spirits that I had not experienced in a long time.

"You will stay for the stew, right?" asked Marlon, facing me, his fingers on my skin, a flicker of worry in his eyes.

"I owe the world the truth about those leeks."

He smiled.

"Maybe we can take a walk or something later," I said, looking at the brilliance of the sky outside his window. "Or we could take a train somewhere. You could show me that flea market."

"That sounds nice, Mira."

CHAPTER TWELVE

JANUS GAVE ITS employees half days on Fridays through the summer months, bowing to the publishing industry's summer Friday tradition. On that day, the office was usually desolate, with only a handful of assistants or a diligent intern at work even in the morning hours. Ulrike usually worked from home the entire day. It had been a few months since Joy had found me, and my nights were covered with a familiar thin film of semi-wakeful unease that would break in the mornings at the first hint of light. I welcomed work as I had three and a half years ago, finding solace in a rhythm and absorption that felt like I had some use in the world. One Friday, I walked in early, at eight, but Ulrike had beaten me to it.

"Mira," she said in surprise, as she spooned coffee into the gleaming asteroid of a coffee machine in the kitchen.

I opened the fridge and pulled out an orange juice. "Are you here to see who really shows up on Fridays?"

Ulrike laughed, tamping the grounds down. "I couldn't care less who shows up as long as they get their files to production in time." She closed her eyes in ecstasy, inhaling the fragrance of the coffee. "God, thank goodness they let me buy this thing. It's like nectar. Do you want one?"

"No nectar for me. Been sleeping badly. Trying to limit it to one cup a day."

Ulrike pressed a few buttons on the machine and peered at me. "Is it the accident? Do you have any pain?"

I shook my head. "I'm okay."

She regarded me, curious. After a moment, she narrowed her eyes.

"You seeing anyone?"

I laughed, surprised. "I—kind of. There's a dude. I mean, we're not really seeing each other—"

Ulrike set down her coffee and clapped her hands together. "Oh, good. So it is sex. A lot of it?"

I checked to see if anyone else was in earshot and turned back. "Yes, a lot of it. Since I'm not sleeping much anyway, it seemed to be a good idea."

"You like him," she said, delighted.

"Yes."

Ulrike looked as surprised as I felt by the admission. Neither of us had thought of me as capable, even three and a half years later, but Marlon was a soft spark inside of me that I knew would give some hope to Ulrike that I might finally be exhibiting a glimmer of moving on.

"This is marvelous, darling," said Ulrike, sipping her coffee, contentedly. "What good timing for this *dude*. Now you're really back in town."

I drank from the juice box, the cold drink seeping through my chest. "Ulrike, I—I appreciate you—not saying anything to Joy."

She looked at me, a long moment. "She found you anyway," she said, sympathy in her voice.

I looked away, pressing the condensation of the carton against my wrist. "A while ago. I don't think I can talk about it."

Ulrike nodded, her eyes gentle.

I stood against the fridge, awkward. "Got any plans for the weekend?"

"I'm headed to the Hamptons this afternoon," said Ulrike. "Jitney at one. Thought I'd pop in for a bit before."

"Oh, fancy. Just to get away?" I took another sip of the juice. "God, I'm so tired. Gigi said orange juice works the same as caffeine."

Ulrike snorted, derisive. "Gigi believes that birdshit on Chanel brings good fortune." She paused. "Greg and I are celebrating," she said. "Thirty years." She smiled at me, suddenly wistful. "Instead of a party, just the two of us on the beach, marveling that we made it through."

We would never talk about missing years and the love affairs that had all but ruined us, and yet there was a current of knowledge between us, a friendship that lay steady in the unspoken.

I hugged her. "Thirty fucking years. What a feat. Congratulations, and jubilation."

"Thank you." Ulrike smiled. "'Two roads diverged in a yellow wood / And sorry I could not travel both / And be one traveler, long I stood / And looked down one as far as I could / To where it bent in the undergrowth.'"

"Ah, Frost—ever depressed, ever accurate," I said, when it felt like the silence had turned to melancholy.

We laughed and I felt grateful to have Ulrike in my life. "Maybe I'll take a nectar after all. Who needs sleep?"

"God, you're about to have your mind explode," said Ulrike, turning back to the asteroid with enthusiasm.

AT MY DESK, in the face of Ulrike's potent brew, the fog of the past seemed briefly to dispel. To hell with family, I thought to myself, buoyant as I sorted through the stack of mail on my desk. There was an invitation to a conference of pastoral poets and their publishers in Georgia, a reminder from my dentist that biannual cleanings were not optional events, and a copy of Cake Zine, a magazine that I subscribed to, that described itself as "a hedonistic exploration of history, pop culture, literature, and art through sweets." Pleased, I leafed through the glossy pages as I bookmarked an article about pie as a metaphor for rejection. Really good writing was impossible to replace, I thought, regretfully setting the magazine aside ten minutes later, in an effort to begin the day's work. In the hands of the gifted, the experience of a too-sweet dessert might easily transform into a heady allegory on contrition. Not for the first time, I felt a keen sense of pleasure at the work that I did and its refuge, even as the words I had whispered to Joy, my deliberate bloodthirst, came back to me. I pulled my laptop closer, warding her off, the cold metal soothing under my fingers. A large yellow envelope, the kind that likely held a thick manuscript, sat on my desk. I had missed it in the mail pile, distracted by the zine. The label bore my name and the office address, without a sender or a return, unusual in every way for professional mail. The envelope was about two inches thick and as I slit it open, a manuscript slid out. On the front page, it said in bold font: *The Wild Lings*. Beneath that, *a novel by Finley Maria*. My immediate instinct was to take my palms off the manuscript. We had instructions to never read files, hard copies or digital, that weren't sent to the official submissions address or email. This was marked specifically to me even though it wasn't poetry but an entire novel; why hadn't it been sent to the fiction editor? My heart beat a little faster as I touched the pages again. Throughout my life, a sense of the inevitable had followed me around in specific moments that later felt as if it might be part of a more sweeping conclusion. In that moment, it felt as if something was quietly clicking into place.

A FEW HOURS later, I knocked on Ulrike's door, nervous because the blinds were drawn, which Ulrike only did if she had a headache or was upset. Or maybe she had already left for the Hamptons. She swung the door open, clad in a shapeless linen dress, a burlap sack of an outfit, and plastic slippers, her hair twisted into a short ponytail at the base of her neck, sans her usual oversize, classic pieces of jewelry, a wide brimmed straw hat in one hand.

Ulrike laughed. "From the look on your face, I don't think we've ever been to the beach together." She waved a carefree hand at me, tendrils of her hair clumping around her face. "These past few years, after that damned plague, I've just let myself be a little. I know, I look like somebody's coastal grandmother. Who cares?"

"You look happy," I said.

She sat down at her desk, transferring items from a leather purse into a straw tote that matched the hat. I realized with a little jolt that I had never seen her without eye makeup before.

"Thank you, darling," said Ulrike. "Now, what is it? I have to catch the Jitney in thirty minutes."

"It's—it's this manuscript. Someone sent it to me. I don't know who."

Ulrike took the sheaf from me.

She frowned. "Who's Finley Maria?"

"I don't know. Nothing came up online so either it's an invented name or someone scrubbed themself off of the internet. No representation either. But I read the book."

Ulrike lifted her eyebrows, still perfectly shaped despite her new avatar. "You read an unsolicited submission?"

"Yes. I'm sorry. Something made me start reading and—it's really good."

Helen, puzzled, flipped through the pages. "Is it in verse?"

"No. It's not a poems sub. I think whoever sent it just wanted me to read it. But if you're okay, I'd like to send it to Bin and Gigi."

"Is it any good?"

"Ulrike, I'm telling you. There's something exceptional about this manuscript."

Ulrike frowned, reading. "The prose feels so light. But literary."

"Exactly, exactly." I stood in front of her, my heart hammering in my chest. "It's almost Austen-esque. Frothy, but satire of the sharpest kind. The heroine, her name's Ginger Ling and she's from this rich Chinese-British family that's always moved in predominantly white circles. Until Ginger falls for a Chinese man, a first-generation immigrant who forces them all to confront their, well, whitewashing. She's got a big family—siblings and parents and a stepmom, so it's a real romance meets family drama and such a great portrait of British and Chinese society. I don't know that I've read anything like it in a long time—a kind of blazing comedy of manners." Breathless, I stopped.

"You really love it," she said, bemused.

I nodded.

"Well, I'm not opposed to publishing an anonymous excerpt if Bin and Gigi are as taken by it," said Ulrike, as she continued to flip through the pages, reading at her lightning pace. "Who do you think sent it? One of your Brits, you think?"

"There was a note," I said. "It said that Finley Maria was a pen name. That the author would like to remain anonymous, but if I liked it, to email the address in the note."

The skin around Ulrike's eyes crinkled with pleasure. "Good god, may it be Elena Ferrante, please, for the love of all the publicity gods."

I lifted the manuscript off her desk. "I'll have Masha make a copy and email it to you. I have your blessing then, to circulate?"

Ulrike looked at me, sharp. "What's the matter? What aren't you telling me? Shouldn't you be happier?"

I shook my head. "It's nothing. I just—the writing—it feels familiar."

She elongated her neck, as if listening for an unwelcome sound, on guard immediately. "What do you mean?" she asked.

"I feel like I've read it before." I faltered.

"Mira. If you think you have an idea who the author is, and you're keeping that from me, you don't need me to tell you how ill-advised that is," said Ulrike, now the fearsome protector of *Janus*.

For a moment I said nothing. "Jack," I said at last. "It feels like Jack."

Bewildered, Ulrike looked at me. "Jack Smith? Sam's brother? But he's a man. And isn't he a lawyer?"

"He's always wanted to write. He loves British television. He once said that love stories were the greatest and hardest stories—that more men should write them."

I looked at my shoes, trying to focus on them—crimson felt loafers with black embroidered swans that I had bought at a London flea market, Ulrike's cream carpet swirling beneath them. "He spent a year abroad in Bath," I said.

When I looked up, Ulrike had softened, her pity too much for me to stomach. I looked away, feeling a bristling under my skin. "I realize it sounds ridiculous, but he always said he wanted to write books. The voice, its observation—it's all so familiar."

Ulrike took off her glasses. "Why would he send it to you?"

"I don't know."

For a few minutes, Ulrike said nothing, allowing my misery its privacy. She looked at the manuscript in my hands.

"Hope is the most fatal of all poisons," she said softly.

I swallowed. "Ulrike, I'm not an idiot. I'm not sitting here hoping that it's him. That he's trying to tell me it was a mistake. We both know"—I choked on the words—"there's no going back." The air in the office felt glutinous, the patterns on every surface too much as they rose and swirled around me. "I'm just telling you what I feel in my bones. If I'm wrong, great. No harm no foul. It's still excellent."

Ulrike touched the tips of her fingers together, briefly lost in thought.

"The thing that gives me pause from dismissing this immediately is that I trust your taste very much, as you know," she said, at last. "Let me be clear, I don't want any sort of circus for the magazine."

"I understand," I said. "I wouldn't be standing here if I didn't think the manuscript was really good."

"Okay," said Ulrike, dubious. "Send it to Gigi and Bin. And don't tell them you love it. Let them tell you. If it's really that good, everyone's vote but yours will count."

We both knew that I had just asked Ulrike for a favor and that she did not like it. That if it were true, and that Jack had found a complex, silent way to communicate with me, there might be a precarious path ahead. If we published an excerpt and the piece got any buzz, it would take one internet troll to go doggedly down a path and piece together the jagged edges of the puzzle. But if it were true, I had something to hold on to, the smallest sliver of light in the abyss inside me. In the early months, well into the year after Jack had left me, I saw signs everywhere. There was nothing more American than falling for a guy named Jack, ubiquitous in fiction or film, someone's cousin, the new hire, a character in a play. Jack, a mailman, Jack a muse, Jack a love song, Jack-a-lantern Kerouac Lemmon Nicholson. His favorite candy, a Starburst wrapper, lay crumpled and incongruous on the streets of London as I stared at it—had he come after me, had he made a mistake, could the universe reverse its tectonic shifts after all?

IN THE EVENING, Gino lay in my lap, half asleep and sticky with sweat and the remains of a cinnamon pastry, as I cradled him, rocking back and forth in the back yard in a chair that had belonged to Lena's grandmother. Lena was stretched out on a blanket at my feet, watching Mirabel and Alice feed a large white rabbit with pink eyes.

"How long do you have to keep the rabbit?" I asked, stroking Gino's flushed cheek, his skin warm from the sun.

Lena let out a dramatic sigh. "Well, each kid in their class has to do one week of animal husbandry but because there's two of them, I have the singular pleasure of scooping limitless quantities of rabbit poop for two weeks."

Gino stirred at my touch. Contrite, I hummed "Vincent," the Don

McLean song that my father had often sung to put me to bed as a child. Marlon, grilling chicken with Sebastian in the backyard, turned to look at me. He smiled, holding my gaze before he turned back to Sebastian.

"Sebbie really likes him," said Lena, watching me.

"And you?" I turned to Lena.

Lena closed her eyes and lay flat on her back in the grass, reluctant, I knew, to answer.

"There's something so delightful about Marlon," she said, after a pause.

"But?"

Lena ignored my interjection.

"It's like he's genuinely interested in people," she said, wrinkling her forehead in the way she always had when perplexed. "Nobody's ever *really* interested in my day, but he is." Lena frowned deeper, opening her eyes. "But there's also something about him that's on guard, that I can't put my finger on."

She sighed.

"Maybe it's because I just want to make sure that the next person you're with is a saint."

"He's a nice guy and I would drive a saint crazy," I said, under my breath, so that Gino wouldn't wake up. "Also, *I'm* interested in your day."

Lena propped herself up on her elbows. "How nice?"

"*Very* nice."

"Ah, the joys of early-romance sex. I'll just sit here in my rabbit poop, jealous."

Alice screamed as the spray from the garden hose that her sister was holding hit her shoulder.

Lena craned her neck and said calmly, "Mirabel, please. Do not point that hose at your sister."

Gino's eyes flew open and he began to cry. "Mama," he wailed.

Reluctant, I handed him over to Lena as Sebastian separated the twins, pulling a pouting Alice onto his lap with a mild rebuke to his other daughter as he wrangled a gushing garden hose with one hand, an expert in all things fatherhood. Mirabel, chastened but not dispirited, wandered over to Marlon. I watched as Marlon crouched down to her.

"At least he's good with kids," said Lena, with a grin at me.

Gino, soothed, stared up at me from her lap, his dark eyelashes wet with tears as he sucked his tiny thumb.

"Don't you go down that road." I shook my head in warning at Lena.

"What? You came together tonight. It's got to be more than just the ecstatic fucking."

"Stop it, Len." I shook my head again. "I'm still such a mess. And you're right, I think there's a mystery, a woundedness to him. Maybe that's why I'm so drawn to him."

"Just be careful, okay?"

I nodded. Satisfied, she turned to look back at Marlon. "But I will say, Mira, look at this man. Be still my beating ovaries. If you don't want him, can I have him?"

We giggled, our teenage selves again. Marlon said something that made Sebastian laugh out loud.

"It's also that he seems to have fallen like a ton of bricks for you, pretty quickly," said Lena, reflective, as she kissed Gino's forehead. "I mean, I get why, but it's a touch suspicious in this era. If he turns out to not be a dick, it would be very nice for me. But the jury's out."

"You talk a tough game but all you want is for me to buy the brownstone next to you guys and have a couple of babies to carpool with yours," I said, laughing.

Lena had an ease with marriage and motherhood, home and hearth, as much as with her career. Occupying her universe—husband, children, office, cat, rabbit, fresh rolls, garden hose, the recriminations and thrill of toddlers, had made her the happiest she had ever been.

"I mean, think about it. We would have the mommune we've always dreamed about," she said.

"That was your dream. My version was doing psychedelics and reading about the stars."

"Fine, fine. Live your debauched life." Lena placed Gino gently into his rocker. "It's not like I'd make you go to church or anything."

"Is that—are the kids—?" I stumbled on the words.

"Are they going to church with us? Of course." Lena raised her eyebrows in surprise. "It means so much to Sebbie. And I've come to feel a real belonging with the community."

I nodded. Lena touched my hand.

"When they're grown, if they become debauches like you, we'll love them just as much," she said.

I tried to smile. "Religion is just"—I let out a burst of breath—"more structured than I want anything to be."

"Not necessarily," said Lena, stretching out, content. "It's what you make of it."

When Lena had begun to go to church with Sebastian, it had felt like a loss. Lena had virtue embossed into her DNA, but neither of us had ever subscribed to anything save the power of art, or humanity. It had been one of the reasons we had become friends, bound by a reverence only for what felt free and real to us. By the time I came to cherish Sebastian's friendship and appreciate what mattered to him, I also realized that Lena's effortless transformation to a life of domesticity focused on home ownership and carpools and raising money for her community was what made her happy now. And yet she had remained the Lena that soothed me as she did her children and husband, seeing what we needed in the moment.

In his sleep, Gino smiled. "He's so beautiful," I said.

Lena looked up at me. “Yeah. Maybe you’ll take him to Durga Puja in Lexington sometime.” She smiled. “So he can belong to your world, too.”

I looked at her, grateful. “Ma Durga, my favorite goddess of all,” I said to the sleeping boy in his rocker. “A thousand stories about her, to read to you.”

When I looked up, Marlon stood above us, backlit by the sun, his shadow cool against my skin. “Lena, would you mind if I taught Mira my favorite poem?” he asked.

Lena cocked her head in confusion, the sun in her eyes.

“Mirabel, I mean,” said Marlon. “She called herself Mira.” He laughed. “I didn’t mean M.”

“By all means, teach me your favorite poems,” I said to him.

Lena smiled at Marlon. “Mirabel is named after *this* Mira actually. What’s the poem?”

“‘We Real Cool,’” said Marlon. “By Gwendolyne Brooks. She asked me what my favorite rhyme was and that felt like a good one.”

Lena and I burst out laughing at the same time.

“Are you telling me, Marlon Hughes, that your mother never taught you ‘Ring a Ring o’ Roses’?” I asked.

“My mum was more the Langston Hughes kind.”

The electricity between us was unmistakable and Lena looked away, as if making the discovery anew. She waved in the direction of Mirabel, who stood with her arms crossed, a frown on her cherubic face.

“Have at my child, please,” said Lena.” Just make sure I’m not spending happy hour answering questions about gin or death.”

Marlon laughed. “I promise. I’ll be back with some chicken in a sec. Sebastian’s almost done.”

“Two pieces for me, please,” said Lena. “Gino might want some in a bit.”

The sun faded in a final flourish as the evening began to take shape around us—crickets, the click of Marlon's beer against Sebastian's, his soft voice as Mirabel giggled, the terrace across the street growing noisier as a dinner party drifted upstairs, our drinks sun-warmed, the ice in them melted, Lena and I made languid by it all.

"Have you—thought about what you're going to do?"

Lena had been waiting for the right moment to ask me her burning question. I shook my hair loose from a hair tie, feeling my scalp with my fingertips. A gust of breeze wafted over us, the smell of spiced meat and wet earth in the air.

"I'm going to see him," I said.

"Jack?" Lena's face froze in shock as she clutched at Gino's rocker.

Despite myself, I laughed. "No, you idiot. My dad." I paused. "We've been talking on the phone a lot but he's upset I haven't been to see him yet."

"Oh." Lena said the word in a rush of relief. "I thought that silly manuscript had you in a tailspin." She pushed the rocker, absent-mindedly. "You love him so much; it is pretty nuts you've been able to stay away."

I looked away. "I had to."

Lena did not say anything but I knew that she understood the terrors I lived with, of running headlong into my past.

"But it's time now," I said, mustering cheer into my voice.

"Mama," protested Gino, waking as his rocker sped up.

I leaned down and reached into my purse. The late afternoon light illuminated Gino's cocoa skin as I handed him the toy duck that I had bought at the pharmacy earlier.

"Ducky," screamed Gino, happily.

"When are you going?" asked Lena. "Do you want to borrow our car?"

Marlon and Sebastian began to pile steak and chicken onto a platter. Mirabel and Alice, sisters again, danced in a circle around them, as if the men and meat were their sacrificial offerings to the hot grill.

"Tomorrow, for lunch. I'll take the train up to Manhattan."

The moon had come up, as the afternoon had faded. I wished Lena would stop asking me questions because I was happy in the peace of the evening and any joy was so fragile and fleeting that I wanted no part stolen.

"So she's going to be there? Mira, are you sure you're ready? Do you want me to come?" Lena, fierce, held my wrist.

"It'll be okay," I said. "It had to happen sometime." I smiled at Lena, encouraging, unwilling to let her see the drowning I held at close bay.

"I don't like it," she whispered angrily, as Marlon began to walk toward us, balancing three plates. "Joy doesn't deserve you."

"I'm doing it for Baba," I said, as I looked up at Marlon, a brilliant halo encircling him, created by the lights that were strung across the backyard.

CHAPTER THIRTEEN

ON A SATURDAY, the trains from Brooklyn to Manhattan felt pressurized with the bodies and anticipation of New Yorkers emerging for air into the promise of a weekend. Everyone was a different color, skin and teeth and hair meshed together, yet alone, inside of a headphone or an open book, siloed in the way New Yorkers could be, both intensely aware of and yet seemingly oblivious to the trials of the man performing cartwheels to James Brown in the center of the subway car. Nobody would have made note of me, silent and pleasant, moving when I was supposed to, making way for the space of others, absorbed in the Arctic Monkeys, an unremarkable attendee likely enroute to a fourth date or a picnic in the park or perhaps a taker of a weekend language class. Nobody would have thought to themselves that here was a woman, her skin on fire, cold beads clinging to the cotton fabric of her summer dress, on her way to be bitter and cold to a devious sibling, consumed by the fear of becoming an orphan, incapable of rising above the underground that we hurtled through, the chatter and scream of Union Square, now Times Square, now Seventy-Second street echoing their noises in my head, as we approached a world that had gone on without me.

AS A DISTRACTED teenager, I had often forgotten to look both ways before crossing the street. Eddie, our super, had kept an eye on me, more than once yanking me out of the furious paths of the city's overworked drivers. Eddie stared now as I walked into the Savannah. I felt an intense familiarity take hold of me.

"Well, I'll be damned," said Eddie in a version of the dark suit he had worn through my childhood years, his glasses bifocals now, as he hugged me.

Growing up in a predominantly Jewish neighborhood, Eddie and we—my father, Joy, and I—had been the only people of color on the block for a long time. Indian families did not often own property on the Upper West Side, but my soon-to-be-absconding mother had wanted to be close to the university and my father had wanted to feel more American than he was. We were the gold-star model minority. Eddie had watched over Joy and me, spurred on possibly by our motherlessness and as the father of two daughters himself. He had seen us through high school and on into our adult lives. When Jack had left me, there had been no time to explain to tender-hearted Eddie why I might have chosen to disappear, but in the end, he must have understood. He stepped back to look at me.

"Are you taller?" he asked.

I laughed. "You've been saying that every year since I was four."

"You look taller. You look like you used to when you came home from camp." Eddie squeezed my shoulder. "It's good to have you back, Miss Senior G."

I felt hot tears at the back of my throat, this homecoming a relief from something, the nagging crater in my life that I had refused to look at for five years.

UPSTAIRS, THE SMELL of mint and chili permeating the hallways, I knew that my father was cooking the six-hour pork that I had demanded in vain on weeknights as a child. I knew that my childhood bedroom would be the same, untouched by our new realities. I could take home my Bach and Fleet Foxes records, I thought, striving for ways to focus the shaking of my hands. I pushed the unlocked front door open, carefully setting down a galette—blackberry and sesame, my father's favorite—that I had schlepped from Brooklyn. My father had an intuition that had served him well in his legal career and equipped him in his mellowed, older years for the sorrows of his children. This crucial time alone in the living room, getting a sense of my bearings before the sensory overload of the kitchen, was a gift from him. That he was near, that I might finally hold him in person, beloved arms, beloved heart, was suddenly overwhelming. I walked into the kitchen, galette-armed. Joy, barefoot, towering a few inches above my father at five ten, tasted from a wooden spoon as she bent over the pressure cooker that my father had brought back from India in the eighties. He stood next to her, impatience on his face.

"Needs salt, but it's, oh god, so good," she said as she licked the spoon clean.

"Don't put *that* back in there, ma," said my father just as Joy stuck it back in the pot, the two of them erupting into laughter despite his exasperation.

This world, their little universe of sauces and aprons and jokes and spills—all of this had existed while I had wasted away in London. Joy was the first to turn around, as if feeling my gaze, jerking away from the pot and my father, the spoon slipping slowly into the meat. But it was my father's face that unraveled me. He was thinner, frailer, parts of him unfamiliar, like the slump of his shoulders, his body seemingly shrunk by the time we had spent apart. Yet, he burst forward with the energy with which he had infused dinner parties all his life and folded me into an embrace.

"My dear girl," he said, as I laid my head on his collarbone.

He was cardigan-clad even on a warm day, his specific smell a transportation into childhood. I felt a piercing relief—he was not too old or debilitated or teetering on the edge of something I had failed to notice in my weekly calls from London, during which he would entreat me to return. My father was himself. Joy had deceived me, as was her way.

WHEN JOY HAD been about four or five, playacting was a part of our lives. My father and I would sit on the floor and she would thrust toy tea cups into our palms, imperious as she held court. From her imagination, she would serve up delights on plates the sizes of our palms while we enacted the emotion that might come from sucking on enormous lemons or thrusting our tongues and faces into fistfuls of invisible whipped cream. Now my father sat at the head of the table, as he had a thousand times, and Joy tiptoed around me, setting plates and silverware in motion, the pork in its urn as centerpiece to our performance.

"Let us eat," said my father, ushering us toward an activity that would keep our mouths and hands busy, such that Joy and I might only look from our food to him and back again, she stealing glances at me. Mid meal, my father, misty, touched both our shoulders.

"I cannot tell you both how happy this makes me," he said, looking at me.

I looked away. Urn, cucumber salad, rice, plate, pork, fork, the floral patterns of the unfamiliar tablecloth.

"Thanks for cooking," I said.

We ate politely, with requisite sounds of appreciation. My father beamed at the praise—he had not lost his vitality in the kitchen or any part of himself. I felt the exhale in my body and it softened me.

"You look so healthy, Mira," said my father. "When you called me in February about the car crash, my imagination—it went to the worst places. I said a prayer."

"Since when do you pray?" I asked.

"I don't. But you can spend all of your life being a nonconformist and the second your child is in trouble, you'll believe in dancing dragons."

"It worked. I got lucky," I said to him, placing my hand on his wrist. "And we talked five times the next day, so you know I was doing fine."

In my periphery, Joy looked away for a beat.

"Did you go to a doctor?" she asked, Joy's first question of the evening to me. "To make sure there weren't any internal injuries? The impact had to have been hard on your body in that kind of multiple collision."

Something curled up inside of me as I sliced into a cube of pork, the fat opaque and tepid. A sudden wave of nausea entered my throat, a souring in the spaces beneath my ears. My father's expectancy hung in the air between us as I remained silent.

"No," I said finally. "I feel fine."

I heard my own voice, stilted and removed, as a silenced Joy and my father began to eat again.

"Have you settled back into the office?" asked my father, cheerfully, as if the last few minutes or years had, in fact, not occurred. "Is Ulrike still there?"

Ulrike had always made my father feel special. She would throw back her head and laugh at his quips or appreciate the devotion with which he read *Janus*, firmly out of his pulp fiction wheelhouse. There had always been a special pep in my father's step after a conversation with Ulrike.

"She's celebrating her thirtieth wedding anniversary in the Hamptons," I said. "She sends her love." Involuntarily my eyes slid to Joy, whose pale skin, unlike mine, flushed easily. *Not to you,* I said silently and she knew it from the way in which I looked at her, the first time we had made eye contact since Lee's.

"Ah, the love of Ulrike. How fantastic. Isn't that fantastic, Joy? Tell her we send our love, too." My father raised his glass and drank from it. When Joy was upset, she turned defiant, her chin upturned, her lips pursed with the hint of a tremble, her eyes, identical to mine, narrowed. I chewed slowly, staring at my plate. The color of her hair was different. Darker, like mine, with wisps of bangs that she had not had before. She was wearing a silk blouse, the color of milk chocolate, that I had never seen before, and her nails were done in the French style, the tips white, the cuticle glossy. Some part of me registered that Joy was older, more manicured, her body more contained.

"Mira?"

I looked up to see them watching me.

"Sorry. I was thinking about work," I said to my father.

He nodded. "I just wondered if you might want to go to the park after lunch. The way we used to."

Nothing is the same, I wanted to scream at them. It didn't matter how well we had our parts down, how much we had rehearsed our sides—it was all gone to rot. But I nodded carefully, once and then a second time, at my hopeful father. The pain we had caused him, Joy and I, was as irreversible as the debris of our sisterhood.

You must understand, Mira. Family is family. You only have one sister. If you want a sister, this is the one you must forgive. Over the phone in London, his voice had had the coldness of a command, flat, legal, communicating the facts of a plea bargain to a client.

"You should sue the state," said Joy, fracturing the heavy air, her voice raised.

Reluctantly, I looked at her, full throttle this time—some sort of pearl eyeshadow (new), silver drop earrings that I had given her on her sixteenth birthday, no other jewelry, a darkening under each eye (lack of sleep, or a sister), her eyes wide with the power of knowledge (Joy loved this power more than anything else). She looked at me with what seemed like relief—could it be that we were capable of looking at each other again? The back of my brain tingled at the idea.

"Here," she said, thrusting her phone's screen toward me, teacup-brandishing toy queen again. "The Tort Claims Act allows you to sue the government for personal injury and premises liability cases, including car and bus accidents. Who knows how much emotional damage you've been through, how many hours of work have been compromised, what damage it's done to your mental acuity? You could square away your student loans with this thing." Joy looked insane, and ecstatic, as if she had solved a crime on the spot.

As the three of us sat in silence, I wondered if it was just me who had experienced the missing years. Had it even happened if we could so thoroughly ignore it? I felt myself begin to laugh. Joy, the only one I wanted to sue, was sharpening my knives for me, so that I might go after others. The absurdity of our life, eternally interwoven as half-bloods, when we might have had some modicum of peace had we never had to set eyes on each other again. I doubled over laughing until I was coughing, Joy and my father infected by me, laughing too, the three of us trapped in the farce that life had dealt us.

"You're not a fucking personal injury lawyer," I said, tears rolling down my face, the only ones she had seen in five years.

"I'm a great lawyer," said Joy back at me, throwing her neck forward, delight transforming her features to the girl she had once been, containment thrown to the winds. "I could be *your* great lawyer," she said, collapsing with laughter.

My father, chuckling, eager to join, to hold on to whatever this was: "You're not allowed to swear in front of me," he said, fists on the table, tears downstream his cheeks too—a collective need to shed them.

Slowly, we subdued, my breath shuddering to a halt. Outside, a hummingbird screeched, the same kind that had hovered over our growing years, trying to safeguard its territory, its nest in the same crook of the elm's elbow that all of the previous generations of hummingbirds had guarded fiercely. When the nest was destroyed by season or storm, a few weeks later the hummingbirds would rebuild. It would be as if the nest had never been broken, a magic trick. When I turned back to Joy, there was familiar fear in her eyes. Since the afternoon Jack had told me the truth, I had looked at her rarely and only with hatred.

"If I'm not doing anything on a Tuesday afternoon sometime, I'll think about suing New York," I said to her. "On account of the rats in my building's laundry room, if nothing else."

Joy stared at me. After a pause, she smiled weakly.

"I can definitely be your lawyer for the rat situation. Class action, I think."

I nodded and turned to my father, for whose approval I had released a syringe of reconciliation into the air. He nodded, almost imperceptibly. I knew that I had made him happy. Until he died, I was required to be Joy's sister. This was my role to play.

IN THE PARK, the leaves were the verdant British hue they took on before the rust of fall. There was a wetness in the air, even though it had not rained, the sky suddenly cloudless yet gray. As children, in the depths of the park, we had always sensed magical creatures lurking beneath the earth or between branches or under large, misshapen rocks. If you walked long enough into the sprawling wild green, like the three of us had so many times, there were streams, ice cold and gurgling, or brambles heavy with berries, or a school of watersnakes or migrating birds overhead, scaring butterflies into hiding. As an adult, the park still felt occupied by those who knew other worlds than the one we occupied. I breathed in the cooled air and imagined my lungs firming with purity. There was a lake we had found years ago, smaller than the other lakes in the park, the water warmer, a tiny pool of silken pale green. Joy and I had leaped in even as our father protested, terrorized by his own father's fears—*who knows how deep it is, what if you drown, it's illegal to swim here, get out of that water at once.* But we were unafraid that summer, her five-year-old body squirming in my iron grip. I had been almost thirteen, unwilling to let her swim out of my sight even though she was the better swimmer, already more fearless and stronger than me, both of us fused together in delight as we held our breath under the clear water.

"The lake is to the left of the smaller sugar maples—you have to go past the urchin water fountain and then it's definitely behind the line of sycamores," said Joy, confident.

"They're not sycamores, they're London planes," I snapped. "It's further, behind the planes, past the dog park."

Joy looked uncertain—our newfound truce was alternately seething and melancholic. Even she knew that it was too soon to retort back at me. That afternoon, in the make-believe land we had entered, some part of my brain had clouded over. Was pretense so bad, after all? Ulrike had once told me that in order to feel happier, one had to perform the physical act of smiling for an extended time. The brain might then be tricked into firing neurons toward synapses of manufactured happiness. In London, I had tried, my skin and teeth stretched taut with the effort. But in the park, with my father and sister, I felt my fury sag, my skin cooling as Joy hooked her arm around mine, tugging on my elbow, pulling me toward a line of imposing, magnificent chalky sycamores that had borne many worse storms than we. She stood gleaming with satisfaction in front of the lake we had once swum in as sisters.

"You were right," I said to her.

She nodded, but there was a grief to Joy, who loved me as if I were half of her self. I had known that the greatest punishment to Joy would be to deny her my presence in her life. Even if I could not access the vast love I once felt for her, I could attempt to be empty, devoid of the poison that had eaten us alive. My father, slower than usual, meandered toward us, out of breath.

"Take it easy, Baba," I said through the thicket, my voice looping in thin echoes, around the trees. "Come and sit by the lake. We found it."

"I found it," yelled Joy, alight with mischief even as she wavered on the tightrope between us. She extended her hand toward me. "Come on. Let's get in before he catches up."

I looked at the water, flecks of sun emerging from the sky, making their way into the lake. My father had stopped to look at us, holding on to a sycamore as he caught his breath, his joy plain on his face. It was a tale older than time that to be his daughter fully, I would have to take Joy's hand. Joy whipped off her blouse and shorts, shimmering like the water in her golden swimsuit beneath. She leaped in, both legs momentarily suspended in the air, an effortless geronimo into the lake. I ran behind her, unbuttoning my dress, flinging it off as I plunged into the cold water in my underwear, my body knotted and unpracticed, both of us submerged, trying to hold on to each other for dear life, the lake deeper than we had remembered. It would take only a few motions to drown the other. It was the first time our bodies had touched in years. In our leave of absence from sisterhood, she had become a formless, recurring dream that shape-shifted in the distance. That she was so alive and real felt impossible. *I'm sorry, we love, we hate.* When we came up for air, our mouths were open, gasping, our arms wound around each other's heads and limbs, water in our sinuses. Joy's laughter rang through the woods. In the distance my father lay beneath a sycamore, so peaceful that he might have been sleeping, but even before I leapt out of the water, running toward him, I knew that he was dead.

CHAPTER FOURTEEN

I SAT IN the manic churn of the hospital, its fluorescent lights pulsating as our father was taken away. Joy had taken charge; she had called the ambulance and then herded me into a taxi as we rode to the hospital. She filled out the paperwork and procured his insurance card from his wallet. She was on the phone, organizing and informing and arranging for dry clothes to be sent to us from the apartment. As she hung up, my sister leaned against the hospital's coffee machine, waiting for the pale brown liquid to trickle into two cups. She brought the coffees over to where I was seated and glowered in the direction of the nurses who sat at the entrance of the emergency room.

"I can't believe they've had him for over an hour and don't think it's necessary to give us an update," she said, handing me a cup as she drank from the other.

I took a tentative sip—the brew was acidic but warm, and felt comforting.

"They're trying to save his life," I said.

She looked up even as I heard the sharpness in my tone.

"Thank you for the coffee," I said.

Joy nodded, silent. We both knew that she excelled at being in charge and I was better at holding my father's hand, or breaking difficult news to him, or giving him reassurance. But we chafed at what the other could do better and this had been the story of our lives, never fully uniting to form a team.

"Are you—okay?" I asked, hesitating on the words.

She nodded, stoic. A different Joy from the sister who confided in me constantly through our lives.

"I just want him to be okay," she said.

I nodded. "Me too."

Maybe in the intervening years since I'd been gone, Joy had transformed her headlong emotions into a poised restraint. In sudden, fierce longing, I wished that she would cry and that I could cry with her. But we sat there instead, turned to stone, watching the stream of injury and illness pass us by. After what felt like hours but had been forty-two minutes, a petite nurse with eager eyes and rust-brown locs piled on her head materialized in front of us with a clipboard. She touched me on the shoulder.

"Miss. Are you okay?"

Why wasn't Joy talking? I thought to myself.

But Joy had vanished, either into the bathroom or for more paperwork. If my father was dying, would I have to take care of her in any way? I was the one who ran, Joy was the one who stayed. In his absence, what would remain of us?

"Miss?"

I heard the nurse's voice again, her beauty odd in the sterility of the crowded ER. She was alert now, an octave more focused, scrutinizing me for something—fatherlessness or the feeling that I, too, might die, as she touched my elbow this time. "Do you need an exam?"

I shook my head. "Our dad—he's inside."

"I know," she said, crouching to be level with me, radiating compassion.

She looked at the clipboard, touching my knee.

"He's had a NSTEMI heart attack—which essentially isn't a full-blown one, sort of like a mini version of one."

Her badge said PALOMA. She had to be in her twenties—how did one learn languages of grace so young?

"Is he going to be okay?" asked Joy, her voice high and breathless behind the nurse.

"Yes," said the nurse, turning around. "They've stabilized him. For now." She rose to her feet, tiny against Joy. "We looked at his records. He had complained of chest pain and shortness of breath back in January. He was supposed to schedule an echocardiogram, and his doctor prescribed medication, but it seems he didn't make the appointment. And I'm guessing he hasn't been taking the medication either. The doctor's going to come out and give you two a more detailed picture of what's going on and what he needs, but he can't just go on living life as if it's a little asthma or something. His GP warned him a few times last year that this could happen—I was just on the phone with her."

ALTHOUGH I HAD not believed her, Joy had been right to warn me about my father's health. As a family we specialized in looking away, from wounds open and closed. If my father had looked a little more tired, a little more drawn than usual in the past few years, I had been oblivious, looking away from the screen and absorbed in my own pain, pain that he, too, had prioritized over his own. He had lied to both of us—there had been no pronouncements of clean bills of health—he had the same weak heart that his father had died from. In secret, my father had been living with an artery partially blocked, choosing to pretend that he was untouched by pain. This was what we excelled at, telling our extended family, our friends and our acquaintances, how fine we were in the face of terror. But Joy had never been that way. She had always looked us in the eye and demanded the truth. She had made rigorous note of every time he had sat down too quickly and the long morning walks that had progressively shortened over the last few years, even though he had repeatedly assured her that nothing was out of the ordinary. My father had always exercised complete control over his own life; that was the patriarchal way. And in accordance with that tradition, we had never pried, asked after receipts, medical records, or finances, or commented on what he chose to eat and drink. As I watched Joy stare out of the waiting room window, I realized that we were going to have to assume a change of guard in the roles we played. Joy was watching a family of ducks waddle across the tiny pond in the gazebo garden that the hospital had constructed in view of the wing with its wealthiest patients, who were able to stay longer than the average insurance would allow. She sensed me behind her.

"I knew it," she said intently, to the ducks, without turning around.

This, too, was Joy, who would inform us that she had told us so, had warned us of outcomes that my father and I, too romantic for reality or frightened by it, were ill-prepared for. I felt a seizure of anger at her tone.

"If you knew it, why didn't you tell him to . . . " I began to say, inflamed, but Joy had turned to me, and there was a vast suffering on her face, in the curved hunch of her shoulders, her sorrow physical.

I felt something long forgotten stir inside of me, so buried in the depths of my being that it was hard to believe that it was real—this tiny, piercing spear of love for a sister. Yet, it fluttered, possessed by my father's heart, and beat its angry little wings inside my stomach, a buzzing creature of insistence. Joy leaned, childlike, into my arms as her body, taller and imposing, folded into mine, her face damp on my neck, yet still not weeping.

"I'm sorry, Didi," she whispered but I did not know whether it was an apology for her imagined lack of vigilance over my father or for our older, deadlier war.

I held her tighter, breathing in her smell, so long gone yet familiar. As Joy calmed, my phone began to vibrate. We let it ring through, unwilling to separate from this fragile new state, an extension of the moment at the lake. When it buzzed again, through the pocket of my skirt, Joy shifted against me.

"It's probably Ma," I said, reluctant. "She called a few minutes ago, too. Maybe someone told her about Baba, and she's going bonkers at the thought."

Joy lifted her head from my shoulder. "Take it," she said. "I told the cousins on the text group so one of the aunties must have told her."

"Nothing like the aunty news corp to get information across the Atlantic," I said.

Joy smiled, a hint of eye makeup streaking along her face. I pulled my phone out and saw that it was Marlon.

Joy stared at my cell phone's screen. "Isn't that—who is that?"

Automatically, I slipped the phone back into my pocket, shielding it from her. "I'll call back in a bit," I said.

A flash of hurt shone in Joy's eyes.

"He's a friend," I said, releasing my shoulders, willing myself to relax again in her presence.

"Isn't Marlon the guy running Lee's bar?"

Joy's questions were more plea for sisterhood than curiosity, I knew. But the last few years had been too much for me to trust her ever again. Quickly, a palpable sadness took shape between us.

"Lee still owns the bar," I said, breaking the silence. "Marlon's his brother."

Joy nodded. "Yeah. He said."

Her voice sounded small and I felt a sorrow overwhelm me. "We're—dating," I said. "Or something like it."

"Wow," said Joy, amazed. "Something like dating is big."

I looked away. "It's new."

She nodded. "I'm really happy for you," she said, touching my hand.

I extracted my fingers, unwilling to navigate the subject of Marlon with Joy. "Listen. Baba's going to need us. He's going to need taking care of, no matter what he says." I paused. "We're going to have to do this together."

"I've been doing it for the last few years on my own," said Joy, belligerence sliding into her voice.

"I'm back now. I want to make sure he gets better."

"We both do," said Joy.

Our old standoffs were unchanged in tone or nature. I let my shoulders sag, my breath deflate. "Things have got to change," I said. "We can't keep fighting over him. It's no good to him, and it's a waste of our time. We can't change—what's happened. But I'm willing to work on doing what's best for him."

The old Joy returned for a brief moment, emotions passing through her features in the space of seconds, obstinance and offense morphing to misery, then hope.

"What's best for our family," she said, her voice smaller still.

"Yes." But the lake felt far away. In the coldness of the hospital, the desire to love Joy came and went like the ambulances.

"It's all I want, Didi," said Joy. "To be a family again."

She held my shoulders, embracing me. I could feel it in her breath, in the thrust of her beating heart, like a bird in a fist, erratic and wild. She wanted us to be sisters again, in service of our father, and all I could do was hope that it was possible.

"I need to make a call," I said, disengaging from her. "Will you text me if the doctor comes out?"

"Yes. Didi?"

"What?"

"Are you going to call Marlon?"

I shook my head, amused despite myself. I could feel her snicker as I walked away. Joy's bravado, her boldness and lack of boundary, were all intermingled in some odd combination that rattled me to my core as much as it made me long for her.

"HI." I WHISPERED into the phone, looking around to make sure I was out of Joy's earshot, even though I was in the gazebo downstairs, next to the pond. The ducks had returned to the water as nightfall descended. It was almost nine and the gazebo was dark and empty, a relief from the relentless ER.

"Why are you whispering, M? Are you okay?" Marlon sounded urgent.

I paused in confusion. "Yes, of course. I'm okay. Didn't I say I was coming up to Manhattan to see my father? I'm sorry I missed your calls."

"We were going to meet for dinner. You said Han Dynasty at seven thirty. God, I thought something had happened to you."

The worry in Marlon's voice sent a warmth through my unsettled limbs, the effect soothing, like an embrace I did want. "I'm so sorry," I said.

"It's okay," he said. "Did you forget?"

"No. My father—we went to the park. Swimming. And he—he had a heart attack. Or something like it." The words rushed out of me and I felt myself gripped by feelings I had barricaded around Joy. "He's okay," I said. "The nurse said he might be able to go home in a day or so. They need to monitor him. I'm such a wreck though. The idea of just losing him in an instant. And my sister, who I haven't talked to in years—she's here, too, and the whole thing is too much. It's too much."

It struck me that it was Marlon I was talking at and not Lena, that he did not have any of the context. And yet, in his quiet way, he seemed to recognize and comprehend the violence of families without being told.

"I'm so sorry, M," he said. "What do you need?"

I had not thought about what I might need. Unlike Joy, who always knew what she needed and went after it, I only knew the impermanent relief of flight from hurt. "Thank you for asking. I'm not sure. I think maybe a doughnut."

"Where are you?"

"In the gazebo. Which is a fancy name for a patch of lawn with a little structure in the middle of it. At Mount Sinai. On Madison at East Hundred and First Street." I sounded hysterical to my own ears.

"It says I can be there in forty minutes, plus fifteen for doughnuts," said Marlon, after a beat.

I swallowed. Marlon was a salve I wanted but the idea of involving him in Joy, in my father, in the depths of my troubled family, felt like a freewheel. "What if I come by for those doughnuts as soon as I can?" I asked.

I heard the silence in which he registered my saying no.

"Sure," he said, easily, swiftly.

I leaned my head against the cool pane of the gazebo window. Two floors above, in the ER, Joy was outlined in the window, staring outside again, the protective cover of night eluding me from her vision. I felt an odd satisfaction at being able to study her without her knowledge. A duck splashed into the pond's water, startling me as I turned around.

"You still there?" asked Marlon.

"Yeah. I just don't know when I'll be able to get back to Brooklyn."

"Whenever you do, those doughnuts will be waiting."

"You're going to have to show me a flaw or two, or I'm going to think you're some sort of psychopath," I said.

"Wow. Just can't be a basic-ass nice guy these days."

I laughed, studying the duck dipping in and out of the water, moonlight glinting off its oily feathers.

"One way to get to know someone's warts is to spend a lot of time with them, y'know. No place to hide, etcetera etcetera," said Marlon, his voice low.

My body recognized his tone from when he was naked, beneath me, holding my hips. I took in a breath, my desire alive even in a place where I did not know what might happen to my father.

"You do know how to take a girl's mind off her worries," I said.

"Well, good. Call me anytime—I'm here."

I hung up the phone, made lighter by his effervescence, whether or not he was a fleeting rebound or some sort of unanticipated missile. I looked up at the night sky, the moon at half mast, an airplane sauntering past the navy skyline. When I looked back at the window above me, where Joy had stood only moments ago bathed in the acrid light, there stood Jack. Jack, as I remembered him, of the beloved, curious face, a patient softness between his furrowed brows, his ordinary freckled features cascading into an extraordinary, gentle manner that had warmed almost everyone we met, his jacket the same faded khaki color that I remembered. Jack, whose arms comforted my sister as she leaned into his shoulder, in the same way she had leaned into mine only moments ago, their flawless union steadfast and dizzying to any stranger that might chance upon them in that flickering, fluorescent room. Jack, in whose arms Joy shed her first tears of the day, her release so acute that I had to look away. Jack, as he held my sister, who had married the only man I had ever loved—so much that losing him had made me afraid of losing myself at every juncture.

PART FOUR

CHAPTER FIFTEEN

MONTHS BEFORE I had left for London, I had wondered if Jack had fallen out of love with me. But the notion that he might be having an affair had never occurred to me. It was not blindness, so much as the unthinkability of what had happened in plain sight. Before our romance, Jack and I had built a friendship so steady that I worried that, instead of ongoing passion, we might have slipped back into the latter's easy rhythms and placid motions of pizza nights and falling asleep on the couch, initially a new kind of intimacy, but dangerous territory for a young couple to tread for too long. I read wellness journals and purchased a set of handcuffs and wore lingerie to bed instead of oversized T-shirts, but in the end, it had not been the suffocating or mundane domesticities of a long-haul love. Red-faced and wretched with the exertion, he had confessed that he was in love with someone else. That a storm had descended into his life months ago, and so powerful was the feeling that he turned whole in her presence, that his life had never found its real roots until he had felt love for her, a love that he was afraid of because it was like looking at the sun. I had laughed despite the feeling that I might be swallowed whole, so florid was his delivery. But Jack had been serious, as if he were telling me that he was terminally ill, that despite anything I did or said, there was no turning back. As I sat on our bed confronted by his demons, I wondered if I would survive it, but surely people had suffered worse.

"I want you to be happy," I had said, afraid that I might die, wondering if I should scream. "But if you left me, I don't think I could be happy again."

I had stated the fact as if we were talking about the best route to take to the theater during rush hour and if he might reconsider his path in light of this new information. He had said he could not. Not because he did not want to (leaving me was the last thing he had imagined wanting, he had said), but because he could not conceive of a life without her. I had nodded, as if agreeing to take the A train instead of a cab, wondering if I should throw a cleaver at his head, paralyzed by something godforsaken in the DNA of my ancestors, polite until the end.

"Does she know I exist?" I had asked in a voice so shrunken that it was foreign to my ears, emanating from a new, spurned body. Did she know that I was a human person who shared a life and two bedrooms and a yard with him, whose possessions were in drawers with his, whose laundry was, at that very minute, intermingled with his, intimates upon intimates, his spoon left in my yogurt in the sink, our toothbrushes interchangeable, the swell of grief inside of me noiseless as it corroded my insides.

Jack had looked up at me, impoverished.

"It's Joy," he had said, almost inaudibly.

I had been uncomprehending. What had Joy done? Had she found out before me and assailed him? I did not understand.

"I'm so sorry," he had said. "The day I met Joy, when we began to talk, something insane took hold of me. I didn't understand it at first. I didn't want to, God in heaven. But I love her, MG. It just happened to us. I don't think I could live without her."

He had begged me, as if somehow I was the person in charge of what he did.

"God knows she wants to try to live without me," Jack had said. "Neither of us can imagine doing this."

To you. He had not said the words out loud but it was me that the doing was being done to. The Victim, formerly known as MG, the burning bridge between true lovers.

Clues that had been carelessly littered around me now fell into place, my horror a silent scream. I left Jack and Joy's lives silently, without reproach to either of them, ice entering my veins, a freezing over of my soul as I left the apartment with nothing but my wallet, passport, and laptop. At Lena's, I packed a few borrowed clothes into a duffel bag and left for London. Joy wrote me emails that I printed out and deposited, unread, into the fireplace of the *Janus* office in Greencoat Row. To watch them physically consumed by the flames felt like the only relief I had access to. That Joy had eventually relented as I knew she would, giving in to the first great love affair of her life—marrying him the following year in a tiny ceremony that had used the pandemic's aftermath to exclude any extended family's confusion over who was marrying the groom (not the bride they had thought!)—felt like an order of events that were the sequence of an enormous practical joke. Afterward, everywhere that I went, despite the fact that I was an ocean away, it felt like she might leap out of bush or curtain or street corner, to shout, surprise Didi, it was obviously a prank, my goodness.

AS I CLIMBED the stairs to where they sat in the ER, waiting for me, I realized it was the first time that the three of us had occupied the same space since it had happened (to me). At the entrance, I watched them, their heads bent toward each other, a viscous, invisible togetherness between them, so real that it felt as if I might gag on it. Jack, ashen, his eyes tired, let go of Joy's hand, rising to his feet as I entered the waiting room.

"Mira," he said, MG having died so long ago. "It's so good to—I'm so glad that you're okay."

He was referring to the televised accident of light-years ago, I realized dimly.

"Thank you," I said.

It felt implausible that he might wear clothes that I recognized, bear the same tiny scar above his eyebrow that an incident with a German shepherd at Millie's dog park had given him, or stand in front of me as my sister's husband.

"Did the doctor come out?" I asked, rubbing my temple to get at the mild reverberation that had developed behind it. Suddenly I felt parched, a burning in my throat, every inch of my skin wrinkled and aging.

Joy nodded, something aflame in her eyes. "They want to keep him tonight and tomorrow at least, but maybe longer. He's sleeping now but we can see him in the morning."

I looked in the direction of the circuitous hospital hallways.

"Do you want to see him now? I—could come with you," said Joy.

I felt a sharp pop of hysteria bubble up inside of me, the image of Jack, Joy, and I leaning over my father as he came to, like a scene from an absurdist play, in which my father might question if he had died and gone to hell. I shook my head, unwilling to make eye contact with her. "I'm going to go home."

"We can give you a ride," said Jack.

I watched them exchange a look as an older couple in the waiting room examined us with curiosity. Joy and I were obviously related, they must have thought. Sisters, you could tell. The man with us, nice-looking, sweet-faced, the taller sister's boyfriend, their energy unmistakably that of a couple. Oh, wedding rings. Husband and wife. Jack and Joy did not need rings, so thoroughly had they become versed in the language of each other, little gestures everywhere, his palm hovering over the small of her back as it had mine whenever he had felt the need to offer protection. I turned from them, a stinging at the back of my eyelids.

"I'll take a cab," I said over my shoulder as I picked up my canvas tote, still damp from the lake, and left the ER, running down the stairs as soon as I knew I was out of their field of vision. They had consumed too much of me already—I would not allow my grief to be theirs, too.

DOWNSTAIRS, THE YEARS came flooding back. Where did they live? Was it a beautiful home? They were both neat where I had been messy. Did Joy choose the furniture, as was her way in our family? Did Jack have his beloved grandfather's fedora hanging on their wall, as it had in our apartment? Had they had sex before Jack had told me? Did they order in or cook? Images of them making my father's recipes together, of them sleeping in the bed that Jack and I had once shared, assailed me.

"Mira."

I heard his voice behind me, but I did not turn to look.

"Mira," he said again, now nearer.

I stepped backward, in desperation to feel further away from him, my ankle slipping on the edge of the curb as Jack caught my wrist. I straightened, recovering my balance as he let me go.

"My Uber is six minutes away," I said, gripping my phone as evidence.

Jack looked back at the hospital where my sister presumably still remained.

"Joy's in the bathroom," he said, though I had not asked. "I just wanted to say that I hope..."—Jack faltered—"someday, we can just—"

"Be a family?" I heard a bark of laughter escape me, the sound unfamiliar.

Jack looked at his hands, clasped together, his phone between his palms. "I feel like I killed someone."

A young, sprightly valet, dressed in the maroon and blue shirt that the hospital staff wore, pulled up in a black Jeep.

"You still have the Jeep," I said.

Jack blinked, looking at the car his parents had given him after law school, as if it were not his. "Yeah."

The valet held the driver's-side door open for Jack. Jack walked over and handed the eager boy a bill he had had all along in his palm, ever the master of a sleight of hand. We would joke that Jack might have been a magician, but being a lawyer was sort of the same, he said.

"I don't know that you can ever forgive me, MG. But"—Jack's voice broke—"if I've destroyed the relationship between you two forever, I don't know how to live with that."

He had called me MG. I stood there on the street, the Jeep between our bodies.

"I'm not here to help you," I said. "I should never have had to see you again."

Jack looked away, at the Saturday night stream of traffic into the hospital. "I deserve everything you've got for me," he said, headlights illuminating the soft outline of his forehead and mouth. I wondered what might happen if one of the cars drunkenly swayed in our direction. If Jack and I were erased from her life, what would Joy have left? I thought of my father, slight in his hospital bed, connected to tubes as he slept. My cab pulled up behind Jack's Jeep.

"Maybe someday I'll forgive you," I said as he turned to me again, shadows from cars dancing across his face. "You loved one woman and then you met another and you stopped loving the first one and wanted the new one. It's a story we've all heard before. You fell in love with someone else." I shrugged. "I get it. It happens. It's been five years. Maybe someday, it'll be okay and we'll say happy birthday to each other once a year."

Jack shook his head imperceptibly, as if to make sure he had heard me correctly.

"But she took something I loved more than anything else," I said. "Joy did what she does—she saw something I had that she wanted, and she took it. She had to compete. She had to have it." I felt hatred for Joy actualize inside of me, almost a relief to experience it so clearly. Jack must have seen some part of it because he winced.

"I'll never forgive her," I said.

As I slipped into the backseat of the car, I saw Jack lift a hand in a wave in the distance, to signal to an emerging Joy that he was where he had said he would be, waiting for her.

BACK HOME, I was sleepless. Of my own volition, I had reentered the war-torn minefield of bitter fury. I went online, trying to excavate every detail of their lives, examine every post and thread for signs that their union was anything but the exclusive refuge I had witnessed. The internet was an abyss that I had skirted for years. As I went headfirst into it, I felt a madness descend into me, scouring vacations and dinner parties and comments for ragged scraps of information that I might piece together, like a junk dealer in search of something whole. They had refrained from posting too much—potentially out of pity for me, the thought enraging my overheated mind further. But they were tagged in dozens of photos from a community that loved them, including friends that had once been both Jack's and mine, my cousins, strangers who did not know me and a few taken by Sam. I could not breathe, sucked into a feverish devouring of their marriage. When I was able to slam my laptop shut, I poured a shot glass of the bourbon that Ulrike had given me as a housewarming present, but no amount of alcohol could numb the brink that I was teetering on. I put on my running shoes and as I went out into the unexpected coolness of the night, I felt some relief.

MARLON OPENED THE door of his apartment with astonishment.

"M," he said with pleasure. "How's your dad? I've been texting you. Come in. Have you been running? At this hour?"

Each time I entered Marlon's home, I felt a synaptic comfort akin to the stew of the first time and the ease that Marlon embodied. But that night, I was chilled by the night air and the sweat dripping down my back.

"Sorry," I said. "I should have called before coming over."

"You kidding? I'm so glad to see you. Come here." Marlon pulled me close, and shut the door behind us.

"I'm sticky," I said, prising myself out of his arms.

Marlon let me go. I fidgeted under his gaze as he leaned against his kitchen counter.

"Are you my DoorDash delivering the dumplings I ordered?" Marlon smiled at me, gentle.

"You ordered dumplings at one a.m.?"

"Of course I eat at one a.m. I run a bar. You're welcome to some. They'll get here eventually."

"Okay." I looked at my running shoes, willing myself to say something that might explain why I had just pushed him away.

"Maybe a movie? Help us both fall asleep?" Marlon extended his hand.

"Okay," I said. If Marlon saw that I was wounded, he did not show it and I was grateful for that.

"Do you want a glass of wine?" Marlon disappeared into his kitchen.

"Do you have any bourbon?" I untied my shoes as Marlon chuckled from inside.

"Really? I've never seen you drink any whiskey."

"You barely know me," I said.

In the kitchen, Marlon was opening a bottle of bourbon. "You get a hall pass to be mad today," he said, affable. "Should I be flattered that you're taking it out on me?"

I watched as he poured the alcohol into glasses. "Sorry," I said.

Marlon nodded, handing me one of the glasses.

"What movie were you going to watch?" I asked as I drank too quickly, the liquid sliding down my throat in hot bubbles.

"*Sabrina*." Marlon watched me as he took a sip from his own glass.

"Which one?" I asked, momentarily surprised.

"The good one. From the fifties. It's a great rewatch."

"That is the good one. I can't believe you like it."

"Why not? Sabrina not man enough for you?" Marlon raised an eyebrow.

I exhaled, feeling the respite of his company. "You're an interesting guy."

"I am trying very hard to be interesting to you, it's true." Marlon smiled. "Is your father okay?"

"He will be. Can I have another drink?"

"Sure," said Marlon, easily. "Want a cube this time?"

"No thanks."

He nodded, pouring. In Marlon's presence, there was an uncomplicated way to occupy silences. He was comfortable in them and often made me comfortable. But tonight, I wanted anything but silence. Another moment spent inside of myself felt dangerous.

"I ran into my ex today," I said, taking the drink from him.

Marlon frowned, nonplussed. "You ran into your ex? When? Before your dad's thing? The guy you told me about?"

I nodded. "And his wife."

Marlon whistled. "You had a bad day."

There was a space between us that he might have moved to touch me in, but Marlon seemed uncertain.

"Did you know he was married?"

"Yes." I drank more bourbon. "My dad told me when I was in London."

"I'm sorry, M." Marlon sat on the barstool in front of his kitchen counter. "That had to be tough."

"People can so easily move on from one life to the next, replacing only the protagonist of their last life," I said. "It felt surreal." I held my glass out. "Sorry, can I have a little more?"

"Of course." Marlon took the glass from me and refilled it. "Can I ask you a question, M? It feels weird to ask while you're thinking about your dad, but we're on the subject."

I nodded.

"Are you still—are you over this dude?"

"He's married. There's no going back, ever. I told him I forgive him, even."

"Forgive him for what?"

"He cheated. On me."

"With the woman he married?"

"Yes."

Marlon nodded, slowly. "That's good of you. It was a long time ago, right?"

"Yes. I didn't want to hate him when I saw him. I wanted to feel—something, anything other than hate, actually. It feels like it's her that I can't get past, her act of just taking someone who was in a loving relationship." I let out a dry laugh. "I know I sound like a pastor, but it wasn't exactly the most feminist thing to do either."

"Did she know you were with him?"

"Yeah," I said, beginning to shift on the seat. "Can we just drop it? You're right. It's weird to be talking about it here."

Marlon crinkled his eyes, as if thinking through a math problem. "Look, it's none of my business. But the last thing I'll say is that it doesn't feel right to only hold her responsible. Giving him a clean chit doesn't feel very feminist either. But they've caused you a lot of hurt. And I'm sorry about that." Marlon touched my cheek. "I don't know why I said that. I guess I want you to be done with the guy. He sounds young. You're too good for him, M."

I felt the urge to agree, that in fact it was none of his business. "Did you just call me sexist?" My voice sounded higher, straining to be jokey.

"Absolutely not. But when we're hurt, we tend to...go blind a little." Marlon's fingers rested on my knuckles. "You know when I'm upset, I take a bath. Like a whole-ass bubbles-and-bath-salts kinda bath. Usually with a glass of something cold and great." Marlon stepped closer to me, mock whispering, as if in the voice of a cartoon spa attendant. "Imagine it now," he said. "You sink, slowly, into my nice, deep tub, lavender bubbles everywhere."

I drained my bourbon, set it down and put a hand on Marlon's chest, stopping his advance toward me. "What if you had sex with me instead?"

Marlon blinked, taken aback. He let out a half-amused exhale but something in my face made him serious. "Mira—"

I kissed him with force, the liquor on our breaths mingling with my urgency as I wrapped my legs around his waist. Marlon yielded, his body responding immediately as his arms went around me, both of us without abandon as he carried me to his bedroom. I felt the first real release that I had all day as I straddled him on his bed, stripping us both of our clothes.

"Let me get the light," I heard Marlon say, as he extended his arm toward his nightstand, but I restrained his wrist.

"No," I said. I pulled him on top of me. "Just get inside me. Please."

"Mira, love, let me, let's just, here, come here..." Marlon slipped an arm beneath me as he kissed my neck.

I pushed his face away, pulling his waist toward me. "Marlon, please. Just please do what I'm asking. Just fuck me." My eyes were closed and I felt a heat behind them. "Please."

For a moment, neither of us moved. I felt Marlon pull me toward him, in one quick motion, his strength gentle even as I felt him take charge. He rolled me on my left side and lay in front of me, facing me, but I could not open my eyes. As he slid into me, his breath grew more ragged as we bucked, a sudden animal exchange of need as my nails and teeth dug into his skin, no inch of space between us, the darkness a relief. I screamed as the wave took hold of me, his breath shuddering out of him as we both came.

We lay in the dark, breathing that our lungs might refill. I placed a palm on his chest again, both of us sweating, signaling my desire to be freed. Marlon lifted the arm that held me to him; I rolled away. I made my way to his bathroom, disoriented by the brightness in his hallway. As I shut the door of Marlon's bathroom, his navy bath mat plush beneath my feet, his deodorant and toothbrush sitting on his sink next to a tiny potted cactus and a pocket-sized, yellowing Wodehouse paperback, I felt myself begin to cry, my hands pressed to my mouth.

WHEN I RETURNED to the bedroom, showered, Marlon was sitting up in bed, in a T-shirt and boxers, wearing his glasses as he read a copy of *Rolling Stone.*

"Did I mention you're not allowed to read any magazine but *Janus*?" I said, my tone teasing.

Marlon looked up at me, serious. "Are you okay?"

"Yeah, of course." I sat on the edge of his bed, near his knee.

Marlon frowned. "You're fully dressed. I thought you wanted to eat and watch the movie. You could sleep here."

I smiled, apologetic. "I've got an early morning. We're going to go see my dad at the hospital."

Marlon hesitated, then nodded, still unsmiling.

"I—that was great," I said, touching his calf.

Marlon looked away, and then back at me, as if trying to articulate something unpleasant.

"What is it?" I asked. "Are we okay?"

"That was"—Marlon shook his head—"a little weird."

I raised my eyebrows, mock-affronted. "Because it got a little intense?"

Marlon held my gaze. "Because it felt like you weren't here."

I felt my cheeks beginning to warm, the alcohol making its way into an insistent strain behind my eyes. "I should go. I've had a long day. Whatever this is, I don't have the energy for it. I just came over for— "

"For what?" He looked genuinely curious, as if trying to finish a puzzle. "Did you come here to fuck me? Because if you did, that's okay. I want that." He raised his palm to his chest. "Believe me. I wanted that just now. Maybe I want something else, too. I don't know." He shrugged, shaking his head again. "You and I, we can take our time figuring this out. You know what I don't want? I don't want to feel like I'm not invited. Whatever was going on with you tonight, M, whatever that was, I didn't feel like I was any part of it. That, I don't want."

"I'm sorry," I said as I rose from the bed. "I'm really sorry. I have to go."

"Mira." I heard his voice behind me, but I was already running, my shoes on the carpet, then stairs, then asphalt, the click of the gate behind me as I made my way back into the darkness.

WHEN I REACHED my apartment, I felt a sorrow that threatened to submerge me. I composed a text in my head to Marlon. *I'm sorry. Let me call you tomorrow. I'll explain. Please know that I really like having you in my life.* But when I picked up my phone, it glowed up at me, harsh LED glow in the lamplight.

MG, please talk to me. We're family now. Let me make this right. Or at least livable. Please. And a second text after that, as if an afterthought, or the buried lede. *I miss you.*

CHAPTER SIXTEEN

IN THE MORNING, I had a headache that felt as if it might fracture my skull. My mouth was dry, my heart palpitating, as if I had been frightened in my sleep. I reached into the back of my closet and located a green shift I had bought years ago on holiday in Spain. In the bathroom mirror, I worried about the back, craning my neck to examine its plunge. Adding gold earrings that Joy's mother had left me, and lipstick, I took a photo and sent it to Lena.

"Too much?"

Lena wrote back immediately. "No cure like gilding the lily. And it can't hurt if you look like that when you apologize. Take doughnuts or something."

"Don't know how you have time for me and your real babies."

"I've known you longer than I've known them. Listen, be good to yourself today, ok? Maybe come over later?"

"Can't. Going to the hospital after work."

"Ok." The three dots bubbled as I waited for Lena to say what she really wanted to.

"I'm worried about you."

I looked at my reflection, even as my stomach heaved. "I've always figured it out. Love you."

AT LEE'S, I felt even less certain of my ability to figure anything out. Marlon was nowhere to be seen. Deedee had served me a glass of water while I waited for him, a box of doughnuts on the barstool next to mine. Deedee raised her eyebrows in amusement as I winced from the smell of bacon.

"What about some eggs or something?" she asked. "Always does the trick for me."

I shook my head, visibly pained. Deedee's electric pink T-shirt felt like it was hurting my eyes, making its way into the throbbing in my head.

"Just water, thanks Deedee."

"Okay," she said, twirling her blonde braids, simultaneously a girl and in her fifties. "You look so pretty though. That slinky lil number in that color." Deedee made a smacking sound with her lips. "Really does it for you. No one will know you're a wreck inside."

"Who's a wreck inside?" Marlon stood behind Deedee, putting his apron on.

"Oh, Mira's just havin' a day after a rager," said Deedee. "Can't look coffee in the face. But look how cute she looks."

Deedee flitted to the other end of the bar while Marlon rang up a teenager's coffee. I had not seen him come into the bar but when Marlon was not happy, there was a formidable silence to his presence. I had only seen it once before, with a very rude customer who, drunk, had been persistently urging the woman next to him into conversation that she had clearly not wanted to engage in. When the man had laid a palm on the woman's lower back, Marlon had walked over to their side of the bar. He had said very few words to the man, but his presence, as he leaned against the counter and made eye contact with the man, had unsettled me. The man had left quickly. The grateful woman had thanked Marlon and asked what he had said to the man. Marlon, shrugging, had said that you just had to make it clear when someone was not wanted. I had the feeling that day that somewhere in his being, there was something dangerous about Marlon. But I knew in my body that I did not need to be afraid of it, and so there was an electricity to the experience, as if he had given me permission to learn something illicit and private. Later, Marlon had told me about the men in his neighborhood that had made his mother feel unsafe for his entire childhood.

As he finished ringing up the coffee, Marlon turned to me, grim.

"What can I do for you, Mira? It doesn't look like you're here to eat breakfast or purchase a beverage."

"Does Deedee know we're dating?" I tried to smile at him.

Marlon narrowed his eyes in disbelief. "She would know more than I do, if that's the case."

I swallowed, stung by his coldness, nausea riding up my throat. "I'll never drink again?" I said, with a little laugh, pitiful to my own ears.

"If this is about last night, I don't think the issue was alcohol."

I pushed the doughnuts toward him. "Earl Grey and chocolate ganache. I stood in line even though it made me want to throw up."

Marlon lowered his voice, decisive. "Mira, I can't do this. I'm not some lovesick teenager. I like you. But I won't let myself be yanked around. I've got too much to do."

He turned around and began to stack newly printed evening menus next to a pyramid of cocktail coupes.

"If you're hungover, you've got to sleep it off before you drink again," he said, without looking at me. "Those are just the rules. A little more alcohol is going to make you feel better in the short term. In the long term, you're going to feel like shit." He finished the stack and turned to look at me. "Same rules apply to life. And I don't want to be made to feel like shit just because you do."

I shook my head to allow the aching to make way for clarity. "Some life stuff, you can't get over. It's not time or the person—I promise it isn't him. It's how it happened and how impossible closure seems to feel. Twenty years later, I'm probably going to feel the same horrific shrinking at the memory of what happened to me. But because I will run into them, again and again, it will get easier every time. I will have developed the muscle of 'fuck it.' I told my ex last night that I could see a future where we were polite to each other. That future is within reach for me. But I just got back to this city. And I saw his marriage up close for the first time yesterday. Should I have expected it? Yes. Can you still be blindsided by pain? Tell me you haven't been blindsided by being human. Give me a little leeway here."

Over newspapers and breakfast sandwiches, a handful of diners at the bar strained to hear me. Deedee studiously looked away. So what, I thought. I was surprised at how important it felt to win back Marlon's affection.

"I didn't think you cared how I felt," he said, slowly. "I didn't mean to upset you."

He put a hesitant hand on my shoulder. I realized I must have looked near tears.

"I haven't felt this—this feeling, for a long time," I said. I reached out to touch his hand. "I'm sorry about last night. The idea of losing my dad. And then seeing them together. It just—it made me feel like I wasn't a real person. Like I was this tiny shell of myself. I was desperate for something that could make me feel better, and the answer was you. The answer these days seems to, pretty often, be you. But I shouldn't have just showed up like that—it wasn't fair to you."

"I like making you feel better, Mira."

The bar was getting busier and I was grateful for the clamor that drowned us out. Marlon took my left hand in both of his but he was frowning.

"When we started, you were clear with me that you didn't owe me anything," he said. "You don't have to feel any guilt. But I might be in a little trouble here, if it's just sex. I want to see what else there could be between us. It doesn't have to be right away, but if we're going to keep going, I need to tell you that things have changed for me."

I nodded. "I don't know where we're headed. But it felt

incredibly important to to ask you to forgive me and keep doing... what we're doing."

"And what are we doing?" Marlon leaned closer, his breath a combination of toothpaste and coffee, an intensity in his frank eyes.

"This," I said. "If you want to. When I think about you, it makes me feel like it's—nice weather or something and things feel easier and maybe there's fruit to be eaten from the trees. God, I can't believe how stupid that sounds out loud."

I leaned over and kissed Marlon. When I drew back, he smiled.

"I never know what to expect from you, Mira."

"I expect better from myself when I'm with you," I said, surprised that it was true.

The line at the counter was snaking out of the door and Deedee was looking increasingly desperate.

"I should let you get back to work," I said. "But maybe you'll see me tomorrow night?"

Marlon nodded, still wearing his surprise. "Can I ask you a question?"

I nodded, fearful.

"This guy—his wife. They're here, right? In New York? They were your friends? Is that why you think you'll keep running into them?"

"It would take a lot to not run into them, yes. When I first returned, I thought I could live a life where I wouldn't ever see them. I was kidding myself."

Puzzled, Marlon regarded me, even then with kindness.

"I must seem like the least desirable prospect in Brooklyn at the moment. But would it be crazy to just ask you for some time? Just a little time for me to get used to this new world, where I'm making my peace with things. Where, someday, I can tell you what happened, and it wouldn't feel like the worst thing in the world to revisit?"

Marlon paused, looking in the distance, over my shoulder. It occurred to me that Joy might have turned up again, but when I turned around, the doorway was empty.

"Take all the time you need," he said. "I'm here. You're a bit of a surprise in my life, and I'm not sure what to make of it, but I'm not willing to let it go either."

I felt a surge of emotion as I held his fingers to my face. "I've spent so much time, wasted time, wondering who to blame. All I want is my life back."

A soft warmth spread itself around me. Marlon grinned.

"You're hungover as heck, huh? You zipped straight through a half bottle of bourb last night."

I nodded, fragile as I moved, the interior of my stomach shifting with me. "I took something for my head. Now I just have to make sure I can get through the day at work without throwing up on Ulrike."

"Wait here. Do you have five minutes?"

Marlon, when alight, was impossible to resist. "I have five minutes," I said.

As he disappeared into the kitchen, I felt myself emerging from the fog. The simplicity of being around him was too tempting not to dissolve into. The early light of the day trickled through the slats of the windows onto my face, the soft strains of Debussy piping through the bar overhead. I closed my eyes. When I opened them, he was standing in front of me again.

"That color against your skin. Something luminescent about it. Like you're from the ocean."

He said the words softly and I laughed, but something in his voice made me refrain from deflecting with a joke. Marlon held up a to-go mug.

"My famous all-purpose cure," he said. "Hangovers, heartburn, heartbreak, you name it. Coconut water for electrolytes, avocado for potassium, berries, collagen, chia, greens, the works. And a spoonful of almond butter."

I took the container from him, gingerly. "Have you talked to big pharma about this miracle?"

Marlon laughed as I got off the barstool.

"See you tomorrow?" I asked, wanting to make sure he did.

"Yeah. Hey, M?"

"Yeah?"

"I think you'll be okay. I have a good feeling about it."

I looked at the mug in my hands, steadying myself. I looked back up at him and nodded. "I think so, too."

IT WAS ALMOST ten by the time I reached work. The office was in its usual pre-deadline upheaval, exaggerated this time by the anniversary issue. As I closed the door of my office, my phone vibrated with a text from Marlon.

—Earl Grey was my favorite but they're all superb. All gone. After you left, the bar lost its charm so we decided to close it down for good.

I laughed, looking at my phone.

—Wait till you tell Lee that. Smoothie was vile but it worked a miracle. I'm cured x

"What's so funny?" Gigi loomed over me.

I hadn't heard her come in and, startled, dropped the phone on the floor. Gigi looked amused as I bent to pick it up.

"What're you up to, Mira G.?" she said. "You look positively... suspect."

"Nothing beyond nursing the crushing guilt of being a privileged first-world citizen in this era," I said, standing up.

"You can't fool me, girlfriend. Look at this outfit." Gigi snapped her fingers. "An emerald queen."

"Oh, thank you. I'll put that on my business card. 'Emerald queen. Will edit you. Beware.'"

Gigi crossed her arms over her chest and leaned her head forward, conspiratorial. "Are we... dating?"

"Just a little." I held up a thumb and a forefinger in a pinch.

"I knew it. No one looks like that without an agenda."

I leaned forward in my chair and cupped my hand to my ear. "Can you hear it? The sound of feminism dying?"

"Oh pshaw." Gigi waved a hand in my face. "There's a difference in the way someone looks when they're trying to make an impression. When they're texting the person they're making impressions on." She squeezed my shoulder. "I want to hear all about"—she held up her fingers, mimicking mine—"the 'little dating.'"

"Maybe Friday after work at Franny's?" I said, reveling in her delight. For too long, they had been on tiptoe around me.

"God, I cannot wait for a gossipy Friday Franny."

I stood up. "Well, I look forward to regaling you with disappointingly tame information. I better get to it now before Ulrike asks where the hell the edits on the issue are."

"Oh lord," Gigi clapped her hand to her heart. "The reason I've been looking for you since the crack of dawn. That manuscript. *The Wild Lings*." She placed both her hands on my desk in emphasis. "I love it."

Gigi's hyperbole was infamous but her taste was nimble and instinctive. I could see she meant it.

"Bin loves it, too," said Gigi. "It's been a while since I've read anything that captured me like that. And her writing is so fun but meaty, with this potent lens on race. Where did you find this woman?"

"I—it's anonymous. It was in my mail. Might even have been sent to me as a mistake." I felt my heart ricochet in my chest. "I mean, it's a bit frothy, isn't it? Does it really make sense for us to consider an excerpt?"

"But that's the beauty of it," said Gigi, emphatic. "It feels incredibly literary but almost incognito, like Cheever or the Brontës."

"That's high praise from you," I said, quiet to my own ears.

Gigi's eyes narrowed again, but this time with scrutiny. "It isn't you, is it? I won't tell Ulrike, I swear. But you've got to tell me. I could see you sneaking off to write some fiction. I mean, Mira, this is *good*. Good like we don't get too often."

I nodded. "I wish it were me. But really, I have no idea. There was an email address on the cover page."

Gigi sighed. "I wish it were you, too. Or me. Fine, I'll email her. I wonder if it's someone awful and canceled and they can't write under their real name, so this is the only way out. With my luck, that would be it."

"Something about it feels like it came from a pure heart," I said.

Gigi stopped to stare at me. She cackled and shook her head. "God. To be as bananas as the poetry people. Okay, I'll go off and email your pure heart. Maybe you can drop her a line too, in case you're the favorite. 'Anon, anon, good heart. Anon, reveal thy mysterious self.'"

"Ha-ha-ha," I said, after a laughing Gigi.

But inside I felt as if a forgotten anchor had crept up, sinking me just as I had come up for air. I was wrong, I had to be—how could Jack have written a novel during these years? He had talked about it when we were together, a void in his heart shaped by regret, the kind that any one of us might carry. It had sounded like a once-possible dream that had left a little longing in its rearview and nothing more. I had asked him what he might write about, and he had looked at the sky and laughed.

"Love, I guess. What else does anyone ultimately write about? Isn't that the only interesting thing?"

BUT THE BOOK itself was more than a stormy, elliptical love story, littered with Jack's preoccupations. It was an incisive examination of the politics of skin color and assimilation, class and wealth disparities, simultaneously lyrical and sharp. It told a story that was both new and as old as time. As I read passages a third, fourth, fifth time, it felt like Jack was speaking the words to me, in his idiosyncratic way, both deeply personal and specifically informed. I tried to dig through my memory, to see if there might be anything I had missed, anything of significance that might be a sign or symbol pointing in the direction he wanted me to go. I wanted to find any reason to be wrong—why would he have written a book in between marital bliss and a frenetic legal career. Yet something inside me recognized him clearly, between the lines and commas and the quiet flourishes of his prose.

Dear Finley Maria,

Thank you for your manuscript. It made me sit up straighter, laugh out loud, and at the end of it, I was moved. Very rarely does a novel do all of that, in such a singular way. My colleagues are convinced you are a woman and I cannot be sure of your pronouns, because your writing is so fluid, and your observation, as it switches character, so lucid and honest. I cried and felt hope for all of them. In Ginger's neuroses, I see parts of myself, but also contemporary children of immigrant families like the Lings everywhere.

The fiction department would like to, upon communication with you, add in an excerpt from The Wild Lings in our twenty-fifth anniversary issue; we pay a decent fee, which they'll also talk to you about. It is a very last-minute addition, but I can see how they felt that they must. I hope you are prepared for success, because it feels like you might have some. In great success, like in great failure, anonymity becomes harder because the world is curious about both. But there are those who know how to possess it. My advice, unsolicited, would be to sign with an agent so that you turn over the nuts and bolts of this—and future—deals to them. I can suggest a few names if need be. If nothing else, I am such an admirer of your work.

My best wishes,
Mira Guhathakurta

AT A QUARTER to four, as I was hurrying to turn over the first-pass pages of the issue to Ulrike, Joy arrived below the office. *Here!* said her text, brimming with optimism, fifteen minutes earlier than planned, as I had known she would be. I did not want her to come upstairs, and she did not ask to.

Need 5 more minutes, I texted back.

What Joy imagined my colleagues thought of her was likely much more monstrous than their liberal curiosities and empath tendencies might harbor. But I was willing to let her live with that, I thought, as I finished proofing the pages.

She was parked on the opposite side of the street, under a TOW AWAY ZONE sign. Spotting me, she waved as if we might have been long lost sisters.

"Hi," she said, her eyes wide with happiness as I crossed the street to the Lincoln Continental sedan she had purchased the summer she had returned from London.

Jack and I had gone with her to the dealer and helped pick it out, a gleaming olive beast of a machine, designed to fit a family of spies. We had laughed at her for wanting it, but Joy had insisted it was who she was, christening it Jitterbug, and driving it proudly through the clogged streets of New York, where owning a car was an anomaly by itself. Jitterbug had always been meant to hold Joy's family. The thought pierced through me as I slid in.

"You're not supposed to stop here," I snapped. "There's a sign."

"I know, Didi. But that sweet man," Joy pointed at a young construction worker in a hard hat, eating a sandwich a few feet away, "said I could, just till I picked you up, and no one would know."

As Joy rolled Jitterbug into traffic, the man beamed at us, still under Joy's spell.

"You look pretty," she babbled on. "I've never seen that dress before."

She turned the radio to 88.3; Coleman Hawkins trickled into the car. Despite my desire to remain on guard, I felt my shoulders relax as I leaned my head against the tinted window, the sky above turning lilac, promising a cool evening ahead.

"Majorca," I said.

"Oh, that's right. Didn't you almost wear that to Bunny's wedding but then you thought that the aunties would think it was too slutty?"

She tittered as she swept through the streets. Joy had never cared what aunties or anyone else thought of her. In Majorca, she had told me to wear the dress, but instead I had chosen a sari, like the rest of the good Indian girls.

"How's Lee's brother? Is it going well?" Joy's voice was warm with delight, like Gigi's had been in the morning. "What's his name again? Brandon?"

"Marlon."

"That's right. Marlon Brando. He's so handsome."

I heard the anticipation in Joy's voice.

"Dr. Ho said they may have to keep Baba another night," I said. "If they do, I can head to the hospital directly tomorrow morning. We will have wrapped up next month's issue, so I'll have time to take the train."

"It's no problem to pick you up. It's on the way. My client is in Bed Stuy."

Joy's voice had diminished and I felt something slice through me. This was to be my punishment. The desire to do her harm coupled with the fact that I could not bear her unhappiness—it had always been my undoing. We listened to Hawkins's cascading melodies in silence as she drove. As we sped past the bridge and neared the hospital, Joy looked at her watch. "We're early—visiting hours start at five."

"You were early," I said.

"Are you hungry? Maybe we can find a café somewhere? Get a snack and a coffee?"

My breath caught; the idea of ordinary activities with Joy, terrifying.

"Can't you just get something at the cafeteria?"

"God, you're such a museum piece sometimes," said Joy angrily.

Involuntarily, I laughed. Surprised, Joy turned toward me.

"Look at the road," I said, but we were both laughing as she swerved to avoid a parked truck.

AT THE HOSPITAL, we were told the cafeteria had had a plumbing leak and was closed for the day. Joy, petulant, shook her head in disbelief at the stoic nurse who imparted the news to us.

"What are visitors supposed to do?" she asked, in a temper. "What if someone was having a medical emergency, like low blood sugar?"

"Do you have low blood sugar?" asked the nurse tiredly.

"No, but that's a pretty important hypothetical situation that you guys should take into account, don't you think?" Joy's pale cheeks inflamed with righteous indignation. "I'm going to the bathroom," she said. "I'll meet you outside Baba's room."

"I'm sorry," I said to the nurse. "My sister gets insane when she's hungry. Always has, since she was a kid."

The nurse shrugged. "Not the worst news I've had to hand out today. There's vending machines and coffee stations on every floor."

MY FATHER HAD been moved to a private room and the difference from the ER was remarkable. My mother, overwrought, had been outraged when she learned that the hospital's private suites were fully booked. Calling on every influential (wealthy) academic connection, she had managed to have my father moved into a room with a couch in the corner, a heated duvet on his bed, and a view of the park where he had almost died.

"This is so nice," Joy said as she sat next to me in one of the white waiting-area chairs, each of which had a cream striped cushion on it, as if we might be at a coastal restaurant, waiting for a table to eat crab claws.

"Ma pulled trustee strings."

"That's nice of her," said Joy. "Tell her I say thank you."

To Joy, my mother was a mysterious, generous aunt-esque figure in England who had sent us both presents since Joy had been a girl, to which she had written dutiful thank-you notes in return. To me, Ma was an absentee mother not to be taken too seriously but enjoyed like a distant relative who occasionally wanted to know the personal details of my life, as if catching up with the newest research in her field of interest. We had talked on the phone a few times during the time that I had spent in England, in hiding from Joy and Jack, but she had known that I wanted to lick my wounds in private and that she would be unable to offer me any real comfort. She remained the best of friends with our father however, their phone exchanges meaningful, each always caught up on the other's passing years. For Joy and me, it had felt like an undeserved competitor for our father's affections. But ever since Jack had married Joy, my mother had ceased all communication with her. I heard the hurt in Joy's voice, but I took some satisfaction in the fact that my mother had had at least enough maternity to take my side. I picked up one of the two coffees I had obtained from the small kitchen on the floor and handed it to Joy.

"Where did you get that?" she asked happily, taking gulps from the cup immediately. "Thank goodness. I've been up since five a.m. Goddamn class action."

She looked at the chocolate bar in my hands.

"Is that for me?" she asked, greed in her eyes.

I unwrapped the bar and handed her half.

"Why didn't you just get two?" said Joy, annoyed.

I shrugged. "To piss you off."

After a beat, Joy chuckled, chewing on chocolate, inhaling it whole as was her way. The the door to my father's room opened and the lanky doctor emerged.

"He's good as new, ladies," said Doctor Ho. "Ready to run a marathon."

My father was sitting upright in a hospital gown, his thinning hair wild from sleep, a vibrant cheer to his face.

CHAPTER SEVENTEEN

BUT MY FATHER was not as good as new. The ride back to the Upper West Side left him depleted, short of breath, and he needed help to climb the few steps up the front porch of his building. As I helped him into his bed, he squeezed my hand, but the touch felt unfamiliar, lacking the strength that he had radiated my entire life.

"I'm glad you're here, Mira," he said.

I smoothed down his stubborn curls. "You sure timed it perfectly."

"If you had lived in London any longer, I would have pretended to have a heart attack in any case, so the universe has simply spared me the trouble."

"You need a haircut, Baba," said Joy, walking in with a tray of pills and fruit juice.

"I'm told Julie is in Warsaw till August. I can't drink pills with juice. Get me some water, please, Joybird."

"Who's Julie?" I asked.

"The only goddamn stylist he'll see in the city," said Joy, pouring water from a jug on the nightstand into a glass. "The juice is the mango-carrot from Citarella."

"My favorite," said my father, with pleasure.

"What happened to Jairam's salon?" I asked. In the years that I had gone missing, Joy seemed to have learned all of my father's patterns, armed with intimate knowledge of new favorites, new prescriptions.

"Jairam married a white lady and zoomed off"—my father made an ascending motion with his palm—"to the English countryside where without a doubt, he trims the balding heads of our colonizers."

He laughed and immediately leaned back on his pillow.

"I'm tired, girls," he said.

We sat on either side of him, our anguish mirrored in each other as we watched him try to swallow the pills.

"It's the damn tube they shoved down my throat," said my father and sighed.

Joy moved the tray to the nightstand and held his hand. "You should sleep, Baba."

My father looked at me. "My girls, together again."

I looked away. "You'll be back on your feet in no time."

"Will you come to lunch on Sunday, Mira?"

My father was half asleep already, semi-lucid from his medication, but when I did not reply, he reopened his eyes.

"Please? I want to eat a meal as a family."

Something stiff and painful lodged in my throat. My father reached for my hand and repeated words he had said to me before.

"This is the family you have. This is the sister you have. We can't change these things. If you want a family, if you want a sister, this is the one you must make your peace with."

When I looked up, Joy was in tears. He had always specialized in asking enormous things of us. Yielding was natural. Yielding was duty. But yielding was also the specific brand of love he had earned from me. I nodded at my father, his stubborn fingers laced with mine.

"I'll come," I said.

AS HE SLEPT, I stood in the kitchen of my childhood home, drinking a glass of water from the tap, feeling the need to steady myself as I had in Marlon's bar in the morning. My life seemed to have become shaky, in need of constant grounding. Joy sat near me, at the breakfast nook, her knees up on the chair, huddled into herself.

"He's going to be okay, right, Didi?"

But it felt like she was talking to herself. I had always thought that I loved our father more than Joy did. She had had more luxuries and things paid for as we had grown older, an advantage of being the younger sibling, arriving when my father had had more success in the workplace and was more softened at home. Even so, she had been dismissive of his importance in her life, easily annoyed by his deeply Indian ways and his inability to demonstrate love in the way that Western fathers did. She was right in that our childhoods were not littered with affirmations, embraces, or patience. Yet to me, he had been steadfast and filled with humor, the bedrock that never shifted beneath me as my mother had. But as we were confronted with his old age, I felt the same dawning terror as Joy, that one day he might leave us to our own devices. I extracted a bar of chocolate from my purse and placed it on the table, in front of her.

"I did get two," I said.

Joy picked up the bar, turning it around with her fingers. For a moment, I thought she was going to cry.

"You always get the plain dark but the good one has hazelnuts and more milk," she said.

We looked at each other; something opaque and large reared inside of me, the distant memory of an enormous love between us. The doorbell rang.

"Philistine," I said, turning back to the sink to refill my glass.

I heard Joy's soft laugh behind me as she rose to answer it. I drank the water, cool and sweet, so different from London's slight bitterness. I had been homesick without knowing it. When I heard the first bark, I wondered if a neighbor with a pet had stopped in to inquire after my father's health. Like me, Joy loved animals, a trait we had both inherited from our father. The second bark was intensely familiar. The sound of a big dog overjoyed to see her owner, the sound of Joy stepping backward, making an exclamation of affection and surprise, my jolt of recognition at the unmistakable volley of barks, as I watched Millie greet Joy in the hallway, leaping up onto my sister, one paw on each shoulder, the same way she had greeted me for the first two years of her life. I stood frozen in the kitchen. I heard Joy ask a young female voice how much she owed, as I willed myself to move. Before I did, Millie stood in the kitchen doorway, blinking at me. For a moment, she cocked her head; in the next instant, she had felled me to the floor, licking my face, breathing hard in excitement, her muscular, warm body vibrating as it had when I would come home each night.

"My sweet girl," I said, laughing, but I could feel wet tears on my face as I put both my arms around her neck, Millie and I rolling around my father's kitchen rug.

When I came up for air, Joy was watching us from the kitchen door. Immediately, Millie deserted me, tail wagging furiously, as she ran to Joy.

"It's nice to have her back, huh, Mil?" said Joy, patting her head.

"Does she live here?" I asked, fearful of what Joy might say.

Joy looked away, color creeping into her cheeks, the way it had since she was a child when caught doing something she wasn't supposed to. My dark-brown skin did not redden, its heat internal, and I had always admired the prettiness of the hue even when she was guilty. Joy shook her head.

"We live nearby," she said, softly.

For a raucous moment, Millie on top of me, I had felt real happiness and I strained to remember it.

"Come here, Mil," I said, whistling the low, soft sound that she knew was my call for her.

But Millie went to an empty dog bowl I had not noticed at the far end of my father's kitchen. She picked it up between her teeth, clanging it onto the ceramic, patterned tiles of the floor.

"She's hungry," said Joy, apologetic. "Here, Mil, Didi wants to say hi." Joy whistled and pointed in my direction but Millie picked up the bowl and took it to Joy, dropping it at her feet. Joy must have seen my pain because she looked at me, stricken. "I'm sorry. If you just stay for dinner, she'll eat—and then afterward, she always wants to cuddle."

I stood up, brushing Millie's fur off my shift. "I don't need your sympathy, Joy."

"What? No, that's not what—"

"I should really be hearing some shame instead."

Joy flinched, as if I had hit her. Millie clanged the bowl on the floor again.

"You should feed your dog," I said, the hardness in my heart making its way into the rest of my body.

Joy began to cry. "I can't bear it. When you talk to me like that. I can't. Not with Baba like this, too. I'm sorry, Didi. I'm sorry. What can I do? How many times should I say it—I'll say it as many times as you want. I'm a terrible person. Please, please, forgive me. If I could change it, I would."

Tears began to stream from Joy's eyes as she wept, her face contorted, as a worried Millie clambered around her, trying to offer solace.

"No, you wouldn't," I said. "And this has nothing to do with Baba's illness. Don't you dare make it about him. You don't get to club what you did, with that."

Joy wept harder, beginning to hiccup. Millie began to bark until Joy quieted, patting her head to soothe her.

"You seem shocked by what this has done to me," I said. "To us. What did you think was going to happen?"

I felt a clinical curiosity even as bitterness rose inside of me, sour and vicious. Joy shook her head repeatedly in desperation. Millie jumped up on the couch and laid her head on Joy's shoulder, licking her new parent's ear.

"I'm sorry," she said. "I'm sorry. I thought in the hospital, that it could be okay."

"It'll never be okay," I said, an exhaustion settling into my bones.

"What can I do? How can we just stop being a family?" Joy began to cry again, softer this time.

"The problem is, you've forgiven yourself," I said. "Enough time has passed, in your opinion. I'm just expected to get with the program. Move on, or tell you what to do to fix it. It's what you're best at. No consequences, ever. But not this time. This time, you made me stop wanting to be your sister. I don't love you anymore, Joy. I couldn't even if I tried."

I picked up my purse and walked out of the kitchen, through the darkening hallway and living room that would need lamps switched on to dispel the evening's gloom. As I left, I heard Millie whimpering, as she tried to comfort my sister.

OUTSIDE, I FELT as if I needed to weep, too. Joy had passed her insidious sickness into my own cells; there was no reprieve to be had in confronting my killers. I took in large breaths of air, relieved that Eddie had gone home for the night. The street was busy, New Yorkers rushing, on their way to dinner or their families, the soft lights glowing against a cobalt sky, the night ushering in. My phone began to vibrate in my purse. It was Lena and I walked quicker, away from my father's building. When I had crossed the street, I stopped and sat on a stoop. I was sweating, my face hot despite the evening breeze.

"Hi," I said.

"I called a million times. Are you okay? I want to know what happened."

"With Joy?"

"With Marlon, this morning. What happened with Joy?"

When I did not respond, Lena let out a guttural exhale. “I cannot believe she has the temerity to come barging into your life this way. You think she’d leave you alone in the least.”

“I told her that I could never love her again.”

Lena’s voice tightened. “It *kills* me to watch you in this kind of pain.”

“It felt good. And then it felt terrible.”

“I wish you hated her. It would make all of this so much easier,” said Lena, furious.

“Most people get dumped and it’s fucking awful. But they don’t have to see the person’s new life through his new wife’s rose-colored POV every fucking day. If this doesn’t kill me, I’m probably invincible, right?”

“I’m so sorry, love.” I heard the sorrow in Lena’s voice.

A passing child stuck out his tongue at me, a little boy with dark hair.

“Stop that, Brentie,” said his mother as she made apologetic eye contact with me.

The boy and his mother disappeared into the entrance of the subway station.

“Tell me something sweet Gino did today,” I said.

“That little jerk. He found my nipple pasties in the bathroom and of course, devotee that he is, took them immediately to his sisters. The three of them cut the pasties into what they describe as “starfish shape, Mama.” Now every lamp in the house has my nipple pasties all over them. Sebbie won’t let me peel them off.”

I laughed. “Gino’s a genius.”

“They do have a nice glowy effect on the living room lighting,” said Lena. “Of course Alice wanted to know why I had ‘such huge nipples’ after that.”

“Your nipples are perfect,” I said.

“Thank you. Is the Marlon conversation a good one or a bad one?”

“Good, I think. He let me off the hook.”

"You were a goddess in that green silk."

"You should see it now, wrinkled like a Kleenex. I took doughnuts, the ones you recommended."

"I'm beginning to like him," said Lena. "He makes you happy."

I heard the sound of a train rushing past, the ground vibrating beneath my feet. "Len?" I said.

"Yeah?"

"When I got to the house, all through the afternoon, every time the doorbell rang— " I stopped.

"What is it?"

"I wanted him to be there. I kept wanting him to show up. I kept looking at the door for when Jack might walk through it."

The breeze had grown into a steady wind, its gusts blowing my hair around my face as more people hurried into the subway.

"Who doesn't want to look like a fox when they run into their ex, right?" said Lena at last, lightly. "It's natural, love. Don't give it another thought."

"Yeah."

I heard the soft rise and fall of Lena's breath, as we stayed on the phone in silence, the same way we had at any time the other had needed it, through our lives.

PART FIVE

CHAPTER EIGHTEEN

A FEW WEEKS later, Jack came to see me at work. The summer had turned into a boil, the sidewalks too hot for dogs to walk on, the swelter only relieved by thick blasts of air conditioning. My father slept and read and ate small meals that he barely had any appetite for, all within the cool recesses of his apartment—a longer recovery than any of us had anticipated. The Sunday lunch he had begged me to join had never materialized. His body had lost its initial burst of adrenaline at being released from the hospital, and since, he had refused to venture beyond bedroom and balcony. Joy and I had reached silent agreement on an alternate-day system of visiting him or driving him to medical appointments, giving each other the distance we needed in order to function as daughters. Occasionally, I would find a cluster of gooseberries or crisp small apples or a slice of dense chocolate cake on the counter, in Tupperware marked by a Post-it that said *Didi* on it. In this manner, I understood that she had continued to bake, despite the rigors of her career, and that the two of them often visited Jack's aunt upstate in the Hudson valley where he and I had once eaten fruit from her Honeycrisp trees and gooseberry bushes, the scent as alive in my memory as when I took them home in Joy's containers and ate them over the sink. I returned the plastic tubs washed and empty at first, and then with leftovers of meals I had cooked—a quarter of a roast chicken, an eggplant salad that we had loved as children, leftovers of a pint of blackberry ice cream I had made for Gino and the twins. It did not feel like any version of a truce, but I was loath to decline a gift, lest my father find out, and loath to let her be the only one capable of largesse. But what felt like virtuous performance eventually morphed into a peculiar satisfaction. I was not a sister again, but there was something in the contactless exchange of things that could nourish us separately.

The afternoon that Jack was waiting in my office, I had just returned from a long lunch with a group of student poets who had been riveted by my reluctant account of a career adjacent to the medium of poetry. I had tried to impress upon them, in vain, that I was no longer a poet nor had any remaining appetite to be one. My hope was that I would prove a cautionary tale and they would keep writing. When I walked into the office, Binyamin was putting on his jacket.

"Leaving already, Bin?"

His eyes widened slightly, startled, as he looked at me.

"Oh, I'm just heading off to place an order at Gertie's for dessert."

I blinked.

"For the anniversary party," said Bin, patiently.

"You're going yourself? Why not send Masha?"

Bin grinned at me. "Gotta personally make sure about the rainbow cookies or it'll be some fancy low-fat thing again."

I laughed as he looked over his shoulder at Gigi, who was in conversation with Wren, our art director. Gigi, serious, nodded at Bin and rose from the desk she had been perched on.

"What?" I frowned as Gigi came toward me.

"See you in a bit, Mira," said Bin, his exit hasty.

Even before Gigi could say the words, I knew.

"It's Jack," said Gigi. "Jack Smith. He's here. Waiting for you in the conference room. I tried to call but you didn't pick up."

Gigi looked mortified as I stood rooted to the ground. It could not have escaped any of them that the last time Jack had been in the office, we had been in love.

"Hey," I said, touching her arm. "It's okay. It's probably something to do with my dad."

THE CONFERENCE ROOM at our office was a former master bedroom, renovated to be a space where we could talk with writers and poets, or each other, for our weekly meetings. It was flooded in the mornings with natural light streaming in from large glass windows. An extra-long, worn dining table that might have belonged to an expansive farm family stood in its center, flanked by the same mismatched chairs that dotted our office. Jack was examining a framed poster of the 1999 spring issue of *Janus*. It was a line drawing of a child on tiptoe with a popsicle in his right hand, and a miniature adult, presumably his mother, sitting on the other palm. It was my favorite of the past covers—a mixture of whimsy and comment, quintessential *Janus*, but I could not remember if I had ever told Jack that. I said his name aloud as he turned around. The air-conditioning was cold enough that I felt myself shiver, but what shocked me was how normal it felt to be alone in his presence. If it should have felt dangerous, it felt the opposite. During our loving years, Jack's deep appreciation for the quiet pleasures of domestic life had turned him into a stable home for me. He had had the opposite of my disregard for institution and had made a convert of me after it was too late. A memory of how he had always disavowed divorce, having been at the receiving end of his parents', came back to me as he turned, his strained face brightened by a smile that transformed his eyes.

"MG," he said, then faltered, pausing. "I can call you Mira, if—that's what you'd like?"

"Is it Baba? Has something happened?" I shut the door behind me, terse.

"What? No, of course not. I'm sorry," said Jack, running a hand through his hair, the air of boyish confusion perpetually hanging off his frame, working its way into the motion of his shoulders. "I guess I should have said that first."

I did not want to speak of Joy to Jack, but he must have seen it in my eyes because he shook his head.

"It's not anything specific. Well, it is. But nothing to worry about. I wanted us to talk."

"You thought coming to my workplace was appropriate?"

In the years we had been together, even when we had fought, I realized I had never been inaccessible to Jack. That he had never heard true hardness in my voice.

Jack looked at me, wounded. "I didn't know what else to do," he said softly. "You won't answer my texts. I don't know where you live. No one will tell me anything about you."

There were years' worth of things that I wanted to say to him, but none of them rose to the surface. I pulled out a chair from the dining table and sat down too quickly.

"You always want the impossible," I said. "At work, in your life, in everything. You go after the hardest cases, you spend three days drinking only water to test your body's ability to fast. You want what other people would be scared by or would have the sense to not want. You are impossible. What you want from me is impossible."

I exhaled, my anger sliding out of me with the pent-up words. His aftershave, an excruciatingly familiar bergamot, filled the closed room.

Jack shook his head, imperceptibly. "If that's true, I don't know how to go on."

"Why are you here? To try to convince me to play at happy families? You must be mad. At least with Joy, I get it. As long as Baba's alive, she and I are stuck together"—I heard the bitterness curdle my voice—"but you and I, surely we can just pretend like the other lives on another continent. Is that really too much to ask?"

Jack looked like he wanted to weep and it filled me with grief.

"Why are you here?" I leaned forward and held my head in my hands because it felt like I needed support.

I heard Jack move and before I looked up, I felt his nearness.

"Ever since I've known you, the best thing in your life has been Joy," said Jack, standing over me. "She was the one person you let in all the time, past all your guardrails. No matter what she did, you came to her rescue and defense. And it's the same with her. She can't sleep, she can't eat. It's like part of her has gone missing."

No, I wanted to shout at him. No true sister would have been capable of such staggering betrayal. Jack knew that, since the day she had been born, a peculiar desire to protect Joy had taken hold of me. Yet something about the diluted quality of our blood had apparently given Joy permission to kick over sacred fencing. And in a world where she was my assailant, there was nowhere for our love to live.

"Have you told yourself that you're here because you care about me?" I asked instead.

"I do care about you. I care about this family. And I know what I've done to it."

I felt a slight shudder to his breath, regret etched into his strained face.

"They hate you. Ulrike, Gigi, Bin. Everyone." I said the words matter-of-fact, hearing their petulance, wishing I could scream at him.

"I know."

"Yet, you're here."

"I'll do anything, Mira," said Jack, alive with desperation.

I shook my head. "I eat her fucking gooseberries and I put food in her fucking Tupperware and I return it on the table and that's all I can do at the moment. I don't know what else you think I can do."

"You said to your dad that you'd come to Sunday lunches again. The three of you," he added hurriedly. "I think it would mean the world to him. And seeing each other more frequently, or at least sometimes"—Jack searched for the words—"maybe things could get easier between you two."

I looked at him in disbelief. "Did Joy send you here? Is that what this is?" Fury clutched at me again. "Is this you and her bonding over what to do about me again? Isn't that how you fell in love?"

Jack bowed his head. For a few seconds, we were both silent.

"I'm so sorry, MG. You can't know how sorry I am."

I pushed the chair back and went to the window. Despite the fiery temperature outside, I needed air. The panes creaked under the force with which I tried to lift them. Behind me, I felt Jack. He placed his palms underneath the window and as he lifted, the warm air rushed in, an attack on the manufactured chill inside.

"I don't need your help." I sat on the ledge, the devastation unfurling inside me.

He sat next to me, miserable.

"Joy didn't send me," he said. "And I know I have no place in your life, but it feels like I have to try to repair this gulf between the two of you. Your dad said you'd promised to come to lunch with Joy and him, but you never did. It felt like enough hope for me to try."

"He's too sick. That's why we haven't done it."

"He walked outside today. Asked me to bring over a ladder—he wanted to refill the nectar in the hummingbirds' feeding station."

Despite myself, my lip curled in amusement. "That crazy old loon. You did not let him."

"Nope. I was like, I have no idea what that is, and how to do it, but you're going to sit on this comfortable bench, Mihir, and explain to me exactly what you need me to do for these damn birds."

"Bet he loved that," I said, a shard of pain going through me at Jack's saying of my father's name, with intimacy.

"He glared at me and explained from the bench the many ways I was doing it incorrectly," said Jack. "I was in a suit. On my lunch break." Jack examined my reluctant smile with caution. "He's just like the both of you. Incredibly independent."

I looked away, unwilling to be in any club with Joy. "Please. You won him over on day one. You've been his favorite child since."

When Jack did not say anything, I looked at him, outraged. "The least you could do is deny it." The sounds of the busy office trickled into the room, merging with the city outside. "You know, when we were together, it felt like you were perfect in some ways," I said. "And then you went the other extreme."

"No one in the history of time has ever been more imperfect," said Jack, desolate.

I felt a surge of laughter. He had always been endearing when upset, sadness permeating his being in the way a child's might.

"What exhibit did you see?" asked Jack.

"What? Oh." I touched the sticker on my blouse, above my breastbone. "I didn't—I was on a panel. Talking to some Columbia grad school poets."

"They want to be you," said Jack.

"I suspect that's the last thing they need. They want to write things, make things. Those who can't do, y'know, edit." I shrugged.

"That's bullshit. You're the lifeblood of the poetry section. Even these past few years, you've had such a voice in *Janus*. What you do, brings it to life," said Jack, impassioned.

I looked at him. "You read the magazine? When I was gone?"

Jack nodded. "Every issue. It was the only bridge to you."

I looked away, tears filling my eyes, unexpected.

"Mira, you can't think—that you didn't leave an incredible void."

I looked at Jack's face and saw he was telling the truth. I took a breath and stood up.

"My marriage hasn't been easy." Jack went on, pleading. "Without you in her life, she was never again fully herself. And losing you like that, made me feel never fully myself. I think about children, and I realize that without you, the family will never be complete. You can't just be this ghost that exists on the periphery. If anything, it should be me. If it makes things better, I'll try to be as invisible as possible in your lives when you and Joy are together."

I held up a palm and took a step backward. "Stop. I'll think about lunch. But stop. I can't do this."

Jack held up both his palms, nodding in acceptance. Behind him, the air seemed to balloon, even hotter. It had made the room sticky, an unnatural scald to the season. The temperature had driven us all to extremes, I thought.

"I have to get back to work," I said.

"Okay," he said again. "I'll use the back entrance, through the kitchen."

We both knew that he knew the ins and outs of the office by heart. As I made my way to the door, I stopped, my hand on the knob.

"Can I ask you a question?" I asked.

Jack nodded, wary. Questions had become minefields where neither of us might anticipate losing a limb.

"A legal question," I said, turning to face him.

"Of course." His shoulders relaxed and his hands slid into his pockets, relief settling into his jawbone, an immediate, assured slide into lawyerhood.

"An anonymous author sent me a manuscript. It's—very good."

Jack blinked twice in rapid succession. After a pause, he frowned. "Fiction?"

"How did you know?" I asked. I felt beads of sweat beginning to form in the humid air, on my forehead.

"I didn't. Something about the way you said it. Sounded like fiction."

"It's a novel. *The Wild Lings*."

"Wildlings," he said, rolling the syllables off his tongue. "Good title. Sounds mysterious. Are you guys considering it for an issue?"

"We want to publish an excerpt. But if it turns out that this author knew me—that there was a personal connection between us—do you think I'd get in any legal trouble?"

Jack's forehead delineated into deep ridges, the way it did when he was looking for a solution. "But isn't it always easier to publish something if you know someone in the business? Doesn't everybody do that?" he asked.

"We just have to be careful in an era of transparency," I said. "I can't look like I published something as a favor. Especially if the person was a friend or family."

Jack looked at me, his face blank. "You think this person is a friend or a family member?"

I held his gaze. "I just want to make sure I know what I'm getting into."

Jack nodded. "I think the technical answer is no, you can't get into legal trouble. You should maintain records of texts, emails, any communication with this person and every person you've sent the book to—proof of your lack of knowledge, per se, like a chain of title—but if that's on record, I can't see how you're guilty of anything other than doing your job. And even if you were guilty of nepotism, it certainly isn't illegal. You might just be on the receiving end of some public ire, which I'm guessing Ulrike doesn't want."

"No." I stared at Jack. "I did email with her. The author."

Jack nodded. "Sounded like it."

"Okay. Thanks."

"And you really have no idea who the person might be?" Jack's face relaxed into curiosity.

"I think I do."

Jack studied me for a beat. He smiled. "I can't wait to hear how this turns out."

"Why would a good writer hide?" I said. "I find the need for anonymity fascinating."

Jack laughed. "Of all people, you should understand it. You're always undercover, in one way or the other, MG." His face changed shape, into regret again. "I'm sorry—that was stupid. I didn't mean—"

I nodded. "I think you're right, actually. Maybe that's why he sent it to me."

AS I WENT back to my desk, I felt an exhilaration, as if I had run a marathon I had not known I was capable of. The woman who had returned from London seemed to me a different person, uninterested in the old set of rules by which I had lived my life. Perhaps it was imperative, in the new and overheated world we occupied, to remain undercover. Perhaps it was the only way to survive.

CHAPTER NINETEEN

FOR THE MOST part, Marlon drove a motorcycle, a 1963 Harley Davidson Sprint that he spent a few hours each week tinkering with and marveling over in the toolshed of his building. Overall, the bike added to his slight air of audacity as he sped through the streets of New York. My first experience of being a biker chick had felt intoxicating as I held on to his torso, a panic and liberation pounding in my veins. But to meet my father and Joy, Marlon had chosen his athletic Subaru, a car primed as much for adventure as it was for soccer moms. It sat outside Lee's, by the curb; I examined it from a barstool inside, both disappointed and relieved that my father's first sighting of Marlon would not be as he roared up on a motorbike, me in tow.

Deedee brought over the coffee pot, her braids swinging as she leaned over the counter to refill my cup. "Going somewhere special?" She winked at me. "Marlon only busts that car out when he's trying to look like a good boy."

I laughed. "I don't know that he has to try too hard. Last night, on our way back to his apartment, he literally picked up every piece of trash on the street. This is New York City. I told him he was going to catch something doing that."

Deedee nodded, vehement. "I didn't think anyone could be a greater boss than Lee, but Marlon gave me a second advance last month so I could pay rent. I went out too many times. I'm in a panic, you know. What if I don't find someone before I turn sixty? And lose control of my bladder or something." At this, Deedee leaned her elbows on the counter, arching her back, her forehead creasing in real concern. "Marlon gets it. He's a real doll."

I nodded. "He is. You're going to go dancing every Saturday at Ciao Ciao when you're ninety."

Deedee arched her back again, but something sharp, a whisper of sadness, passed through her. "I have all my friends at the club," she said, vacantly. Almost immediately, she was restored and rolled her elbows on the counter, leaning forward, gossipy. "So where you guys going?"

It had not been an event of any consequence when I had planned it, but as I said the words, I felt an anxiety. "Just to see my father, in Manhattan."

Deedee's eyebrows lifted into her bangs as she lifted a calf behind her in a stretch. "No wonder he got out his wheels."

I wondered if Marlon felt that it was indicative of a forward motion in our relationship. I rubbed my temple. "It's just dinner."

Deedee finished her arch and straightened, a scrutiny in her bright eyes. "He's been through a lot, you know? Boy's mother dies, he goes to prison, moves to Australia, closes his shop, moves here, whatnot. He deserves some happiness. You know?"

For a moment neither of us said anything. The air felt oppressive even though the front door to the bar swung open at a regular interval. I nodded, feeling the tightness in my vocal cords. "Of course he does."

Deedee flashed a smile at me then, wide and brilliant. "You're a good egg. I can tell. You want a coffee to go?"

FROM INSIDE HIS Subaru, Marlon leaned over and opened the passenger door for me.

"Who has a car, and a bike, in New York?" I asked, as I strapped myself into the seat. "You live in a city with a subway that's as disgusting as it is effective."

"It's nice to see you, too," said Marlon, kissing my neck.

"You smell good," I said, breathing him in. "And look at this crisp shirt. It's got little rosebuds on it?" I peered at the pattern. "You look fantastic."

"I wanted to make a good impression." Marlon grinned at the road as he drove.

I leaned over the seatbelt to fiddle with the radio. "I mean, it's just dinner. No biggie." I found the classical station and Brahms floated into the recesses of the car. I exhaled, easing the space between my shoulder blades.

Marlon turned to look at me. "You okay?" he asked.

Boy's mother dies, he goes to prison.

I nodded. "*Vier ernste Gesänge*," I said. "*Four Serious Songs*. He wrote it inspired by the Luther Bible. This one is the second, I think, about death and the transitory nature of life."

"It's beautiful," said Marlon.

I watched him as he listened, experiencing the music for the first time, his eyes flickering in pleasure at its intense, emotional movement. I wondered what he had done that someone had thought merited prison. I wondered why he had not told me, and thought of the many things I had not told him. The singer's baritone took hold of me and I felt a wave course through me. I closed my eyes, yielding to it.

As the piece ended and the next one began, I heard Marlon repeat the words: "You okay?"

Unwilling, I reopened my eyes. "Music like that can sometimes be too much. It's almost too beautiful."

Marlon nodded, bemused. "Like looking at the sun."

I turned to him. "Can I ask you a question?"

He raised his eyebrows and laughed. "You sound serious."

I shook my head. "No. But I'm curious."

He nodded, wary, but did not say anything.

"Do you think people are entitled to their secrets, even from loved ones?"

Marlon frowned. "In relationships? Or families?"

"Anywhere. I've always thought that a secret was that ultimate private part of yourself. And to reveal it to someone, well, it takes a lot. You have to earn it. And that's okay."

Marlon let out a laugh but it seemed more of a short breath. "Is it even possible to not have any?" He paused, deliberate. "I think there's a trust between two people, an unspoken understanding of what you can keep to yourself, based on that relationship. And what you can't. But yes, I do believe that people are entitled to their inner lives. To privacy. I don't know that anyone can be fully known, anyway, even to themselves." He angled his head to one side. "Are you saying I have to earn your secrets?"

Marlon was making an attempt at humor, but I could see that he was confused. I felt lighter, as if freed from something. It felt as if he might understand, when he inevitably learned the truth.

"I've just been thinking about a manuscript I'm reading at work and it made me realize that people deserve to keep parts of themselves hidden for as long as they need to."

Marlon drove without responding but I felt his attention focused on me. The music reached a familiar, haunting crescendo and I felt my heart beating faster, in response to it.

"The world can demand that you turn all of yourself over too quickly," I said. "So often, we do it before we are ready, and then the discovery lacks context and becomes just fact without nuance." I shook off my shoes, gripped by something.

"You really are talking in riddles today," said Marlon, amused but there was a seriousness to him. "I think I like it."

I wondered again what he had been convicted of, but it was

impossible to believe that the man next to me was capable of harm. I shuddered.

"Are you cold?" he asked.

I shook my head. A car cut in front of us, but Marlon did not react.

"Speaking of secrets," he said.

I felt my spine stiffen. In that moment, I wanted Marlon to stay exactly as he was to me, without the shifts that new information might bring.

"I read your poem."

A wave of hysteria bubbled inside me, but I did not laugh.

"I'm sorry if you didn't want me to. You must not have, since you never brought it up. But—I looked you up. And, well,"—he shrugged. "You were famous."

This time I laughed. "Hardly."

He wrinkled his forehead. "The poem was everywhere."

"For a brief moment, yes. And then something else took its place."

Marlon said nothing and I felt a familiar prickling.

"I wrote it so long ago," I said. "It feels like a different person wrote it. I haven't written anything else that I'd show to anyone."

After I said the words, I realized that the last sentence hung in the air between us, like an object. We stopped at a red light; Marlon turned to me, his eyes frank.

"I really liked it," he said. "That's all I wanted to say."

Something thick made its way into my throat. He did not say more and I was grateful.

"My sister Joy and I—just so you know—we have a strained relationship. Things haven't been easy since I came back. I just wanted to warn you."

Marlon nodded. "I saw it when she came to the bar. In the way you looked at her."

"We have different values," I said. "Things she thinks are okay, I consider wrong. And she probably thinks of me as an unfeeling bitch."

Marlon looked at the road, reflective. "She asked me if I knew you or had seen you around, that time that she came to the bar. I said yes. There was something intense about her, in the way she lit up. There's love in there."

I turned the dial of the radio again.

"Too much death and transience for me," I said. Doja Cat sprang to life. "Ah," I said, leaning back. "Much better. Doja knows something about living."

"Bet Brahms would have loved her."

I swung to the music and rolled down my window, letting the evening air in. Marlon turned off the air-conditioner.

"I shouldn't have said anything about your sister," he said, apologetic. "That was presumptuous."

"Families are complicated."

"Yeah," he said, as we descended from Dumbo down through the sweep of the bridge, the cityscape gleaming silver and concrete to my right, the Hudson a clear blue in front of it.

I HAD AGREED to come to dinner on the condition that there would be lamb, and no mention of the past would be made. I could smell the shanks simmering in their cumin gravy from the elevator as it halted on my father's floor. When I opened the door without knocking, Jack was unpacking groceries from a large Whole Foods tote. Startled, he looked at me, as if caught stealing. Joy emerged from the kitchen in an apron with the word *Hellraiser* embroidered on it in cursive that my mother had abandoned light-years ago.

"Did you remember the pomegranate molasses?" she asked Jack, a wooden spoon in one hand, wiping the other palm on the apron. When she saw me, she halted mid-wipe, alarm in her eyes.

"Sorry," said Jack to me, holding an orange mid-air. "I was just dropping these off."

Despite myself, I laughed. "For god's sake," I said, setting down the bottle of Gamay that Marlon and I had bought. "Stop acting ridiculous. You can't hide him away all the time," I said to Joy.

The two of them stood silent in the living room, like children in trouble.

Exasperated, I shook my head. "I've got a guest tonight. Don't make it weird, please." I looked at Jack. "Are you staying for dinner?"

"He isn't. Of course not," said Joy, in a rush. "Baba just needed some groceries. And you're—early."

"You're welcome to, if you like," I said to Jack. "It's fine. We're all grown-ups here."

"Are you sure, Didi?" Joy looked at Jack, uncertain.

I shrugged. "Whatever. Just stop making it weird all the time."

"If you're okay with it, I'd love to stay," said Jack, quietly.

I nodded, taking in a deep breath. "Where does he keep the wine openers these days?"

Jack and Joy reached for the opener simultaneously, from a bowl on my father's bar cart, synchronized swimmers in their domestic pond. Joy giggled, nervous as she handed me the opener—a lacquered gold merman perched over the drill tool. I raised my eyebrows.

"A present from his friend, Mrs. Murphy downstairs," said Joy meaningfully, as Jack handed her the jar of molasses. "She wants to be the next Mrs. Guhathakurta."

As I opened the bottle, Joy pulled out glasses from the cupboard.

"Where's your guest?" she asked.

"Parking," I said. "Where's Baba?"

"Showering," said Jack. He sat down at the far end of the dining table and this I knew was his effort at becoming invisible.

"Who's the guest?" asked Joy, her eyes rounded with curiosity. "Lena?"

"Marlon Hughes," I said, pouring wine into the glass that Joy had handed me.

She raised her eyebrows, an identical gesture to mine. Ignoring her,

I took a sip of the wine. In my periphery, I felt Jack's eyes on me. Delighted, Joy clapped her hands together.

"Thank goodness, I bought enough lamb to feed a wedding," she said.

I HAD FORGOTTEN to tell Marlon what floor my father lived on and my phone remained in my purse, so by the time I rescued him from a beaming Eddie and brought him upstairs, my father had emerged from his bedroom, his hair still damp from his shower and combed neatly into a middle part, like a schoolgoing toddler's might be, instead of his usual unruly mop. In place of his pressed slacks and shirts, he was dressed in sweatpants and a T-shirt, even thinner and seemingly more content than I had seen him in years.

"Hello sweetheart," he said to me as I reentered the apartment with Marlon behind me. "I made Joy follow the lamb recipe, line by line, no modifications."

"Except the orange juice I threw in at the end," said Joy from the couch, where she sat with her knees tucked under her, on her phone. My father looked at her horrified and Joy rolled her eyes. "Just kidding."

My father hugged me, a faint medicinal scent to his skin. I held him by the shoulders. "Are you sure you're up for this, Baba?"

"My dear, I've never been better," he said. For the first time, he noticed Marlon in the doorway. "Hello," my father said, with surprise.

My heart began to beat faster; on the way to his house, I had wondered if my father's subconscious held any of the embedded racism that my extended family of Indian elders would casually proffer when confronted by the Black community. *Where is he really from? What will your children look like? A bartender? Boy's mother dies, he goes to prison.*

"This is Marlon," I said, as Marlon stepped inside the apartment.

Recovering himself, my father held out a hand. "Mihir," he said, smiling with a pleasure that made me swell with love for him.

"It's very nice to meet you, Mihir," said Marlon, shaking his hand. "Mira talks so much about you that it feels like I know you already."

"Really?" My father raised an eyebrow, in the exact manner Joy and I did. "Not all bad, is my hope," he said.

"I think she might think you're perfect," said Marlon.

"That's right," said Joy. "This is the problem. She thinks he's perfect and won't hear a word otherwise. Hi. Remember me?"

"Of course," Marlon said. "Joy, in search of a sister. How could I forget?"

Joy laughed, as she held out her arms. "That's me."

As Marlon and Joy hugged, I looked at Jack. He had risen to his feet. For a moment, we held each other's gaze. The circumstances that had brought us to that moment seemed so ludicrous that it felt necessary to be gentle. I willed myself to smile at him. Jack nodded imperceptibly and came closer to where we were standing. He held out his hand to Marlon.

"Hi, I'm Jack."

Marlon stepped forward, his body lithe and eager to make contact. "Marlon." As they shook hands, Marlon turned to look at me.

"My sister's husband," I said.

"Ah," said Marlon. "Pleased to meet you, mate."

"Likewise," said Jack, sliding his hands back into his pockets.

For a moment, the four of us stood in silence, in a circle around Marlon. I thought of the things I had prepared for conversation but my mind seemed to have erased its notes.

"Shall we eat?" asked my father, a quickness to his words. "Marlon, in this house we do not believe in appetizers, we go straight for the jugular. Let us get you a drink while we bring out this beautiful lamb that my grandmother taught me to make when I was a boy."

BUT THE LAMB had not finished cooking. My father inspected the meat with disappointment. As he gave us each last-minute instructions, Joy added molasses and pistachios into the Dutch oven the meat was cooking in, I fried parathas, Marlon plated roasted peas and Jack was assigned a salad. Marlon excelled in the kitchen and at putting people at ease. As he wove his way around my family, finding pepper and a knife and handing my father a glass of water or Joy a lime from the fridge, I watched the instantaneous affection that they extended to him, and felt relief that, even briefly, I was capable of something other than anger around Joy. My father sat at the kitchen table, doing the crossword as he held court. Jack sat across from him, slicing cucumbers. As Joy and I stood over adjacent burners of the stove, I realized there was a new confidence in the way she occupied the domestic terrain of kitchens and family. It was the product of having built her own home, and the realization made me turn away from her.

"Joy, not that much garam masala," said my father. "You need a delicate touch. Mira, please don't burn those—add a touch of ghee."

He turned to Marlon, who was seasoning peas as instructed. "My grandmother would rise from her ashes in the Ganges to haunt us if she knew that neither of my daughters were able to make parathas and we were in the prepackaged business now."

"If only you had taught us to make parathas instead of insisting on careers, Baba," said Joy, opening the oven and inserting a thermometer into the lamb with vigor.

"Not that hard, Ma. You don't want to break up the meat," said my father. "It's true. I raised excellent girls. Doesn't mean you can't learn to roll out a paratha."

Marlon laughed. "What do you do, Joy?"

"We're both lawyers, Jack and I," said Joy. "I work for a private firm that specializes in corporations and malpractice. Jack's got the more exciting job."

"Is that why you gave me the least glamorous kitchen task?" asked Jack, disgruntled as he peeled garlic for his salad.

He had been silent for the most part, and hearing his voice felt like a surprise.

"Garlic is the singular reason I didn't become a pro chef," said Marlon. "You have to start by chopping and peeling and grating thousands of cloves. Gets in your bloodstream. Couldn't do it."

"I hear you, man," said Jack. "When I'm not making salad around here, I work at Universal Music. Part of their inhouse legal—I look at copyright specifically."

"Cool," said Marlon. "You listen to a lot of music?"

"From the minute he wakes up, to when he drifts off at night with earbuds in his ears, listening to jazz," said Joy. "It's twenty-four seven."

"Like Mira," said Marlon. "She won't go ten minutes without a tune."

"That's right," said Joy, easily. "I got my first education in music from my big sister and my second from my husband."

"Is dinner ready?" asked my father. "I'm about to collapse." When Joy and I looked at him, he smirked. "I jest, my dears."

AS WE ATE, taking pleasure in the meal, it felt oddly natural, and I wondered if my father had been right. If one played at pretend long enough, perhaps the sensation might transfer from external sound and motion into one's being, taking on the shape of truth. It felt like I was home with my family, who were mildly disguising an interrogation of my new boyfriend and, slowly, I had tricked my senses into enjoying it.

"And which do you prefer, Marlon—Australia or England?" asked my father, helping himself to cucumber salad. "Do you enjoy cricket? Jack and I watch a lot of sports, when he has the time. Girls, I've had half a piece of lamb. Surely I can have a little more?"

"Absolutely not, Baba," said Joy.

"Maybe a little gravy, though," I said. "On your rice."

Joy let out a sound of frustration. "There are new rules now. We need to be careful."

I watched as Joy poured a measured spoon of lamb gravy over his single scoop of brown rice. I had been the one to ask for lamb, and guilt flooded me as I realized my father could no longer eat red meat at will. Jack gave me a sympathetic smile.

"Our father is ecstatic that I married a real bro," said Joy. "The sports fan he never managed to procreate."

Joy rolled her eyes at her patient husband and sliced him a piece of lamb that he had not asked for but happily accepted. Something painful made its way through my heart. Joy talked to Jack in a way I never had, teasing and arguing, her best and worst versions on display around him. She took care of him in an intense, *wifely* manner that could not have come naturally to me if I had tried. But I had wanted it and might have learned the ways of wifedom. The truth was that Joy had coolly possessed what I had never had with Jack—the definitive, infinite nature and reassurances of marriage—light-years from the tenuous, disposable fabric of being the girlfriend I had been.

"To be honest, I didn't really play much sport growing up," said Marlon. "My mother read a lot of books and then she'd go to work—she was a pediatric nurse at King's College hospital—and I had unsupervised access to her shelves. Jackie Collins, Harold Robbins, bodice rippers, but she also read *Rebecca, The Thorn Birds*, Anaïs Nin, *Jane Eyre*, all that stuff. So my main hobby was alternating between steamy and serious women's fiction. I did like riding bikes and watching Formula One though."

"That's hilarious," said Joy. "I'm picturing you as a twelve-year-old, reading an erotic novel."

"Formula One is a fine sport," said my father approvingly.

"Joy went to King's College for law," said Jack.

"Oh, right on," said Marlon. "Is that where you guys met?"

I felt a shock in my veins. To have to answer the question felt impossible. Joy, next to me, did not look up from her plate.

"I went to college with Mira. That's how Joy and I met."

I heard the words come out of Jack, as my father helped himself to more salad. I waited for the wave of memory and bitterness to descend, but instead, I felt absolved of a burden.

"We were concert buddies," I said.

Perhaps in this new manufactured existence, we might all subscribe to a reality in which Jack and I, concert buddies, had overseen the greatest love story of Joy's life.

"Cupid," said Marlon, delighted, in my direction.

"That's me," I said, wry. My father rose to refill his glass of water. I heard a soft laugh escape Jack, and I laughed, too.

"What's so funny?" asked Marlon.

"Just life," I said, looking at Jack.

Joy craned her neck, stretching it out as she did when she was uncomfortable. I caught a flash of Jack reaching for her knee, beneath the table. A silence descended, the three of us on edge and at attention. I could see that it confused Marlon and after a few moments, he looked up from his plate.

"So what kind of concerts did you guys go to?"

"Do you remember that Kamasi Washington concert we went to at Brooklyn Bowl?" Jack asked me. "I still think about it."

"You guys saw Kamasi live?" asked Marlon.

I nodded. "Before he was famous. It blew our brains out. That you could have this big, oceanic kind of jazz fill a tiny space and soar in it like that. I think it's my favorite concert ever."

"I felt it in my chest and knees. That music was inside me," said Jack.

"Sounds like a time," said Marlon. "We should go to more concerts, Mira."

Ever so slightly, Jack flinched, even as I watched him color it over with chewing. A peculiar pleasure took hold of me.

"We should," I said.

"What kind of music do you like? Mira's mostly an alternative and jazz girl," said Jack. "Andrew Bird, Dev Banhart, Sufjan, Al Green." Jack rattled off the names, looking at me. "Remember Al Green inside that church in Georgia? That might have been the most spectacular concert I've ever seen. You would have loved it, Mihir."

"Did he play gospel music?" asked my father. "I saw him in my twenties with your mother, Mira. He was a young man then, just like me."

I shook my head. "It was at his church—he was the pastor, but it was just his own music, with his Sunday choir backing him up. It was beautiful. Actually, that one was pretty special, too."

"I hope he tours again," Jack said, looking at me.

I nodded, smiling. Joy extracted her knee from under the table and rose.

Jack looked up at her. "What do you need, honey?"

"Just getting some more wine," she said.

But I knew he had caught the flash of belligerence in her eyes. Concerned, his eyes followed Joy's retreating body, her shoulders square in the kitchen doorway.

"You like a lot of Indian classical music too, right?" Marlon asked me. "And Brit-pop? M was blasting the xx the other morning in her kitchen," he said to Jack.

"No way," said Jack. "Not pop." He looked at Marlon. "She's always loved Hindustani classical."

I shrugged. "I had a colleague in London who took me to an xx concert. I loved it. Big Harry Styles fan too, as of 2023."

Jack examined me, his semi-stranger sister-in-law whom he had once known by heart. Joy returned with a replenished glass and an open bottle of wine and sat down with a briskness. Jack put an arm around the back of her chair.

"Do you have a favorite concert, Marlon?" asked Joy.

"Tough question," said Marlon, thinking. "My biggest memory with my mum is a Radiohead gig in a converted Yorkshire house. I was fourteen and it was the year before she died—kind of a difficult year for us. It made me feel like music could be the thing that always brought me back to center, you know?" Marlon hesitated. "I wax on for no reason."

I touched Marlon's elbow, feeling Jack's eyes on us. "I know exactly what you mean," I said.

My father poured himself a half-glass of the wine. "Even as a child and as she grew, Mira always chattered on about music, and poetry when she began to fall in love with it. Of course, much of it inherited from her wonderful mother."

Joy pointed to the wine in my father's hands. "Absolutely not, Baba," she said.

"Good grief, can't a man be left in peace for a moment, Joybird?" said my father, annoyed. "It's for Mira. She likes this brand."

Joy, chastened, drank from her own glass of wine.

"Thanks, Baba," I said, as he handed me the glass, reluctant.

"Jack remembered the name," said my father. "He brought it from the natural wine shop."

"I assumed your taste in wine, at least, had not changed," said Jack.

"It hasn't." I watched as Jack refilled his own glass. "I think my favorite concert was Springsteen, now that I think about it. Lena, Seb, Jack, and I sneaked in hip flasks and knew every lyric."

"You can't have three favorites," said Joy.

I heard the strain, in the guise of a friendly dig, in her voice, but this time, Jack did not make note, his arm still around Joy's chair.

"We had VIP tickets—someone from *Janus* got us those, right?" asked Jack.

"Yes." I warmed at the memory. "Ulrike was invited by *Vanity Fair* and wasn't exactly a Springsteen fan. Sweaty music, she called it."

"Sounds like her." Jack grinned.

"Maybe Kamasi's playing an arena somewhere," said Marlon. "We could all go?"

"Sure," said Jack, looking at Joy. "That sounds great, doesn't it, hon?"

Marlon reached for my hand under the table and I felt my family register the moment, as I slipped my fingers through his.

"Where did you meet?" asked Jack, bemused.

"Lee's Bar," said Joy. "He's Lee's brother."

"That's right," said Marlon. "My brother's away for an extended honeymoon and I'm managing his bar at the moment."

"Lee's Bar?" I heard something in Jack's voice and the image of us, laughing with Lee, on so many nights of the past, flashed into my brain.

"Yeah. He's my brother. Different mothers," said Marlon.

Jack flushed. "I didn't mean it that way."

"Of course not—I just love telling people that detail. Makes Lee more interesting," said Marlon with a grin. "One of the first things I said to Mira."

"No dessert for me, I'm afraid—doctor's orders," said my father. "But we do have a chocolate mousse that is my youngest's specialty for the four of you to enjoy. I will just watch every bite you take and regret the day I met that damned Dr. Ho."

"I'll get it," said Joy, pushing her chair back with force.

This time Jack looked up, his eyes slightly widening in recognition of his wife's unhappiness. He began to rise but I was already on my feet.

MY FATHER, HOPING to turn Marlon into a sports fan overnight, was passionately explaining the pros and cons of the Knicks team that season. Jack, participating half-heartedly, watched me clear a few dishes and go into the kitchen. Since we had been children, Joy and I had sensed when the other was upset, even when the world remained oblivious. Yet, I was unprepared for the sight of her hunched over the sink, paper towels clutched in her fists. She turned around as soon as I walked in.

"Is my mascara running?" she asked, her face inflamed.

I shook my head and set the dishes down into the sink.

"Bobbi Brown," she said, low through her tears. "Although you've never needed mascara. Did you know I once got Jack basketball tickets worth a couple thousand dollars and it was the wrong team? Nets. From New Jersey. Not the Knicks." She looked at me. "It feels like I'll never know him the way you do. And I'll never know you the way he knows you."

"This was never going to be easy, Joy," I said, my heart hardening.

Fresh tears welled in her eyes. "But it's so awful."

The sound of the men laughing outside drifted into the kitchen alongside notes of the ghazal my father was playing on his record player.

She shook her head in disbelief. "All I want is for Jack and you to be friends again. For us to go back to the way it was. But then we're all at a table, and the two of you talk to each other as if nobody else exists, with these"—she looked at the paper towels, crumpled in her hands—"*things* that connect you, all those years, and I hate it." My sister looked up at me, defeated. "I don't know what to do. I want it so much to be easy but usually the ex isn't sitting right there, at the table, talking about concerts they've been to. And here I am. Wooing her. Begging her to stay for dinner."

I felt anger rise in me as Joy wiped her eyes, this time streaking dark lines across her face.

"Joy, I'm the ex. And it's just as much my table as yours. Think about what that feels like."

"I know," she said, her face crumpling, like the towel, into grief.

"We were never friends. I was in love with him, even in college."

Joy looked up, horrified. "You never—said that."

I looked at her, incredulous. "What difference would it have made? And what did you think it was exactly? We were living together when you visited us, remember?" I paused. "He was the first man in my life to mean anything to me."

Joy stared at me, but it felt like she was looking past me. I wondered if she understood it, if she might fathom that the only poetry to come from me that the world had acknowledged had been a result of the night Jack and I had spent together, that Jack and I had the kind of history you couldn't erase quickly, especially in a sister. Joy covered her face with her hands. Shreds of the paper towel floated to the floor. "I don't know what to do," she repeated.

We stood there in silence, the sound of the television turning on in the living room. My father, hoping that his daughters talking in the kitchen might amount to something. Jack, hoping, for what exactly? Marlon, in the dark. I felt familiar exhaustion permeate me. "There's nothing either of us can do. There's no magic trick to the three of us coexisting. We're going to have to take it one day at a time. Right now, all we need to do is get through dessert."

I leaned across the kitchen counter, to where the paper towel dispenser sat. Plucking two sheets off the top, I went to the sink. Joy moved aside as I dampened the towel with a few drops of water. "Hold still," I said, turning to her. I held her face in my left hand as I wiped off the mascara with the other. "Bobbi's not that good. There. I fixed it."

Joy stood in front of me, motionless for a few moments.

"I'll do anything to have you back, Didi," she said.

I took in a breath, the lamb still perfuming the kitchen. "Where's this mousse of yours?"

DESSERT WENT BY quickly, Joy returning to some amount of cheer in her usual pivot, the mousse so delicious that Marlon and Jack both ate seconds while my father looked away, melancholy. I covered his hand with my own, after the table had been cleared and we had moved to the couches.

"We'll do this new diet together," I said. "I eat too many sweets anyway."

My father sighed with an air of tragedy, as he settled into a large cushion. "No, no. Live your life. Why should you pay for my sins?"

Jack had disappeared into the guest bathroom. In the kitchen, Joy and Marlon were loading plates into the dishwasher.

"I can see you really like Marlon," said my father. "I like him, too."

Jack reentered the room as my father said the words and our eyes met for a brief moment; he began to clear away the remaining glasses on the table. As he left the living room, my father squeezed my hand.

"I did not think a night like tonight was possible, Mira. It makes me very happy." He leaned back into the couch, and closed his eyes.

Joy and Marlon returned to the living room.

"Jack's taken over the dishes," she said, happily.

"You really give him the worst jobs," said my father. "He's such a good boy."

"He offered," she exclaimed. "Didi, Marlon, can I interest you in some of Baba's port?"

"It's going to waste anyway—you might as well drink it," said my father, sulky.

I stood up. "I'm actually really tired." I looked at Marlon. "Did you want some port?"

Marlon stood up, too. "I'm okay. Ready whenever you are."

GOODBYES WERE AWKWARD and stiff, like everything else that I had needed reintroductions to. Hugging Joy was no longer natural to my body or instincts and yet we put our arms around each other as my father watched, pulling away in seconds. I walked to the kitchen where Jack's arms were covered in suds in the sink.

"Bye," I said.

He stopped the tap mid-rinse. "It was really nice to see you."

I nodded and left the kitchen quickly. In the living room, my father and Joy were on the couch.

"We're going to watch a movie," said Joy. "It's a Danish whodunit."

"Marlon's gone to get the car," said my father, hopeful. "You can tell him to come back up if you want to stay a little longer?"

I smiled and shook my head. "Tomorrow's Monday."

A pang of what felt like loss went through me in the elevator. Downstairs, Marlon was waiting for me in the Subaru. As I climbed in, Kamasi Washington was playing.

"A little something for the ride home," said Marlon.

I let out a long breath, as if I had been holding it in my ribs. "I should have snuck out some of that port in my purse."

"I thought it went well," said Marlon, turning to look at me as he drove. "Didn't it?"

"Yeah. They're just a lot. Of course, they're charmed by you—why wouldn't they be?"

"I like them, too," said Marlon, pleased. "I could tell your dad was surprised. You didn't tell him you were seeing someone?"

"He was probably just surprised because you're not my usual type. And I hadn't said you were definitely coming."

"What's your usual type, darlin'?" Marlon tucked a strand of my hair behind my ear.

"Well, you're definitely the most laid-back, immediately likable person I've dated."

Marlon smiled at me. "You've never had a Black boyfriend, is that it?"

I looked at Marlon but he seemed easy with the question, asked with his usual candor. I felt a rush of affection for him. "I haven't, no."

"Did that make you nervous, taking me home?"

I felt some embarrassment but decided on honesty. "A little, but my parents take pride in their open minds and I should give them more credit. My aunts and uncles and grandmothers would be problematic with their inherited bullshit around model and problem minorities. I did wonder if Baba would interrogate you about your job. If there's anything Asian families are united in, it's elitism where careers are concerned. But he loved that you ran a bar." I looked to make sure Marlon had not taken offense, but he seemed in good spirits.

Marlon nodded. "He really did. Told me he wished he had started something, a business of some kind that surrounded him with people. He said that retirement gets lonely."

"I think the thing he was most taken aback by was how easily you fit into the family," I said.

We sped past Chinatown, its fluorescence blazing, the stillness of Manhattan behind us. I felt a sadness at Marlon's words; my father had not told me that he was lonely but I had never asked him.

"Do you want to get a nightcap?" asked Marlon. "We could go to Henry Public. Someplace that isn't an establishment I own?"

"Wait till Lee hears that you're calling yourself the boss now." I leaned back in the seat, the smell soothing, of the leather mixed in with the objects of Marlon's life.

"I actually did put some money in the place, recently," said Marlon. "I've been thinking about staying and Lee could use the help."

"What do you mean, some money?" I sat up a little.

"I co-own the bar now, with Lee. I made some cash from a business I owned in Perth."

"What do you mean, you're staying?"

"Here. In New York. I wasn't sure when I first got here but I am now." Marlon looked over at me.

"You're so mysterious," I said. "I didn't know you were ever trying to leave."

We stopped at a red light. He leaned over and turned my face to him. As Marlon kissed me, I felt a sense of hot shame. He drew back, still holding my face. "You've got me in a tizzy, Mira," he said, desire on his breath.

The SUV behind us honked, an elderly woman scowling at us in the rearview.

"The light is green and that lady is mad," I said.

Marlon laughed and began to drive. As the lady passed us, Marlon looked at her and placed a hand on his heart. Begrudgingly, she smiled at him.

"You're not easy to remain uncharmed by," I said.

"Please tell me you're not trying. But I don't want to rush this." He looked at me. "I mean it. Take all the time you need."

Marlon kissed my left shoulder and backed into a parking spot across the street from Henry Public.

I turned off the music. "Marlon, there's something I have to tell you."

"Was the tizzy thing too much?" He grimaced. "I should get better at holding it in. I'm really not trying to speed anything up. I was just in a mood."

"It's not that. It's about me. My ex actually."

A flicker of uncertainty passed over Marlon. Wary, he leaned sideways against his seat, facing me.

I tried to muster a laugh. "It's actually not a big deal. I've just missed the boat on telling you earlier, and so it's a little awkward now."

Marlon said nothing. The inside of the car suddenly felt oppressive but I did not want to roll the window down.

"My sister and Jack—they've had a complicated history."

"They seem happy enough," said Marlon, when I paused.

I closed my eyes and opened them again.

"Jack was my boyfriend. We went to college together and later, we met again, by accident, and I fell in love with him. We were together. We talked about having kids. When Joy came home after law school, when she moved back, something shifted between Jack and me. We began having problems, not just the little arguments but bigger ones, fundamental differences. And he and Joy had become close friends. The further we drifted apart, the closer they got and I thought it would help...that it would help the relationship"—I felt my voice begin to crack—"but it didn't. I thought I was going to be Jack's wife, but it didn't work out that way."

I looked up at him, afraid, regret beginning to flood me. Marlon had gone still. He turned his body away from me and looked ahead at the darkened street.

"Jesus," he said.

"I can't tell you how it happened. I've never asked them the details. But it happened. They fell in love. When I found out, I felt like I'd been punched in the stomach. A part of me just felt like it died at that moment. So I disappeared."

"To London," said Marlon slowly.

"Yes."

"Four years ago?"

"Almost five now. Yes."

"Good god, Mira." Marlon exhaled. "How could he do that to you?"

I shook my head, desperate for the conversation to end, for something to happen that might relieve the shame and pain I felt.

"I don't know but I know that he's got a good heart. He said he couldn't live without her. So he must have believed that." I rolled the window down a crack and breathed in the outside air. "Tonight was the first time I've seen them properly, since I returned."

Marlon shook his head in disbelief. "Why wouldn't you tell me this? It's not like you did anything wrong. This happened to you. But why not tell me?" He shook his head again, swallowing, his Adam's apple bobbing up and down, pronounced. "Why let me walk into your father's house thinking that I was meeting the family?"

When I said nothing, Marlon brought his hand down on the edge of the steering wheel, hard. I flinched at the impact.

"I feel like an idiot, Mira, going in there trying to impress your family when it had nothing to do with me."

For the first time, I heard fury in his voice as our breathing filled the car.

"I'm sorry," I said, my mind suddenly blank. There were a thousand things I wanted to be able to say to him but instead I said the first thing that came into my head. "If anyone could understand keeping something private, I figured it was you." I heard the plea in my voice. "I know I let it go too long. I'm sorry."

Marlon's jaw and shoulders clenched, his eyes dropping to his hands around the wheel. Something—shame? resignation? I could not tell what exactly, so far had he gone from me—passed through his face.

"What do you mean by that?" asked Marlon, so quietly that it sent fear through me.

"Deedee told me. I couldn't care less. It doesn't matter to me, I give you my word. But you didn't tell me. And I'm just saying—I'm just saying that I understand that."

Marlon looked at me, and I understood that this was the face he had presented to the lecherous man at the bar—smooth and flat, his eyes so cold that it felt he might be capable of anything. Even so, I wanted him, in that moment, above all else, to not leave my life.

"What do you mean, Mira?" he asked again, as if I was a rogue stranger myself.

"Deedee told me you had gone to prison."

It felt like I had accused him of a crime myself. His body went slack, as he breathed in.

"And you assumed it was natural, given that I was a Black man."

I flinched. "That's not fair."

He laughed, bitter. "You're a hypocrite, Mira. Talking about fairness and your family's prejudices when you've lied to me this whole time. You're blind to your own biases. What did you think I was in for? Good old-fashioned murder? Or something a little more basic, like drugs or larceny?"

"You don't know anything about me if you think that," I said, hotly. "I wanted to hear it from you, yes, but that doesn't mean I feel any differently about you. All I'm asking is that you extend me the same courtesy."

"I have no idea who you are, Mira." There was contempt in Marlon's voice and it was a knife through me. I reached out to touch his hand through my tears, but he recoiled, opening the door on his side, swinging his legs out.

"I have to get out of here," he said.

Marlon dropped his keys into the cup holder and got out of the car. As the door slammed shut behind him, I flinched again. There was a finality to his anger that scared me. I imagined never seeing Marlon again, as I sat in the car. We were casual, so what did it matter anyway, I asked myself. A few moments later, I picked up the keys and got out. He had already walked a block before I was able to catch up.

"Marlon, please, listen to me."

I caught hold of his hand, breathless. New Yorkers passed us by, unseeing just another couple fighting on the street. Reluctant, Marlon slowed, but there was a seething in his eyes I had never seen before and it felt like he had lost all feeling for me.

"You *were* meeting my family. I didn't know he would be there. I'm so sorry I didn't tell you earlier, but having that secret makes me feel like a freak, as if I have a second head. Every single person in my life walks on eggshells around me, but you never have. I didn't want you to start. I didn't want to change the way you looked at me. I didn't want this."

Marlon shook his head, and turned away from me. As he walked away, even quicker this time, I did not go after him. I was stained with what had happened to me, too broken for someone else's affections, made a liar by my humiliation. I turned and walked in the opposite direction, then sat down on a curb in front of a bodega and leaned my head into my knees, closing my eyes. I stayed like that for a long time. At some point, the owner of the bodega came out and I thought he might ask me to leave, but he handed me a bottle of cold water. I accepted it, wordless, his kindness threatening to unravel me, and the man went back inside. I held the icy bottle against my cheek and laid my head in my arms, wondering if I should hail a taxi, but I was paralyzed. At least my friend in the bodega would keep an eye on me, I thought, hazily. A few moments later, I felt a body next to mine. Marlon was beside me, on the curb.

"I gave you the car. Why are you out on the street? You can't just be sitting here."

I shook my head at him, unraveling again, apologizing through thick tears. Marlon touched my hair.

"Being deceived by you scares me, I think. It made me feel like a pawn."

I felt a hot bitterness for Joy and Jack, who had turned me into this monster.

Marlon softened, a sorrow emanating from him, too. "You shouldn't feel shame," he said. "You didn't do anything."

I looked out at the bus stop across from us, miserable. "I feel like I let it happen. That something about who I am, some sort of defect in me, allowed it to happen."

This time Marlon reached for me, wrapping his arms around me. I huddled into his chest. "This isn't your fault, Mira," he said.

A bus trundled up and I rose from the curb, my body still on alert for the unpredictabilities of large moving vehicles, after the accident. Marlon followed me to the bench in front of the bodega. The owner inside gave me an imperceptible nod, and I sat down. A child on the bus pulled away from a tired woman and pressed her nose against the window. I thought of Gino. Marlon took off his glasses and rubbed his eyes.

"I was nineteen," he said, a toughness in his voice. "My first year of college, in Canberra. Most people were white and the Asian kids had it the hardest, but I was still trying to fit in. We were at a party one night—my buddy Mikey was white and popular and took me with him and he was trying to get with this girl Renee but she liked me, I could tell. It was in Belconnen, which was a bit of a sketch neighborhood. The police were always hanging around to find something, and we were idiots and didn't clock shit. At some point, the party became maybe fifty or sixty kids. Spilled into the porch. Anyway, Mikey and our other buddy, North, they were passing joints around, half hanging out of a window. When the cops showed up—there were five of them, bored and looking to make a stink—North shoved the bag of weed into the couch."

Marlon's voice had grown an octave higher. I imagined him as a boy.

"I wasn't even smoking. Those damn cops threw me, Mikey, and Renee into the cooler. North went scot-free because he said he had asthma and his mom backed him up. Mikey was a cocky motherfucker and a Greek major. He decided to sign his name in Greek at the station and this cop nearly punched him, but his dad got there in time. Renee's parents got her out, too, and I think she felt bad because no one was going to show up for me and I was the Black kid in there for the night. She told the cops I didn't smoke any. They let me go a couple hours later but it went on my record, and Lee jokes about it sometimes. That's probably where Deedee got a scrap from and invented the rest in her head."

An ambulance screeched by us and I wondered where it was going and who it had happened to. I looked up at Marlon, feeling something akin to heartbreak in my chest.

"You had a friend called North?"

Marlon grinned. "That was his name, yeah. He was a dingbat."

I took Marlon's hand and this time he did not pull away.

"I am very sorry," I said.

I wondered if I should elaborate—it felt like I had so much to be sorry for—but he nodded and let his hand remain in mine. I felt slack with relief at his touch and wondered how Lee's brother and I had arrived at this point.

"This must change the way you feel about me?" I said.

Marlon extricated his hand and put his glasses back on. "I don't know how to change what I feel for you right at this moment. So, no."

Shame burned through me—Marlon had said the words in anger but he had been right. I had become adept at avoiding all self-examination, making assumptions about him that now sickened me. It felt like I didn't deserve his feelings for me. We sat there, bathed in the odd rainbows of Brooklyn's night lights, warm yellow from the spill of the clustered restaurants, the neon glare of the bodega's signs, police cars rushing past us, their red and blue chasing past our faces, as the green traffic lights changed.

I thought about what I had said to Joy, that nothing was ever going to be easy again. But the truth was that it was me for whom things were always going to be difficult. Somehow, in all of the events that had transpired, Joy had emerged unscathed, husband and father in tow, sister within arm's reach, the world having accepted that things had changed. Joy had slipped past the door that had slammed in my face, and I was the one who would have to reckon and reconcile, daily, with the new order we occupied.

"You're still in so much pain, Mira," said Marlon, softly, watching me. There was a shift in his tenderness, a newly guarded quality to him that wounded me to my core, despite my deserving of it.

"But I'm here. That has to mean something," I said.

After a pause, Marlon nodded. I rested my head on his shoulder.

"Can we go home?" I asked.

"Yes," said Marlon.

CHAPTER TWENTY

IN THE MORNING, I awoke to three missed calls from Ulrike and one from Gigi. I looked at the clock next to a still-sleeping Marlon. It was six thirty and immediately I felt panic; it was too early for anyone at work to call me. Something had to be wrong. I picked up Marlon's T-shirt from the floor and slipped it on. Inside the bathroom, I called Ulrike. She answered on the first ring.

"What's wrong?" I asked.

"Why are you whispering?" demanded Ulrike.

"It's early."

"Oh?"

"I don't want to wake Marlon up," I said, rolling my eyes. "Happy?"

"That does make me happy," said Ulrike with approval.

"What's wrong? You called three times."

"Good god, Mira. Haven't you looked at emails or seen *The Bookseller* yet?"

"What? No. What did I miss? Did we sell a lot of copies of the anniversary issue?"

"Oh, we will. Here, do me a favor. Open your TikTok."

"I don't have TikTok, Ulrike," I said. "Just tell me, please."

"You are in a mood this morning."

"Sorry."

"Just look at any social media and search for *The Wild Lings*. And Finley Maria."

I sat down on Marlon's toilet seat. As I typed, Ulrike chewed, presumably her breakfast of ten raw almonds and a coffee.

"You really must get the Tok," she said, between grinds of her jaw. "We've got to keep up with the times."

The internet was spotty in Marlon's bathroom but eventually, the page opened. I stared at my phone. "What in god's name?"

"And that's just a fraction of it," said Ulrike, with relish.

On my screen, thousands of people liked and tweeted and spiraled over the way the excerpt from *The Wild Lings* had made them feel. As I scrolled, I felt my heart quicken in my chest, my feet suddenly cold against Marlon's bathroom tiles.

"Two days after the story was online, some book influencer said that Ginger was the Asian heroine that a generation had been holding their breaths for," said Ulrike. "And here is my favorite; on Instagram, from a freelance critic who writes for the *Times* and *Globe*: 'the most original portrait of whitewashing, in the guise of a carbonated romp, conceived in modern times.' Six thousand–something people retweeted that in a matter of hours and last night, the whole thing exploded all over the internet. #WhoIsFinleyMaria is the number one hashtag on all the handles. The second"—here, Ulrike took a triumphant pause—"is #JanusMagazine. Every board member has rung or texted me this morning. We are more *relevant* than ever."

I had never heard ecstasy radiate from Ulrike's voice before. "Ulrike," I said. "I'm worried."

"Why?" She sounded astounded. "This is your win. We're going to tell the story forever, about how you found it buried in your mail."

"But I've *told you*—" I felt my voice rise and tried to lower it. "I told you I think it's Jack."

There was silence on the other end.

Ulrike sighed. "Mira, this is the best thing that's happened to *Janus*, and your career—all our careers, in a long time. We've been beloved by our niche but struggled to place ourselves in the zeitgeist. This thing, this phenomenon, whatever it is, has squarely done that job for us. This morning alone, more twenty-somethings have purchased subscriptions to our little magazine than ever before in its history. They may be discounted trials that will be canceled in under a month but they are something. You did that and we did that. And whatever your suspicions, we went in, eyes wide open. So my strong advice is, outside of owning and celebrating the story of how we discovered this writer, no other details should be discussed publicly or privately outside this call. Whoever this is, it's a good thing for them and for us. We knew what we were getting into," Helen emphasized.

Not like this, I thought, but I did not say it.

"*The Bookseller* reported that the author received both offers of representation and publication simultaneously this morning. For the fifteen minutes that Finley is King, may we be participants in some of her shine. I must go darling, but see you"—she paused and I knew Ulrike was looking impatiently at her father's gold-banded Cartier watch that she had worn every day of the time I had known her—"very soon."

WHEN I EMERGED from the bathroom, Marlon was sitting upright in his bed, shirtless, with his glasses on, drinking from a mug and reading the paper.

"You're up," I said. "Sorry, I took your shirt."

"Looks better on you. I made coffee," he said, pointing at a second mug that stood on the dresser.

After we had returned to his place the night before, neither of us had said much. We had brushed our teeth and climbed into bed and we had not had sex, but he had held me until we were both asleep. I let the coffee warm my palms as I carried it back to bed and climbed in next to him.

"It's delicious," I said.

"Brand called Overlook," said Marlon, without looking up from the paper. "The one you liked so much, the first time you came over. We just started carrying it in the bar."

I drank in silence. "Are we okay?" I asked, at last.

Marlon looked up from his paper and took off his glasses. "I think so. But it's going to take a little time. To process."

I nodded.

"I heard you on the phone," said Marlon, looking at me.

I looked away. "It was Ulrike."

Marlon sighed. "I didn't mean it to sound like that. You're perfectly entitled to take a phone call wherever you like in the apartment. You've just never made one in the bathroom before. And I guess I'm a little on edge about secrecy."

"I didn't want to wake you," I said. "I heard you get up several times in the night."

"I couldn't sleep so I was looking at my phone," said Marlon. "Listen, I have one more thing to say about last night."

I nodded again, fearful.

"I do believe in an individual's privacy, even within close relationships. You can't really have the room to breathe and have agency without it. But there's a crucial difference between that and secrecy that causes harm to the other person or to the relationship. That, to me, is unacceptable." Marlon took a breath. "Please just trust me with the truth. I promise to try to understand it, whatever it is. And if I have a hard time, you can help with that. But this"—Marlon touched my cheek—"won't work unless we're honest with each other."

"Okay."

"Feeling like I didn't belong as a kid has made me prickly about feeling on the outside as an adult," said Marlon, with what I could see was an effort. "I felt like an outsider, when you told me what was really going on at dinner. Like I didn't matter. I'm sorry I got so wild about it. I give you my word that you can tell me anything."

"You had every right to be furious," I said.

Marlon leaned toward me and kissed me, the paper rustling between us. I kissed him back, hard.

"Let's turn the page, okay?" he said, his breath mixing with mine, as we came apart.

"Okay," I said.

We went back to our reading. Under the duvet, his leg touched mine and we settled into the intimacy of the morning.

"It was Ulrike with good news," I said, after a few minutes. "The phone call in the bathroom."

"Oh?" Marlon looked up again.

I nodded. "A story I discovered—an excerpt from an unpublished novel actually—made it into the magazine. And Ulrike called to say that it went viral. The internet went bananas for it. Apparently, the author has agents and publishers lining up."

"Mira, that's fantastic," said Marlon, turning away to set his coffee cup down. Turning back, he hugged me. "Congratulations," he said, holding me tighter than usual. "That's wonderful. The author must be incredibly grateful." His happiness filled the bedroom.

"This is a big deal," he said. "You're happy, right?" He looked at me with curiosity.

"Yes." I tried to make sense of my feelings. "I mean, of course. It's great for us and the author."

"But?" Marlon propped himself against the pillows, focusing his full attention on me.

"It's always interesting also, to think about what captures people's imaginations. Multiplies that quickly." I took in an involuntary breath.

Marlon nodded at me, slowly. "I know exactly what you mean." He looked at his ceiling. "The word *viral* comes from the Latin word *virus*, which translates to 'liquid venom.'"

"Yes," I said. "Most things that can have that effect are usually part of some instant gratification response, a quick orgasm for your emotions. You get off, quickly, cheaply."

Marlon laughed. "I read a *Smithsonian* article about the emotions that went viral the most. Their conclusion was that joy moved faster than sadness or disgust, but nothing was speedier than rage. You have to get people ecstatic or fuming. I can imagine someone reading that, stirring, preparing a formula, in a lab."

I thought of Joy moving quicker through life than me, a quick pierce under my rib. I shook my head, dispelling her. "But sometimes, as in this case, the material is very good," I said. "And the writer's instinct taps that emotional vein, but with some sort of original truth. It gets you to that giant gulp of recognition at a visceral level, when you feel both seen and heard. The same reasons we fall in love. Something about *The Wild Lings* has made people feel that way." I exhaled and slid down the pillows, lying flat on my back. "Sometimes you go through life thinking you're the only person who could feel a certain way, and then it turns out, the world gets it, harder and faster than you might think."

Marlon looked at me, amused. "You love this book. I've never seen you this worked up."

He put an arm, heavy, around my waist. I yielded, curling into him.

"Sometimes the virus can turn to poison, eating itself, in the form of trolls," said Marlon. "Are you worried for your author?"

"No. I think the author might be good at a defense, if it came to that."

"Really?" He raised a good-humored eyebrow.

"Yes." I drew back and faced him. "There's more. In the spirit of honesty. Like you said."

Marlon leaned on his side, against the headboard of the bed. Still holding my waist, he regarded me.

"The writer—Finley Maria—is anonymous," I said. "It's a pen name and it was sent to me at work, with just an email address."

"You don't know who it is?"

I shook my head. "But I have a strong hunch. I believe it's Jack."

Marlon's eyes flickered as he angled his neck to his right, then left, as if stretching out a knot. After a beat, he removed his hand from my skin and sat up. He picked his mug back up and drank from it.

"I'm sorry," I said, quickly, sitting up. "I know it's too soon, after last night. But I wanted to be honest."

"What makes you think it's him?" he said, his eyes narrowed in disbelief. "It could be anyone, right?"

"It's him," I said, with the certainty I felt. "I know him. I know the way he thinks."

Marlon pushed the duvet aside as he swung his legs off the bed. He stood and looked out of his bedroom window, the sun soft on his face, his skin almost copper in the sunlight. "You two have so much history," he said softly, to the sugar maple outside, its branches swaying in the morning air.

"And now you know it all," I said, still sitting on his bed.

"I thought he was a lawyer."

"In college, he wrote articles for the school magazine. And short stories. Said he had dreams of writing a novel someday. And his brother, Sam, is a novelist."

It felt as if, once again, there was an ocean between Marlon and myself, even though he was only a few feet from me.

"Why would he send it to you?" he asked, turning to me with genuine curiosity. "He seems okay. Even happy in his life. He could have sent it to his brother."

"I don't know. It was right after I got back from London, before we reconnected. He wanted a bridge to me, is my guess. He said the magazine was the only way to have any access to me. Maybe he did it for Joy."

"You think he did it to have some sort of connection to you," said Marlon, even softer this time, turning back to the tree. When I said nothing, he paused, shifting his weight from one foot to the next. "Has he ever hinted to you that it might be him?"

"No," I said. "But I think he knew that I would know. There are things in the book that feel like he's talking to me."

"What's it about?" he asked, without looking at me.

"A love story, of sorts. And about a Chinese family who have successfully assimilated into their very white neighborhood. It's incredibly sharp and ultimately as much a story about who gets to be an insider. The protagonist is their daughter, Ginger Chan."

"Wouldn't it be more likely it was someone Asian who wrote it?"

I shook my head. "It's as much about the white man she falls in love with, as it is her. I promise you, it's him. I know the authority with which he writes, his voice."

"It makes you think, who has the permission to write stories like that. Always seems to be a white dude."

"Jack isn't like that. The book isn't like that," I said, hotly. "The perspective isn't an appropriation in any shape or form."

"Okay."

His stillness at the window felt disconcerting, as if he had walled me off. I exhaled. "We were friends for a long time. I know him. Like you said, we have history. But that's all it is." I heard the defense and plea in my voice.

He gave me a brief nod. "I have to get to the bar," he said. "I'm going to go shower."

There was a silence where neither of us moved.

"I should get to work, too," I said.

Marlon disappeared into the bathroom. As the water began to run,

I dressed quickly. When I was ready, I leaned against the closed bathroom door.

"Bye," I said, but the shower was still running and there was no response.

After a few moments, I picked up my purse and left.

THERE WAS AN electricity in the air at the office. Ulrike had ordered champagne, and a three-tiered monster of a confection studded with chocolate and berries stood in the kitchen.

Ulrike raised a plastic flute. "To Finley Maria. May she be the gateway to a new generation that finally reads *Janus*."

Bin raised his glass. "I never thought I'd see the day, but my nineteen-year-old niece called to ask if I worked at the '*Wild Lings*' magazine. Of course, I had tell her we were actually called *Janus*, but she still thinks that's rad." He shrugged, bewildered. "I'm rad."

Despite the melancholy that seemed to never fully shake itself from my shoulders anymore, I felt a thrill. This had turned into something so unexpected, it was like a signal from the universe. To trust myself. To plunge more often into the unknown, be that as it may an abyss.

"I've sent Finley's agent a cake of the exact same size and weight as this one, with instructions to get it, while still edible, to her client, so if someone checks into a city ER with a chocolate overdose, that's our girl," said Ulrike, shining with excitement as she made eye contact with me. "To our team, who made this happen." She raised her glass again.

I raised my flute. It was ten a.m. and I did not want the alcohol, but the air of celebration had proven infectious. I felt my phone buzz in my pocket and pulled it out quickly, but it was not Marlon and I felt a stab of sadness. I walked away from the cheer, and closed the door of my office behind me.

"What's wrong?" I asked, into the phone.

"Well, hello to you, too," said Joy.

"I was in the middle of something," I said.

Despite the closed door, the raucous sounds from the kitchen floated into my office.

"Sounds like a party. Aren't you at work?" Joy, ever curious.

"We're celebrating an author's success." I felt a flash of dread as I said the words and imagined the second three-tiered cake sitting on Joy's kitchen table. "Was there something you were calling about?" I asked.

"You don't have to sound so grumpy. I can call back if you're busy."

I sighed, sitting down at my desk. "I'm not busy."

"Oh good. Listen, I've had an idea," said Joy, cheerful again.

"Yes?" I combed through my mail carefully, the phone held between my ear and shoulder, looking for anything that Finley Maria might have sent me since the excerpt had been published.

"Do you remember Anita Maupin, that musician friend of yours from Los Angeles who was out here for a few years?"

Anita, a friend of Lena's from Brown, had eventually become my friend, too. She had started out playing Joni Mitchell covers in college before she had evolved into a folk artist in her own right, writing songs that had wrung me out. Anita loved Cat Power as much as I did and when she had covered a few of Chan Marshall's songs hauntingly close to the originals, I had known every lyric. She had returned to New York seven years ago, this time as a beloved alternative musician with records of her own. Jack and I, then dancing around acknowledging our love, had gone to see her perform.

"How do you know Anita?" I asked.

"Well, Jack listens to her on Spotify sometimes," said Joy, apologetic.

"I have to go back to work, Joy."

"Wait, listen. Apparently she's singing at the Music Hall of Williamsburg in the fall. Mid September, I think."

When I said nothing, Joy continued: "Jack said he wanted to see her live. So I bought tickets."

I stood up, unwilling to hear Joy's voice any longer. "Sounds fun. Did you call to tell me your plans? I really do have to go."

"God, you're always such a burn. Can't you listen to me for a second?" Joy's voice rose in hurt.

"I'm listening."

"I think Jack will be thrilled I bought tickets, but I don't know any of her music. I could try to catch up, but we all know it won't really be my thing. I thought he'd be much happier going with someone who shares his enthusiasm. You." Her voice turned a fraction smaller. "The other night, he looked so happy, talking to you about music and stuff. Your friendship was so important to him and I get that."

Joy paused a beat.

"I'm sorry I was a child about it. I didn't want to be."

I looked at Ulrike, passing my office, her face alive with purpose. She waved to me as she entered her own office.

"I want him to be happy," said Joy. "If you're game, I think it would be good for both of you to just hang out. Like old times."

I sat back down, slowly. "What are you doing, Joy?" I asked, finally.

"It felt like a nice thing to do," said Joy, an edge of desperation in her voice. "All I want is for things to feel a little normal again. I keep trying to prove that to you."

"And the solution is for Jack and me to become best friends, all of a sudden?"

"No. But maybe you could just figure out a way to get back some of the old friendship. I feel"—Joy stumbled on the words—"I feel like I took that away from both of you. That if he was married to anyone else, the two of you might have found a way to be on friendly terms again."

At my silence, Joy entreated: "Look, I have the tickets. There were only a couple left. Just think about it. You don't have to decide immediately. Please?"

I breathed in and out. Joy with a bone was relentless. "I'll think about it," I said.

"Really? Oh, thank goodness. I for sure thought you were going to shoot me down like a sheriff in heat."

Despite myself I laughed. "Do you talk like that at your firm?"

"It's why they love me. Imagine me, on your side, opening an argument with that phrase. I always win."

You sure do, I thought, but I did not say it aloud.

"Okay cheerio, and a very good day to you. I'll see you soon," said Joy, her merriment trickling down the phone.

CHAPTER TWENTY-ONE

SUMMER CAME TO an end, but the season seemed to only get hotter. Wildfires stormed across Canada and the skies turned amber, a beautiful hellscape. It felt like the earth was gasping for breath in the same way we did when we walked around the city, overheated, the humid stickiness clinging to our bodies. My father did not venture out much, except in the early mornings when the air felt cleanest. Joy and I resumed visiting him on alternate days. For the last few weeks of summer, the wealthier set of New Yorkers either went to the Hamptons or the Amalfi coast. Those that remained kept to their apartments, the streets emptied of the city's frenetic quality. Like Finley Maria, we existed online, or in each other's devices, our sentences curated and careful. Yet the season felt filled with longing, a desire to emerge unscathed from the tyrannies of weather. I felt a perpetual ache but I could not have said for what.

Without holding a grudge against her, Marlon had left Deedee in charge of the bar for a few weeks while he visited friends in New Orleans. He had not invited me to join him, and in his absence I felt a curious wound. We had not ended anything, and yet the pall of separation hung over our polite text exchanges. If I asked how he was, he responded in single sentences.

Good. And you?

Most of the book and magazine industry had slowed for the month of August, yet *Janus* remained busy, the afterglow of *The Wild Lings* having left a sheen on us. More submissions flooded our inboxes than ever before. The weather was both muggy and smoky, and Ulrike let us work from home. I found myself cramped into my beloved apartment, able to run and stretch my limbs only in the coolness of the nights. One morning, I woke up to an email.

—Is Wild Lings the novel you were telling me about? The one you needed legal protection for? Are you the genius who discovered Finley Maria? Is this still your email or am I writing into the ether?

—Am I a genius? Ok! Wouldn't go so far as to use the word discover though. It was waiting for me in my mail and only an idiot would be blind to that book's extraordinary quality. I'm sure you heard about the bidding war? Lena's mad I didn't slip it to her first even tho there's no way that she could have bid enough to win it—7 figures!

—No way Finley stays incognito much longer. Stakes too high. A star is born and the world must know?

—Wouldn't it be nice if the world knew a little less? If we could let Finley have the privacy Finley wants?

—MG, it's you. You're Finley. I knew it.

—I am Finley. Or it's you. Are we all a little Finley inside, trying to both entice and escape the world? When I read that book, I felt like Finley knew me. That it was me, she was talking about. Is that why it's so good

—Can't wait to read. It's midnight. Why are you up so late? Are you writing the next Finley?

—I'm standing outside my building in a face mask made of mud and aloe. Smoke is pouring out of Mrs. Lechner's kitchen and the fire brigade are storming the place. Slightly less glamorous than writing a novel.

—Moving to text.

A MESSAGE POPPED up on my screen.

—You okay, MG?

—Madame L was roasting a chicken (at 12:02 AM). An unfortunate experiment with coconut oil renowned for its low smoke point. I heart NY. Firefighters muttering about how they see one of these every week.

—Have you heard this Bobby Womack studio album ? His 27th and last one. Very good.

—God, I spent the whole subway ride listening and it's insane. Missed my stop and was twenty minutes late to a meeting. Ulrike looks grumpy. How did I not know about this?

—Me too! Flew under radar. Wait, here's a remastered version.

—Can I put it in Janus' Staff picks? Maybe Bobby will go viral too. Ahahahahaha.

—I'm sitting in a meeting with my whole legal team and this post punk rocker who's apparently a wunderkind. He's wearing boxer shorts and a hoodie. We're all in suits. Trevor is ten seconds from offering to smoke a joint with him to get him to sign with us.

—Picturing the whole team running around Manhattan high. Is punk kid good?

—Really good. Not our usual scene but maybe it should be. I'll send you his demo

I OPENED MY photos app and scrolled through it, clicked on one and hit Send.

—Look at this photo of Lena and me that she sent me today! Brown!

—Angels in ripped denim jackets. Great hair. Why am I not in the picture?

—You weren't invited, skater boi. We were too cool for school. Well, Lena definitely was. She's got one kid hanging off a hip and another screaming for a snack right now. I'm at her house.

—Bet she makes it look cool. Do you need a photo of a chicken on a skateboard? No? Here it is anyway.

—I like to think that you look at this stuff in meetings where someone asks you what clause number 24-59 is and you say, "I'm sorry, I didn't catch that." Thank you for the delight. Ulrike is in a MOOD and skaterbird made me laugh out loud.

—Here's a photo of me on a skateboard sans chicken, circa age fourteen. Macho.

—BANGS. You're a baby Bieber.

AND SO IT went, that over the course of those arid weeks, something in the debris-filled air breathed new life into our old friendship, into the good-natured ribaldry with memes and songs and photos that had been our origin story. We slipped back into it so naturally that sometimes it was with a jolt that I remembered the truth, as if awaking anew to the fact.

One afternoon, on my way back from taking my father to a doctor's visit, we stopped at Zabar's for smoked fish and the late season's heirloom tomatoes so that I could make him lunch before I went back to Brooklyn. As we entered his apartment, my father looked exhausted.

"Why don't you lie down, Baba?" I said, trying not to exhibit any trace of worry. "I'll make us the sandwiches and we can eat in your room."

"All I do is spend my days in that bedroom," said my father, sulky. But he did not argue with me.

"Remember that you have to slice the tomatoes extra thick, with the serrated knife, and then salt them with Maldon," he said as he sat down on the couch and began to untie his shoes.

I rolled my eyes. "God forbid that I should bring you a thinly sliced tomato."

"A pity to waste the season's finest," said my father, disapproving. "It cost the earth a lot of water and sun to create that perfect specimen."

"Far be it from me to waste the season's finest." I went into the kitchen and dropped the tomatoes into a colander. As I began rinsing, the doorbell rang.

"I've got it," said my father from the living room.

"You should be lying down," I said, under my breath. A few minutes later, I looked up and Jack was standing at the doorway of the kitchen.

"Well, hi there," he said, his face breaking into a grin of pleasure. "I hear you're on tomato duty."

"Jack is going to get ESPN to work on my bedroom TV," called my father from the couch.

"I could have done that," I said, rolling my eyes. But I was pleased to see Jack.

He set down his laptop bag on the dining table and rolled up the cuffs of his shirt. "Please let the expert do his job, MG."

"Okay, Mister Man. Want a sandwich?" I asked. "Whitefish, tomato, mayo."

"God, yes," said Jack. "Mihir, I'm going to gift you the sports channel subscription of your dreams. Let's go."

BUT WHEN I carried in my father's tray, Jack raised a finger to his lips. ESPN played silently on the flatscreen television. It was only five, but the sun had already begun setting and my father was fast asleep, peaceful in the light of dusk. I placed the tray on his nightstand.

"I'm going to bring another plate to cover the sandwich," I said, whispering. "Want to eat on the patio?"

Jack nodded. "Glass of wine?"

"White," I said.

As I covered my father with his beloved cotton *lep* from Kolkata, for the first time since my return to New York, I felt a sense of peace. As if, finally, I had found my way back home.

OUTSIDE ON THE balcony, Jack sat in the acacia chair where my father read his morning paper. He had poured wine into glass tumblers filled with ice. I set down our plates and immediately, Jack picked his sandwich up with both hands.

"Challah, good god. I haven't eaten one of these in so long."

"Almost five years," I said.

Jack looked up, mid-chew, but I smiled. "It's a long time to go without one of my tomato sandwiches," I said.

Jack shook his head. "Too long," he said, his mouth full.

The air had finally cleared itself of ash and I breathed it in, freed of something. I was suddenly as hungry as Jack, taking an oversized bite. I drank the cold wine and the ripe tomato disintegrated in my mouth.

"God, that was good," said Jack, setting his plate down. "Do you remember when we'd picnic with Lena and Sebbie in the park, after work? You'd make these and it'd be dinner and we'd ice our wines."

I nodded. "I have a photo of you trying to squirt a bottle of mayo into your mouth."

"That's right. Just what a Kewpie fan does," said Jack, with a vehement nod.

As we laughed, Jack looked out at the sunset, the sky striped with a muddy lavender light.

"I miss them both, but especially Lena," he said, with sadness.

I nodded.

"I deserved it. Of course she cut me off. That's not what I'm saying." He looked at me.

"I know," I said. "I think she misses you, too."

I saw his chest lift and fall, sorrow filling his face.

"It's good to talk," I said. "For so long, I was so lonely, grieving by myself. The grief of us. It's really only the other person in the relationship who understands what's been lost. So often in London, it felt like if I could only talk to you, it might make things better."

Jack nodded. "Every morning, I'd wake up and think of different ways to reach you. A letter but I didn't have an address. You changed your number. You disappeared. I thought about it over and over again—if there was some way to reach you, to make contact. It felt like a part of me had died. I even thought of disguising myself, like a mailman or something, and turning up at your door, but I didn't know where it was."

In the years in London, I had only thought of Jack as blissful in his new life, and the thought that he had felt my absence felt like a sharp relief. I looked at a passing school bus on the street beneath, emptied of its charges.

"So you wrote a novel and had it sent to my office, huh?"

For a moment he looked taken aback. "Duh," he said after a pause. "Of course I did." Jack shook his head. "I wish that's what I'd done. Written the greatest thing possible and then you'd have to talk to me."

I looked away from Jack. The sky was darkening quickly, the days shortening each hour. "You can be honest with me. You know that, right?"

After a pause, he nodded. "Yeah."

We sat in a few moments of silence.

"I'm really sorry, MG," said Jack, quietly. "You know that, right?"

"Yes."

Jack drank from his glass. "If you ever want to ask me anything, or talk about what happened—"

I raised my hand. "I don't. Let's just be here, now."

Jack looked at me for a brief moment. Then, he nodded. "Okay. Can I ask you one question though?"

I looked away, unwilling. "Depends on what it is. But you can ask."

"Do you think Lena and Sebbie ate tomato sandwiches in the park without us, after you left?" Jack looked serious enough that he might be arguing a case. I laughed and he laughed with me. "Wouldn't put it past them, those rascals," I said. "Thank goodness they have three screaming children to keep them home these days."

"Three?" Jack looked astonished. "Lena had a third? Good god."

"Gino. He was born a few months after I left. He's a darling."

"Do you have a picture?" Jack looked genuinely sad. "I can't believe there's a whole child of Lena's that I haven't met."

"My phone's dying, but I'll send you one later."

"Okay." Jack stretched his legs out and leaned back. "Her twins are so beautiful. Such personalities." He smiled at the memory.

"Do you still want kids? The way you used to?"

Jack held my gaze, even as he flushed in discomfort. After a moment, he sighed. "More than ever. The older I get, the more I feel like fatherhood is a bone in my body that's missing. I feel its absence."

"Does Joy know?"

"She knows."

When Joy was ten, she had found out that pregnancy had killed her mother. That night, she had told me that she never wanted to be pregnant. At nineteen, she had wondered aloud to me if she should remove her ovaries. The year before she had met Jack, she had mulled over whether any man would want her, given her disinclination for motherhood.

"And has she told you how she feels?" I asked.

Something in Jack's throat shifted, his pain palpable between us. "She was completely against it in the beginning but I think she's softened. I mean, given what happened to her mom, I totally get why she's horrified by it. I would never push her to be pregnant. But this past year, it's felt like she might be open to surrogacy or adoption, even." He shrugged. "It gives me hope. But if she doesn't, we still have a family."

I felt a quick burn of pain flare like a forgotten sciatic. I nodded, and turned away from him, but we were in darkness now, only lamplight from the streets silhouetting us. Suddenly, as if an apparition, Millie appeared in a tornado of tail wagging and barks, erupting from the darkened living room. She raced between Jack and myself, licking one, then the other, then the first again.

"You crazy girl," said Jack, laughing as Millie leaped up onto my lap in excitement, her body quivering.

I looked up to see Joy staring at us. "What are the two of you doing here?" she asked.

Millie rested her face on my neck. "Good girl," I whispered, my arms around her.

"We were just eating a late lunch," said Jack, standing up. "I came over to fix your dad's ESPN thing and MG was making tomato sandwiches so I stayed for one."

"Or an early dinner," I said with a shrug.

"You were supposed to meet me at Bardolli's at five thirty to go grocery shopping," said Joy, her voice enraged. "I texted you."

"Oh, shit. I'm so sorry, honey. I left it on charge at the office." Jack looked upset and I stood up.

"How could you just forget?" said Joy. "I thought something had happened to you. And you're just sitting here, eating tomato sandwiches."

"Excuse me." I moved past Joy in the patio's doorway. "I have to get going and I should see if Baba's eaten his sandwich. Good girl, Millie," I said, patting her head. Millie whined and followed me into the living room as I switched on the lamps.

From behind me, I heard Jack say, his voice low and upset, "I'm sorry. But do you have to always get so mad? And you're making a scene in front of MG."

"I don't fucking care," said Joy and I could picture the rage on her face, the vein on her forehead pronounced, fury gritting itself into her jaw.

I made my way to my father's room. He was still asleep and I shut the door quietly. I spent fifteen minutes in my teenage bathroom, checking email and fixing my hair. In the cabinet sat my old hair dye, pink lipstick, a curling iron that had once burnt half a lock, purple nail polish, and dozens of lip glosses. I opened a tube of gloss and applied it. Maybe the sparkle of it would return some of the moxie I had as a teen, I thought as I inspected my lips. When there seemed to be silence outside, I stepped out of the bathroom. In the living room, through the glass walls of the balcony, I saw the shape of Jack and Joy's bodies outlined by the shadows of the night outside, the lamplight creating doubles of them on the glass. They were locked in embrace, a perfect union in that their bodies fit each other as if custom-made, a calm after the storm that seemed exactly how a couple primed for a long life together might move past acrimony and make way for greater, more important things such as their dog curled at their feet, a family of three.

CHAPTER TWENTY-TWO

FOR THE NEXT few weeks, Joy did not write her usual texts to me apart from a terse: *No mayo for Baba. Dr. Ho's rules, not mine.*

What makes you think I wouldn't know that?

You made your tomato sandwiches—accusation leaping from each word.

What makes you think his had any?

We reverted to silence. I did not miss her, but the summer had allowed me to become accustomed to her insistent presence in my life. I registered her absence at arm's length, restraining any emotion that the past few months might have given rise to. It felt necessary to confirm that she could no longer invade my conscious thought or cause me intense pain. If the price to pay was that my feelings for her were to be reduced to a throb akin to a minor swelling under my skin, I was more than willing. It was the season for silence. Marlon did not write to me either. My father tired easily on phone calls. And since the fight I had witnessed, Jack had retreated from our daily exchanges. Even Finley Maria had disappeared from my life, though the clamor around the author's identity grew. Readers had loved the book, but the idea of its author's anonymity gripped the feverish imaginations of a bored post-pandemic world in search of dopamine. The word of mouth was reminiscent of the "Cat Person" phenomenon when a singular short story had launched both book and movie deals, and preorders had gone through the roof. Speculation was rife that Finley was a popular female author dissatisfied with her original beach-read fame; or that the mystery author was a canceled A-list male actor with a vocal fondness for the notion of CRISPR babies. Other ideas swirled online—Finley was Volodymyr Zelenskyy, a stay-at-home Mormon mother of eight in Utah, a former secretary of state, Finley's literary agent who had been a former model, a Chinese socialite in Shanghai, a sixty-three-year-old British horticulturist in Bath who had published a viral Reddit post on romance novels and, in an unsurprising turn, me. Occasionally, I would find the odd amateur sleuth in my inbox or at the door of our offices trying to verify my identity, and on one occasion, my bank called to make me aware that someone had been trying to ask questions around my personal net worth in the past few months. When the television rights to *The Wild Lings* sold after a bidding frenzy to a major studio, I began to worry about Jack and if he truly understood the appetite for both adulation and destruction that a screaming spiral of fans might have, the book having been ejected outside of gentle literary ranks into an international hunger. But it did not feel like my place in the world to worry about him, and the thought took shape that there was the chance that Joy, a formidable corporate lawyer, knew the truth and was his chosen confidante.

EACH YEAR, *Janus* hosted an annual salon that was simultaneously a gathering of literary excellence and hedonistic revel. This year's party had been more anticipated than usual because of the anniversary issue, but in the wake of *The Wild Lings*, rumor began to buzz around our circles that Finley Maria might choose to reveal themselves, given that the award for debut excellence was to be presented to the author's agent. Increasingly, the atmosphere around the office felt fraught, and the question of whether we needed security at the event, given the state of affairs in America, presented itself. Could it be true that the author was not American and a recent immigrant from a war-torn region? Might it be that the author was a criminal? In this manner, we remained on edge, hurtling down the rabbit holes of the internet. But when the evening of the salon eventually rolled around, the office felt effervescent with cheer, market lights strung across the low ceilings, a romantic glow to the guests who filled our rooms. Authors, readers, editors, journalists, and the occasional television actor with a penchant for books made their way through the armchairs and low tables studded with wooden bowls of macadamia nuts or canapés on trays toward the bar area we cobbled together out of a few tables each year, or the seating space in front of the makeshift stage where Ulrike was making a passionate speech.

"This has been an extraordinary year for our magazine," said Ulrike, incandescent in a silver sheath, her body a centerpiece as she stood on the stage. "You know this because more BookTokers have been photographed in the wild with copies of *Janus* magazine than ever before. But it has been a long time coming. This team of mine that you see around you has made it their life's mission to discover some of the most original thinking around the world. And the best rainbow cookies in New York State, which is saying a lot. Say a special thank you to head fiction editor and cookie aficionado Binyamin Korn as you delight in both. Thank you all for joining us as we raise a toast to a quarter of a century of *Janus* in our collective consciousness."

As ripples of laughter murmured through the room, I felt a wave of gratitude for the tiny magazine that Ulrike had built from scratch. It felt like the magazine might be my life's work, its poems a piece of my existence that could not be taken away even when everything else might shift. From a distance, a voice carried toward me:

"Ulrike could probably have a cult if she wanted. She's got this way of liquefying a crowd."

I turned to locate Sam Smith's brassy, admiring tone, recognizing its ebullience immediately. He was a few feet from me, at the back of the room, in a corner next to the dessert bar. Next to him, Jack was helping himself to a tiny terrine of chocolate mousse, both of them in linen shirts and slacks, unmistakably brothers despite Sam's heavier, ruddier, taller frame. As I looked at them, Sam's eyes found mine. He stiffened even as Jack looked up and saw me. I lifted a hand in a wave and smiled. Both men smiled back and I watched as Sam said something under his breath to Jack. I turned back to Ulrike's speech, my heart beating faster into my chest. Ulrike had moved on to introducing the first reading—an excerpt from a gothic inheritance plot by a young Sicilian wunderkind. Even before Jack said a quiet hi, I knew that he was behind me.

I turned to them. "Hey guys. Long time no see, Sam."

"Mira, it's good to see you." Sam enveloped me against his chest, genuine in his warmth, his discomfort disappeared. It was the first time I had seen him since discovering that my relationship with Jack was over.

"What's big brother doing here?" I asked, looking at Jack.

Sam shrugged. "Best date in Manhattan, as far as I'm concerned." A second later, he looked at me, stricken.

I laughed. "Sounds about right."

Sam touched my shoulder. "Is your dad doing okay?"

"He's better," I said. "It's weird to watch your parents get older."

Jack and Sam nodded, their heads bobbing in the same way.

"Our hippie of a mom was recently told she couldn't smoke her beloved American Spirits any longer," said Sam. "The Appalachian mountains are thrilled to not have rings of her smoke settling around them hourly, but she's flattened."

"Poor Mary-Lou," I said over the raucous applause for Ulrike's speech.

"Poor Mary-Lou has taken it upon herself to substitute smoking with a desire to play the trumpet," said Jack.

"It's a right nightmare for the mountain people," said Sam, shaking his head. "Never has Asheville and the Blue Ridge been witness to a greater absence of musical talent."

"You should call her sometime. She misses you," said Jack as I laughed.

Sam nodded. "You're family, Mira."

I felt something swell and make its way into my throat. I could not find the words and instead nodded. Ulrike descended upon us in a sweep of silk and rapture.

"Darling boy," she said to Sam, her eyes mellowed with real affection.

"You are magnificent, Ulrike," said Sam, meaning it, as they embraced. Something felt private to them and Jack and I looked away at the same time.

"Do you want to get a drink?" I asked Jack.

"Sure," said Jack, grateful.

Ulrike gave him a brief, dismissive nod. "Jack," she said.

As Jack and I made our way toward the bar, I put a hand on his shoulder. "She doesn't mean to be rude," I said.

"I would excommunicate me if I was your friend." Jack stood at the bar, a sadness in his eyes.

"You are my friend," I said. I felt a quick jolt of shock flit through my stomach as I said the words, recognizing them to be true.

Jack nodded with emotion. "Yeah."

A hush fell over the room as the Sicilian writer read from her book. The prose was startling and compared the physical experience of inheritance with the brutality and endorphins of an ice-cold, naked plunge into a British country river. Our guests listened mesmerized, while Jack ordered two glasses of wine, so softly that the bartender had to strain to hear him. I looked back at Ulrike and Sam, at ease in each other's presence as their heads bent toward one other, almost a photograph in their stillness.

"I don't think I ever realized they had made such a transition into friendship," I said to Jack, as he handed me my wine glass.

"Sam had an Ulrike-shaped hole in his life, after they broke up," said Jack.

I moved closer, to hear him better. The room clapped for the Sicilian author, who bowed, her cheeks reddened with pleasure and rouge.

"I think they both found it easier to be friends than to not have the other in their life." Jack looked at me.

I felt something uncurl within me. The crowd milled around us as people refilled drinks and made exclamations of delight. A jazz band began to set up in the corner.

"The band's really good," I said into Jack's ear. "Subway buskers who Gigi found by accident and fell in love with. They're called Sweet Tooth Tunes."

As the crowd swelled, we were jostled a few times, our drinks on the precipice of spilling. Jack put a palm on the small of my back and beckoned me toward the large window behind the nonfiction editorial assistant's desk. We made our way toward it and sat on the ledge, the gusts of the late-evening air settling its coolness against my warm skin, the tiny corner a refuge from the many dapper bodies that filled the party.

I sighed in contentment. "It's really the mid-party move—finding an open window."

Jack chuckled. "Remember the time we went to that weird electronica concert and got stuck climbing out of the window and then they got really really good?"

"My ankle still rolls a little when I run too long, because of it." I laughed at Jack's horror. "It was worth it."

The band began to play a smoky rendition of Carmen McRae's version of "Take Five." I felt the music move through me, loosening the clench of my spine.

"They are good," murmured Jack.

I nodded. "They're going to play background through the awards and then there'll be dancing."

"Ulrike, the high priestess of galas," said Jack.

As the band finished and introduced themselves, Jack turned to me, as if gathering courage to say something.

"What?" I frowned.

"Speaking of music, are we on for Anita's concert?" asked Jack.

I laughed. "God, I thought you were going to tell me something awful."

"Like what?" The cleft between his eyes deepened. "I can't think of anything awful I would want to say to you."

"Well, this is a great improvement from our history," I said, straight-faced.

I regretted the words immediately, as Jack's body slowed. Then, he laughed. "I've missed how funny you are, MG."

The wine made me feel a little giddy. "I'd love to see Anita. We should go."

"This is great," said Jack, his eyebrows high in delight. "When Joy suggested it, I wasn't sure if you were already going with Lena and Sebbie, or"—he paused—"wanted me to come."

"It'll be fun." I paused, and took a sip of my drink. "I just haven't heard from Joy since that night we ate sandwiches on the veranda. I didn't know if we were still going."

Jack paused for a moment, taking in the band. "You heard us fighting," he said.

I felt grateful for the music, which seemed too full of life to allow me my usual retreat. I nodded, feeling an odd sympathy for Jack.

"I'm sorry you had to hear that," he said. "Lately, things—they've been difficult."

I said nothing and Jack spoke again. "She seems angry, constantly. On edge, in a way that feels new. I can't tell if it's work or something else."

"The 'something else' being me." I heard the flatness in my voice, my anger at Joy bubbling beneath my ribs. Here she was again, her emotions all of our labor, but I did not say it aloud.

"She desperately wants you and me to be friends and she really, really wants you and her to go back to what you had, but somewhere in the middle of that road, she's at a loss as to how to make it all work," said Jack. "She's trying her best. We all are."

There was a defeat in Jack's voice as he leaned against the side of the window.

"You loved me once," I said. "Now you love her. I left the scene but now I'm back and the reality of us being sisters isn't something she necessarily thought through before jumping in. Doesn't Joy have to suck it up just a little?"

Jack winced at the hardness in my voice. "It was me, too. You know that."

"Yes, but you don't demand things from me incessantly, the way Joy does. She wants instant redemption. Pour hot water into a cup and there you have it, sisters again," I said, willing my bitterness to recede.

Jack nodded, tiredly. "Family is the most important thing to her. You're her family. She's in a hurry."

I watched as Ulrike gave Sam a quick kiss on the cheek and made her way back to the front of the room. The sweetness of the linden trees below the building floated up toward us, unfurling their perfume as it combined with the chatter and cigarette smoke out on the patio.

"Can't you get through to her that these things take time?" But even as I said the words, I knew that Joy was a force to be reckoned with when in pursuit of something, especially something she loved.

"I think, when you came back, she discovered you newly, in a way," said Jack. "You're her sister, but you're also the woman I loved." Jack looked up at me, with suffering. "I still love you, MG. It's different but you know that I do."

I looked away. "Yes."

"She can't understand how I could have loved you in that way once, and love her now. She's filled with some sort of strange anger at me and it's killing us."

For a moment, I felt incapable of speech, dread settling into my stomach at the impossibility of what we were all up against.

"Do you remember when I broke up with Leon?" I said.

"University man," said Jack.

"Remember when you described what discovering a soulmate might feel like?"

"You laughed at me. As per usual." Jack tried to smile at me.

"I thought you were my soulmate, even though I didn't believe in the idea. I told Joy that. That it felt like I wanted to go to the ends of the earth with you. That we had found some sort of higher purpose in life by being together."

Jack let his head sink back on the window as I looked away from him, having said aloud the things he had never heard from me before, all of my regret balling up like a fist in my mouth.

"She's got all of that sitting in her head, as she thinks of you as her life's partner," I said. "It's a lot to ask of your marriage, the baggage that the three of us have." I could not help feeling deep sorrow for his visible anguish and willed myself not to touch him. "Just give it time," I said. "It's all we can do."

Jack exhaled as he nodded. "Okay," he said, softly.

Ulrike took to the stage again, triumphant, a two-headed gold statuette of a Greek muse in her hand—the *Janus* logo fashioned into an award. The band performed a ditty of a drumroll, as Ulrike, statuette-esque herself, held a microphone in one hand and the award in the other.

"Janus, god of all beginnings," I said, softly.

"I wonder if Finley will show," said Jack.

I leaned back against my side of the window, to be able to watch him as Ulrike spoke.

"Each year, *Janus* recognizes exceptional ability in fiction, poetry, and nonfiction that we have had the honor of publishing in our magazine," said Ulrike. "The first of those awards is always for a writer who is a first of their kind, whose work blazes a new trail through the vast woods of literature. The winner of our twenty-fifth debut fiction prize is a surprise to nobody. But here are the ways in which it is a first for us."

Jack straightened as Ulrike spoke, his face impassive.

"A novel that is as broad in appeal as refined in literary craft, that with astonishing skill poses as a romp, then catapults a reader into crucial interrogations around race and culture and the ways in which we exist in the world today, even as it reaches for every emotion we have with an unforgettable heroine, a love affair of the ages and two families that will remain in our imaginations, long after we end the last chapter." Ulrike stopped for a breath. "It gives me nothing but great pride to present the 2023 *Janus* award for debut fiction to Finley Maria, for *The Wild Lings*."

Jack sat next to me, his breathing calm and certain. He turned to me, a glimmer in his eyes, and squeezed my fingers. "Congratulations, MG. Your guy made it."

I held his hand for a moment longer, staring at him.

"What's wrong?" asked Jack.

I let go and shook my head. "Just a big night for all of us."

"Yeah," said Jack, turning back, toward the stage. "And quite the night for Ulrike."

Ulrike was presenting the award to Finley Maria's agent of a few months, a long-limbed, striking transgender woman in a white silk suit, with a dramatic curtain of auburn hair down to her waist.

"There's a chance it's her, right?" Jack whispered in my ear as I smiled. "Come on, wouldn't that be great?" he said.

"That's a great commission, if so," I whispered back. "I'm thirsty. Going to get a glass of water from the bar. The next award is Lifetime Achievement."

Jack feigned an exaggerated yawn.

"Don't let him hear you say that." I pointed in the virtuoso's direction, a few feet from us. "Do you want something?"

He shook his head as I stood up, my ankle cramping from having swung from the ledge for too long, the memory of the night it had injured itself eight years ago giving me a private flash of happiness. As

I straightened and looked over the sea of applauding guests, trying to decide the shortest path to the bar area, I met Marlon's gaze. He stood at the entrance of the office, framed by the door, the fluorescent light of the hallway behind him, dressed all in black, a bomber jacket and jeans, his motorcycle helmet under one arm as he watched me.

BY THE TIME I reached the doorway, stepping over stalwarts and the year's crop of fresh-faced scions alike, and trying to escape the beginnings of conversations, it had taken me a full ten minutes to reach him. Marlon smiled at me.

"I almost thought you weren't going to come and say hi," he said.

"Hi," I said. I felt a frisson float through me as I remembered his hands on my breasts, the sudden image startling. "How long—have you been here?"

"About half an hour. I didn't want to come in, in the middle of the speech."

I turned to shut the door of the party behind me, the sound of Ulrike's voice announcing the next award ringing out across the room. As it closed, I saw Jack rise to look at us from the window where we had been sitting, his hands in his pockets.

Marlon took my hand, his fingers intertwined with mine, an immediate electricity between us.

"It's really nice to see you," he said.

"I didn't think you would come," I said, disoriented, the harsh tube light blaring into my senses after the dim room inside.

"It's your big night. I wanted to come," said Marlon, looking at me with his transparent, easy face. "You asked me to, remember?"

I took a step back from him, my fingers falling to my side, trying to center my flailing mind.

"I guess I don't understand," I said, my voice lowered. "You've barely spoken to me these past weeks."

Marlon nodded. "I had a couple of things going on. A bit of a tear.

I'll tell you about it." He took a deep breath. "But I also needed time to think. I didn't necessarily know that but I did. I'm sorry if I came across as distant."

I swallowed. "Think about what?"

"You," said Marlon, with candor. "You make me laugh and you capture my imagination in a way that no one ever has. It's a bad idea; you're on the rebound, and the situation"—Marlon looked at the helmet in his hands—"well, it's bonkers, wouldn't you agree?"

His smile was so gentle that I could have burst into tears, standing there, at the receiving end of a compassion that I had not known I needed.

"Yes," I said.

"But here's the thing. I go to a few places, do some travel. End up in New Orleans." Marlon took a step closer to me. "And I walk around and think of things and I deal with business and the bar and I laugh with friends and take a boat I rent out onto the water and feed a gator called Eleanor marshmallows every once in a while—"

Marlon stopped and took my face in his hands. I let him, wondering what might come to pass if Jack came out in that instant.

"And the whole time, it's you," he said. "It's you in my head, in my sleep, in the phone as I try not to dial, try not to write. It's you in the way I listen to the world, to the music you've taught me to pay attention to, in the way I look at people with more grace. I find myself trying to see the whole thing the way you do, in the way you see beauty even in the dirty dishes stacked in my sink, in the shapes and shadows they create. You've made me more at peace, M, with my own dark places. Less angry at the world. To quote an iconic Australian poet, Mira, can't get you out of my head."

I closed my eyes, touching his palm spread across my cheek, certain that I might be drowned unless I stood very still. The air felt too cold suddenly, and I shivered. As I let go of Marlon's hand, I felt his fingers drop away from my cheeks. When I reopened my eyes, he had a resigned look in his eyes.

He smiled at me, rueful. "Are you still in love with him, then?"

"I don't know," I said, rooted to the ground, afraid of something breaking if I moved.

Inside the party, applause rang out again, a girl's laugh floating in our direction. Thick clouds had gathered in the navy night sky in the window a few feet from us, the smell of rain in the air, the world continuing to move to its known rhythms even as the truth reared its monstrous head and I felt a soft click in my head, the understanding that what lay buried could be contained for only so long.

"Marlon," I whispered, trying not to cry.

He nodded and took my hand again, his skin softened by sadness. He kissed my fingers and looked at me, tender.

"Goodbye, Mira."

He took in a long breath as if it was the last time he would look at me, and stepped back, still holding his helmet in both hands. As he began to walk down the hallway, I waited in case he turned back around, but instead, he disappeared down the stairs, until I could no longer hear the bounce of his sneakers against the concrete.

CHAPTER TWENTY-THREE

FINALLY, THE LEAVES turned. More bursts of rain had cooled the city and the season's new crispness nipped at my skin when I ran in the early mornings. Any chance walk during the day yielded fleeting sun slipping between rust-gold foliage. It felt like an elation had been dispersed into the air by some sort of generous government, New Yorkers visibly happier than the rest of the year, the city taking in the rebirth of the season with a renewed attention to its charms. The second Sunday of fall, Jack and I were going to see Anita Maupin perform at the Music Hall of Williamsburg. It had nearly been canceled—Anita had been afflicted by one of the many strains of COVID that came with any drop in temperature and the rest of her tour had been in question. When I texted to ask how she was and to say that Jack and I would go to her show if it took place, Anita had asked no questions as was her way. Instead she had written back: "I better get better then, ain't that right?" When the evening of the show arrived, I realized I had been holding my breath for something to transpire that would come in the way of this new season for Jack and I, where we, too, might start afresh. Lena and Sebastian were upstate picking some kind of fall fruit with their children and had been unable to join us; I was relieved for it. It would mean that the concert would belong to just Jack and myself. My only desire was to leave the past permanently behind.

THE MUSIC HALL of Williamsburg was a former mayonnaise plant turned alternative-rock club, in Brooklyn between Fifth and Sixth streets, a few feet from the East River. Jack and I had planned to meet at the outdoor market by the water, where you could carry out plates of German food and eat it on benches as you watched egrets, herons, and American oystercatchers fly low and pluck prey from the blue-gray surface. I found Jack on our favorite of the wrought-iron benches, the one with an unobstructed view of both water and skyline, with a slim plaque on its spine that said FOR LOU, FOREVER. Jack was holding two hot dogs, two plastic glasses of beer next to him. It was about five in the evening, suddenly cold enough for his light sweater, the sun bouncing off the water, bright enough for both of us to wear sunglasses.

"Perfect timing," said Jack as I sat next to him, the drinks between us on the bench. "I was getting exhausted holding these. Beef on poppyseed, mustard, and curry ketchup." He held out one of the hot dogs.

"You remembered," I said.

"You made a convert out of me—I get the exact same thing now. Cheers," he said as we touched the tips of our frankfurters, our tradition of eons past. "It's the curry in the ketchup that really makes it sing," said Jack, chewing with pleasure.

I nodded. "And the roll. This is a good roll. That was a good dog."

Jack looked up at my empty plate as I licked my fingers. He laughed.

"You were hungry," he said.

"Starving."

The beer was bittersweet and tasted faintly of orange rind, cold and wonderful as it slid down my throat.

"I told Anita we were coming," I said. "She said to come say hi, after the show."

"God, what's it been, a zillion years?" Jack drank his beer, leaning back, the sunlight reflecting the river off his dark glasses.

"Nine," I said. "The last time we saw her, it was you, me, Frankie, Lena, Sebbie. But she and I kept in touch."

Jack nodded, the lines around his eyes deepening at the memory. It felt surreal to realize that he had aged in the last decade, that so much time had gone by.

"Remember that song she wrote that sounded like a love song, but it was about the Bosnian war?"

I laughed. "'Ballad of Annihilation.'"

"It was the sweetest little melody but filled with so much fury. With her brothers crooning backup."

"I think she's retired the brothers and found herself a few pro crooners now," I said. It dawned on me that Anita's rise into alternative pop stardom had coincided with the entirety of my history with Jack. "I wonder if she'll do any of her covers," I said, instead.

"She had a great one of 'Seasons.' The Future Islands song."

I nodded, happily. There was no one that I was more animated about music with than Jack. "Listening to her in college was a bit of a fever dream," I said. "She had a voice that you heard and wondered—how come that girl isn't famous? And she's a poet, with her lyrics."

Jack chuckled, the sound warm, the chatter of the riverside behind us. "You were right, MG. You're always truffle hunting. Just ask a literary star of recent times."

I sighed. "Hardly. Finley is one truffle I'd love to get my hands on."

Jack looked out at the water. "God, New York is beautiful sometimes. I mean, it's the worst, but sometimes you almost think it's worth it."

"The best of times, the worst of times," I said, my knees tucked under me, my palm propping my head as I looked at Jack.

He looked back at me. "What do you think you'd say to Finley Maria, if you finally met them?"

I lifted my shoulders in surprise. "Where would I meet them?"

A heron came closer, perusing the ground for poppyseeds and breadcrumbs that I had brushed off my skirt.

"That bird is too trusting of humanity," said Jack, watching it. "Makes me nervous. Look, it's right by your foot."

I turned. The heron scuttled off, peaceful. "What's wrong with trusting humanity? You don't think the bird's got one up on us?"

Jack smiled. "What if Finley came up to you at a restaurant and said, 'Hi, it's me'?"

"What would I be eating?" I looked out, over the water.

"Chanterelles in a cream sauce on toast, or something ridiculous like that," said Jack, laughing. "Crab on a cracker."

I nodded in approval. "I want to be doing something that tells Finley it's really me, Mira. Finley's been in hiding for so long—he deserves the real thing."

"What would you say?" asked Jack, amused.

"'What took you so long?'" I said, turning back to Jack. "I'd tell Finley I've been waiting this whole time."

For a beat, we looked at each other. As if remembering a detail, Jack looked at the water, then at the slim leather-strapped watch that his mother had bought him in high school.

"Almost six," he said. "Anita will be starting soon. We should get going."

I nodded, feeling a sense of victory, an emboldening flooding white-hot into my veins. If Jack wanted to keep pretending, he could. But I had had enough secrets for a lifetime.

WE WERE EARLY enough that we could buy drinks and park ourselves at the front of the stage, but in the space of the next fifteen minutes, a crowd in their late twenties and thirties, dressed in a mix of thrift and the wildly expensive, had taken over the concert hall. The building had a sloping ceiling legendarily responsible for its sophisticated acoustics. An old-fashioned red velvet curtain separated the stage from its audience.

“Thank goodness we got here before the hordes descended,” said Jack, with a grin. “Or you’d have had to climb on my shoulders, like the Springsteen concert.”

“I’ve got muscle now,” I said, flexing a bicep in his direction. “You couldn’t take me for more than four minutes.”

“Oh yeah?”

“Yeah,” I said back at him, beating my chest with my fists.

Jack laughed, looking around. “Man, look at this crowd. Good for Anita.”

“Looks like a thousand but I know the license only allows for six fifty because there are only four exits,” I said.

I knew this because Joy had told me but I did not want to bring her up that night.

Jack looked at me, amused. “Since when are you worried about dying?”

“This is America, baby,” I said. “You gotta know the facts.” I jerked my head at the EXIT sign right next to us. “Stick with me and I’ll make sure you get out okay.”

Jack laughed. “Can we try not to die tonight?”

“If we do, it’ll be the best last night of our lives.” I smiled up at him.

Jack put an arm around me and pulled me to him for a brief moment. As he let me go, he shook his head. “I can’t believe we made it,” he said.

I nodded, happiness filling me up in a way that frightened me, the blue and rose lighting shimmering off our bodies. Anita came onstage, ethereal in white, a heron bathed in blue light. The raucous crowd cheered.

“Everyone having a good time tonight?” she asked, her smile knowing, as she strummed the first chords of a beloved song on an acoustic guitar.

We screamed, ecstatic.

SONG AFTER SUBLIME song came and went. It felt like Jack and I had traveled backward through time, and arrived at a station that housed our past lives as friends, so natural was the way in which we knew the other's punchlines, or how to occupy a few feet of space together, dancing, breathing, perspiring as if nothing had ever come between the original version of ourselves. When Anita announced her last song, I felt as if something precious was ending. And then we clapped and begged and she came back, a second and a third time, and in the end it felt like something had changed for good. At one point, Jack and I held hands as if it were the most organic extension of our newfound kinship and the thought struck me, unwilling, that if Joy was with us, she would have completed the circle.

AFTERWARD, WE TRIED to stand in line to see Anita, but her legion of fans had swelled to the point where it looked like an hour's wait. Instead we bought her record and went out into the street.

"God, I'd do anything for a cigarette," I said, shivering in the night air. Despite its full sleeves, my thin shirt was no match for the sudden drop in the city's temperature.

"Really?" Jack looked at me with surprise.

"I haven't smoked in a million years." I shrugged. "I mean, it's heinous."

Jack laughed. "Let's find a cigarette and share it. We'll be heinous together."

He approached a slight young woman in towering boots. Within seconds, she had extracted a cigarette from a slim metal case and handed it to him. There was an invitation in her eyes as she lit the cigarette for him, his head bent over her lighter as she examined the way in which his hair, the color of wheat, fell over his forehead. As he thanked her, Jack ran a hand through his hair and nodded in my direction. The woman and I exchanged a look, a disappointment in hers as she turned back to her group. Jack returned to me, and offered me the cigarette suspended between his index and middle fingers. "Still got it," he said.

"You've always been so good at making friends," I said, sly.

Jack raised an eyebrow at me. "This is the thanks I get?"

I laughed, feeling the shock of the nicotine in my extremities. "It feels like I'm either more alive than I have been in a very long time, or it's instantly killing me a little." I exhaled a curl of smoke with visceral pleasure.

"A bit of both," said Jack, laughing.

"Should we wait for Anita? Or go get a drink?"

Jack looked at his watch and frowned.

"Unless you're tired or have to get home." I took another inhale of the cigarette.

"It's only nine thirty," said Jack, decisive. He took the cigarette from me and inhaled, closing his eyes. "I kinda want to go grab a drink though instead of waiting. Is that okay? Will Anita miss us? Did you want her to sign your record?"

I shook my head. "She'll probably be thrilled having two less people to exchange germs with."

"There's a dive bar nearby and a sports bar another couple blocks away, but I feel like a great cocktail, you know?" Jack finished the cigarette, his head angled to his right side as he did when he was considering something. "God, that was good," he said as he stubbed out the butt and tossed it into the green mesh trash can behind him. He looked up at me and paused. "We could walk to Lee's," he said.

I had not told Jack about breaking up with Marlon, but there was a question in his eyes. "Filthy Diamond is about the same distance," I said quickly. "Nearer to home for me—I could pick up a jacket really quick and we could get the best Old Fashioneds in Brooklyn?"

Jack looked up at the sky. "God bless Brooklyn and all the bounty that comes with it. I've missed you so, favorite borough."

"You're a regular poet," I said laughing.

THE AIR FELT icy as we went deeper into Brooklyn, my eyes watering with the shift in temperature. Jack, too, had his arms crossed in front of him, warding away the wind, his cheeks bright with cold.

"Wasn't it summer, only ten minutes ago?" he asked. "Are we going straight into the fifties from the eighties now?" He looked at me in concern. "MG, I can hear your teeth chattering. I wish I had a jacket for you."

"I'm an idiot. I always forget. In London, it felt like I was either soaked or a cube of ice, all the time."

We were walking at a brisk clip. Jack put an arm around me. "Here, let me warm you up a little. You'll get your sinuses into overdrive as usual at this rate."

Jack, my former lover. Jack, my concerned brother-in-law. Jack, my friend. Jack, who loved us both.

As we reached my apartment building, I fumbled for my keys in my purse. I found them and looked up. Jack was watching me. "What?" I asked.

"What was London like?" he asked, hesitant.

I thought for a second, the keys cold against my fingers, but the chill had left me suddenly. "Lonelier than I've ever been in my life," I said.

Jack nodded, pained. "You used to love London so much. I feel like I ruined that, too."

I shook my head. "I still love London. It was really kind to me." I turned to slide the key into the front door's lock. "But I'm home now."

UPSTAIRS, JACK ENTERED my apartment, tentative as he stood in the doorway. He had been silent on the walk up to my floor.

"Make yourself at home," I said as I walked to my bedroom. "Sorry it's a mess."

In the bathroom, as I looked at myself in the mirror, it struck me that I could have never imagined a world in which Jack and I might go to a concert again, where afterward he might stand in my new living room, in my new life, and yet be the old Jack. It had never occurred to me that ordinary things might be possible for us again, and even in their fragile newness, it was as if a miracle had been performed. When I emerged, cardigan in hand, Jack was sitting on the birchwood seat upholstered with red velvet that had come with the little piano he had bought me.

"You kept it," he said, his palm on the maple surface.

"Yes."

Jack's pain had not yet dissolved. "You play so beautifully."

For a moment we were both silent.

"I mean, I wasn't going to throw it out into the street."

He smiled. "It's weird being here," he said. "In your apartment. It's what our apartment used to look like."

I looked at my desk, papers and books overflowing across it, my throw pillows scattered across couch and carpet, my coffee mug still on the windowsill where I read in the mornings. "Bet you have a lot less clean-up now," I said.

Jack did not respond and I picked up the mug and put it in the sink, self conscious.

"Aren't you going to be cold?" I asked. "Isn't that sweater too thin?"

"It's definitely too thin for this weird weather. Also I just looked at Filthy Diamond on the map and it said it was closed."

"Oh no. I forgot they close early on Sundays. Damn it."

Jack looked at his watch. "Is it too late to go a little further? Maybe Elsie's is open late?"

"They shut after the pandemic," I said. "You haven't been to Brooklyn much in the last few years, have you?"

Jack shook his head. "There were too many memories here."

It felt as if the exuberance of the evening had been lost to us.

"Here," I said, throwing my cardigan on the couch. "Why don't I just make us half-decent Old Fashioneds? It's freezing outside anyway."

Jack brightened. "That sounds great."

I nodded. "Records are under the desk."

Jack rose from the piano seat, awkward. "There's just one thing, MG."

"What?" I asked. I felt impatient to go back to the happiness of the concert.

"You make terrible cocktails. Can I make them instead? Your proportions are always off."

I picked up the nearest cushion and threw it at his head. Jack ducked, catching it.

"Fine," I said. "Make the damn drinks yourself."

"I promise you'll thank me."

"SHOULD WE LISTEN to Anita's record?" I asked as Jack rattled around my kitchen. "There's a bejeweled antelope on the cover."

"Antelope pop, my favorite," said Jack. "Do you have bitters?"

Marlon had left bitters on my bar cart. "Yes," I said, picking up the tiny glass bottle.

I walked into the kitchen and put it on the counter. Jack, entirely at ease as if he had made a thousand things in my kitchen before, was slicing an orange. He had poured pistachios into a small bowl.

"Excellent," he said, unscrewing the bitters and squeezing the dropper into my metal shaker. As he shook the drink, Anita's voice drifted to us.

"She didn't play this tonight," said Jack. "It's called 'Thank You, High Town,' right?"

"Yeah. I wanted her to. It's one of my favorites. From her early albums. It's a bonus re-recording."

Jack poured the liquid with careful precision into two glasses, over ice and orange slices. He held one up to me. "That'll be twenty-two dollars. Finest Old Fashioned in New York state. Made with a slightly wrinkled orange, but still the finest."

"A vintage orange, if you will," I said, taking a sip. "Oh god, this is delicious. I'd forgotten how good you were."

"I told you," said Jack, meaningfully. I threw a pistachio at him.

We carried our drinks over to the couch and made ourselves comfortable. We talked about our parents and the Spice Girls aging, what it meant to see a musician live, what it meant to be mid-career (time enough to switch, and the sense that time might be of the essence, said Jack), the television shows we had not watched together, whether the mayor might seek reelection, if London's coffee was any better (yes), the fact that I might re-adopt the bangs I had had in college (yes, said Jack, with enthusiasm), should bars serve communal peanuts (disgusting in the current era, we agreed), should he try to represent more independent musicians (yes, I exclaimed), how much Millie had grown (an extra foot in length since I'd left, said Jack), the televised fascination with serial killers and artificial intelligence, the sociopathic tendencies of good politicians. Everything but Joy and their life together. And so it went, that we rediscovered what had been crucial for us, the fierce debate and silly conversation that had defined our closeness, that had been lost to us even in the last year of our romantic relationship. It felt like the stuff of magic, a spell that had finally lifted, Jack and Mira awoken from a thousand years of sleep, all poisoned fruit in the rearview, so easily did we inhabit the selves we had been at the start. Jack got up to flip the record we had forgotten about and looked at his watch. Anita began to sing again, her tremulous, fragile song making its way into my body. Jack leaned forward to refill his glass with the expensive Italian red wine I had opened after our cocktails. It was a bottle I had been saving, a parting gift from my colleagues in London that I could not have imagined sharing with the man in front of me.

"I should go soon," said Jack, as he made himself comfortable amongst my pillows.

Despite the alcohol, I felt clear-headed, lighter of heart and mind than I had been in years. "Do you have to work tomorrow?"

"It's a Monday. I can roll in at eleven." Jack looked at me with real emotion. "Can we do it again?"

I nodded. "I've missed this," I said.

Jack looked away. "When you left, it felt like a part of me went missing. Tonight has been the first time in a long time that I've really felt fully myself again."

In the lamplight, Jack seemed younger, his skater self at Brown, the years between the past and present slipping between us.

"I think we were meant to be in each other's lives," I said.

"It's one of the things I've thought about, so much. In all of this ridiculous mess I've made, in this pile-up of hurt and crazy life events, the one thing that's stayed true is that we can't escape each other. We're so many things to each other. Even Millie. She'll be ours forever."

Something took hold of me as he said the words, rising like a crescendo in my ears, warm blood rushing through my body. Jack touched my hand.

"MG, we're always going to have each other."

Anita, silent between songs, rose up, choral as I stilled, the first bars of the piano music taking hold of me. Jack's eyes flickered as he registered the familiar melody and I saw him take in a sharp, quick breath.

"Jack," I said.

I shook my head, very slightly, his gaze on my face as I met his eyes. I saw his pupils dilate in the light as I turned my hand upward, catching his fingers that had rested on my skin moments ago. I pulled, very slightly, and shifted my weight forward, until my face was next to his, the sweetness of his breath familiar.

"Out of here," I whispered.

The lyric was the last thing I would say before I kissed him, Jack unmoving for a second, then yielding to me as his hands gripped my waist, our tongues liquid, our bodies urgent as we moved quicker, his hands sliding under my sweater, his eyes closed as I pulled off his with force, ripping the neck of the soft cashmere, both of us uncaring as he unhooked my bra, his palms on my shoulder blades, and finally, we were skin to skin. It felt like we were breathing each other in, our mouths never leaving the other as we descended to the carpet, my hands furious, unbuckling his trousers, years of need and longing coming to a head. We were naked, the carpet rough beneath us, Jack's lips on my breasts as I wrapped myself around him, trying desperately to eliminate every last bit of distance between us. As the song ended, Jack's eyes flickered open. He raised his mouth to mine, dazed even as we kissed, again. In the silence between one song and the next, I felt Jack still. I willed Anita to start singing again, but the seconds passed, interminable.

"Mira, no," Jack whispered. "Oh god. No."

He looked at me, on the floor beneath him, the way he had once known me. Jack's eyes widened.

"Oh god," he said again. "What have I done?"

Jack rose, looking around, bewildered, as if unfathoming of how we might have lost our clothes and minds so quickly. He reached for his sweater and slipped it over his head, breathing hard. Slowly, he picked up my sweater and handed it to me, our eyes meeting.

"I'm so sorry," he whispered.

I did not know if he was apologizing to Joy or me.

"I should go," he said finally, standing.

I rose from the floor and stood, slipping my arms into my sweater. "If you want to go, you should go. But I'm not going to run from what I feel. This felt right, you know that."

Jack looked away as Anita continued to croon softly to us. Eventually he picked up his keys and wallet and touched my hand briefly before he left. It occurred to me that I had betrayed Joy irrevocably but the idea felt ludicrous in the face of what she had done to me and the enormity of the longing I felt for Jack. But he had left and all that remained was the emptiness inside of me and the silence of my apartment.

PART SIX

CHAPTER TWENTY-FOUR

SUN ON OUR faces, Joy and I screaming in delight as we played catch, pool water suspended in our ears, confetti and glitter and lip balm, ice-cream cakes from Morgenstern's made with towering layers of mint chip and chocolate sponge, wedges melting through our fingers, her swinging off my limbs, our bangs and bobs matching despite the years between us, I, her older sister who could do no wrong, a child myself, worshipped and mirrored by my beloved infant sister.

A WEEK AFTER Anita's concert, it was Gino's third birthday. Lena had hired a face painter. I had made the ice-cream cake that Joy and I had loved as children and asked Lena if I might invite Joy. Shocked, she had asked me why.

"Joy is my sister," I said.

It was better to face up to it, than run from it. We were bound by blood and our father, and as it turned out, we were not all that different. Lena had looked at me for a long moment, eyes narrowed, and I worried that she knew me too well, that she might see past a sudden pivot. But above all, Lena wanted me to be happy, and she therefore had agreed.

At the party, her eyes shining with happiness, Joy had held Gino for the first time. Lena had my permission to forgive her and we watched Gino take immediately to my sister. Lena's mother-in-law, Rosa, a delicate-boned, blunt woman from whom Sebastian had inherited his humor and green eyes, had flown in from Mexico City for the occasion. Because Joy had been in law school during Lena's wedding, Rosa had never met her and was one of the few people in our lives who had little idea of our complex histories as sisters.

Joy and Gino returned from the face painter's cluttered table, hand in hand, to where Lena, Rosa, and I were sitting on lawn chairs, drinking Rosa's signature hibiscus margaritas.

"It feels like he's taller every week," I said to Lena and Rosa.

"Mama, I'm a lion," said Gino, his face painted in gold and orange, the remnants of drying ice cream on his arms and chin. "Joy is a butterfly." Gino pointed at Joy's silver-blue face.

"You're both beautiful," said Lena. "What should Mama and Mira Mashi be?"

Gino looked at Joy, conspiratorial. He whispered in her ear. Joy giggled.

She looked at us, shaking her head. "It's not good news, I'm afraid."

"RATS," shouted Gino, bursting into peals of laughter as he collapsed on the grass, his little body flipping backward into a somersault.

"Careful, you'll hurt yourself," I said, rising to catch him, Rosa and Lena on their feet at once as well. "The ground's too hard for that."

"Joy taught me how—look," said Gino, screaming with happiness as he somersaulted again.

Joy looked at us, apologetic, as she sat on the grass, next to my feet. "It's true, I did. But I taught him the safe way, using your butt, like our dad taught Didi and me."

"Now you, Mira Mashi and Mama and Tita," said Gino as he climbed on my lap.

Lena looked at me. "I guess we're going to be somersaulting rats today. Sweetie, why don't you try the bouncy house? Look, your sisters are having so much fun."

Gino looked at the clown leaping into the air. As the clown jumped, his rainbow wig dislodged and flew into the air. Immediately, Alice and Mirabel, accompanied by their ecstatic gang of friends, pounced on the wig, everything bouncing up and down, the hapless clown on his knees, in pursuit of wig and balance. Gino giggled but he made no motion to get down from my lap.

"Silly clown," he said.

"That poor clown doesn't stand a chance," said Rosa, sipping her margarita.

"You don't think the clown, bouncy house, and a face painter was a bit of an overkill?" I teased Lena.

"Bouncy house was fifty bucks for the day, the clown is Matteo, a former intern trying to make some extra cash, and well, Mirabel begged for the face paint," said Lena, picking up her phone from the rickety folding table that held our drinks. "What on earth are we going to spend our double incomes on if not to bring joy to these little monsters? I mean, we could travel but where's the fun in that?"

I rolled my eyes, laughing as Lena stood up.

"I'll text Sebbie to rescue Matteo," said Lena. "The pizzas have to be done by now."

"I remember how good Seb's pizzas are," said Joy, her eyes greedy.

"Sebastian is such a good father," said Rosa with pride.

Lena rolled her eyes at me. "Dad gets all the credit for a weekend brunch while mom slaves over a hot stove weekday nights after work. Thankless, I tell you."

"Oh please, you're the queen of takeout," I said, laughing. "The best mom on the planet, and the queen of takeout."

"Lena is a wonderful mother," said Rosa, nodding with approval.

"It's the primary teacher in you, Rosa," said Lena, kissing her mother-in-law's cheek. "Handing out gold stars all the time."

"And I like the takeout in Brooklyn," said Rosa, cocking her head.

Sebastian strode out. Within seconds, bouncer-esque, he had separated the screaming children from the beleaguered clown. Handing the clown back his wig, Sebastian clapped his hands. "Pizzas in the kitchen. Plain, sausage, and Hawaiian. Go get it."

Gino slid down my lap in one swift motion.

"PIZZA," he yelled to Joy, tugging at her wrist, her slim gold wedding band glinting in the sun.

I wondered if it had Jack's name inscribed underneath. Gino wiggled his waist to the music.

"He likes James Brown," I said.

"He's such a musical niño," said Rosa. "Always tapping away to something. Maybe there's music in his blood."

"Maybe he'll learn the piano," I said, with longing.

Lena looked up from her phone.

"Maybe you'll teach him," she said. "Save me a bunch of cash on lessons."

I nodded, with happiness. It was a cold, bright afternoon, and we were in sweaters, luxuriating in the best of both seasons. Being in Lena's house around the children as sunlight rippled through the white cedar that spread its branches over their backyard made it feel like Joy and I might find ways to coexist again.

"Joy, come with me," implored Gino again.

"I'm not hungry, Gin-Gin," she said to Gino. "But you eat a slice for me and then we'll go jump in the bouncy house together."

"JUMP," said Gino, leaping in the air, in the direction of the kitchen.

"Gin-Gin," said Lena, impressed. "Should we just rechristen him that?"

"You're so good with him," said Rosa to Joy. "Do you have children of your own?"

Joy shook her head, without missing a beat. "I love kids. They make me feel like a kid myself, and it's the only time I'm like that. But I have zero desire to have my own. I'm happy to be around other people's kids."

Rosa nodded. "More and more young people these days. In my time, it was a scandal to stop at two. What about you, Mira? Do you feel the same way as your sister?"

Lena looked at me, stricken. For a moment, my mind went blank.

"Rosa, you really can't— " Lena began to say.

I felt certainty swell in my chest. "Yes," I said. "I'd like to be a mother. I think I'd make a good one."

"I think you'd make a great mom," said Joy. "I'll be their beloved Mashi who spoils them to death and takes them to expensive concerts. Greatest aunty in the world."

AS WE STOOD next to the front door and put on our coats, I asked Joy why Jack had not come with her since I had asked Lena to invite them both. She looked away.

"He's always working on the weekends these days," she said. "It's as if the music business might come to a stop if he closed his laptop for a few hours."

I nodded, feeling winded. "Probably a big case."

Joy held my wrist, her fingers warm against my skin for a brief moment. "Didi, thanks for inviting me. I know Lena had to have asked you first. It was so incredible to just be somewhere with you, and have it be normal. And Gino's the sweetest baby. I can't believe they have three kids now. I mean, Lena used to give me rides on the back of her motorbike."

Something lurched in my throat. "It was a nice party," I said.

"Can I ask you something?" said Joy, curious. She went on, without waiting for me to say yes.

"When Rosa said, maybe there's music in Gino's blood—what did she mean? Like, she would know, right, if there was?"

"Gino's adopted," I said. "They were trying for a third, but this seemed easier."

"I figured he was adopted," said Joy. "Something about the way Rosa said that. I love that they went that route."

"It's an option, you know," I said. "Adoption." I tied the belt of my coat into a knot against my stomach. "If you ever change your mind."

"Oh." She laughed in surprise. "I'm not going to. You know that. There's nothing I want less in this lifetime."

I LEFT LENA'S house at six thirty when it was already pitch dark, then walked for what felt like hours, all the way to Manhattan, to a chrome and glass behemoth in the center of Park Avenue, with an art gallery and a juice shop on the ground level. Jack had once joked to me that the art and juice were strategic placements by his company so employees might feel as if they had rejuvenated on breaks, when in truth they were underslept and overworked. In the years we had spent together, Jack had always left work at five or six, coming home to me quickly, his core centered as firmly around life as it was around work. I stood downstairs in the marble lobby, jaundiced in the yellow light that streamed from overhead chandeliers. I sat down on a black leather couch that swallowed me whole and pulled out my phone.

"I'm downstairs."

Five minutes later, Jack was standing in front of me, disbelieving. I rose from the couch.

"Good surprise?" I asked.

Jack shook his head. "Mira, I can't— "

"We need to talk," I said, pulling the belt of my coat tighter around me. "There are things I need to say to you."

Jack looked away, dismayed.

"Please, Jack," I said, and he must have heard the break of my voice because he nodded.

"I'll get my coat," he said.

WE STOOD IN the entrance of the juice bar, uncertain, the harsh white halogens beating down on the canary yellow formica countertops. A teenager in denim leg warmers, a minidress, and an apron that said *Juice Yo Life* smiled encouragingly at us.

"You sure you don't want to go to a bar instead?" asked Jack. "There's one around the corner, on Thirty-third."

"No." I didn't want dimly lit corners or music or my own rogue emotions to cloud any clarity that I might be capable of. I pointed at a booth, the furthest from the blenders. "Let's just talk here."

Jack bought us two bottles of water and slid into the booth, opposite me.

"How are you?" I asked.

Jack looked at the yellow tabletop between us. "Out of my mind. With worry. Fear."

"Fear of what?"

"Everything. Losing Joy. Losing you. My family. Losing my mind. How could I have thought this would work?"

Jack looked untethered as he put his head in his hands. I unscrewed one of the bottles and handed it to him. He drank as if he had been parched, finishing the water.

"I'm sorry I haven't called," he said. "I just—I need to figure this out."

I took a breath, willing myself all that I had tried to muster in the last week. "Do you remember the morning after Thanksgiving, that year when you made the potatoes and Baba made the French toast and it was just the three of us?"

Jack said nothing but he did not need to.

"That morning on the balcony, in the snow, I summoned more courage than I've ever needed, because I had to tell you the truth," I said. "To ask you to leave Frankie. To remind you of what we had become to each other."

Jack looked at me, his eyes softening, whether in the memory or in compassion for me I did not know.

"I am here, once again somehow, in the same position of being unable to get away from it," I said. "No matter how far I go, I can't seem to get away from you, and the fact that I love you." I took another breath. "Jack, I'm asking you to reconsider. I think you and I—we can get through this. I think we're meant to be together in this life."

Jack stared at me, disbelief coloring his usual air of reassurance. "I'm—married. To Joy."

"Yes. And yet there's no way you can deny what happened last week. What we still share." I felt my face heat, the tips of my ears on fire. "You knew what was happening that night. You felt it."

"Yes," said Jack, looking at his knuckles on the table, his eyes shifting from me before I could see if there was shame in them.

The blender whirred to life behind us and I turned to make sure it was not Joy who had ordered a juice. When Jack looked up again, there was a bewilderment in his eyes.

"Joy is my wife, Mira. She's the person I chose to spend my life with."

"So what?" I heard the hard ring of anger in my voice as I wrapped my fingers around the bottled water, the plastic crackling in my grip. "That's easy enough to change. It was easy enough the first time round."

Jack flinched, as if I had hurt him physically. I struggled to contain my desire to weep.

"She doesn't want children," I said. "She never has and never will. I promise you that."

Tears sprang to Jack's eyes. "Is this your idea of revenge?"

I laughed, the sound brittle and alien, as if my body had left me for a different person. "There's not enough revenge in the world." The anger left me in a swift drain, leaving only sorrow behind. I shook my head. "I'm okay with asking back what was mine. What she took from me."

"MG." Jack shook his head, blurred by grief. "You don't understand."

"So tell me. What don't I understand? What's wrong with it

having been a mistake? With trying to course correct? What if you just thought about it as if it weren't impossible? How is this fair?" I felt my bitterness return, my voice raised. "At the very least, I've earned the right to have you entertain the idea."

For a while, Jack was silent. In his stillness, I felt his solidity return, the weather of his emotions a map I knew by heart.

"I'm so sorry I hurt you. It is the thing that I hate the most about myself."

Jack said the words slowly, without meeting my gaze. As he lifted his head, I felt an ache spread through me.

"You're right that we didn't have any closure, and that is my fault," said Jack. "I couldn't bring myself to acknowledge it. That there was all of this love left between us..." Jack turned his palms upward on the yellow Formica, as if holding the love we had lost, his ring a mirror of Joy's. "When we were together as a couple, it was the kind of beautiful, poetic love I had not had as a child. My parents were too wild for that and when I met you, it felt like I'd found a new way to live in the world. And you became my best friend."

Tears clumped on the outer edges of Jack's eyelashes, rolling thick and slow down his flushed cheeks. "When I met Joy, it was the reverse of comfort. It was a tempest, the opposite of everything I had thought I wanted in a partner. And yet"—Jack searched for the words, choked by his own emotion (I imagined Love, tall and pale, her eyes identical to mine, burning into him, strangling him)—"it was everything I had ever needed. She's impossible and flies off the handle and nothing is ever easy, but she's the love of my life. I am wildly happy around her. The word wife came to me within months of meeting her." *How many months?* "I imagine her hurt and want to destroy the world. I had never experienced real loneliness before Joy came into my life and when she's gone, I feel it. Without her, I am"—Jack shook his head—"lesser. I can't live without her. Nothing matters as much as Joy."

He said the words as if it were a plea to me. We sat there, our skins made ugly in the terrible lighting, every blemish on display, raw with what we had done to each other, the blender periodically reminding us that we had lives outside of the booth to confront.

"I should have believed you," I said finally. "When you first told me about the way she made you feel."

"I am so very sorry, MG," said Jack, his tears coming fast and loose. "You can't know how sorry."

It occurred to me that I had never seen him truly cry before, the machismo of his Southern childhood not fully left behind. I looked outside, at the passersby outside the glass windows of the juice bar, who did not know the deck of cards that I had been dealt. An older man dressed in dark clothes, Orthodox Jewish, with warm eyes, smiled at me as he hurried past. I wondered if he saw my grief, and who I had become.

Jack wiped his face and blew his nose with tissues from the holder on the table. "I have to tell her. There's no marriage, if I don't. I'll tell her tonight."

"You don't have to," I said.

Jack shook his head, certain. "I do. There can't be secrets. It'll kill us."

"The only thing I can assure you is that my sister will leave you if you tell her."

I said the words with the flatness I felt, the inevitability of what I now knew to be true. In the end, Joy had won.

Jack inhaled, deeply. "I'm going to go home to her. I'm going to tell her. If she leaves me, maybe it'll mean that the two of you will find your way back to each other."

We sat in silence for a few moments. Behind us, the teen was listening to a Korean pop song on her phone that felt faintly familiar.

"There are easier ways to try your hand at sainthood," I said.

THAT NIGHT I dreamt of a navy ocean swirling beneath my airplane window, my reflection hazy in the warm glass. Asleep, I wondered what the mysterious water might feel like, cold and dark against my skin, whether I might disappear into its depths or be soothed by its motions. And then I was swimming beneath its surface, peaceful, almost happy until I looked at my pale arms, my palms turned upward to a brilliant sky, gold ring clear against water, and I realized that I was not Mira and that my body had turned into Joy.

IN THE MORNING, I awoke exhausted as the sun came up, imagining a world in which he had told Joy that her sister had tried to wrest him back. Wicked half-sisters, the stuff of lore. The sun grew in potency, filtering through the thin curtains onto my face. I wondered if she would ask every detail, how far we had gone, where in the house it had happened, the look on my face as I had torn the rounded collar of his sweater. Or maybe she would run away from her pain as I once had, because as time went by, it was impossible to distinguish us from each other. When the phone finally rang, it was not Joy. My father's voice, as tired as mine, floated through to the surface.

"I don't understand what is wrong with the both of you," he said.

I said nothing, my father's shame too much to bear.

"It feels like we've been colonized by this white man," said my father. "That the two of you just go around in circles, trying to win him."

"You love Jack," I said.

"I love you more," he said. "But Mira, I just can't see you both do this to each other."

"Who told you?"

"Joy."

I nodded, alone in my bedroom. Of course she had wanted to tell him first, to even the score. "You taught us to take matters into our own hands and go after what we needed to in America," I said. "Here we are now."

I tried to lighten my tone, but there was no hiding my pain from my father.

"It feels like I've failed," he said. "Somewhere in trying to tell you both to be fearless, I've led you terribly astray. Nothing has turned out the way I thought it would in this country."

My father had never vocalized what we knew to be true—that his American dream had disappointed him deeply over time, with every act of racism toward his beard and brown skin that he had not been able to shrug off. In the same manner, he had never yelled at us, or held us by an errant arm or shoulder, to shake his children and ask them what the matter was with them or why they behaved in this manner and that a punishment was to ensue. The thought struck me that it would be a relief if he did raise his voice and ask me why I had hurt my only sister in this way and things might have been easier if he had said the same to Joy. Instead, his sorrow filtered through the phone line and felt as if it might crumble the remains of my heart.

"You haven't failed," I said. "We're sisters. We'll figure it out. We always have."

My father's breath rose and fell, frailer than I remembered, his voice too soft. "You've both gone too far," he said. "I don't know how you find your way back again."

CHAPTER TWENTY-FIVE

I CALLED IN sick at work. I made coffee and listened to the sound of the rain outside, reading a beloved volume of Jane Hirshfield's poems. I was waiting for Joy. It felt necessary to soothe myself, such that when we were forced into a reckoning (by her, always by her), I might have a reserve of wellbeing. "Ninety percent of my cells, they have discovered / are not my own person." In discovering that her body was largely made up of protein, Hirshfield reflected that the true composition of humans were the people in our lives. It felt like a visceral, shocking truth. A protein traveled through bodies, folding and unfolding to destroy and rebuild, Joy and I traveling through each other's spines, vital to what we needed to exist, microbiomes unable to separate from our single ecosystem even if it might save us. At seven in the evening, when it felt impossible to wait any longer, the cream walls expanding and contracting in on my mind, I put on running shoes and went out into the cold air. When I returned, Joy had used the spare key I had given my father. Arms crossed, she sat at my kitchen table waiting for me.

"FOR GOD'S SAKE," I said even though I had known she would come eventually.

I focused on Joy, her fury alive and trembling in the brightness of the kitchen, her curls wild and piled on her head, my eyes adjusting from the dim hallway outside. She had turned on every light she had found, as if to see anew and fully this wretched sister of hers. I threw my keys on the counter, closed the door behind me, and sat on the small footstool by the door, untying my shoes.

"You spent the whole day with me," said Joy, venom in her words. "On Sunday. You acted as if nothing had happened. What kind of person are you?"

I stood up and walked to my couch, from where I could face the kitchen table and yet put ten feet between the two of us. I sat down and brought a cushion against my chest, crossing my own arms over it, armored by what I held too tightly.

"You spent months falling in love with my boyfriend who I lived with, who I thought every day might want marriage and a lifetime with me. The whole time, you pretended to be a sister. I'm not sure you have a leg to stand on to question my *morality*." I said the words with the indifference that I knew would pierce Joy.

"You can get off your fucking high horse now," said Joy, enraged, her cheeks beginning to bloom with blood as she stood and pushed the chair away from her body. The chair scuttled to the wall, too light for Joy's force. We both heard the crack in its structure as it rebounded and fell on the floor, a sudden still life that returned to me the image of our father, collapsed at the lake.

"That'll be six hundred dollars," I said, from between my teeth. "It was a gift from Ulrike, mid-century and made of walnut, but you wouldn't know that."

I felt lightheaded, so powerful was my urge to hurt my sister.

"You think you're so much better than me, you always have," said Joy, breathing hard, an unfamiliar sneer in her voice. "You swan around, talking about your out-of-print books and obscure music that I haven't heard or read, and think that makes you a better human than me. You think you're so kind and thoughtful to Baba when really, you have no idea what he really needs or the medication or diet that could save his life. You're irresponsible and a flake." Joy stopped to take in air. "And as for *morality*, you're no better than me; you're much worse because you're so deluded about the person you have turned into. You can't ever point a finger at me again."

Joy took a step in my direction, her body a threat. "You came back to do this. To sleep with my husband." She spat the words out, an indictment that we were sisters born of the same gutter.

"Shut up," I said, contempt pouring out of me. "You act like a child, who takes the shiny thing she wants, with no regard for the lives you destroy. It's what makes you good at your corrupt career, the job you do just to be more loved by Baba and trump me. It's the same way you got yourself a husband. It's in your blood to grab at things and think that you own them." I clutched the pillow tighter and stood up. "How long before you discard Jack for a new plaything? What are you waiting for? Me to get a new boyfriend that you can go after?"

"You fucking bitch," said Joy, charging toward me.

Before I realized her body's purpose, she had grabbed my shoulders and thrown me down, back onto the sofa, as if we were in a fighting ring.

"Are you crazy?" I said between breaths, panting and winded, my body flattened as she loomed over me, breathing hard.

"You've never loved me, not in the way real sisters do." She said the words through her teeth, accusing and convinced of them, I could see.

"You stupid *child*," I said, incensed. "You have no idea what I've sacrificed, so that you could have your little life."

Joy's hold on my body went slack as she registered my words in confusion, but I was too far gone in my bitterness. I reached up and grabbed a fistful of the curls that cascaded from her topknot. Joy screamed, spiraling downward, on top of me on the couch, both of us buried in its plush depths. Muscle memory kicked in from when as a child, already inching taller than me, Joy would mock-wrestle me to the floor and I would have to learn the angles and tricks of her body such that I could flip her over or pin an arm down without hurting her.

In this manner, we had come to know each other's bodies blindfolded. But Joy was bigger now, her bones less familiar.

"I'm the one he chose," Joy said, as I held her elbow behind her hip, this time twisting to cause harm as we landed hard on my rug, not soft enough, I thought with sharp regret, to cushion the lengths to which sisters might go. "You and Jack were unhappy," said Joy, a bone digging into my screaming body, its sharpness leaving me breathless. "You fought all the time." She shouted the words, her eyes glittering. "It was me that made you both happy around each other."

"So you took him from me?" I bellowed in her face, yanking on the belt of her dress until she yelped in pain, the fabric stabbing the soft flesh of her waist. I yanked again and this time it came away from the dress's loop, the material screeching as it tore. "The same way you always needed to take Baba's attention away from me?"

Joy screamed as I felt my knee rise into her stomach. She brought her entire body down on mine on the floor, an excruciating tangle, both of us writhing.

"I never meant to," she said, heaving the words out. "You always thought I did it on purpose, but I didn't. You just think the worst of me, all the time. That's not how a sister is supposed to be."

Our breaths slowed in the aftermath of her words.

"He chose me," whispered Joy, a plea this time, her tears falling on my face as I was reminded of Jack, begging me to believe that my sister was the love of his life.

Something flickered and dimmed in Joy's eyes as she softened against my body, giving in. I pushed her away, both of us limp. For a few moments, we lay motionless on the carpet, staring at the ancient brownstone's peeling fresco ceiling. Joy sat up on the rug slowly and curved her spine against the couch, as she held her knees to her chest, rocking herself back and forth, ten-year-old Joy unable to make sense of the world. I tried to stand, suddenly dizzy, and held onto the arm of the couch for support, my head throbbing.

"Didi, you're bleeding," I heard Joy say as I tasted blood against my teeth, my lip sour in its middle, where the skin had split.

I sat on the couch with a thud. Joy raised herself to her feet and went to my fridge. She cracked open an ice cube from its tray in the freezer and brought it back to me. As she sat on the couch next to me, Joy held the cube to my lip.

"I'm sorry," said Joy, with grief. A long breath shuddered out of her. "I really am. I've always been so sorry."

I closed my eyes, reminded of Jack again, the ice so cold against my lip that it hurt. In the end, both of them would have made me a thousand apologies. It was supposed to count for something. Joy pulled the cube away. I opened my eyes.

"I think the last time someone gave me a fat lip, Baba went and gave the parent hell," I said. "Third grade, Chase Katz's mom. In our case, Baba would have to write himself a scathing email, threatening legal action."

Joy did not laugh as she pressed the ice to my skin again, the taste of blood metallic in my mouth. Our faces and bodies were inches from each other as she administered to me.

"Your cheek is scratched," I said, tracing the lines that ran from her left temple to her eyes, microscopic spots of blood rising through her skin to form a constellation.

I took the cube she held against my lip and pressed it against her temple, traces of my blood on her skin. Joy closed her eyes, a defeat in her limbs.

"Baba's so sad, all the time," she said.

The ice cube disintegrated and dripped against my wrist and her jawline. I wiped her jaw with the forearm of my sweatshirt.

"We're his kids, but we're also two humans," I said. "He has to see that." I disentangled myself from Joy's body and got up from the sofa. "You need something on that scratch. Stay there. I'll get the first aid kit."

"I also broke a nail," I heard Joy call, her voice small and upset.

From my bathroom cabinet, I pulled out the plastic box of bandages and ointments that Marlon had left behind after attending to my wounds, the first night that I had brought him home. I went back to where Joy was now lying on the couch and sat next to her head.

"Hold still," I said, as I applied an antibiotic cream to her temple, then cheek, then arm, a reenactment of our youth.

"Things will never be the same between us, will they?" asked Joy, her voice still that of my little sister, from when we were girls.

I tore open a Band-Aid wrapper and spread the plaster carefully against the scratch I had inflicted on her.

"I don't think so," I said. "But maybe we can try to see if we can be something new."

"Sisters, though?" said Joy, a quick fear in her eyes.

"Yes," I said.

I spread another Band-Aid over her collarbone.

"Good," said Joy, her shoulders sinking further into the couch as she closed her eyes.

She was motionless for a few moments as I worked, and for a moment I thought she might have drifted into sleep.

"I left him," I heard her say, as I applied the final bandage to her fingernail.

I let go of her wrapped finger and stroked the curls away from her forehead, but she did not open her eyes.

"I had to," said Joy.

Outside, we heard a group of people laughing, noisy and happy. It felt like Joy and I had been in the apartment for hours, a world in which time had ceased to exist.

"Are you hungry?" I asked at last.

"You always try to feed me when I'm sad," said Joy, opening her eyes. "Do you have jam?"

"Yes," I said.

"Toast," said Joy, closing her eyes again. "I haven't eaten since he told me."

I let my fingers remain where they were, on the slope of her forehead. "There's no one that he's ever loved, the way he loves you," I said. "Not even close."

I felt Joy shiver as I rose from the couch and went to the kitchen. As I turned off some of the lights that Joy had turned on and opened the fridge for bread, I noticed my phone, charging next to the toaster, glowering up at me. I slid two slices into the machine and picked up the phone.

"It's Jack," I said.

Joy opened her eyes from where she lay on the couch and turned her body sideways, to face the kitchen.

"He's called eight times," I said. "Does he know where you are?"

Joy shook her head, almost imperceptibly. "I left my phone at home. I won't talk to him. I won't." She paused and looked away. "Maybe it's you he wants."

I shook my head. "No. It's you he wants."

Joy and I looked at each other for a long moment. I turned away to unscrew the lid of the jam jar.

"Can I text him and say you're here?" I asked, over my shoulder.

"Yes, but I won't see him. It's over," said Joy as she turned back into the recesses of the sofa, lying flat as she looked at the ceiling with certainty.

She's here, I typed. *I think you should give it time.* Immediately, the phone began to vibrate in my palm.

"He's calling again," I said.

Joy said nothing, unmoving.

"I'm going to answer," I said. "I promise I won't let him come upstairs if you don't want to see him."

Joy paused for a beat and then nodded. "Can I stay here with you?" she asked.

"Yes," I said as I answered. "Hello?"

"I'm driving," said Jack, his voice desperate and faraway. "Mihir—he was furious. He called and asked me to come over. He said he wanted us to talk. And then when I got there, he was asleep in his armchair and no matter how much I shook him—I tried so many times, I swear to god—he wouldn't wake up. Eddie and I called an ambulance, and they said he had fainted. They took him to the hospital. I'm on my way there now."

IT FELT AS if we were trapped in a cruel sestina, endings and beginnings, words and times and places, recurring over and over, in and out of order but a pattern emerging that it felt urgent to pay attention to if we were to survive. My father was asleep in a room, an arm holding a pillow to his side, as if he were taking an ordinary nap. Joy and I sat side by side, in Doctor Ho's office, suffused in dread. We had been asked to step into the doctor's office, truant children of the patient's, who alongside the daily news may have been largely responsible for his decline. Joy had clutched my hand in my father's room, either looking to take or give support, her usual air of responsibility drained by the horror we both felt. In the hospital, the doctor's office was a waiting room in disguise, a generic space where one might go privately to receive news that was too much for the larger waiting room. A cherubic nurse bustled in and out in a matter of seconds, extracting an armful of masks from a closet, pausing only to smile at us, enormous dimples cleaving her face with a radiance. Sisters, she might have thought to herself. Ten minutes later, the doctor came in, harried, his white coat rumpled.

"Sorry," he said, smoothing down his dark hair, his unlined face creased in concern. "The day is full of emergencies."

And in a day full of emergencies, where did we rank? But Joy and I were mute, as we waited for him to tell us what we needed to know. He sat down, pausing to examine us.

"What happened to your faces?" Dr. Ho leaned forward, his eyes crinkled.

Joy shook her head, as if in refusal. "Please, doctor. Tell us what's wrong with him."

He pursed his lips briefly, in sympathy. "This must have been scary."

"Why would the ambulance bring him to the hospital if he only fainted?" asked Joy. "Was it his blood pressure? Or something else? Did he have another heart attack?"

The doctor shook his head. "As far as I can tell, he was reading and lost consciousness in his chair. And when he woke up, he was fine. All of his bloodwork, his scans and EKG, have come back normal. Mild arrhythmia, but that's to be expected."

"Why did he faint?" I heard the fear in my voice.

Joy reached out to cover my knuckles with her palm.

Dr. Ho nodded at me, as if in mild approval. "That's the question. We don't know and that's concerning. We do see it in patients who have recently suffered cardiac arrest, and that's why the paramedics brought him in—it's always a good idea to run every test if something like that happens. But as far as I can see, there's nothing that suggests that anything has changed."

"But you asked to speak with us," I said. I imagined my father's body, bloodstreams and organs functioning as they should, only the rogue cells of his daughters flowing through his veins, ebbing life away from him.

"Yes," said the doctor, compassion in his lean features. He paused. "Your father is well, for all practical purposes. On paper, he is a healthy man. But I have known a lot of heart patients. He's losing weight and falling more often and the fainting spell makes me concerned." Dr. Ho paused, seemingly reluctant to say the words. "I recognize the signs that can come quicker for some, especially heart patients."

"Can you just say what you mean?" Joy was fiery, abstraction not for her palate, ever.

Dr. Ho leaned back in his metal waiting room chair. "As his doctor, I've upped his medication and we'll monitor him closely. There is the possibility of the beginnings of congestive heart failure but we are following every protocol. For now, there is nothing more to be concerned over or done." He paused, to let out a sigh. "As a friend, I'm saying, make the most of the time you have with him. There may not be as much time as we want—there never is. I don't want any remaining months or years to feel wasted for your family."

"'AS A FRIEND'? He's not my friend. Is he yours?" Joy stood outside the hospital, her voice shrill, carrying through the stillness of the night.

"He's saving Baba's life. One could argue he is somewhat friendly to our cause," I said.

It had rained while we had been inside the building, the smell of wet earth and a dampness to the air.

"It doesn't give you the right to make a pronouncement like that to someone's kids," said Joy, outraged. "It's quite possibly illegal, in fact. I'm going to have Noah look into it."

"You're not going to slap Dr. Ho with a medical malpractice lawsuit," I said, touching the edge of her sandal with my sneaker. "Maybe Baba coached him to say that to us, to get us to stop fighting."

"It isn't funny, Didi," said Joy fiercely, the Band-Aid on her temple peeling at its edges, her nostrils inflamed with misery.

I looked away. The hospital's gazebo, lit by streetlamps, stretched in front of us. The idea of a world without my father felt impossible to withstand, a physical aching throbbing inside of me, between my breasts and collarbones. "But he's right," I said. "We need to make the most of the time we have. It doesn't matter how long that is."

"But it does matter," said Joy, on the verge of tears. "Baba can't just give up on his body. It sounds like that's what he's doing."

I held Joy's shoulders. "He's not going to give up. He's going to be okay. Let's just go upstairs and in the morning, we'll take him home. Maybe we can start doing Sunday lunches each week and visit him together more often. Let's just give the damn man whatever he wants, for now." Sorrow, persistent and heavy, felt as if it might never leave my body. "It's all we can do."

Joy must have heard something in my voice, because she came closer and took me in her arms.

"Are we allowed to give him lamb and chocolate?" she asked.

I tried not to cry. "Doctor Ho would call the police."

"Maybe we can sneak in a little, every now and then."

I nodded, Joy's body slack against mine.

"Can I ask you something, Didi?" Without waiting for my response, she went on. "If Baba dies, will you still want to see me?"

An owl screeched in the distance, the moon beginning to emerge in soft slices, between rain clouds. The hospital's church bells rang out three times. It would be light in a few hours.

"Yes," I said.

"Do you promise?"

"I promise, Joy."

THROUGH THE NIGHT, the waiting room of the hospital gradually filled with new faces, each wearing its own variant of urgency or the anticipation of relief. I had never been in a more heightened state, yet we became used to it and drifted in and out of uneasy sleep. At five thirty in the morning, Dr. Ho came out again and told us that he wanted to keep our father until the late afternoon, to be on the safe side. After looking in on him still asleep, Joy and I agreed to leave for a few hours, to shower and attend to our respective inboxes. We would return armed with fresh cheer for our father, we said. She was reluctant to leave him even for a short while, but we both needed air that did not belong to the hospital.

As we walked out, the sky had turned a predawn cobalt, the hospital's lamps still lit in the gazebo. On the furthest bench of the green area, between the manicured Japanese boxwood bushes near the entrance, sat Jack, the hood of his windcheater pulled over his head. It looked like he had spent the cold night outdoors. I watched as he made eye contact with Joy and half rose, but she began to walk quicker and passed him by.

"I'm going to find us a taxi," she said to me as we reached the main entrance to the hospital.

There was a question in her eyes as she turned to look at me. "Do you want to wait here?" she asked.

"Joy—" I began to say but she shook her head.

"Didi, don't. You can't be part of this. You can't be part of my marriage. Is that okay? Please?"

"Yes," I said.

Joy's strength seemed to emerge in the most unfamiliar spaces, between the cracks and fissures of cemented things.

"If you want to talk to him, I'll wait in the cab," she said.

There was a calm to her, an unfamiliar air of definition, and I realized with surprise that the feeling inside of me was respect.

"Are you sure?" I asked.

There was a wavering on Joy's face for a second.

"I don't have to," I said.

"No, it's fine." She nodded, firm. "It is."

"I won't be long."

She disappeared through the entrance, toward the taxi stand to the left of the hospital.

ON THE BENCH, Jack sat, unslept and ravaged, his face in his hands. As I approached, he looked up at me, his eyes reddened, his face pink with cold and despair as the morning light broke out over us.

"What happened to your lip?" he asked.

"My sister," I said.

Jack looked at me in disbelief.

I paused. "I think we're going to be okay. Or something that looks like it."

Jack looked away in grief. "She hates me."

I sat next to him, the iron bench icy and wet against the yoga pants I had spent the night in. "No," I said. "But she's stronger than I am. I would have taken you back immediately, but Joy wants a better love for herself. She knows she deserves it."

Jack's breath curled and dispersed in the air between us. "What can I do?" he asked, desperate.

"I don't know," I said. "You have to figure it out. You have to treat her better. She's hurt."

The gazebo smelled of the maples and ginkgos that surrounded it as they soaked in the morning dew.

"But you have a great love between the two of you. The kind that doesn't come along all that often. You have to do everything you can." I rose from the bench and picked up my phone, the only item I had remembered to bring with me.

"MG— " he began, overcome, but I stopped him, raising my palm.

"No. I have to remember this and say it clearly." I took a breath. "Loving you made me capable of a great love too, Jack. I know that now. We were never right for each other and somewhere inside, we knew that, long before Joy came along. No matter how different our values were, or how many arguments we had, I just would have never admitted it. I was too in love with the idea of us, of the great distance we might cover together with love, into old age. It was a poem in my head. I needed to be left by you to see it for what it was. And I think I needed to see Joy again to accept that." I looked away, the ground filled with wet orange leaves that framed my shoes. "Maybe you came to me to find her. You're free now. I am, too."

As I walked away from him, I waited for the old darkness to take hold of me, heavy and cloying in its grip, but instead I heard the song of the chickadees, the orchestral honking of the garbage truck as it careened by the hospital, sirens in the distance, the smell of fresh coffee and fried eggs from a breakfast truck. Joy was waiting for me at the curb, in a taxi with an elderly driver at the wheel. I wondered if he was from Prague.

As I slipped in next to her, she looked at me, her eyes soft and clear. "Ready?"

I nodded. "Let's go home."

CHAPTER TWENTY-SIX

FALL TURNED TO winter, the branches bare once more. One night, as I had known she would, with the same certainty with which she had left him, Joy returned home to Jack and Millie. As the season rose and fell, our father began to pay attention to the cardinal outside his window again. I worked and slept and ran, taking care not to slip in the snow, one day at a time, pausing often to see my family. From the ashes, it felt like we had risen, enough to laugh at dinners together and celebrate each other's successes. Joy was promoted, Jack left his firm to work for an independent label, *Janus* went back to having a niche but devoted audience, Gigi left to write elegant thrillers, my father was able to walk two miles uptown, Millie became best friends with a chihuahua at the dog park, birthdays and Sunday lunches and the new year came and went. Joy and I learned, like the seasons, to rise and fall with some grace, to swim into bad-tempered barbs and seething resentments, into the murky waters of our histories and fears and eccentricities, and stay afloat as best as we could, because the remainder of the time felt like a hard-won sweetness that we could finally taste together.

ONE FEBRUARY AFTERNOON, I asked Ulrike if I could take the rest of the day off. I did not give her a reason and I could feel her curiosity follow me as I left the office, but our friendship over the years had allowed some room for the unsaid. I walked the entirety of Brooklyn

Bridge, my eyes and nose simultaneously frozen and liquid, the wind whipping against my overcoat, an exhilaration in my veins. Tourists stood in the cold sunshine, muffled by their layers, taking photos of the skyline, the East River still blue beneath them. Soon it would turn gray and icy, a grande dame who reigned through the year, unfazed by the shifts above her. It took me two hours, my ankles too warm in my boots, to reach the front doors of Lee's Bar. For a moment, I stood still, my uncertainty in freefall, daylight already disappearing into the late afternoon. I pushed through the doors into the warm light and chatter inside, the air perfumed by beer, jazz, and some sort of soup. Behind the counter, Lee stood, tanned and tall, rounder and even happier than I remembered him, as he poured draft beer from a tap into a glass.

"Lee," I said, still breathless from the walk, overjoyed to see him.

Lee looked up, his eyes widening. "Mira? My god." He set down the glass and came around the counter.

I hugged him fiercely. "It's good to see you."

"What's it been? Five, six years?" Lee looked at me, emotional. "You look good."

"Thanks," I said. "You got married."

"I did." Lee clapped his hands together, a boyish glee to his bearded face. "Wait here."

He went back around the counter and disappeared into the back of the bar. When he emerged, it was with a petite woman with large eyes and red hair woven into two braids.

"This is Zuri," said Lee, with the air of having won a prize. "She's on the wrong football team but I love her anyway. Zuri, this is my pal, Mira. She's been comin' to the bar for years."

I shook Zuri's hand over the counter, her entire body lifting up as she reached for my fingers.

"I can't tell you what a joy it is to have Lee back and to meet you," I said. "I've never seen him happier."

"He needed the honeymoon, is what it is," said Zuri, dry as she blew Lee a kiss.

"Were you guys in Australia the whole time?" I settled into the barstool.

"Aye," said Lee. "Was good to just kick back and see family and introduce Zuri to everyone, especially my old mates from high school. We took care of some business, too. Closed the sale of my brother's bookshop and found a tenant for my dad's old house."

"Oh," I said, after a beat. "I knew Marlon had a store. Didn't know it was a bookstore."

Lee nodded. "Mighty fine little place. Hardwood floors. Wall-to-wall paperbacks. Our second cousin Randolph took it over. Gave us a good price for it, too."

"What'll you drink, Mira?" asked Zuri.

"Does Lee have you working here now?" I smiled at Zuri. "Really making the most of this marriage thing, Lee?"

"Figure I'll help keep the lights on," said Zuri with a wink.

"She's a business whiz, too," said Lee. "Manages the books like nobody's business. A martini for you, Mira?"

"Too early," I said. "Maybe a beer?"

As he poured my beer and Zuri rang up the couple next to me, I looked at Lee. "How's Marlon doing?" I asked.

From the pause that Lee took before he looked up at me, and from the way Zuri's eyes slid to him, I knew that Marlon had told Lee about us. I felt heat slink across my face as Lee set a beer in front of me.

"He's swell," said Lee. "Never been better." Lee flushed, frowning. "I didn't mean— "

"I'm happy to hear it. He's wonderful. It makes perfect sense that he's your brother."

Lee smiled in relief. "I'm glad he got to know you."

Zuri patted Lee's shoulder as she made her way to the tables in the back of the bar.

"Is he going to be here later?" I said. "I was hoping to talk to him."

"Ah, no," said Lee, regretful. "I wish he was. I'd love to see him more. He bought a bit of the bar and then got tired of it, I guess. Went off and got a different job. Likes it much better than having his brother be his boss, I bet."

Lee chuckled as he turned to a customer. I felt a heavy disappointment descend. When Lee turned back to me, I summoned the courage to ask. "Did he leave—because of me? Because I live nearby?"

"Oh god, no," said Lee, leaning forward, his elbows on the table. "He had nothing but darling things to say of you. As he should."

Zuri returned and smiled at me, a whiff of sympathy in her eyes, as she began to make a cocktail.

"Thanks Lee," I said. "I just—I didn't want to leave it the way we did."

Lee nodded, knowing. "He's always at his apartment these days, working. If you wanted to hunt him down."

I laughed. "Maybe a text instead."

Zuri tossed a braid behind her shoulder. "That Marlon's so bad at phone calls. He's never free anymore."

"Bet he'd take her call," said Lee, shaking his torso, meaningfully. Zuri looked amused as I did.

"What's he working on?" I asked, curious.

Lee turned away to fill another glass with beer. "Couldn't tell you if my life depended on it. I've barely seen him these past few months."

"Does he have a new girlfriend?" I regretted the words immediately. "Sorry— "

Zuri laughed. "God, no. That boy works all the time. He's barely got time to match his socks in the mornings."

"He better come to pizza night next week though," said Lee, grim.

The crowd was thin at the bar in the early evening hour. Lee and Zuri were relaxed as they made their way around each other, their language of glances and little bumps and inside jokes effortless, like Jack and Joy's.

"I'm really happy for you guys," I said to them, meaning it.

Lee put an arm around Zuri who looked up at him, glinting with pleasure.

"Got lucky, didn't I? Though I was always considered the catch of the hood," he said.

"This neighborhood? Bushwick?" I laughed as Zuri rolled her eyes.

"He means the four acres of farmland outside Perth that his granny Finley left his daddy," said Zuri. She giggled. "Lee's a stud over in the outback."

Lee swelled his chest and swerved his hips around. "They call me big cat daddy out there."

As they joked, it felt like the world stilled around me for a few moments. I felt a rushing in my ears, a sensation of a sweep of cold air closing in on my chest, clarity leaving me lightheaded, dizzying in its descent as if I had stood up too quickly. Lee and Zuri turned to me, in expectation of my participation.

Lee stopped dancing and looked at me in friendly surprise. "What is it, Mira?"

"Your grandmother. What was her name?"

"Granny Finley?" asked Zuri, before Lee could stop her.

His features had shifted, stricken, his large, happy face frozen in almost comedic panic.

Zuri frowned. "I don't get it. What's wrong with you both?"

Lee and I looked at each other, a long moment.

"Nothing," I said, sliding off the barstool. "I just remembered something, that's all. Lee, can I put the beer on my tab? I probably don't even have a tab anymore."

Lee shook his head, concern spreading itself across his whole body, his shoulders and arms suddenly stiff.

"Time for a new one," he said.

"Okay," I said, as I wrapped my scarf around my throat. "I'll be back, don't you worry."

"Mira, please— " Lee stopped himself from finishing his sentence, a perplexed Zuri staring at us.

I nodded at him. "Don't you worry, Lee," I said again.

IT HAD ALWAYS felt like a big part of my work lay in deciphering fragments of people's imaginations as clues to what lay beneath them. Words swirled together in poetry, often forming kaleidoscopic, unique riddles that I was able to solve for, if I spent enough time with the verse. And yet in life, I so often missed the things that stood right in front of me, shocking in their solidity and definition, such that my beloved might have loved another all along, and never loved me quite the same. This to me was one of life's greatest mysteries, that abstraction and metaphor might so easily morph into the truth of a poem for me, but if Finley Maria had stood in front of me, fully formed the entire time, I would have still looked in the opposite direction, the one that I had hoped he might emerge from. My desire to be loyal to my beliefs was what had propelled me to remain in love with Jack. That desire, in the end, had had little relationship with the truth. On the way over, shock reverberated through me, a pulsing in my stomach. But as I walked up the familiar steps, reaching the second floor, I felt lucid. Marlon opened the door, his face tired, but his body exactly as I remembered it, its sinews and lines as familiar to me as if I had seen him every night instead of not at all in the past months, his eyes still alight with the kindness that was second nature to him. We stood for a long moment in his doorway, taking each other in. He held the door open and I entered his apartment. Marlon closed the door behind him.

"Lee called," he said.

I nodded. He wore a white T-shirt, the soft kind he slept in, and sweatpants. There was a new tattoo—some sort of circular pattern, on his wrist. The smell of his aftershave mixed with coffee somewhere in the apartment, making its way into my senses.

"Your friend, Ming. She was the inspiration for Ginger."

"Yes."

"Ginger Chan, who thought of herself a little like the whales she loved. You went to Leeds. To the writing program. It's one of the best in the UK. I looked you up an hour ago and it was right there. Why did I never look before?"

"People don't look up people like me too often."

I shook my head. "You're right about the world, but you're also wrong. You don't give the world a chance. You're so sure we won't get it. You never gave me a chance."

"You must be upset?" asked Marlon, bemused, studying me. "You must think me a liar?" He paused. "And a hypocrite."

"I was. Why didn't you tell me?"

"I almost did, so many times."

The flatness of his chest and stomach rose and fell as he breathed. Somewhere in the distance, I heard a child cry, a woman's voice soothing after it.

Marlon looked away. "I should have tried much harder. But you didn't want to look in my direction either."

"Yes," I said, ashamed.

"When you became important to me, I worried it would end it between us."

I nodded. "When the manuscript turned up in the mail, that was you. You used me."

Marlon looked up, a flicker of familiar heat in his eyes. "You don't think that."

"I do, actually. I don't mind it. You slept with a girl who liked you just as much as you did her, you heard about her job, you had a book to sell that you thought she could help with, and you mailed it in." I felt a peace settle inside me. "These past few months, I've been trying to see things for what they are, a little more. Turns out it's a steep learning curve for me."

Marlon angled his head, a slight frown wrinkling his forehead. "You can't possibly think our entire relationship was based on my wanting to get published?"

I shook my head. "I don't."

Marlon took in a sharp inhale. "I was in love with you."

"I know." Regret sliced through me. "I was in love with someone else." I paused, my face aflame. "I cannot tell you how sorry I am for believing that it was him who wrote the book. Of course it was you."

Marlon nodded. We stood in silence as the woman's voice floated up to us again, a lullaby shapeshifting through the sounds of the evening beneath.

"I've always wondered what I would say to Finley, the first time we had a conversation." I stared at his face, the shape of his ears and nose. "It's so ordinary really, nothing special to say except that it was light and dark and hopeful and incredibly tragic at the same time. It moved me, Marlon."

"In the end, they make it," said Marlon. "In the book."

I nodded, the skin on my arms and neck alive. "Yes."

"The rest of it, the internet, the five seconds of fame, it's all"—Marlon shook his head—"an illusion. Manufactured by something I don't quite get. Already, I'm yesterday's news. By the time they realize it wasn't someone famous trying her hand at romance and instead just a Black bartender from Australia, they're going to be bored with the whole thing. Or not. But what you felt for my writing from the start, that's the real thing." Marlon took a step toward me. "Every time you talked about the book, I wanted to tell you. That night you thought it was him, it broke my heart a little." Marlon shook his head. "It never occurred to you, even as a passing thought, that it could have me."

I could see the deep hurt and anger that still rankled just below his surface; I said nothing for a few moments. "It turns out I walk around in an alternate reality, ninety percent of the time," I said, slowly. "I am trying very hard for that not to be the case any longer. To not be unseeing of my own blind spots any longer. What happened with Jack—it was an idea that I believed to be true about us. I had always wanted him so much more than he wanted me. When there is an imbalance like that, the relationship—especially its beginnings and endings—is always more heightened and acute than if two people want each other equally. If we had gone on living our life together"—I felt my breath catch in my throat, so acute was the feeling of discovery— "we might have separated naturally, even amicably. We were always meant to be friends." I looked up at Marlon and realized I was shaking.

Marlon softened, but he did not reach for me as he might have in the past.

"But when Joy came along and he fell so fully in love with her, when she loved him back, it became something different. It became about her and me," I said.

Saying the words aloud for the first time felt as if something might erupt and shatter into fragments.

"You've been through too much, Mira," said Marlon, a compassion in his voice.

I took a step backward. "I went to Lee's today to tell you that I'm so sorry for the way I treated you. For the way I behaved."

Something passed across Marlon's face. He nodded slowly, as if arriving at a decision. "You gave me a lot of happiness, Mira." He shrugged. "Besides, I made a killing on that book so it's all good."

I laughed, suddenly light-years younger. "You deserve it all."

"I lied to you, too." He looked at me, hesitant, as if searching for my own anger, but all I felt was relief.

"I think we're even."

Marlon smiled. "Does this mean I have to come out to the world tomorrow? It was going to be a matter of time anyway. Lee said he had to tell Zuri."

I shook my head. "Your life is yours. For as long as you want it. I'll never tell anyone."

Marlon nodded again. He looked at me for a long moment.

The clarity I had felt as he had opened the door hadn't left me, I thought to myself as I moved closer to him. "What if we went back to the start? And you talked to me in a bar and maybe one day I'll take you to dinner and maybe another night, you'll ask me to stay?" I took a deep breath. "What if we did the whole dance again, but as ourselves this time?"

For a few moments, Marlon said nothing.

"We can't erase the past. It's everywhere, in your present," he said.

I blinked. The moment had felt sweet, rich with the promise of something. But there was a reckoning in Marlon's face.

"I was very happy with you, but I was very hurt in the end."

I nodded, swallowing. "Yes, of course."

"You don't know that you're ready to be with someone," said Marlon, with enough tenderness that it made my eyes burn.

I let the wave of sadness settle into my body. When it had, I took a breath again. "You're right, I don't know that I'm ready. But I want to try." I nodded, my peace returning. "And if you're not ready to trust that, I would understand."

Marlon walked to the large open windows behind me, reflective as he looked at the sky outside. Despite the chill of the season, he liked fresh air, a reveling in nature that was his constant state of being. It had been one of the many things I had loved about a man who was so painfully honest yet lived a double identity. Around him, I had always felt a mixture of fascination and admiration, and yet had never stopped to examine why.

"I don't know what we look like in this new world where we know the truth about each other," I heard him say. Marlon paused. "I don't know if it'll work."

I looked at him as he turned from the window.

He smiled." But maybe we should try to find out. I think it could be worth it. Let's do the dance, Mira."

CHAPTER TWENTY-SEVEN

ONE NIGHT, I dreamt that Joy had climbed into my bed, the way she would as a child, her little body scooping into my side, its fragile bones huddled around mine, my arm instinctively flung over her, her breath slowing, her skin warm.

"Joybird," I said in my sleep, making room for her amongst my pillows.

She murmured something indistinct, a brief sound of happiness, as she swam in the waters of my mind, a sharp tug on my duvet. With a start I awoke, the moon so bright that it felt like artificial light, Joy illuminated in the dark next to me.

"Joy," I said, clutching the cover to my racing heart. "What are you doing here?"

She frowned, half asleep. "Couldn't sleep," she said into the crook of my arm.

"You drove to Brooklyn because you couldn't sleep?"

"Uh huh," said Joy, half closing her eyes again.

"Is everything okay?" I asked, propping myself up on an urgent elbow, my sister stretched out over more than half the bed.

She opened both eyes, reluctant. After a pause, she said, "I brought ice cream. I thought we could watch a movie."

"At midnight," I said in disbelief.

"Tomorrow. When we wake up."

I looked at her for a moment. "Is everything okay with Jack?"

"Yes," said Joy happily, sleep clouding her features. "It's nice." She looked up at me, the moonlight almost blue against her skin, her curls streaming over my pillow, a tortoiseshell claw clip buried in their depths. "Is that okay?"

"Yes," I said. I reached into her hair and unclipped the claw. I put it next to the dresser as Joy moved closer to me. "I'm going to fall off the bed," I said. "Scoot a little."

"I told Jack I missed you and wanted to sleep in your bed," said Joy, moving back an inch. She closed her eyes. "This is nice, Didi."

I lay down on my side, facing her, our eyes and noses shaped the same.

"Didi?"

"Yes?"

"Can I borrow your banana silk coat? The beige one with green flowers? We have a wedding on Sunday and nothing I have matches my skirt."

I shook my head at her. She opened an eye.

"Fine," I said. "But you have to promise you won't stain it."

"I promise," she said, as she closed her eyes, our arms around each other as we drifted to sleep.

CHAPTER TWENTY-EIGHT

LENA AND I sat on a bench on the boardwalk, the ocean roiling in front of us with the beginnings of a storm. The fleeting afternoon light skimmed the surface of the water, a lone duck flapping its oily feathers in an effort to join a flock in the distance. Despite the weather, the air had warmed a little in the sun and I breathed in the salt of the waves.

"Did you know, *Helena* means light in Greek?"

Lena looked at me in amusement. "I did know that actually. My dad told me when I was a kid. Though I was named after his favorite aunt. What brought that on?"

"In Hebrew, *Lena* can also be interpreted to mean tower or dwelling." I shrugged. "I was trying to write something down. I looked it up."

Lena put an affectionate arm around me. "Never change, okay?"

"I can't believe Baba would let us come here by ourselves as teenagers," I said, watching a couple that could be no more than fifteen kiss open-mouthed under the closed Ferris wheel.

"Oh, leave them young lovers alone," said Lena, laughing. "Remember when you kissed Gavin Chen backstage right as the curtain went up, in ninth grade?"

I smiled. "Sweet Gavin. We're never letting Gino marry, correct?"

"That's right. He'll be home at forty with his two favorite ladies.

That's the plan," said Lena, nodding for emphasis. A gust of ocean breeze blew her hair around her face. "Baby boy's been asking about learning the piano from you. After Rosa mentioned it, I put the idea in his head and said you knew how to play."

"Isn't he too young?" I looked at Lena in surprise. "I thought we weren't giving him lessons in anything until he could choose for himself."

Lena shrugged. "He's always clanging something around the house to his own beat so I'm not opposed. You'd be doing us a favor. Besides, Serena Williams started young." Lena shimmied an arm at me, for comedic effect. "Gotta headstart a prodigy."

I giggled. "Okay, Gino can be Serena if he wants. Tell you what, I'll let him clang around on it next week on his own and answer questions but I won't teach him anything, okay?"

"Sounds good to me," said Lena.

We sat watching the sun descend into the turbulent water.

"You know, you're happier than I've ever seen you," said Lena, as she looked at the waves. "And I've known you for a long time."

I looked at her with affection. "I am happy."

She nodded. "Do you think you'll ever tell her?" Lena turned to look at me. "You've both come such a long way."

I turned back to the foam-capped water. The duck had finally reached its brood and the birds were flapping around each other in excitement, the water's surface creating circular ripples around them.

"There's nothing to say. Gino's your son. Nothing will ever change that."

We sat side by side, the sounds of Brighton Beach around us. Gulls, children, the foam of the water, a despondent mime left over from the summer, a wrapper making its way into the ocean. "Do you remember that night in London, when he was born?" I asked.

"I held your hand," said Lena.

"I remember thinking that nothing would ever be the same again. That this would be the thing that changed everything. And it did. But we're all exactly where we're meant to be."

Lena took my hand, her fingers cold as the sun made its final plunge back into the ocean, the sky almost purple, the color of bruises and pomp. Another day in our beloved lives had come to an end.

Meteorite

The world had ended.

Mere rock, more brilliant than star sent by the gods.

I was told.
Flattened by collision.
My own heart, lungs, limbs ajar

Moved inside me.

Swift kick shower spark
Of life. Proof that I was alive
in the dark.

Son of god,
son of none, son alone
Of mine, heart.

Blade by blade, we emerge from the earth once more.

You are the ocean.

My light, your shore.

RAISING READERS

Books Build Bright Futures

Thank you for reading this book and for being a reader of books in general. We are so grateful to share being part of a community of readers with you, and we hope you will join us in passing our love of books on to the next generation of readers.

Did you know that reading for enjoyment is the single biggest predictor of a child's future happiness and success?

More than family circumstances, parents' educational background, or income, reading impacts a child's future academic performance, emotional well-being, communication skills, economic security, ambition, and happiness.

Studies show that kids reading for enjoyment in the US is in rapid decline:

- In 2012, 53% of 9-year-olds read almost every day. Just 10 years later, in 2022, the number had fallen to 39%.
- In 2012, 27% of 13-year-olds read for fun daily. By 2023, that number was just 14%.

Together, we can commit to **Raising Readers** and change this trend. How?

- Read to children in your life daily.
- Model reading as a fun activity.
- Reduce screen time.
- Start a family, school, or community book club.
- Visit bookstores and libraries regularly.
- Listen to audiobooks.
- Read the book before you see the movie.
- Encourage your child to read aloud to a pet or stuffed animal.
- Give books as gifts.
- Donate books to families and communities in need.

BOB1217

Books build bright futures, and **Raising Readers** is our shared responsibility.

For more information, visit **JoinRaisingReaders.com**

Sources: National Endowment for the Arts, National Assessment of Educational Progress, WorldBookDay.com, Nielsen BookData's 2023 "Understanding the Children's Book Consumer"